ESCAPES

LESLIE KELLY

JANELLE DENISON

TAWNY WEBER

Published in Great Britain 2014
by Mills & Boon, an imprint of Harlequin (UK) Limited,
Eton House, 18-24 Paradise Road, Richmond, Surrey, TW9 1SR

SULTRY ESCAPES © 2014 Harlequin Books S.A.

Waking Up To You © 2013 Leslie A. Kelly
No Strings… © 2013 Janelle Denison
Midnight Special © 2013 Tawny Weber

ISBN: 978 0 263 91130 5

009-0114

Harlequin (UK) Limited's policy is to use papers that are natural, renewable and recyclable products and made from wood grown in sustainable forests.
The logging and manufacturing processes conform to the legalenvironmental regulations of the country of origin.

Printed and bound in Spain
by Blackprint CPI, Barcelona

WAKING UP TO YOU
LESLIE KELLY

January 2014

January 2014

Leslie Kelly has written dozens of books and novellas for Mills & Boon® Blaze® and other lines. Known for her sparkling dialogue, fun characters and steamy sensuality, she has been honoured with numerous awards, including the National Reader's Choice Award, the Colorado Award of Excellence, the Golden Quill, and the Romantic Times Magazine Career Achievement Award in Series Romance. Leslie has also been nominated four times for the highest award in romance fiction, the RWA RITA® Award. Leslie lives in Maryland with her own romantic hero, Bruce, and their daughters. Visit her online at www.lesliekelly.com or at her blog www.plotmonkeys.com.

Prologue

The Hollywood Tattler-
Superstar No Longer A Bachelor?

Pay attention, ladies, it looks like Thomas Shane, hottest young leading man to come out of Sundance, might be ready to trade in his bachelor digs for a cozy cottage for two. The handsome actor, who set female hearts throbbing in his very first picture, is reportedly in the market for a home in the Laguna Beach area.

Shane, who is rumored to be starring in the next big superhero reboot, has been notoriously picky about his lady friends. But he was recently seen house shopping with a hot brunette who, sources say, was the costume designer on his last film.

If it's true that Thomas Shane is leaving the realm of available men, hearts are breaking all over the world.

Don't go, Shane! Don't go!

1

"WAIT, YOU'RE ASKING me to *marry* you?"

Her mouth open, Candace Reid stared into the beautiful, sky-blue eyes that were the dominant feature of the most perfect male face she had ever seen. Thomas Shane, handsomest man on the planet, hottest young up-and-comer in Hollywood, subject of fantasies and object of obsessions, had just said the words every other woman in America would kill to hear from his lips. And he didn't appear to be joking.

"Yes, I am. Marry me, Candace. Say yes."

"But...but...you're a movie star."

"So what? You're a movie costumer."

She grunted. That *so* didn't count. Her check on their last film was smaller than his by at least four zeroes.

"We've known each other since kindergarten."

"Nursery school. Say yes and I will at last forgive you for stealing my Fruit Roll-Ups during nap time the day we met."

She growled. She hadn't taken the damn Fruit Roll-Ups. "That was Joey Winpigler...don't you remember his green teeth?"

"That kid's teeth were always green."

She groaned, realizing they were getting off topic—off this *insane* topic. "I can't marry you...you're my best friend."

"And you're mine. That's why it's so perfect."

Throwing her arms up in frustration, she exclaimed, "But, Tommy, you're gay!"

He waved an unconcerned hand. "Oh, *that*."

"Yeah. *That*."

"It's really no big deal."

"I disagree. I don't have a penis, and they're right up there with raindrops on roses and whiskers on kittens for you."

"Well, I'll admit they *are* among my fav-o-rite things."

Of course Tommy would get the show-tune quip—he'd starred in every musical in their high school and could tap-dance his way around a chorus line of Rockettes. Not that anyone who had seen him in his last film, taking out an entire terrorist camp single-handedly, would believe that.

"But really, penises schmenises, most men are jerks," he insisted. "I *adore* women."

"Not sexually."

He plopped down beside her on the buttery-soft leather sofa in the living room of his Malibu condo. "Sex isn't everything."

"Yeah, right." For him maybe it wasn't, since his career was his entire focus right now. But for Candace, who liked sex a lot, even if she seldom got it, it was kind of a biggie.

"I think maybe I'll just be asexual from now on."

She snorted and rolled her eyes.

"What? I can love from afar. It'll be all tragic and shit."

"Like the mad crush you had on that guy who played your grandfather in your second film?"

He pursed his lips, looking prim. "Every serious actor has a crush on Sir Anthony Hopkins. He's a God."

"But not every serious actor goes trolling for a little

strange cock when he's out of town, away from the cameras."

"Big strange cock," he retorted. "And that's a secret."

"This is nuts. Stop playing around."

"Babe, I've got to keep my personal life on the down-low for now," he said, growing serious. "If I don't, my superhero action-movie days are over. It sucks, but you know it's true."

Part of her wanted to urge him to be true to himself and stop hiding the man he was. She'd known about his sexual orientation for as long as he had, having realized it in middle school when Tommy had gotten pissy about her landing a date with the hottest guy in their class. It hadn't been hard to figure out who, exactly, he was jealous of. The two of them had talked about it, acknowledged Tommy was gay and that was that.

Her sister, Madison, the only person in the world to whom she was closer than Tommy, hadn't figured it out quite as quickly. But once she had, the three of them had become like the Three Musketeers, fighting for Tommy's right to be himself.

And now he wanted to hide who he was for good.

"There have been rumors," he said, not meeting her eye.

She shrugged. "There are always those kinds of rumors about movie stars." Tommy wasn't the first Hollywood celebrity to worry about in-the-closet stories, and he wouldn't be the last.

He rested his head on the back of the couch and stared at the ceiling. "I've also gotten a few veiled threats."

Oh, hell. "What do you mean? Threats from who?"

"Just somebody I had a fling with last year."

"Blackmail?" she said, indignant on his behalf.

"Not yet. But it could get there. He's making rumbles about supposedly having some kind of proof."

Candace glowered at him for being careless. "Tell me you didn't let some dude take pictures."

"Do I look mentally challenged?" He sounded indignant.

"Sorry."

"And before you ask if I left DNA on a Gap dress, let me explain. It was just some text messages."

"They can be faked," she said, waving an airy hand.

"Yeah, but look at what happened to Tiger."

True. Text messages could definitely come back to bite you. She made a mental note. *Next time you're about to break up with someone, borrow his phone to destroy the evidence first.*

He turned to face her. "So you see why this is so important? With that tabloid article hinting I was going to settle down with you, I think I can put out the fires for a while. Once I nail this franchise, I can get haughty and walk away to do high-minded indie films."

Haughty wasn't hard for Tommy, although she knew it was a pretense. He was almost always in character. Right now it suited him to act the part of spoiled Hollywood star. But playing the role of her husband? That would take some Oscar-worthy skills.

"Please, Candy, I'm begging you," he said. "Just give me a few years—five max. You and I both know it wouldn't be the first five-years-to-hide-the-fact-that-I'm-gay marriage in Hollywood."

Five years. Could she really give up five years of her life? Okay, so she was only twenty-six, she wasn't seeing anyone and had no interest in settling down and having babies until she was in her thirties. Still…it was quite a commitment.

"And there'll be no prenup. You'll get half of whatever I earn."

Her eyes nearly popped out of their sockets.

He saw her reaction and pounced. "You know you could use the money, since you won't let me lend it to you. You can help out your parents and your sister, give your grandfather the money to get that broken-down winery he bought last year up and running."

That was all true. Curse him for understanding her well enough to know exactly which buttons to push.

"And it'll be fun. We'll walk the red carpet together." He dropped an arm over her shoulders and pulled her close. "I'll be all romantic when I give my Oscar acceptance speech and thank the wildly sexy woman who made it all possible."

Hmm. That sounded like fun.

"There is still one big problem," she finally said. "I like sex. Five years is a long time to go without it."

"You don't have to," he insisted.

"Eww," she said, shoving his arm off her. "That'd be like having sex with my brother. My gay brother."

"I wasn't talking about me! You can have affairs."

"Tacky. Besides, that'd *really* cause some gossip. I'm already on the radar of those leeches."

She hated that, truly. Being the subject of gossip was infuriating, and she doubly hated the idea that some people might have decided she got her start in Hollywood because of Tommy. If anything, he'd gotten his first break through her. He'd come to visit her at work at one of the studios one day, met a casting director and the rest was history.

"Look," he said, "we both know you've got a gazillion gigabytes of internal memory when it comes to sex. You've already stored up experiences that helped you through dry spells in the past."

She couldn't argue that, but did stick out her tongue at him. It wasn't nice of him to point out all those dry spells, usually caused because Candace had a bad habit of going out with guys who were far more focused on material things and their own ambitions than they were on her. "Your point?"

"My point is, I'll send you on a trip to France for two weeks. You can boink your way from Bordeaux to Paris, free from the paparazzi. Once you back up some orgasms on your libido's hard drive, you can come home and we'll announce our engagement."

He always managed to make her laugh. "And what if my vaginal computer crashes? Am I supposed to zip off to a bordello to do an emergency dump onto my flash drive?"

"I bet you'd make it two years. Then, when you're crawling out of your skin, I'll pay for you to go to Australia and you can throw a few shrimp on your barbie."

He said the words in a cheesy down-under accent, and she couldn't help laughing. The whole thing was absurd, ridiculous.

But, craziest of all, she was seriously thinking about it.

Not just because she loved Tommy, or because it might be fun playing Hollywood wife. No, because she could really use the money. Her parents were happy in the Florida home where she'd grown up. But since her dad's heart attack two months ago, they'd been stretched thin financially.

Her sister had just finished grad school and had a mountain of debt. And her wonderful, willful grandfather had, indeed, been struck by some wild notion and bought an old run-down winery in Northern California a year ago. The place had nary a grape in sight, and Grandpa had no clue how to grow them, much less turn them into wine. But he was determined to make a go of it.

So, yeah, the money would come in handy. Tommy had offered to help out, but she wouldn't accept charity. She always earned what she got. And frankly, if she had to give up sex for five years, she would earn every penny. Because, no matter what he said, she'd never risk having an affair after their engagement was announced, a time when she'd be more under the paparazzi spotlight than ever. This sowing-her-wild-oats-in-France thing would be it, the full extent of her sexual activity for five long, lonely, vibrator-filled years.

Could she do it? For Tommy? For her family? For the money?

"So what do you say? Pretty please?" he asked, flashing those baby blues and his amazing smile. That grin, that wicked sense of humor and his innate kind streak always made her give in. He deserved the brilliant career within his grasp. No creepy blackmailer should have the right to take it away from him.

"Oh, hell." *Farewell penises of the world.* "I guess I'm in."

"Yes! You are the best friend ever." He pumped both fists in the air, then dropped to one knee. Taking her hand, he stared at her adoringly, playing the man-in-love character. Put him in a Nick Sparks film opposite Emily Blunt and nobody would ever guess he'd once seduced the star football player of their high school.

"Candace Eliza Reid, will you be my bride?"

"Yes, I will. Now get up, idiot. And get your travel agent on the phone because I am *so* taking you up on that Paris thing."

"Or maybe Italy for some spicy pepperoni?"

"Dork," she said as he wagged his eyebrows suggestively.

"Wait…Ireland! I know you've always dug Irish guys."

"Nope, French will do. I don't want my sex toy to speak English. I don't need him for conversation, and I definitely don't want him talking to any reporters who come around."

She doubted she'd come across an absolutely amazing superhunk who would give her five years' worth of orgasms in two weeks, but it was worth a shot. She'd do her damndest, anyway, and nobody was going to stop her

from gorging herself on one last sexual feast before settling in for five hungry years of celibacy.

Before Tommy could make the call, however, her own
cell phone rang. She answered, listened and realized that
she'd been wrong. Somebody *could* stop her. Something
could happen that would totally change her mind and her
plans. Because, when it came right down to it, her need
to stockpile some sexual memories couldn't even begin to
compete with family, especially when somebody she loved
was hurt and needed her. And her grandfather—whom she
adored—was hurt and needed her.

So, within a few hours, Candace was at the airport,
waiting to board a plane, not for France and orgasms, but
for San Francisco and family. She'd be by her grandfather's
side for as long as it took…even if she had to sacrifice any
chance she had of meeting a man who might make her most
wicked dreams come true.

LYING IN BED in the small groundskeeper's cottage that he
now called home, Oliver McKean suddenly found himself
wide-awake, wondering what had roused him from his
slumber. He was exhausted, his body aching after a long
day of hard work, followed by an evening in a hospital.
After twenty hours on his feet, he'd been totally wiped.
When he'd gotten home, he'd showered, hit the mattress
and been sound asleep in minutes.

Until now.

He lay there in the stillness, blinking, looking up at
the ceiling that still didn't look familiar, though he'd slept
beneath it for four months now. A long silent moment
stretched out, broken only by the faint far-off howl of a
coyote. Coming from L.A., he still hadn't grown used to
the silence up here in Northern California. Sonoma was
known for its famous wines, but its landscape was pretty
spectacular, with thousands of acres of untamed wilder-

ness. The estate on which he lived sometimes felt like it was in the middle of a deserted island.

Which was exactly the reason he'd come here, chucking his old life and heading north, choosing the wine country both because of his family's ties to the area and his own love of the region. Being away from the seething mass of humanity in L.A. had sounded like a good way to regroup, regain his sense of self. He also wanted to regain his sense of right and wrong, which had started to slip away as he'd fallen further into the trap of career and ambition. He needed to take a year or so, to drop out of the world, do penance for the wrongs he'd done and to figure out what he was going to do next. One thing was for sure—it *wasn't* returning to the Los Angeles County D.A.'s office.

"Been there, done that, never going back," he whispered. His job as a prosecutor had demoralized him, savaged his optimistic streak and left him with a strong distaste for his chosen profession.

Glancing at his clock and seeing it was almost three, he settled back into his small, lumpy bed, which had come with the furnished cottage. But right before he closed his eyes again, he noted the shadows playing across the ceiling. *That's* what had awakened him. Not a noise, a light.

When he'd gone to bed at 1:00 a.m., it had been pitch-black outside. The sky had been overcast for a couple of days, leaving the stars and moon—usually brilliant up here away from the city lights—hidden behind a bank of clouds. He could hear the soft fall of rain now. But there was light coming from somewhere. It was noticeable against the utter blackness, and sifted in through the uncurtained window.

He got up, walked over and looked toward the main house. A warm, golden beacon shone from within, shattering the darkness.

Strange. He didn't think he'd left a light on, and the

house was supposed to be empty. The owner, Buddy Frye, was lying in a hospital waiting to have surgery for his broken hip. Frye lived alone, with Oliver occupying the groundskeeper's cottage nearby. Nobody else was within a few miles. Oliver had talked to his boss's daughter earlier, and she'd said she would try to catch a flight from Florida in the next few days. But no way could she have made it this soon. So who was skulking around in the house?

He hadn't been away from L.A., and his job prosecuting some of the most violent criminals in the country, long enough to assume the visitor was simply a friendly, concerned neighbor. Huh-uh. Buddy was pretty new to the area. He didn't socialize a lot; much of the community thought he had to be crazy to buy an old ruin of a vineyard estate that had been on the market for three years.

There had been reports in the news lately about break-ins in some of the outlying areas, even some squatters taking advantage of the abandoned foreclosures. And while Buddy didn't have a lot worth stealing in that glorious old ruin he called a home, no way was Oliver about to let the man get victimized while he was lying helpless in a hospital.

He reached for the jeans he'd taken off a few hours ago. They were crusted with dirt from the long day he'd put in yesterday. He hadn't even had time to change into something else before racing after the ambulance that had taken his kindly old boss to the emergency room. But hell, if they were good enough for the doctors and nurses at the Sonoma Valley Hospital, they were good enough for Mr. Prowler.

He left his small house, following the illumination. His bare feet slipped in the wet grass, and the cold rain jabbed his chest since he hadn't bothered with a shirt. Passing the toolshed, which stood between his place and the main house, he reached out and snagged a rake. He didn't want to have to protect himself, but better safe than sorry.

Strange that anybody would choose *this* house to rob.
The place might once have been a showplace—Oliver had
seen pictures of it from its glory days, when it had been
owned by his own family. It had been passed down from a
great-grandfather who'd been a silent movie star. His uncle
had sold it a decade ago, and that owner had gone bankrupt. Now Buddy Frye, its current owner, was trying to
restore it. Oliver hoped he succeeded—the bones of a beautiful mansion were still there. As for right now, though,
it was a falling-down heap, held up as much by the layers
of paint on the walls as by any remnants of a foundation.

The porch creaked—the third floorboard being the
loudest—so he avoided it as he approached the door. He
reached for the knob, which twisted easily in his hand.
That wasn't a good sign. He remembered locking it tonight
before heading to his place. Buddy often didn't, feeling
safe out here in the country, but Oliver hadn't lost that big-
city need for security.

Stepping inside, he almost tripped over a small carry-
on type suitcase, and was immediately curious about this
burglar who carried Louis Vuitton.

Clanging emerged from the kitchen. So the prowler
had decided to make himself a sandwich? A little ham and
Swiss to go with the breaking and entering?

Nothing about this added up.

The kitchen was at the back of the house. Edging toward it, clueless about what to expect, Oliver paused at
the doorway. When he peeked in, he froze in uncertainty.

It wasn't a prowler. At least, it wasn't the sort of prowler
he'd ever seen or envisioned, unless prowlers now came
disguised as tall young women with thick masses of honey-
brown hair that hung in a wave of damp curls halfway
down a slender back. She stood at the sink, filling two
things: a glass with water, and a pair of jeans with the most
amazingly perfect ass he'd ever seen.

His breath caught, his heart lurched and all parts south woke up, too. As he watched, she lifted a shaking hand and swept it through that long hair, weariness underscoring every movement. Her slumped shoulders reinforced that.

He ran down a list of possibilities and lit on the most likely. *A granddaughter.* Buddy had mentioned that one lived in L.A. She must have come up when she heard about her grandfather's accident.

Welcome to Northern California, sweetheart. And thanks for improving the view by bringing that gorgeous ass with you.

He blinked, trying to clear his mind. He'd done enough staring for one night, especially at the posterior of a woman whose grandfather was one of the few men Oliver truly respected.

"Ahem," he said, clearing his throat.

She dropped the glass. It fell from her hand onto the floor, exploding into a volcano of tiny slivers, splashing water on her pants. Spinning around, her eyes wide and her mouth falling open, she saw him standing there and let out a strangled cry of alarm.

"Whoa, whoa," he said, realizing what he must look like, shirtless, wearing dirty jeans and, he suddenly realized, still holding a sharp, threatening-looking rake. The woman, who was beyond sexy, with a pair of blazing green eyes and a beautiful face surrounded by that thick, honey-colored tangle of hair, was eyeing him like he'd popped up in front of her in a back alley.

"I'm not going to…"

He was going to say *hurt you.* But before he could say a word, a pot flew toward his head. He threw up an arm to deflect it, groaning as the metal thunked his elbow, sending him stumbling back into the hallway. He barely managed to stay upright. If not for the rake on which he suddenly leaned, he might have fallen flat on the floor.

But the rake couldn't help him when the frying pan followed the pot.

One second later, he *was* flat on the floor, rubbing the middle of his chest. He focused on trying to catch his breath, which had been knocked out of him as if he'd been KO'd by the love child of Ali and Tyson. That skillet must have been made of cast iron, and she'd flung it like a discus wielded by an Olympic champion.

He held his hands up in surrender, trying to form words, though his body had forgotten how to breathe and his ribs were screaming for her head on a platter. Meanwhile, the rake, which he'd been clutching as he fell, toppled forward. Just to add a little insult to the injury, it landed on his shoulder, then clanged to the floor beside him.

Pain, meet agony, pull up a chair why don't you?

"Get out, I'm calling the police!" she ordered as she scrambled to grab another pot out of the sink.

"Whoa, lady, cool it," he finally gasped. "I'm not... going to...hurt you."

"That's what any sick, raping, ax-murdering psycho would say."

If his chest didn't hurt so damned much, and if he wasn't afraid she would reach for the knife block next, he would have mulled that one over, wondering which she thought him to be: sick, raping, ax-murderer or psycho. All of the above?

Active imagination on that one.

"I'm the...groundskeeper," he said with a groan as the ache in his chest receded, only to remind him of the ache in his elbow. *Funny bone, my ass.* "I work here."

She froze, another pot in one hand, a cell phone in the other, and stared at him from a few feet away. "You work here?"

"Yeah, for Buddy. My name's Oliver McKean. I saw the lights and was afraid somebody had broken in."

She eyed him, her stare zoning in on the blood he could feel trickling down the side of his arm. Obviously she'd broken skin, if not bone, with her mad pot-slinging skills.

Nibbling on the corner of a succulent lip, she whispered, "Oh, dear."

"Yeah. Oh, dear. That's some swing you've got there."

"I'm so sorry. I'm Candace Reid."

"Oliver McKean."

"You said that."

"I know," he mumbled, realizing he wasn't making any sense. The one place she hadn't hit him was his head, but his thoughts were still a whirl as he tried to figure out why on earth he was reacting so strongly to a woman who'd just tried to kill him.

"Are you Irish?" she asked with a deep frown, sounding more concerned than when she'd thought him a maniacal ax-killing rapist.

"My father is. We lived in Cork for a few years when I was a kid," he admitted, wondering if his voice still held a hint of an accent. Also wondering why it mattered.

Not seeing the need to discuss his ethnicity, he staggered to his feet. He was none too steady on them, and his lungs still burned. She'd practically knocked him senseless. Dizzy or not, he was incredibly lucky neither of those flying missiles had hit him in the head. They *really* could have done some damage. But worries about what might have happened dissipated as he stared at her from across the room. Now that he wasn't afraid for his life, he found himself struck into silence by the beauty of her gently curved face. Dark brows arched over expressive jewel-green eyes that were still widened with fear and surprise. Beneath a pair of high cheekbones were soft hollows that invited tender exploration. Her amazing lips were made for lots of deep kisses. Her chin was up, determined and strong, as if she wasn't about to let down her guard completely. He liked that…he especially liked that she remained firm even though her long slender throat quivered and worked as she swallowed down her instinctive anxiety and mistrust.

She wore a delicate, filmy blouse, all cloud and color. It clung to the edge of her slim shoulders, revealing a soft expanse of chest and collarbone. Her skin was creamy, smooth, and his fingers curled together as he imagined touching that softness. The scooped neck of the blouse fell to the tops of her full breasts, revealing a hint of cleavage that left him more breathless than he'd felt after taking a frying pan to the chest.

He continued his perusal, seeing those curvy hips from the front—just as delightful—and the thighs clad in tight denim, on down to the high-heeled boots. Hell, she should have used *those* things for a weapon; the spiked heels could have carved out a hole in his heart.

Hmm. He suspected this woman could carve her name on any man's heart. If, of course, he had one still capable of opening up and being carved.

"You're Buddy's granddaughter, I presume?" he finally asked, once his brain started working again.

His words snapped her out of her long moment of decompression. Apparently realizing she wasn't about to be raped, ravaged by a maniac or ax-murdered, she nodded quickly. "Yes. I'm such an idiot. My mother told me that Grandpa's groundskeeper had been the one to call with the news that he was in the hospital. I can't believe I took you for a home invader." She spun around and grabbed a handful of paper towels, striding toward him, her eyes glued on his bleeding arm. "I really am sorry. Let me help you."

When he saw that she was still armed, he took a step back. "Drop the lethal weapon first, would you?"

Looking down at the pot, she nibbled her lip sheepishly

and did as he asked, opening her fingers and dropping the pot to the floor.

Well, not *quite* to the floor. It had his bare foot to land on first.

The pot fell to the floor with a bang, crushing his toes, then rolling onto the linoleum. "Ow, Jesus," he yelled, grabbing his flattened foot and hopping on the other.

Her beautiful green eyes saucered as she realized what she'd done. With a strangled sound, she reached for him, but he leaped out of striking range and leaned back against the wall.

"Stay back. Please. Just stay away from me." His entire body throbbing, he added, "Jeez, lady, you ought to come with a warning label."

She threw her hand over her mouth in dismay, and bent over at the waist. Sounds like tiny sobs were bursting from her lips and her body trembled.

Great. Just great. Tears.

He quickly shoved away his instinctive reaction, realizing she'd had a hell of a night. Obviously she'd raced up here from Southern California to be with her injured grandfather. She'd been high on fear and adrenaline even before she'd thought she was about to be attacked by a shirtless stranger wielding a rake. Anyone would be a little overwrought.

Realizing she was really mortified, Oliver dropped his foot, praying there were no broken bones, and tried not to wince as he tested his weight on it. "It's okay... I'm all right. Accidents happen."

She straightened and peered at him, those green eyes assessing. But she didn't lower her hand, and her shoulders were now shaking as she made muffled sounds. Funny, her eyes weren't glossy, as if filled with tears. In fact, if he had to guess, he'd say they were almost twinkling instead.

A sneaking suspicion entered his mind. He reached out,

yanked her hand away from her mouth and realized the truth.

She wasn't crying. She was giggling almost uncontrollably.

2

"WAIT, YOU'RE *LAUGHING?*"

Oliver couldn't contain his indignation, not sure whether to retaliate by dropping a pan on her foot or shaking the laughter off her oh-so-kissable lips. She was damned lucky he was not the violent sort, because the shaking thing was definitely winning the internal battle in his mind.

She was also lucky he wasn't the ax-murdering-maniac sort because wringing her neck was a close second.

Then his gaze landed on those kissable lips, and he thought of something else he'd like to do with them. A few somethings, in fact.

She sucked them into her mouth, obviously trying to control herself. "I'm so sorry," she said, her laughter deepening and sounding a little frenzied. "That was just so... so Three Stooges!"

"You break my arm, smash a few ribs, crush my shoulder, pulverize my toes and you think it's hilarious?" His voice was tight with anger. Maybe tomorrow he'd look back and think the situation was funny, but right now he was too concerned about a punctured lung to join in the hilarity.

"I really am sorry," she murmured.

"Yeah, I can tell."

Her laughter fading to the occasional little snort, she explained. "I laugh when I'm stressed. It's awful, I know."

"Awfully strange, anyway," he snapped.

"It's just been such a long day. I was in the middle of a surreal moment even before I got the call about my grandfather. I have been so afraid for him." She swept a shaking hand through her hair, which looked like it had been swept through a lot recently. "The flight up here was a jam-packed nightmare. The kid beside me spent an hour flinging Cheerios and boogers at my head."

Eww.

"The cab ride to the house was an exercise in nausea. I needed a drink, but Grandpa appears to have hidden his stash the way he did when I was a kid. And to top it all off, you skulked into the kitchen, looking all big and bad and scared the shit out of me."

Okay. At some point in that litany of woes, between the boogers, the liquor and the big-n-bad, he got the picture.

She was hysterical.

He understood the reaction. He'd worked with witnesses whose terror had revealed itself via uncontrollable laughter and knew that deep inside, she was churning with anxiety. The laughter had held a tinge of frenzy, her fear and reaction to his presence had been a bit extreme, and now she looked like she was going to… "Oh, hell, please don't," he muttered.

But she did. She segued from snickers to sobs in the drawing of a breath. Before he could even take a second to remind himself how utterly useless he felt around crying women, he saw big fat tears roll from her eyes and drip down those soft cheeks.

"Is my grandfather okay?" *Sniff.* "And are you?" *Sniff sniff.* "Do I need to take you to the hospital? I can't believe I attacked you. Believe me, it was my first assault and battery."

She literally wrung her hands in front of her, clenching and gripping them, as if needing something to hold on to. He had to imagine she was running on empty emotionally and was imagining the worst.

He knew of only two ways to calm her down, to make her stop trying to maim him with kitchen utensils, snort herself to death laughing or sob until she had no tears left.

He started with option one. Reason.

"Buddy is going to be fine, I promise. His doctor said he'll need surgery and then rehab, but when I left the hospital he was high as a kite on pain meds and pinching the nurses."

Her lips twitched, and she managed to lift them a tiny bit at the corners.

"And I'll be fine, too." He eyed the kitchen sink and tried for humor, hoping to coax another laugh, or even a tiny snort out of her. "Just don't ever flash a pot at me or I'll go into post-traumatic shock and instinctively dive for the floor."

The lips curled a wee bit more. But he didn't get his hopes up yet.

"How did it happen? My mother didn't give me any details, just that he'd broken his hip."

He hesitated, before admitting, "He fell down the front steps off the porch."

Another sniff. "Such a short fall and so much damage."

"It happens," he said, knowing brittle bones could easily be broken. "But he's going to get a brand-new hip and come home better than ever. Before you know it, he'll be running marathons."

"Oh, great, then it'll be his other hip or his knees."

He wished he'd quit while he was ahead. She was obviously now picturing her grandfather's much-loved arms and skull being shattered. Sure enough, to prove it, the bottom lip began to stick out the tiniest bit and she welled up again. Those churning emotions just weren't going to let her go without a fight.

"C'mere," he said with a sigh, knowing he had to move on to option two.

Not giving her a warning or a chance to get away, he gently took hold of her shoulders and pulled her closer. She resisted for the briefest moment, as if unsure of his motives.

He reassured her, sighing deeply as he wondered what on earth he'd done to deserve this. Having to act like a wailing wall for a gorgeous woman who was totally off-limits, considering she was his employer's beloved grand-daughter, simply wasn't fair.

"Just let it out, darlin'. You've already maimed and injured me, so you might as well use my one good shoulder to cry on."

That elicited a sob that verged on a giggle and she gave in to the invitation. The tall, soft woman melted against him. Burying her face in his neck, she wrapped her arms around his waist, as if it was the most natural thing in the world that she should snuggle up against a half-naked stranger in her moment of need.

He stroked the small of her back, felt the wetness of her tears against his neck and murmured consoling words in her ear. She calmed—her slow shudders growing further apart as she took what he was offering. They swayed a little, as if dancing, and he mentally acknowledged that needing a shoulder to cry on wasn't just an expression. Sometimes that was just exactly the right solution to a problem. Not for nothing was he known as the best brother in the world to his two sisters.

Only this woman was not one of his sisters. Oh, no. She was a beautiful, vulnerable stranger, who, he soon realized, felt incredibly good in his arms. Soft and pliant, warm, all curves and skin and heat and sex appeal. He could feel her gentle exhalations against his bare skin, feel the faint brush of her lips on his nape and was slowly going crazy at the scrape of her nipples through her silky blouse against his chest. He had never been more aware of being shirtless in his life.

He stiffened. Some parts more than others.

He should never have let his mind wander from her mood. Because, while the embrace had started as a comforting offer to a stranger, now he was much too aware that he hadn't had sex in months and a woman shaped like a centerfold had curled up against him like a vine around a trellis.

Shifting back a little, he hoped like hell she wouldn't realize he was getting hard while she wept. But she didn't let him make a gentlemanly getaway. Instead she edged close again, pressing even harder against him. He could feel the warmth at the apex of her thighs, which, with her deliciously long legs, was lined up just perfectly with his groin.

She noticed. She had to notice. Because suddenly, she lifted her head and stared at him. Her soft face was tearstained, but her eyes were wide with shock, confusion and awareness.

Her lips trembled. She licked them, and he held his breath, wondering what on earth she was going to say. Was she about to snap at him and slap his face or issue an invitation? What?

In the end, his wild guesses didn't even come close. Instead, with a soft, regretful sigh, she drew away and whispered, "Why, oh, God, *why* did I not meet you in Paris?"

A SHORT TIME later, after Candace had asked the sexy stranger a dozen questions about her grandfather's condition, she finally allowed herself to think about something else. She now knew for sure that Buddy would be all right. She'd see him tomorrow, but for tonight, she could do nothing else.

Slowly, her fear and worry began to ease away and she let her thoughts drift in another direction. Enough so that, as she sat at the kitchen table and slowly sipped sweet, hot tea with the sexiest man she'd ever seen, she found time to wish two things: that she'd left the pots in the sink, and that she'd never even thought about him in connection with her canceled trip to France.

If she hadn't seen him, reacted like a high school virgin defending her hymen from a horny football team and attacked him to the point of bloodshed, she wouldn't have gotten all giggly, weepy and hysterical. If she hadn't gotten giggly, weepy and hysterical, he wouldn't have taken her into his big strong arms. If he hadn't taken her into his big strong arms, he wouldn't have drawn her against that rock-hard, rippling, sweat-tinged, powerful male body. If he hadn't drawn her against his body, she might not have felt the rigid proof of his virility pressing deliciously against her sex.

And if he hadn't gotten hard, she wouldn't be sitting here vacillating between worrying about her grandfather and wondering when this hot stranger would wake up and smell the estrogen, and realize she was sitting in damp panties.

She shifted in the hard chair. *Seriously damp.*

Of course, fair was fair. He'd been seriously hard.

Yum.

No. Not yum. You can't have him.

Sighing, she inhaled the fragrant tea and murmured, "If you give a mouse a cookie…"

"I don't think your grandfather has any milk," he replied, hearing her. "He's lactose intolerant."

She had to smile that this strong, rugged-looking man understood the reference to a popular children's book. Especially since his voice was all deep and gravelly, sultry and alluring, and completely inappropriate for uttering rhymes to a little kid.

Uttering sexy, needful growls to an adult woman would be much more up his alley.

"I have a niece. She's four," he explained with a shrug. "You?"

Are you asking if I'm single?

She curled her left hand around the cup. The bare left hand. The left hand that was not yet weighed down with the five-carat diamond she suspected Tommy would put on it the minute she got back to L.A.

Remembering Tommy, and everything that ring would entail, she gave a guilty start and dropped her hand into her lap, reaching for the cup with her right one.

"Younger cousins," she finally replied.

There was no point in letting this man know she was single. No possible reason to want him to realize she had gotten all gooey inside the moment he'd pulled her into his arms to offer her some warmth and human comfort. And it would be pure insanity to hope he'd figure out that the goo had boiled into lava once she'd felt the volcanic rock in his pants.

She didn't allow herself to feel terribly flattered. Any bare-chested, slick, hard, virile—*stop with the adjectives*—man would probably stir at the feel of a woman pressing herself against him like she wanted to climb into his skin. That's what she had done, she realized with embarrassment. She might as well have asked him if he could pretty-please comfort her on top of the hard, broad table, or up against the refrigerator. And wouldn't it be nice if the comforting didn't include clothes?

You're engaged, remember?

Right. Engaged. Which meant the Candace Volcano was going to be all Mt. St. Helens from here on out—i.e., dormant. There might be rumbles, but there would be no eruptions for a hell of a long time. Five years, at least. *Oy.*

She would be staying here to help her grandfather for as long as he needed her, which meant there would be no time for a trip to Paris. No chance for a wild fling. Tommy wouldn't want to wait too long to announce their engagement, and she couldn't blame him. She'd have no time to sow any wild oats and bank some sexy memories. But she couldn't truly be upset about it. She adored Grandpa and would do anything for him. Including missing out on her one-and-only chance to be a sex tourist.

So go for the gardener.

She flicked the thought out of her head, not for the first time. That wasn't going to happen. A spring fling in Paris had sounded ideal, but there was no way she was hooking up with someone who worked for her grandfather. She'd wanted someone from out of the country, preferably a stud who didn't speak English. Gorgeous, hung, with a penchant for oral sex and dumb as a rock would have suited her just fine.

This man—as far as she knew right now—had only two of those qualities. He was gorgeous. And oh, had he felt hung.

As for the rest? Well, that mouth looked like it could give a woman incredible pleasure. But he certainly didn't appear dumb. He spoke the language. And, worst of all, lived in her own state. Once she became fodder for the paparazzi, they could easily track him down. They would be very interested to hear that Tommy Shane's beloved fiancée had been having a wild, outrageously sexual affair with a man right before she'd said, "I will."

Mmm. Wild. Outrageously sexual. Oh, did she suspect it would be.

Just her luck that she'd met a man who appealed to her
on such a deep, powerful level on the very night she'd
agreed to give up sex for five years and marry her best
friend.

"Warming up a little?" he asked.

She had been, sip by sip. Grandfather's house was old,
damp and chilly, and she hoped her suitcase got here soon
with her warmer clothes. "Yes, thanks."

"The nights'll get warmer soon," he said. "Or so I've
been told."

"You're not from around here?"

"No." He hesitated, then added, "I moved up from L.A.
a few months ago."

Ahh! The plot thickened. Had he been some kind of
gardener to the Hollywood elite? She suspected any number of starlets would have been happy to have him trim
their hedges and do some deep planting in their gardens.

"Why?"

"It was just time," he explained, his expression and tone
telling her that was all he was going to say.

Talk about cryptic.

The silence between them resumed, though it wasn't
an uncomfortable one. They both merely sipped their tea,
as they had been for the past few minutes. Oliver—that
was his name, Oliver, and what a strong, solid, sexy, old-
fashioned name it was—had gently pushed her into a chair
and insisted on making her some tea. He obviously did
know her grandfather well. A cup of Earl Grey was Buddy
Frye's solution to soothe all the ills of the world. Tea had
cured Candace's scraped knees and hurt feelings, broken
hearts and hangovers. And now, it had made her finally
relax and brought her tension down a few notches.

She wondered if Oliver had adopted the habit from his
employer, of if he was a similar type of man—a calm, deliberate man who always seemed to know how to offer

comfort in exactly the right way at the right moment. Whatever the reason, like the hug that had gone from sweet to smokin', it was a nice gesture, one she appreciated.

Of course, she would appreciate it more if the man would put a damn shirt on so she wouldn't have to keep shoving her eyeballs back in their sockets every time he moved.

Deltoids and pectorals and biceps, oh, my!

The last thing she had expected to find when she'd let herself into her grandfather's house, which she'd only ever visited once before, was a hunk of masculine sex appeal showing up in the kitchen. Her mother had, indeed, mentioned a groundskeeper when she'd called earlier today. But she hadn't said anything about a groundskeeper with nearly jet-black hair, thick and wavy and hanging a little long around his stubbled, two-days-past-needing-a-shave jaw. Nothing could have prepared Candace for the dark dreamy eyes, the strong brow, the slashing cheekbones or the powerful body. Absolutely nothing.

She'd met a lot of handsome men in Hollywood. Probably some who were more handsome than Oliver—Tommy among them. But in terms of raw, masculine sex appeal, she'd seen nobody better.

"Better?"

"Not a single one," she mumbled.

"What?"

Realizing she'd spoken aloud, she quickly backtracked. "Sorry, I mean, I am better. Much. Just tired, that's all."

"So, you said you came up from L.A.?"

"Yes. I headed for the airport right after I got my mother's call. I figured I should come and see how Grandpa was doing myself. I'm really hoping I can handle things so Mom won't have to fly out here."

His brow shot up. Knowing he'd been on the receiving

end of her mother's telephone panic, he had to be wondering about that.

"My father had a heart attack two months ago," she explained. "He needs Mom there with him in Florida. So if I can be here for Buddy and set my mom's mind at ease about my grandfather, that's what I'll do."

He frowned, encircling his teacup in his hand. "Buddy might be in rehab for weeks."

Weeks. Well, that wasn't great, but it was doable. She was an independent contractor and was in between movie projects right now. She'd been asked to submit some preliminary sketches for a depression-era drama that could be a major motion picture in a few years, but that was still in the early stages. She didn't have the assignment yet, and she could work on the prelims here. Besides, Leo DiCaprio, who was supposed to be starring in the film, was the easiest guy in Hollywood to dress. The only thing that might call her back to Southern California earlier would be her famous—infamous?—engagement.

"I'll work something out," she mumbled, wondering how long Tommy would be willing to hold off. She wouldn't want to announce anything while she was taking care of her grandfather. The last thing the elderly man would need once he got home was reporters and photographers knocking at the door. "I don't have to be in L.A. right away."

"What do you do?"

Oh, I'm in the movie business. Costume design. Did you see the last Cameron film? That was me.

That was the standard reply, often said with a slightly superior tone, just because that's how everybody in L.A. rolled. But she just didn't feel like playing that game. Not here, in the middle of the night, with a stranger. Not after the day she'd had. "I'm involved with fashion design."

His eyes didn't immediately glaze, the way most men's

would. "My sisters would probably love to meet you. I think they were each born holding a copy of *Vogue*."

She ran the tip of her finger across the rim of her cup. "Not that kind of fashion. I work for some of the production companies doing costuming."

He grunted. "Movies, huh?"

Her back stiffened as he reacted just as she'd expected him to. Most people were awed by her connection to Tinseltown. This one, this earthy, swaggering man, just didn't seem the type. He looked like he could live out some macho, shoot-em-up action film rather than having to sit through one. Of course, what such a man was doing working as a groundskeeper, she had no idea.

"What's wrong with the movies?"

He shrugged.

"You don't like films?"

"Sure I do. I just don't have much respect for the people who make them."

The vision of him being at the beck and call of some spoiled, rich-bitch movie star popped into her head. She had a hard time envisioning this man taking orders from anyone and wondered if he'd gotten tired of being propositioned by his clients. "Interact with a lot of Hollywood types, do you?"

He eyed her then shifted his gaze away, muttering a cryptic, "Not anymore."

Meaning, he had once upon a time?

Something suddenly occurred to her, which could explain why he seemed like such a fish out of water. "Wait. Tell me you're not a method actor up here in the wilds of Northern California getting ready to audition for some back-to-nature film," she said, horrified at the very idea.

He barked a harsh laugh. "Not likely." His lips twitching as he lifted his glass, he added, "What about you? Did you come out here all starry-eyed, looking for your big break, and end up shifting gears into costuming when the acting thing didn't work out?"

"I couldn't act my way out of a speeding ticket if my car was on fire and the cop who pulled me over was my uncle."

His brow scrunched. "Why would you drive a burning car?"

"I...what?"

"If the car's on fire, why would you keep driving it? Why wouldn't you pull over and get out?"

"Are you always so literal?"

"Do you really have an uncle who's a cop?"

She growled, low in her throat. Seeing the twinkle in his eye made the growl louder, so she continued the game of Answer a Question with a Question with a question. "Do you always bait strange women?"

"Only women who specialize in death-by-kitchenware." His tone was deadpan. "And those I make tea for in the middle of the night."

The faintest hint of his smile made her spine relax a bit. He might not look like he had much of a sense of humor, and his gruff voice sure didn't sound like it was used much for laughing, but she suspected there lurked a good-humored man beneath the superhot, strong-and-silent exterior.

She lifted her cup. "Speaking of which, you make a very good cup of tea. It was just what I needed. Thanks again."

"Tea was a staple in our house. It's one thing I have in common with your grandfather—he does like his cuppa."

"So he does."

The way he said cuppa warmed her up inside. She did love an Irish accent, and while his was buried under a couple of decades of blunt Americanism, she still heard the lilt every now and again.

Another sip. The tea was cooling now, her cup nearly drained, and she knew it had to be close to 4:00 a.m. By all rights, she should be tucked in bed in one of the drafty upstairs guest rooms. But something made her stay. She just didn't want to be alone in this big house. Especially because she still couldn't quite reconcile it as being Grandpa's. He'd lived in a condo in St. Petersburg when she'd been growing up, for crying out loud, about as far from this wild, untamed landscape as one could get.

"What's he doing here, anyway?" she grumbled.

"Who, Buddy?"

"Yes. What on earth possessed him to come out here and buy this place?"

"He's living the dream, from the sound of it. He told me he's always loved wine."

"I don't ever remember him drinking anything but Riunite Lombrusco when I was a kid," she retorted.

"I think his tastes have matured a bit."

"Are there even any grapes growing around here?"

"Not yet. That's my department."

"When's that going to happen?"

"It's a long way off. Probably next summer."

"Seriously? You aren't even going to plant for a year?"

His shrug was decidedly rueful. "It takes time to prepare the soil, especially since it's been ignored for so long."

"Have you worked at a winery before? Are grapes your specialty?"

"Not exactly."

"So what did you do before you came here?"

He had tensed during her questioning, and she figured she was being pushy. But asking him about his past was better than asking him how on earth he managed to find shirts that fit over all those muscles.

"Let's just say I've been digging in the dirt a lot in recent years. This job makes me feel a whole lot cleaner."

That was mysterious, but his clipped tone said it was as much as she was going to get.

"Now, your grandfather's surgery is scheduled for 10:00 a.m. Why don't you grab a few hours' sleep and we'll try to get to the hospital at around eight?"

"All right."

Rising, she picked up her cup, and his, carrying them over to the sink. She noted that, while brewing the tea, Oliver had stuck the pots and pans in the dishwasher, as if to get them out of throwing range. Candace still couldn't believe she'd thought a few kitchen items would stop him if he'd really been some kind of villain. With that body—those strong arms and the table-wide chest—he could pick her up and break her in half.

Or, a wicked part of her realized, just *split* her in half with that amazing power tool in his pants. Not having had sex in a while, she couldn't be entirely sure her memory wasn't faulty, but if she had to guess, she'd say that had been a good eight inches of jackhammer straining against his zipper.

"Need a hand?"

She started, not having realized he'd left the table and walked up behind her. It was bad enough to be caught thinking he had an amazing body, but even worse to be standing here wondering about the size of the man's johnson.

"No, thank you," she said, hearing the breathiness in her voice. He was just so close, so big and warm. All she could think about was how it had felt to be pressed against him, his hands on her hips, his salt-tinged skin against her mouth.

It had been a long time since she'd been close to anyone. Honestly, the thought of not being held in a man's strong arms for five years was almost as upsetting to her as knowing she would not be filled and possessed by one in the most raw, sexual way.

Almost.

"Okay, meet you outside at seven-thirty?"

She nodded, turning to face him, hoping her cheeks weren't pink. She was not the blushing type. Still, she feared the heat in her face hadn't been caused by the steam rising off the hot water in the sink.

"Thank you. And again, I'm sorry I attacked you."

He shrugged. "Wasn't the first time."

She quirked a brow. "Incite a lot of women to violence, do you?"

"Not recently."

But he didn't say anything else. He merely nodded good-night and left the kitchen, leaving her wondering what the real story was behind Oliver McKean.

3

CANDACE REID WAS as good as her word. Despite having probably only gotten the same few hours of sleep he had the night before, she was waiting on her grandfather's front steps when he walked out of his cottage at 7:30 a.m.

She looked like crap.

Bloodshot eyes, pale cheeks sans makeup, sopping wet hair slung up in a ponytail—definitely not the Candace he'd met at 3:00 a.m. She wore a shapeless, heavy hoodie that would be much too warm in a few hours when the day shifted into typical Northern California mode, with its wildly swinging night-to-day temperature changes. The jeans weren't designer; in fact, they looked worn and scruffy. And the functional sneakers in no way resembled the spike-heeled do-me shoes of the night before.

He knew he wasn't seeing her at her sexy best, but couldn't help thinking he liked this not-so-put-together version of the Hollywood costume designer. In her real life, with all the feminine trappings women relied on, she probably would have blended into the stylish crowd to which he had become so accustomed when living in L.A. Hell, he'd even been a part of it on occasion. But here, out of her element, obviously uncomfortable and not making any pretentious efforts to impress anyone—including him—he found her vulnerability refreshing.

Huh. Part of him should be a little disappointed that she wasn't making any effort to impress him, considering how thick the sexual tension between them had been the night before. It had filled that kitchen like an invisible fog. He'd definitely thought about her long after he'd gone back to his bed.

But he hadn't come to Sonoma to get caught up with a woman. He'd chosen this area because it was his favorite place to vacation—he loved the scenery, the pace and the people. He'd needed to reevaluate, to recover a sense of peace and tranquility that had been lost during his years running in the rat race with some huge rats. This period of solitude was about regrouping, finding his focus and doing penance for the shitty things he'd done to get ahead in the Orange County D.A.'s office.

Taking a sabbatical from the spotlight hadn't been a bad side benefit, either. The press had had a field day with him when he'd blown the lid off some of the shenanigans taking place in the courthouse. Rising young stars in the prosecutor's office weren't supposed to refuse to railroad an innocent man in order to close a big case, and they definitely weren't supposed to blow the whistle on the misconduct of others. Oh, yeah, he had definitely been front-page fodder, which made him persona non grata with the legal types in L.A., and would for quite some time. Frankly, that was fine with him. He wanted to forget about that period of his life, and wanted everyone there to forget about him.

So, no, having a hot affair just didn't fit in with his plan of atonement. It was just as well Candace had dialed her sex appeal down a notch, even if nothing could really eradicate the beauty of her face or the curviness of her body.

If her appearance today was meant to send him a message, he'd gotten it. Loud and clear. She wasn't interested.

"You sleep okay?" he asked as he walked over, already knowing the answer to his question.

"Sleep? What's that? I feel like the princess from the fairy tale, only there wasn't a pea under the mattress, there were cantaloupes the size of my head."

"I don't think your grandfather has had a chance to re-decorate. A lot of the furniture came with the house, so it's probably pretty old."

"Who owned it before? Fred Flintstone?"

He couldn't contain a chuckle. "The house was built by an old silent movie star, and it remained in his family for several decades until it fell into ruin. He supposedly threw some wild parties with his Hollywood buddies."

"Huh…my kingdom for a Westin heavenly bed. I'd rather be comfortable than sleep on the mattress that once held Charlie Chaplin." She winced and rubbed her shoulder. "And still might, given the bony lumps inside it."

The old Oliver, the one who'd once been young and carefree and had done killer impressions that cracked up his sisters, might have tottered side to side and swung an invisible cane.

The new Oliver—hardened by the things he'd seen, the things he'd *done*—barely even remembered that ide-alistic guy.

"Ready?"

"Sure."

She stepped into the passenger seat of the beat-up old truck as he got in behind the wheel and together, they headed toward the hospital. He could feel her tension and her anticipation. She sat forward on her seat, as if urging the old bucket of rust to go faster.

"Would you sit still?" he grumbled. "Visiting hours don't even start until eight."

"If we keep going negative-two miles an hour, we won't be there until it's time for Grandpa to go in for his surgery."

"If we were going negative-two miles an hour, we'd be going backward."

She smirked. "Now you're just being silly."

Unaccustomed to being called anything of the sort, he tightened his hands on the steering wheel.

"So how did you end up working for my grandfather?"

His grip grew even tighter. "I was just wandering. We ran into each other and he told me he was looking for help to get the old place up and running. Lucky for me, I had some time and experience."

His experience with grounds keeping had been limited to his lawn-cutting business during high school. But that had been enough for Buddy, who, he suspected, had hired him because he wanted the company as much as Oliver's strong back. And it had helped that Oliver was connected to the estate. He also suspected Buddy had sensed Oliver *needed* to be there, to work hard, not think and stay away from most of the world.

The old man had asked him if he was a criminal hiding out from the law. When Oliver had sworn he was not, they'd shaken hands and that had been that. Four months later, after studying everything he could find on the wine business, Oliver had calluses on his blisters, muscles in places he'd never known he'd needed them and the beginnings of a clear head.

"Sorry, but you just don't look much like a gardener," she said, obviously realizing he was prevaricating.

He cast her a sideways glance and let a faint smile lift the corner of his mouth. "You don't look much like a fashion designer, either."

Instead of taking offense, she barked a laugh and lifted a hand to her sopping ponytail. "Touché. I know I'm a mess. Aside from the horrible bed, a cricket kept chirping somewhere inside the house. And the water in the shower ranged from cold to frigid."

"Devastating," he murmured.

She continued, "There's not a hair dryer in sight, because, of course, Grandpa doesn't need one. I almost stuck my head over the stove but figured that might be pushing it."

"Knowing how dangerous things tend to happen when you're in a kitchen, that was probably a good call. And we don't want to tax rescue services with a call about a fire. They were already out here once this week."

"Did I mention that the airline misplaced my big suitcase? I only had my carry-on, which is why I'm wearing the old clothes that my sister left here when she came to visit a year ago."

Judging by the clothes, the sister was a different type of dresser altogether.

"We can run by a store later if you need to shop," he said.

"If the airline doesn't show up with my things within a couple of days, I might have to take you up on that. I had the basic necessities in my carry-on, but I'll be out of stuff pretty soon."

"Are you really going to stick around for a while?" he asked, wondering if she truly intended to stay for weeks. Man, he hoped not. He was supposed to be enjoying a retreat from the real world. But this talkative, beautiful woman had brought it crashing in on him like the winds of a hurricane.

"Maybe. I'm between projects and was supposed to be going out of town for a couple of weeks anyway," she said, crossing her arms and leaning against her window to look out at the passing scenery. "This isn't exactly France, though."

"You were going to France?"

She nodded but didn't look over.

"Why would it have been better if you'd met me there?"

She jerked and swung around to stare at him. "What?"

"You said that last night."

She bit that succulent bottom lip.

He prodded her. "Your exact words were, I believe, 'Why, oh, God, why didn't I meet you in Paris?'"

She huffed. "Jeez, what are you, a transcriptionist?"

"I have a very good memory."

"Obviously."

"So?"

"So what?"

She was obviously trying to deflect, and he considered letting her get away with it. But something about that sad face and those slumped shoulders made him want to rile her up a little. He'd been raised with sisters, so he knew that nothing worked better to get them out of a sad slump than giving them something to be mad about.

"So, why would it have been better if you'd met me in Paris?"

"I was hysterical. I didn't know what I was saying."

"Not that hysterical. As I recall, you were pretty damned calm at that point. Sedate even."

Her eyes narrowed. "Shall we talk about how *you* were at that point?"

Hell, if she thought he was going to apologize for getting a hard-on when he'd had a gorgeous woman in his arms, she had another think coming. "I have a Y chromosome. And you're beautiful."

Her bluff having been called, she looked away.

"Paris," he reminded her.

Crossing her arms over her chest and harrumphing, she said, "I just meant if I was going to end up in some hot guy's arms this week, it should have been in the city of light, not in my grandfather's kitchen."

He made a mental note of the *hot,* wondering if she

even realized she'd just revealed a little more about her thoughts of last night.

Casting him an arch look, she added, "By the way, it could have been any guy's arms."

"Hot."

"What?"

"You said any *hot* guy's arms."

"It's like I'm riding with a digital voice recorder."

"Like I said. Good memory."

"The point is, I was just speaking in *general* terms about how a run-down old kitchen can't compare to the most romantic city in the world. That's *all*."

He wasn't buying it. "Didn't sound that way."

"Would you stop interrogating me?"

There was fire in her eyes now, and color in her cheeks. Indignation wafted from her, and he congratulated himself on getting her mind off her troubles. Let her be annoyed at him, and engage in a little verbal sparring. At least it would be a few minutes less she spent worrying about her obviously deeply loved grandfather.

"Why were you going to France?"

"Did you miss the part about not interrogating me?"

"It's just a simple question."

"One that's really none of your business."

"So, not for work, then."

She just huffed.

He speculated aloud. "If there was a possibility you'd end up in some random guy's arms, you obviously weren't meeting up with a boyfriend."

"Did you also miss the part where I said it was about kitchen vs. Paris and *not* about a stupid man?"

"Your boyfriend's stupid?"

"Argh!"

Defense attorneys hadn't called him the Honey Badger

of Hollywood for no reason. Oliver had been born with a persistent gene. "Was that an answer?"

"I *don't* have a stupid boyfriend."

"Well he can't be very smart if he lets you come alone up to Sonoma to be stalked by a potential ax-murdering maniac in your grandfather's kitchen."

"There's no boyfriend, okay? Stupid or otherwise!"

He'd known that's what she was saying but was glad for the confirmation, anyway. He couldn't say why that certainty sent a hint of relief gushing through his veins, but it did. "Well, that's good. I'm afraid I'd lose a little respect for you if you liked stupid guys."

"Right now, they're sounding very appealing," she mumbled.

"Low standards, huh?"

"No, I just wouldn't have to be couching every word I say so it couldn't be used against me in a court of law."

That was striking a little close to home. "Because a stupid guy would understand you better?"

"No, because I wouldn't give a damn if he didn't!"

"You calling me smart, and saying you give a damn?" He wondered if she could see his half smirk. "Gee, hot and smart in one conversation. Better watch it, Miss Reid, or you'll make my head swell."

"Shut up, all right? Just. Stop. Talking."

He finally started to laugh. The sound felt a little rusty; he didn't make it very often anymore. And after a few seconds, she slowly joined in.

"You did that on purpose."

"Maybe."

"Women must threaten your life on a regular basis."

"I guess."

They were silent for a moment, then she sighed softly and said, "Thank you."

She didn't have to elaborate. He knew what she meant. So he merely replied, "You're welcome."

A few minutes later, they arrived at the hospital. Seeing it ratcheted up her tension again, and she was yanking the handle and hopping out of the truck the second he parked. He caught up with her at the hospital entrance and escorted her to Buddy's room.

After a soft knock, they entered to find the old man dozing. He was still hooked up to machines and a morphine drip and probably looked pretty bad to his granddaughter. But compared to how he'd looked after he'd fallen yesterday, this was quite an improvement. Oliver wasn't sure he'd ever get over the terror he'd felt when he'd heard the loud cry of pain and he'd run around the house to see Buddy lying on the ground, looking like a fragile, broken porcelain doll.

"Grandpa?"

The eyes shot open and the old man turned to stare at her, his blue eyes shining with vitality and affection. "Candy-cane, what are you doing here?" He cast a glance at Oliver. "I told you not to worry anybody."

"Don't be silly," she said, bending to kiss his forehead. She tenderly brushed away a long strand of silvery hair—used in the ultimate old-man comb-over to cover the sizable bald spot on his pate. "Mom was going to come herself..."

"Ridiculous! She needs to stay in Florida and take care of your stodgy old fart of a father."

Seeing the smile on Candace's face, and the matching one on Buddy's, Oliver could only think theirs was a close-knit family and the joke was an old one. Buddy had to be at least eighty, but he was usually as peppy and energetic as a much-younger man.

"Well, that's why I came, to scope out the situation and see if she needed to visit."

"She doesn't!"

"You certainly seem peppy."

"I'm feeling no pain," he admitted. "You really don't have to stay."

"Of course I'm staying. I'll be here when you get out of surgery, and I'll be at your house waiting for you when you come home."

He didn't argue anymore, looking visibly touched and showing just the faintest hint of vulnerability. Buddy might not want to be a bother, but when it came to being in the hospital, nothing beat having family nearby. The old man hadn't said anything about being nervous about his operation, but considering he hadn't been expecting any such thing twenty-four hours ago, he had to be worried about it.

"I think I'll give you two some time alone," Oliver said. "Buddy, I just wanted to say I'm here and hope everything goes well with the surgery. I have no doubt you'll be kicking up clods of dirt and rocks in no time."

His boss nodded. "Thank you for bringing my grandbaby to see me."

"Not a problem."

"You'll make sure she's okay out there at the house? It's awfully lonely and desolate for a helpless young girl on her own."

He saw Candace roll her eyes at the description. "I'll be fine," she insisted. "I certainly don't need a babysitter."

"Humor an old man. Promise me you'll let Oliver look after you."

She glanced back and forth between them, her mouth opening and snapping closed. Obviously she didn't want to promise any such thing. However, she didn't want to upset her elderly relative, either. Finally, she hedged. "If I need anything, I'll be sure to ask him."

That could range from needing a roll of toilet paper to

needing a spider killed. What it wasn't was an agreement to let him watch over her.

"Promise?"

She obviously didn't like being pressed, and mumbled, "If there's a dire emergency, Oliver is the first one I'll call."

Buddy didn't appear thrilled by the concession, but apparently knew he'd pushed hard enough. "All right." Then he extended his hand. "Thank you again, Oliver."

Oliver walked over for a handshake, but when he tried to end it, the old man didn't let go. Instead, Buddy clutched his hand, while also holding his granddaughter's.

"So, you two are getting along okay?"

If Cupid had ever suffered from a broken hip, he'd probably have taken a day off. Not so for Buddy Frye.

"Grandpa," she said warningly.

"She's already tried to kill me," Oliver said, caught off guard.

Buddy snickered. Obviously the pain meds were still in fine working order. Eyeing Candace, he said, "Did I ever tell you about what your grandma did to me once, back when we were dating? She shoved me in front of a moving car."

"No, you didn't tell me, and I don't believe it," she replied a little primly. Then she gave Oliver a look that said, *Don't you dare make fun of me about this.*

"Yep. She said I was smiling too much at a waitress, so she pushed me into the street. My, that woman loved me."

"She had a funny way of showing it," Oliver couldn't help mumbling. "Imagine if you'd ever really flirted with someone. You'd have been nose-to-nose with a freight train."

Candace obviously heard and her lips quirked.

"I just want you two to get along," Buddy said, settling deeper into his bed and arranging his covers over himself.

He wasn't looking at either of them. "I think you probably have a lot in common."

"I doubt it," Candace said, her tone saying the subject was at an end.

Oliver didn't back her up, or offer her a reassuring glance. He couldn't deny he found the idea of her grandfather playing matchmaker pretty cute, even if the very idea that she'd need him to was ridiculous. The woman was smart, beautiful, funny…she wouldn't need an elderly relative fixing her up. He suspected she could have just about any man she wanted.

She wants a stupid, foreign one, he reminded himself. *Not you.*

Which was just as well. He'd already decided he was not getting personally involved with Candace Reid. So the less time he spent in her company, the better.

She could take care of herself, of that he had no doubt. He would remember Buddy's request and help her in the case of a major emergency, like if the pipes burst or a robber turned up. But as far as spiders and toilet paper went, she was on her own, and he was steering clear.

It was better that way…for both of them.

4

It was the size of a Volkswagen.

Big, hairy, with a million eyes and fuzzy spiked legs and probably a sac full of poison hidden on its bulbous body.

Spiders. God, she hated spiders. Especially spiders who were blocking the only exit from the kitchen, where she stood, wearing a filmy, short little bathrobe, freezing her butt off because she'd come down to put coffee on right after she'd gotten out of the cold-as-ice shower.

"Go away," she ordered in a quivery voice.

The spider ignored her and remained planted right in her path. Beady little pinpoint eyes stared up at her, red and angry—or maybe not, but they looked that way to her—and she knew if he had a mouth, it was smirking.

She edged backward toward the stove, thankful she'd glanced down before walking out of the kitchen, because if she'd placed her bare foot on that furry little beast, she would have screamed loud enough for Tommy to hear her back in L.A. Besides, the little creature looked big enough to have flung her off rather than being smashed flat.

Candace wasn't scared by much. Snakes didn't bother her; she had been skydiving so she wasn't afraid of heights. She'd even bungee jumped off a bridge in Mexico once.

She'd stared down more than her fair share of grubby dudes with cheesy come-on lines on the street.

But bugs? Spiders in particular?

The little bastards terrified her.

"Candace?" a voice called. A voice that was familiar, even though she hadn't talked to him much in the past few days.

She and Oliver, as if by unspoken agreement, had spent little time together since the morning her grandfather had tried to fix them up. When they'd left late that day, after visiting with Grandpa in the recovery room, Oliver had brought her to a car rental place so she could get her own vehicle. She didn't want to have to rely on him to run her back and forth to the hospital, which was where she spent most of her time. They ran into each other there on occasion, had grabbed coffee or a quick lunch and engaged in a little small talk. But as if they both realized they probably shouldn't spend too much time together out at the house, where they were entirely alone, they'd avoided interaction. They exchanged mostly waves as they were coming or going, or when he was working out on the grounds, and she was watching him while pretending she wasn't at all interested.

Any woman would be interested. It was bad enough seeing him inside at the hospital, clothed and respectable. When he worked, when he stripped off his shirt to wipe his sweaty, dirty face, and those muscles rippled and gleamed, he was male beauty in motion. The few times they had talked at home, she'd done everything she could to keep from revealing how incredibly attracted she was to him. Sometimes, though, she caught him staring at her, and suspected she wasn't doing a very good job.

She only wished he would do something to reveal whether or not he felt the same way. So far, he hadn't. He'd been cordial and polite, never more than that, as if she'd suddenly become his employer now that Grandpa was out of commission.

Got a task for you there, Mr. Groundskeeper. How about doing a little plowing for me?

She scrunched her eyes shut, muttering, "Not French, not stupid, off-limits."

"Candace? Are you here?"

"In the kitchen," she said, not sure whether she was hoping he would turn right back around and leave, or that he'd stride in and accidentally squish Mr. Spider so she wouldn't have to (A) deal with the arachnid herself, or (B) technically ask for Oliver's help.

"I just wanted to let you know your suitcase has finally made it. The delivery service just left it on the porch. I signed for it."

Oh, thank goodness. She'd been fighting with the airline about it all week, fearing she would have to put in a claim to replace everything she'd packed for the trip. She'd run out of her sister Madison's left-behind clothes and had had to wash and rewash the few items she'd had in her small carry-on bag. Especially the panties. Hmm. Funny how she'd gone through panties at a record rate since she'd met Oliver. That man ought to buy stock in Victoria's Secret.

"I'll bring it in. Do you want me to haul it up to your room?"

She nibbled her lip, wanting no such thing. Oliver in her bedroom, near her messed bed with the silky nightie tossed carelessly on top? Him filling her private space with that delectable, intoxicating man smell?

Hell, no. She was already having the most intense, erotic dreams about the guy without ever having to picture him near her bed. No way was she going to invite even hotter ones.

"No, it's okay. You can just leave it in the hall."

She waited to hear him bring in the bag and leave.

Waited for an acknowledgment—something. But there was nothing but silence. Frowning, she risked edging a tiny bit closer to the doorway, never taking her eyes off her fuzzy enemy, who showed no signs of moving out of the way. She briefly considered jumping over him, but had the most horrible vision of him launching up while she was split-legged above him. For all she knew, he could be the bug world-record holder at the high jump. Considering she wore nothing but the short robe, she wasn't prepared to even think about where he might land if he leaped. Her vajayjay might have grown cobwebs from disuse, but that was taking things a step too far.

She desperately wanted to go out and make sure Oliver was gone, then dash up the stairs and put some clothes on before he could come back, but it looked like she was going to be involved in a spider standoff for hours. Thinking, she finally grabbed the broom and tried waving it in his general direction. But it wasn't until she got the bristles to within six inches or so that the thing began to move.

Straight toward her.

"No—get away from me!"

A hard pounding emerged from the hallway. She recognized it as running footsteps just as Oliver burst into the kitchen. He didn't hold a rake this time, but the look on his face said he expected trouble.

"What is it?" he snapped as he scanned the room. "What's wrong?"

"Uh, nothing," she said, forcing a smile. Though, when she saw where he stood, she didn't have to force it any further. Because unless the creepy crawly had moved really fast, he was right now stuck to the bottom of a man's thick-soled work boot. Although she loved most creatures, she wasn't about to start playing a dirge for that one, who'd looked like a mad scientist's experimental cross between a bug and a dinosaur.

"Who were you talking to?"

"Nobody. I thought you'd left."

"I was bringing in your suitcase," he explained, walking closer, studying her face to see if she was lying, perhaps covering for a bad guy hiding in the pantry. He obviously wasn't going to go away without an explanation.

Knowing she had to, she admitted in a voice a little above a whisper, "There was a spider."

His frown disappeared. A twinkle might have appeared in those dark bedroom eyes, but he had the courtesy not to smile. "One that speaks English and follows orders?"

"Ha-ha, very funny. That thing was *huge.* I mean, it could have been wearing a mask, swinging from webs and looking for the Green Goblin!"

"Comic book fan, huh?"

"Movie biz, remember?"

And considering Tommy was hoping to be cast as the latest comic hero, he'd made her watch a bunch of them recently. She wasn't a huge fan of the genre, but had to admit, some of those guys did an awesome job filling out their clingy costumes. She'd become a huge Jeremy Renner fan in the past year and fantasized about getting to dress him. Undressing him would be a mighty fine experience, too.

"So where is this huge mutant creature?"

"Gone."

"Where'd he go?"

"I think onto the bottom of your shoe."

"You sure? I didn't hear anything that sounded like the crushing of a colossus."

"Well, he's not..." Her voice trailed off and her eyes rounded as she saw a black leg disappearing behind the table leg. She squeaked, grabbed his arm and ducked behind him. "Oh, God."

"What?"

Keeping her voice low, as if they were facing a ravaging tiger, she replied, "He's right over there."

He followed her gaze and snorted. "That's your monster spider? He's tiny."

"That thing's as big as my hand!" Closing her eyes, she begged, "Please take it away, Oliver. I'll pay you.... I'll bake you a cake, cook you dinner. Just *please* get it out of here."

"Are you a good cook?"

"The best. Excellent. Cordon Bleu. Restaurants vie for my services."

"Are you lying?"

"Oh, hell, yes. Right through my teeth. Now would you please help me?"

"I thought you didn't need any help except in the most dire emergency."

"This is dire."

"Are you an arachnophobe?"

"If that means I am utterly terrified to my bones and feel like I'm going to throw up if I so much as glimpse a spider, then yes, that's me."

"Gotcha."

He didn't tease her anymore, as if knowing she wasn't playing the weak girlie-girl in some effort to entice him. Not, she hoped, that he would ever expect her to. Turning, he grabbed the dustpan, then unhooked her death grip from the broom. Drawing on his primal, caveman-hunter genes, he stalked the monster, deftly swept it into the pan and carried it toward the front door.

"Are you just going to let it go?" she asked, following him. "What if it gets back in?"

"I'm sure he'd be too afraid to risk it. You're pretty intimidating."

"Are you sure you shouldn't squish it?"

"Bloodthirsty, aren't you?"

She thought about it. She wasn't, really. Still, some things were just beyond the bounds of humanity, and sharing a house with a big honking spider was one of them.

"You'll be glad for him during mosquito season."

"Maybe if they're killer mosquitoes carrying the ebola virus. Otherwise, I'll invest in calamine lotion and take my chances."

He opened the door, walked outside and was back with the broom and dustpan a moment later. Leaning them both against the wall, he said, "All gone."

Relieved, she drew in a deep breath and whispered, "Thank you."

"You're welcome. You okay now?"

She nodded slowly. "Oh, sure. Fine."

Her pulse finally stopped racing and her muscles loosened. The nausea receded, as did the panic. Not for the first time in her life, she found herself wondering if an older cousin had dangled a spider in her face when she was a baby or something. Because her phobia about them had been lifelong and was, even she could admit it, a little obsessive. Now that her heart wasn't thumping hard enough to beat out of her chest, she could acknowledge she might have overacted just a teeny, tiny bit.

Feeling almost normal, she waited for Oliver to turn and walk out the door. Considering he usually avoided her, that's what she expected him to do. But for some reason, he didn't leave. He just stood there, two feet away, drawing in slow, even breaths as he studied her.

Finally, he murmured, "Cold in here."

Her spider terror having receded, she paused to remember just what she was wearing—not much.

Her skimpy robe hung to the tops of her thighs, leaving her legs completely bared. The robe also gaped over her breasts, revealing a deep V of cleavage. The whole thing was held together only by a loosely knotted sash.

"Yes, I guess it is," she replied slowly, wondering if he had been making small talk or offering a sideways comment on the fact that her nipples were hard, poking visibly against the silk sliding so sinuously over them.

He continued to stare, falling silent. She knew the answer to that question. He'd finally noticed her apparel—or lack thereof. Oliver was definitely reacting to it. Looking at her. Staring at her.

Visually devouring her.

Her lips parted on a tiny helpless sigh. He didn't acknowledge the sound, instead merely swept that dark-eyed attention over her, from damp-haired top to bare-toed bottom. The gaze was like a touch, lingering here, skimming over there, and she reacted to it instinctively. Here went soft, there went hard, and her most vulnerable places went all hot and wet.

She knew she should yank her robe more tightly around her body and glare him into stopping, or else turn and flounce up the stairs, but she couldn't bring herself to do it. She'd been looked at by men before, of course. By lovers, by potential lovers, by strangers, but she had never felt as thoroughly studied as she did now. It was as if he was examining her, tucking away every detail of her into his prodigious internal memory bank. His dark eyes gleamed, and he made absolutely no effort to disguise his focus or make her think he was doing anything other than memorizing all the things he could see, and imagining all those he could not.

He wanted her. It was stunningly obvious. He was imagining what wild, wicked things they could do together, of that she had no doubt. She knew because she'd been thinking the same thing since the night she'd arrived. So how could she blame him?

A mental voice shouted a warning. But another part of her—the part that had been trying to figure out if he had been avoiding her for the past few days because he *wasn't* attracted to her, or because he *was*—appeared to be calling the shots.

She couldn't walk away from him now. Not just yet.

"This is a really bad idea," he muttered.

She knew what he meant but still replied, "What is?"

He swept a hand through his dark hair. The movement made his arms bulge against the white T-shirt he wore, and drew the thin fabric tight against his shoulders. "You standing there, looking like that. Me standing here, looking at you looking like that."

Her mouth went dry.

Turn around, Candace. Go upstairs. Pray your vibrator is still safely tucked in your suitcase and wasn't pawed over by some luggage guys, dig it out and remember you don't technically need a man to give you orgasms.

But she remained still, as if her feet were glued to the floor. Her vibrator couldn't fill her the way she so desperately wanted to be filled. It couldn't hold her, stroke her, touch her, lick her. It couldn't make her feel as utterly jittery with excitement as she felt just standing here, knowing he wanted her.

Besides, she suddenly realized she *couldn't* run away up to her room. Not while he was standing at the bottom of the steps. Her robe was short and tiny, which was why she'd stuffed it in her carry-on bag, and she had never been more conscious of the fact that she wasn't wearing any underwear. Although she and her sister had done their share of mooning during her younger, wilder days, the only way she wanted to wiggle her bare bottom at this man was if she got on all fours and invited him to make her howl.

Unfortunately, it seemed a bit early in their relationship for that kind of invitation.

No relationship. There's not going to be any relationship. Remember?

"Go upstairs," he ordered, his voice strangled. That was pretty far from an admission of lust.

She instinctively shook her head.

He stepped closer, scowling, almost threatening, as if he could intimidate her into going. "Walk away, Candace. Please."

"No. *You* walk away. The door's right there."

"I can't." His hand rose and he stroked the sleeve of her robe, fingering the silk. He didn't look down, never took his attention off her face, and she wondered if he even realized he'd moved so close. So incredibly close.

"It has to be you," he insisted.

"Why?"

"I need you to turn your back on me, to make it clear that you want me to leave."

He waited. She didn't turn.

"All right, at least say it," he ordered. "Make it clear."

She knew what he was asking, but she couldn't give him what he wanted—a verbal command to go. Not when she suddenly wanted, with every fiber of her being, for him to stay.

"Tell me to go," he pleaded.

She wordlessly shook her head.

He muttered a curse. Reaching for her, as if unable to control himself, he caught hold of the silky bathrobe tie at her waist. He tightened it a little, maybe not even realizing he was doing it, as if he was fighting an inner battle between pushing her away and pulling her close.

But she realized it. Her nerve endings were roaring now, her heart thudding in her chest. There was something almost predatory in his expression, and the tightening of the sash around her waist made her feel somehow claimed.

If he pushed her away, she would be devastated.

If he pulled her close, she'd be lost.

"Go upstairs," he insisted.

"I don't have to."

"God, you're stubborn." He leaned in closer, until his pant legs brushed her bare calves. The fabric was deliciously rough and warm from his body and she couldn't help stepping closer, sucking up that warmth. The early morning air was still chilly but heat wafted from him, like he'd absorbed the first sunbeams of the new day and could now reflect them back.

He inhaled deeply, as if he needed her scent in his lungs. She knew she smelled fresh, soapy and clean, not perfumed or lotioned, but the man looked intoxicated all the same.

"This is not why I came in here." His face was so close to hers, she could feel the gentle fall of his exhalations on her skin. A slight shift and there was the most delicate rasp of his stubble upon her cheek.

"You came to bring my suitcase," she murmured, not really thinking about the words they exchanged, able to focus only on his closeness. His power. The scent of his body, the roughness of his strong jaw. She wanted that roughness scraping all over her, knowing his soft, delicious mouth could kiss away any soreness.

"Right. And now I have." He moved his body even closer. Their thighs came together.

"So you can go." She arched against him, sighing as her hard, aching nipples met that masculine chest.

"You want me to?" One of his hands dropped to her hip and he squeezed lightly, again making her feel claimed.

"The choice is yours." She tilted her head to the side, offering him the bare expanse of her neck.

"I'll go then." He moved his face to her throat, not kissing, not tasting, just breathing in and out, a millimeter from her skin, increasing the tension, heightening her senses.

So close. So incredibly close.

"If you say so." She closed her eyes, swaying slightly

on her feet, willing him not to go, and, for heaven's sake, to just stop talking about it and kiss her.

"I'm going."

"Don't let me stop you."

"Damn it," he muttered as if he'd finally realized she wasn't going to order him to leave, and had finally snapped himself out of the sensual spell. But he still couldn't back away completely, and brushed his cheek against her hair. "Do you always have to get your way?"

"Ask me in an hour."

And she gave up, stopped playing coy and took what she'd been wanting since the night they'd met. Not giving him a chance to fight it anymore, she twined her fingers in his hair and pulled him to her. His eyes flared and he tensed. Then, with a deep groan, he gave in to her and lowered his mouth to hers.

Their lips parted, the kiss hot, sensuous and wet. There was nothing tentative about it, no hesitation, no regret. He simply devoured her and she let him, tilting her head, loving the feel of his tongue in her mouth. Their bodies were pressed together, his hands at her waist, hers tangled in his thick hair, and the kiss went on and on, deep and hungry. She had sensed this man's mouth had been made for kissing, and now she knew. He dined on her, sipped from her, swallowed her exhalations as if he needed her breaths to expand his lungs and fuel his cells.

Against her groin, she again felt the rigid heat that proclaimed his desire for her more than words ever could. Clad only in the robe, with his body slammed against hers, she couldn't help but notice the rock-hard strength of him. She moaned, low in her throat, and rocked toward it, so filled with need she thought her legs would give out.

He suddenly tensed, as if realizing they were one step away from too-far-to-stop. Dropping his hands, he ended the kiss and pulled away, staggering back a step to punctuate the end of their embrace.

The sound of their ragged breaths filled the silent air. Candace felt certain every ounce of blood in her body had pooled in her most intimate places, which now throbbed and boiled with demand. Her breasts hurt, the nipples so sensitive that the scrape of the silk robe was almost unbearable, and she knew nothing would make them feel better but his hands, his tongue, his lips.

But the look on his face said she wasn't going to get any of those things. His hands were shoved in his pockets, his tongue was back in his mouth, his lips were sealed tight and turned down in a frown.

He was trying to pretend he regretted the kiss.

She knew he didn't.

"That was…unexpected," she admitted, hearing the weakness of her voice.

"Yeah." He cleared his throat. "I'm sorry, I didn't mean to…"

"Oh, of course you *meant* to. Just as I meant to."

"Maybe you're right. But that doesn't mean it can happen again, or go any further."

She opened her mouth to argue.

"You're only here for a short time, you're my boss's granddaughter and he trusted me to look after you."

"I think he was sort of hoping you would romance me," she said, her tone dry.

"Yeah, but not bang you up against the front door."

"Is that where we would have ended up? Gee, and the sofa is right in the next room."

"Damn it, Candace."

She held a hand up, palm out, stopping him from saying anything more. "Forget it. I know you're right. I have reasons of my own for not insisting you rip off your clothes and do me until I can't remember my own name."

He coughed and laughed, both at the same time. Then, as if the laughter—and her saucy words—had snapped some kind of spell, he reached out, put his hands on her shoulders and spun her around so she faced the staircase. Gently pushing her, he ordered, "Go."

She spun back around. "I can't."

His jaw turned into granite. "You're being ridiculous."

All because he needed *her* to be the one who walked away and ended this before it really began? As if he had no free will? As if he wouldn't be able to stop himself from doing to her exactly what she'd practically dared him to do unless she removed herself from his presence?

You don't want him to do it, either, remember? You know you can't do this.

Her grandfather was being moved to a rehab facility today. He'd be there for about a week, and then he would be coming home. But coming home to what? Her having an affair with his groundskeeper, then the descent of the paparazzi once her engagement was announced? Did he really need that while he recovered? Did Oliver, who was obviously here for reasons he hadn't yet revealed to her? Did she need the scandal? Did Tommy?

No. She might want Oliver, and having sex with him might even be worth what she would go through afterward if people found out. But nobody else deserved it. She needed to cool this, here and now. She had to be the one who walked away.

Which still wasn't going to be easy.

"I'm telling you, you really don't want to watch me walking up those stairs."

"Yes. I really do."

"And you're honestly not going to get out of here until I do?"

"No."

"You'll regret it."

"Hell, I already regret it," he said, tunneling both his hands through his hair this time, leaving it more tousled than before.

"Not as much as you're about to."

A helping of anger had been heaped upon her sexual frustration. Yes, she'd decided she couldn't have him, but did he have to be so damned insistent about it?

She hadn't been kidding that he was going to regret it. Because she was ready to give him what he was asking for…and wondered if he was ready for what came along with it.

Without another word, she spun around again, squared her shoulders, stiffened her spine and ascended the stairs. He stood below, watching her, and when she reached the fourth one, she couldn't help pausing to glance over her shoulder at him.

"Oh, Oliver, do you want to know why I didn't want to walk up the stairs until you left?"

He didn't reply, just gave her an inscrutable look.

She told him anyway. "Because of this."

Candace took another step, knowing she'd reached the point of no return. Knowing full well he could now see what she was *not* wearing beneath her robe.

She wished she could say his strangled, guttural cry of helpless frustration made her feel better about walking away from what she sensed could be the best sex of her life.

But she just couldn't.

5

EVER SINCE HE'D started getting involved with females, Oliver had known how to handle them. Maybe it was because he'd had sisters, lots of girl cousins and parents with an honest, loving marriage in which nobody held the upper hand. Maybe because he'd had girls after him since he hit puberty. Maybe he'd just been born with the gene.

The point was, he'd always been sure of himself when it came to women. He'd always known when one was interested and when she wasn't, been able to gauge how soon was too soon, or when it was too late and he'd missed his shot. He'd set the pace, led the dance, taken the right steps at the right time.

Until now. Until her. Until Candace.

She had him twisted inside out and upside down, not knowing what to do or say next. He didn't know whether to resist or keep on fighting. Part of him wished she'd never shown up at Buddy's house, and another part dreaded the day she would leave.

"God, what a mess," he muttered that evening as he finished taking inventory in the wine cellar. He hadn't even realized there was one in the house until today, when he'd gone to visit Buddy in the rehab center. He'd watched for

Candace to leave the room, heading to the cafeteria for lunch, and then stopped by, not wanting to run into her after what had happened this morning. Coming face-to-face with her would have been more than his heart could have taken, even a couple of hours after she'd marched her bare little fanny up the stairs.

No, not little. Round, supple, perfect.

Just right for cupping in his hands, or pounding against as he took her from behind, the way he'd been dying to as he'd watched her sashay back to her room.

He swallowed hard, wishing he hadn't allowed himself to go back there in his mind. He'd managed to avoid thinking about her most of the day, but now the images came washing in. He was again overwhelmed by the memory of the gorgeous, naked ass she'd flashed at him as she'd ascended the stairs. He suspected he would keep seeing that vision for a long while, every time he closed his eyes. "You're a complete idiot," he muttered to himself. "You're the one who insisted she walk up the stairs while you stood there like Pavlov's dog, drowning in your own drool."

To give her credit, she had tried to warn him. No, she hadn't come right out and told him what would happen—that he was about to be given a free peep show that would drive a grown man to his knees. And he suspected his own stubbornness had inspired hers. Still, he wasn't sure he could ever forgive her for showing him what he could have had, if not for his own foul temper and his need to keep punishing himself by not taking anything he truly wanted. Being noble was all well and good, but if it came with blue balls, he'd far prefer being selfish.

"Enough," he reminded himself, trying to return his focus to the task at hand. The wine cellar. He still couldn't believe it was here, or that it held so much.

Buddy had found a treasure trove in the basement right before his accident, one he hadn't even realized was there until he'd started trying out keys to locked rooms. That's what had sent him hurrying down the porch steps to find Oliver. He'd intended to show it to Oliver and ask him to help inventory it.

Now that it looked like Buddy wouldn't be doing any stair-climbing for a while, Oliver had promised he'd get started. Buddy had agreed gratefully, telling him to help himself to anything he found…unless it was worth a king's ransom, in which case he would need it for his medical bills.

He hadn't even thought about that, but now that his employer had brought it up, Oliver couldn't help worrying about it. Buddy had sunk his life savings into this place. God, he hoped this accident didn't bankrupt the man.

Caught up in the old man's excitement, he'd stopped by the store to pick up reference books with grades, rankings and values of old wine. Once he'd found the room and gotten started, he'd been shocked by the sheer quantity of bottles. Obviously, his own great-uncle, who'd bought out his siblings, including Oliver's grandmother, hadn't even realized what he had in his possession. He'd been from back East and never done a proper inventory on the place. The group that had bought the estate from *him* had intended to get investors to renovate it into some corporate retreat, but had never fully investigated, either.

Buddy had bought the whole place—and its contents—out of bankruptcy and was legally entitled to everything here. Including this treasure trove. If the previous owners had realized what they'd had, this stuff would have been on auction blocks around the world, not still stored in this secure room, created solely for keeping wines in pristine condition.

Okay, there was dust. A few cobwebs—Candace would hate the spiders. But for the most part, the setup was ideal and the bottles—more than one hundred of them, possibly close to two—looked sealed and correctly colored. It was very likely many of them were aged to perfection.

This collection could be the answer to Buddy's financial problems. Some of the bottles weren't easily cataloged and an appraiser would have to do it. Many, though, had been listed in the books he'd brought with him as being worth thousands of dollars. There was a small fortune within these walls, and, frankly, Oliver couldn't think of anyone who deserved it more.

They weren't all gems. He had found a few broken ones, dry corks or just plain duds according to the books. Some that *were* good wines still weren't worth much, even if in mint condition. Those included vintages that had been bottled during a surplus production year and just weren't collectible.

It was one of those he was eyeing now. A 1971 burgundy from one of his favorite vintners that was still around today. Buddy had told him to feel free to help himself to anything that wasn't too valuable, and this one wasn't worth more than about a hundred bucks.

He deserved a hundred bucks worth of wine, especially after putting up with Buddy's sexy, infuriating grand-daughter.

"How's it going?"

Said sexy, infuriating granddaughter who almost startled him into dropping the bottle. He spun around, seeing her eyeing him from the doorway. "Oh. You're back."

Obviously he had lost track of time down here. It was probably a good thing she'd come looking for him—fully, if sexily, dressed in a pair of slim-fitting jeans and a lightweight pink sweater. With his luck, he'd have consumed the bottle of wine and headed upstairs after she was home and ready for bed, wearing that flimsy little bathrobe and nothing else.

His horny-man brain quickly rebelled at the idea that

that would have been *bad* luck. But he shut that part of his brain down.

"Visiting hours are over. It's after eight. I saw the lights were on upstairs and thought you might still be here. Grandpa told me where to look for you."

She looked like she wanted to come in, but was carefully eyeing the cobwebs and shadowy corners.

"All clear," he told her with a smile, knowing what she was looking for. "I think the mutant spider from outer space is still trying to find his way home."

That was a lie—there were enough webs down here to house the spiders from Harry Potter's Dark Forest. But he wasn't about to tell her that.

She managed a weak smile and slowly entered, her attention focused on shelf after shelf of bottles. She whistled as she walked around the twelve-by-twelve chamber. "Wow. He wasn't exaggerating, was he?"

"Definitely not."

"Amazing!"

"You have no idea."

He quickly filled her in on what he'd discovered, and saw her eyes light up with hope as she realized her grandfather might have actually stumbled into a treasure to help him make this old house into the showplace he envisioned.

"Are you sure?"

"I'm no expert," he told her. "I can only judge by what the books say. Buddy will have to get an appraiser out here. And of course it depends on whether the wine is any good, or if it's gone over." Then he lifted the bottle, holding it up against the milky light coming from the overhead bulb. "I was just about to crack open a bottle of the cheaper stuff and check it out."

She nodded anxiously, looking like a kid agreeing to a dare. "Oh, yes, let's!"

"Are you a wine fan?"

"I'm a woman. Of course I'm a wine fan."

Reaching into his pocket, Oliver drew out a multifunction tool that had a wine opener on it and almost held his breath as he uncorked the bottle. He was careful not to shake it in case of sediment and immediately smelled the air for any scent of vinegar.

Nothing. So far, so good.

Testing the cork and finding it completely moist and not at all crumbly, he began to hope they weren't about to drink a bottle of salad dressing in the making. "This really should be decanted so it can breathe."

Her face fell.

"But there's no point in going upstairs to find a decanter and glasses until we know whether it's worth drinking." He lifted the bottle and extended it to her. "Ladies first."

She didn't put on any fussy airs or complain about drinking out of an old, dusty bottle. Wiping the rim with her hand, she lifted it to her mouth and took a tiny sip.

Her eyes closed. She remained very still. Then she sipped again.

When she opened her eyes, they were sparkling with delight. "Unbelievable. That is the best wine I have tasted in my life! If that's the cheap stuff, I think the really good wine would bring on an instant orgasm."

She immediately caught her bottom lip between her teeth, obviously regretting making that remark.

He regretted it, too. Mainly because, as he took the bottle from her extended hand, and lifted it to his mouth, all he could think about was giving her that instant orgasm.

He could. Of that he had no doubt.

Trouble was, he knew he shouldn't. He didn't have that right. He was in no place to offer her anything and in no condition to take anything. Having sex with her would be about one thing and one thing only—instant gratification. And she just didn't seem like the one-night-stand type.

Nor was that what he suspected his matchmaking boss had in mind for them.

He placed his lips right where hers had been, tasting her lipstick, wishing it wasn't via second degree of separation. Then he sipped, and felt the most delightful burst of flavor in his mouth. He caught smoky undertones, but the tannins were light, unobtrusive. There was also a hint of cherry, or plum. Not sweet, just rich and full-bodied. It went down smooth, the finish just as perfect as the opening, and he couldn't resist taking another healthy sip.

"Fantastic," he said when he lowered the bottle. "Should we go for the decanter?"

"Absolutely!"

She spun around and hurried out the door, leading him up the stairs to Buddy's living room. They were like a pair of kids who'd been given their favorite candy and could hardly wait to dig in.

And they definitely dug.

An hour later, they'd finished off the first bottle, and most of a second one he'd gone down to grab. The second hadn't been quite as perfect as the first, even after a fifteen-minute decant, but it beat anything he'd ever ordered at a fancy California restaurant, hands down. And the book only valued it at forty bucks. Something about age definitely made all the difference.

Dividing what was left between their two glasses, he listened as she went over a list of things they needed to check and do tomorrow. That included finding the closest expert who could come out and do an appraisal. By their own unscientific research, Buddy should come out of this at least two hundred thousand dollars richer. One bottle in particular, a 1945 Château Mouton Rothschild, could very well bring in fifty thousand on its own.

Fifty. Thousand. Dollars. For a freaking bottle of wine.

Damn, he was glad he'd bought the reference books and hadn't dared to just grab a bottle and open it!

Candace sat beside him on the couch. She'd been bouncing with excitement every time he flipped a page and spied a familiar name, pointing to its corresponding mention on his list of Buddy's wine cellar. Her excitement had been infectious. It had also been so spontaneous that, once, she grabbed his thigh and squeezed.

He'd managed to hide a groan, wondering if she was really clueless about the effect she was having on him. And it wasn't just a wine-inspired reaction. Oh, no. Everything about her simply called to something inside him. Her soft scent filled his every breath; her long hair brushed his bare forearm. Their legs touched, hips, too. She filled his every sense, and if he'd thought the attraction was dangerous when they'd first met, he knew he was really in trouble now that he liked her so much.

She was delightful, smart, funny and so sexy it hurt to look at her. Their nearness—and, okay, maybe the wine— made the idea of never having this woman seem not only a shame but a crime against humanity.

"I am thrilled for Grandpa," she said when they'd finally reached the end of the list. She tucked one bent leg beneath her and turned toward him on the couch. "This is going to help him make all his dreams come true."

He nodded, unable to take his eyes off her burgundy-drenched lips, feeling the thrum of excitement that reverberated from her. She was relaxed and happy and he'd never seen her looking so beautiful.

"Thank you," she said, reaching out to grab his hand and squeeze it.

He couldn't resist. Twining his fingers in hers, he lifted her hand to brush a kiss on her palm.

She sucked in an audible breath and edged closer. He continued to kiss his way across her palm, until he reached her wrist. Pressing his lips there, he noted the frantic thumping of her pulse and realized her heart was racing.

He dropped her hand. "I didn't mean to go there."

"Don't stop."

"It's a bad idea, Candace."

"What is? You kissing my hand?" She licked her lips and lowered her voice to a sultry whisper. "Or my mouth?"

Or any other part of her? *Every* other part of her?

"Kiss me, Oliver," she dared. "One real kiss to celebrate. What do you say?"

Intriguing. "Only one?"

"Yes. Just one. I promise I won't ask for more."

He stared into her deep green eyes, wondering whether she was telling him that one would really be enough, or that it would do for a start. Nor could he be sure what he wanted her answer to be.

Not until he spied the list on the table, with Buddy's name scrawled across the top. He was in his friend's home, a little high on his prized wine, contemplating kissing his granddaughter. That alone was enough to convince him he couldn't take any more than the single kiss she'd asked for.

"All right, Candace. Just one."

"You're sure that will be enough?"

Hell, no, it wouldn't be enough. But it was all he was going to allow himself. Period. At least until he didn't feel like the biggest heel in the world for taking advantage of his boss's granddaughter…and for letting himself get close to a woman when he knew he had absolutely nothing to offer her.

He didn't just mean financially. It wasn't just his lack of a career or a house or even his own car, all of which he'd left behind in L.A. He meant himself. He didn't have any emotions to offer any woman. He'd felt adrift for months, and it would take more than a hot flirtation with a beautiful brunette to change that. So he wasn't about to allow himself any more than one small glimpse of the physical pleasure he knew he wasn't entitled to and didn't deserve.

"I'm sure," he finally told her. "*One*. And then we say good-night."

"If you're sure. I mean, remember what we talked about the other night, if you give a mouse a cookie…"

"He's going to say thank-you and walk out the door."

She studied him, gauging his seriousness, and nodded. "All right, Oliver. One kiss, and then we say good-night."

They might have shaken hands given the serious way they made their deal. And a deal was all it was.

One kiss. One and done.

God help him.

ONE KISS? Yeah. Sure. Right.

She couldn't believe he'd really be able to do that, but just in case, Candace was determined to make it a kiss for the ages. She knew from this morning that the man's mouth was ambrosia, and knowing she was going to taste it again was enough to make her whole body shiver and quake in anticipation.

He noticed, and let go of her hand. "Are you cold?"

She shook her head slowly, inching closer to him on the sofa. Untucking one leg, she didn't hesitate to make sure he couldn't change his mind and get up. Giving him a look that was half demand, half plea, she rose onto her knees and slid one leg over his thighs, straddling him.

"Candace…"

"I want my kiss," she insisted as she hovered over his lap. Maybe the wine was making her bold, but she suspected it was pure physical attraction. If she'd been stone-cold sober, she still would have wanted this kiss. This wicked, stolen moment.

"This is a little more than I bargained for," he admitted.

"You're not a very good bargainer," she replied, licking her lips. "You didn't even try to negotiate any ground rules."

"Should I have?"

She smiled wickedly. "Probably."

"I'm guessing it's too late for that?"

"Much too late."

He sighed deeply, but she'd swear his eyes gleamed with excitement and amusement.

"Just one," he reminded her.

"Oh, all right."

She moved down, lowering herself onto him. Her knees rested on the couch on either side of him, the position very intimate. She could feel the heat and power between her thighs and knew he was already aroused. He probably had been for quite a while, judging by the undeniable hardness straining against his zipper.

Yet he wanted only one kiss? The man obviously had an iron will to go along with that iron shaft.

Her blood pulsed and pooled in her groin. She was unable to resist rubbing against him, just a little, taking the heat, the strength and that hardness, and pleasing herself with it. Their clothes were in the way, of course, but she still felt waves of delight pulsing through her as they ground together.

His flexing jaw indicated he was gritting his teeth, as if striving for control, and she made a promise to herself: someday, she'd make him lose it. That control would be long gone before the day they said goodbye. Maybe it wouldn't be tonight. Maybe they would just have one single kiss, as he insisted. But someday, she'd have the rest of him, even if she had to wait five years.

He lifted his hands and twined them in her hair, fingering the strands as he pulled her face down toward his. A quick inhalation, two thudding hearts finding a common rhythm, a last glance of certainty and their mouths finally came together.

It was soft, slow and easy at first, a gentle exploration of lips. Giving, taking, molding, sliding, not a hint of demand in it, just a tender, sexy build.

This wasn't like the kiss they'd shared this morning. It was far more lazy, as if knowing that since one kiss was all they'd agreed on, they both intended to make it not merely the journey but also the destination. It might only be one, but as far as Candace was concerned, this kiss could go on for half an hour and they'd still technically be following the rules.

His warm tongue began to test the corners of her mouth, and she opened for him, sliding hers out in welcome. The kiss deepened, their tongues thrusting together in a deliberate, sultry tango. He tasted warm and spicy, with wine adding even more flavor to his already-delicious mouth. She lifted her arms around his neck, and he dropped his hands to her hips. Digging his fingers into her bottom, he pulled her even more tightly against his erection.

She groaned in the back of her throat, resisting the urge to toss her head back and grind herself into a climax. The kiss deepened as the frenzy increased, and she noticed he was thrusting up slightly, as if making love to her.

Damn their clothes. Damn his conditions.

They might only have one kiss, but he hadn't said anything about what they could and could not touch during that kiss. So without pulling away she reached for his waist, tugging his shirt up so she could touch and stroke that flat, muscled stomach. He sighed against her lips, but didn't resist, merely followed her lead. When his hands tugged her blouse free from her jeans and he encircled her waist with his big hands, she wanted to jump for joy.

She settled for continuing to kiss him, turning her head, going deep then shallow, hard then soft.

His strong hands caressed her, moving up to stroke her midriff, then higher, until his thumbs were resting at the edge of her bra. Whimpering and arching toward his touch, she shuddered with relief when he finally scraped those thumbs over her taut nipples, teasing them through the lace. Sparks erupted as he tweaked and toyed with her.

Her cries of satisfaction seemed to urge him on. Without her asking, he pulled the material down, out of the way, so he could pleasure her more, until she was writhing on his lap, almost desperate with need.

But still the kiss didn't end. It was as if they were both determined to remain true to their terms and see just how far they could go without ever letting their mouths separate.

Pretty damn far, she soon realized as he slid his hands back down her body and unfastened the button of her jeans.

"Oh, yes," she whispered into his mouth.

She suspected he hadn't been waiting for permission.

As he slowly lowered her zipper, she lifted herself up a little, giving him access. He pushed her jeans down just enough to allow him to slip his hand into the steamy crevice between her thighs. When those knuckles brushed against her most sensitive spot, she let out a cry, needing so much more.

He seemed to realize she was right on the edge. Thrusting one hand into her hair to cup her head, he deepened the kiss, making love to her mouth with hungry determination. His other hand remained still, but just as she was ready to pound on his shoulders to demand more, he reached under the elastic edge of her panties. Tangling his fingers in the soft thatch of hair, he moved deeper, until the rough pad of one found her clit and began to work it.

Heaven.

Not being able to pull back and look down was painful. But she didn't want to end the kiss, didn't want to break the spell, for fear everything would stop. All her senses were on overload as she smelled his musky scent, tasted every inch of his mouth, felt his body pressed against hers, saw his handsome face and heard the small groans of pleasure he didn't try to disguise.

Just as she was on the verge of coming, he moved his hand away. This time, she did pound on his shoulder, but he responded with an evil chuckle that she tasted as well as heard. When she realized he was moving deeper into her panties, so that he could slide a long, warm finger into her, she forgave him his every sin.

God, it had been so long since she'd taken anyone into her body. Her muscles clenched him, squeezing, drawing him deeper. He thrust in, drew out, mimicking what he would do when he really made love to her, until she was squirming on his lap.

As if knowing she was desperate for more, he gave her another finger, plunging both deep, stroking her way up inside until she began to shake. And when his thumb moved back up to cover her clit, a warm pulse of pleasure burst out and rushed through her. Every cell in her body felt on fire, from the bottoms of her feet to the tips of her hair, and she could no longer control herself. She threw her head back, gave a long, utterly satisfied cry, and rode out the orgasm that left her quaking and weak.

When she finally came back down to earth, she felt completely spent and collapsed onto him, her head on his shoulders, her arms around his neck. Oliver was kissing her temple, stroking her stomach and then her lower back.

But their mouths had fallen apart. The kiss had ended.

She held her breath, wondering if he was going to say to hell with their deal and make love to her the way his rigid, throbbing cock said he was dying to.

When he gently lifted her off his lap and sat her back down beside him on the couch, she had her answer.

"Seriously?"

She didn't have to say another word. He knew what she was asking; she could tell by the look on his face.

He rose to his feet and tucked his shirt back in.

"Thank you, Candace. Good night."

She gritted her teeth and zipped her jeans, reminding herself that this was entirely her fault. She'd promised one kiss and no more. No, she hadn't exactly invited him to stick his hand down her pants and finger her into oblivion, but it had seemed within reason as long as they were sharing that one kiss.

He was just playing by the rules. Damn the man.

She rose, tucking her blouse back in, and lifting her head, as if she was totally fine about how this whole thing had played out. "Good night, Oliver."

She turned her back to him and began to pick up the bottles and glasses, tidying up the room. He stood there for a moment, watching her, as if waiting for her to throw a fit, call him a jerk or beg him to stay. But she didn't. If he wanted to play this straight, that's what she would do. If he wanted to change the rules of the game, he needed to be the one to say so.

In the end, he didn't say anything. He just nodded, headed to the door and walked out into the night.

6

OLIVER SPENT THE next day wishing he hadn't consumed so much wine the night before, and steering clear of Candace.

He took care of the wine with some aspirin.

Her decision to visit her grandfather for almost the entire day took care of Candace.

That was good. He wasn't ready to run into her again. Not when every time he closed his eyes, he saw her beautiful face, suffused with pleasure, so wanton and gorgeous, he knew she would haunt his dreams forever.

Sometimes, doing the right thing just sucked.

He had thought it was the right thing at the time. Unfortunately, right now, he couldn't remember the reason why.

He'd tried to work out the frustration, spending the day laboring in the storehouse, which still held a number of antique vats. Buddy was hoping to restore and use them. Having tasted the amazing wines aged in antique wood last night, he had to agree that they were worth salvaging. And fortunately, the work was hard enough that he was able to put Candace, and the amazing moments they'd shared on that couch, out of his thoughts. At least, for the most part.

Finally, though, when he glanced at his watch and saw it was after six, he knew he had to call it quits. She would probably be heading back to the estate soon. He intended to go down to the rehab center to visit Buddy. Hopefully, their cars would pass in the night and they wouldn't run into each other, there or here. He just couldn't take another evening of sexual tension with the woman. Not when he knew how sweet she tasted, and how those feminine cries of pleasure sounded when she came apart in his arms. Not when he was dying to slam his cock into her and forget the rest of the world even existed.

As he toweled his hair dry and eyed his jaw in the mirror, he realized he ought to shave. Not because he intended to rub his face on someone sinfully soft and wanted to prepare, but because he was beginning to look a little scruffy. Buddy had made a point of mentioning it yesterday.

"It's not about that soft skin," he told his reflection. "Not about that stomach. Not about those breasts." God, had he been dying to end the kiss if only so he could look down at the perfect breasts he'd held in his hands. He swallowed, seeing the condensation he left on the mirror as he breathed ever harder. "It's not about wanting to bury your face between her thighs and see if she tastes as good as she feels."

Somehow, though, as he finished shaving and stared at his smooth-cheeked reflection, he knew he was fooling himself.

No, he didn't deserve her. No, he had no business taking up with her. But oh, hell, yes, did he ever want her.

Yesterday, when she'd walked up those stairs, giving him a glimpse of heaven between two limbs, it had taken every ounce of his strength not to follow her. He'd pictured it, a flash of erotic images storming through his brain. He'd seen himself pounding up after her, three steps at a time. Stopping her before she got to the top. Guiding her down onto her knees. Gently pushing her forward until she was on all fours and he could take his place a few steps below. He'd instinctively known how perfect it would be to position her sweet, wet sex above him, to bury his face in it, lick into her until she bucked and cried, then to drive into her before she'd even stopped screaming over the multiple orgasms he'd give her.

Oliver closed his eyes, willing the images to leave his head. But they wouldn't. They were imprinted there, the vision so real it was almost memory.

Then came the images from last night. He could still taste her lips, still feel the softness of her skin, still remember how it had felt to slide a finger into that slick, tight channel and play with that pearly little clit until she whimpered.

He groaned, reached down and found his cock hard and erect.

"Damn it, Candace," he muttered, grabbing himself, squeezing, pumping. His hand was in no way as good—wet, hot—as she would be, but it was all he had. All he would allow himself.

It didn't take long. No longer than it had taken the previous night when he'd gone to bed and let himself replay the moments he'd spent with her on the couch. He came in a hot gush, spewing his essence over his hand, knowing he'd give a year off his life if he could do it in her instead.

"But you can't," he told himself, feeling even more sexually frustrated than he had before his second jacking-off session of the past twenty-four hours.

His hand just didn't cut it. He wanted *her* hand. Her body. Her mouth. More than he'd ever wanted anything.

He tried to forget his sexual needs as he drove down to the rehab center. He definitely tried to disguise his desire as he visited with Buddy and gauged how the elderly man was doing with his new hip. Fortunately, he'd been right about guessing Candace wouldn't be there. She'd apparently stayed until dinnertime, leaving shortly before he'd arrived, so he wouldn't have to pretend he hadn't spent the past twenty hours fucking her senseless in his mind. Hopefully he would get home late, find her rental car in the driveway, see all the lights were out and go to bed, having managed one more day of resisting her.

To make sure of that, he intended to go out for a bite to eat and maybe have a few beers at a local watering hole before heading back. He'd even picked the place.

After they'd spent a half hour talking about the amazing find in the wine cellar, Buddy said something that made him wonder if fate was conspiring to bring him and Candace together.

"You ought to see if you can catch up with Candace at Wilhelm's. I told her they have the best burgers in town and she said she was going to stop there for dinner."

So she could avoid arriving home in time to see him? That was funny, considering she was dining at the very bar at which he'd intended to stop. Now, though, he figured drive-through fast food would do him just fine.

"I should probably get home and make an early night of it. I'm going to get back to work on the old vats tomorrow, see what else we can salvage."

Buddy frowned. "I'd feel better if you swung by and checked on her. Tonight's Monday. Adult softball league night."

"So?"

"So we both know the teams all converge on Wilhelm's for brewskis and wings after their games. It can get a little raucous. I'd hate to think of my girl having to fend off some guy who downs a little too much liquid courage."

Oliver tensed at the very thought of it. No, he didn't have any claim on her, and had told her he didn't want any. But damned if he wanted another man making a move, welcomed by her or otherwise. That was probably pretty selfish, but, frankly, he didn't give a shit.

Since he met her, Candace had been putting off some

strong signals. Her body was dying for some action, she needed sex and she needed it badly. And last night, when they'd kissed and he'd stroked her into an orgasm, she had been like a cat in heat, so obviously ripe and ready that he had smelled her arousal—hence his drooling hunger to bury his face in her sex and eat her like a kid ate an ice-cream cone.

He'd be damned if any guy with less-pure motives and less self-control was going to take her up on what she was silently offering.

"Will you at least go by and check on her, make sure she's okay?" Buddy prompted. He wore a slight frown, but Oliver saw the tiniest hint of a smile on his face, as well. The old man was matchmaking again. Under normal circumstances, that would have sent Oliver running in the other direction, away from the local pub where Candace might now be putting off those vibes he'd been picking up on since the night they'd met.

But because of those vibes, he just couldn't.

"Okay, Buddy. I'll go by and make sure she's all right."

And make sure she wasn't entering into negotiations with any other guy for one tiny innocent little kiss. After giving her that orgasm, he'd left her high and dry last night. Over his dead body would any other man get her low and wet.

HER GRANDFATHER HAD been right. Wilhelm's had great burgers. After Candace swallowed the last bite of hers, she wiped her mouth, reached for her tea and thought about dessert.

Not that she was still hungry. Honestly, the burger had been huge. She never ate like that, and could almost hear her arteries screaming in protest. But she was not ready to call for her check, get up, leave and drive back to Grandpa's place. Not while it was only eight o'clock. Not when there was a good chance Oliver would be up, the lights on in his small cottage, tempting her to find some excuse to wander over to see him.

He'd avoided her all day today. As if his rejection last night and the finality of his goodbye hadn't been enough, he'd made it a point to avoid coming outside at all until she'd left the house this morning.

He had the will of a monk. Or a eunuch. The flash of her cootchie as she'd walked up the stairs hadn't elicited more than a frustrated groan from the man. She couldn't deny she'd slammed the door to her room because he *hadn't* stormed up after her, overtaken by lust. Then, last night after their wild, erotic kiss that had involved a whole lot more than lips and tongues, he'd still stuck to his terms and walked out on her.

She'd gone to bed full of need and hunger, dying to be filled. Thinking about it later, however, she forced herself to concede she'd been lucky. She'd already listed the million-and-one reasons why she couldn't get involved with Oliver right now. A little wine and the offer of a kiss had made her forget them, but there was no harm done. He'd ended it, and she was glad.

Maybe if she told herself that often enough, she would begin to believe it. "This sucks," she mumbled.

"What's that sweetheart?" a voice asked.

She looked around to see a bunch of guys in dusty gym clothes and ball caps, who had just sat down in the booth directly behind hers. One of them was leaning over the back of his seat, invading her space, and her contemplation.

"Nothing, sorry," she insisted, her tone polite but cool.

"Hey, we won our game, how about joining us for a celebration?" said another of the men.

Good grief. Did men really think single women eating alone in restaurants were just praying a table full of sweaty dudes would invite her to join their six-some? The guys looked harmless—stockbroker, businessman types, in matching gym shorts and shirts and pricey sneakers. She didn't feel threatened. Nor, however, was she at all interested. "No, thanks."

Before she had to elaborate, she heard a ringing from her purse. Coming from L.A., where people's cell phones were connected to their heads by magnetic beams or something, she'd developed a loathing for anyone who yakked on one in public. Especially in a restaurant. But now, the excuse to cut short a conversation with some overly friendly jocks was most welcome.

When she saw the name on the caller ID, she was even more grateful. She'd talked to Tommy a few times since leaving home and he always managed to distract her from her troubles…usually by talking about his own.

His were always more interesting, anyway. *Hmm, this sexy rock star or that studly NBA player? Decisions, decisions.*

"Hey, sweetie," she said, her voice louder than technically necessary, just to underscore the point with the on-the-make guys. One of them continued to hover over the back of her booth, so she upped the lovey-dovey factor. "I've missed you so much."

"Missed you, too, sugar lips," Tommy said with a laugh. "Who's listening? Grandpa? Biker gang? Jealous she-hag?"

"Nothing of the sort. I'm at a pub, where I just finished dinner. It looks like it's a popular hangout for the local athletes."

"Any delicious athletes?"

"I honestly wouldn't know."

"Oh, come on, girlfriend, you losing your vision?"

Maybe for some things. She hadn't really been able to see any man since meeting the only one she wanted.

"Maybe just my enthusiasm."

Not to mention her opportunities.

"Any idea when you're going to be able to leave there yet?"

"I suspect I'm going to be here until the day you need me to come back," she admitted.

He grew serious. "Is your grandfather doing that badly?"

"No, he's doing very well. But I want to be around to cheer him on during rehab—it's tedious and painful. Plus I want to be at the house for him when he first comes home."

"When will that be? Will it leave you enough time for a trip? Maybe you could go to Montreal? They speak French. Or hey, there are lots of hunky Spanish-speaking dudes in Mexico. Doesn't Cancun sound awesome?"

"I don't think so. But I won't stay too long after he gets home. He'll have home health aides come in, and Madison said she could fly in from back East to relieve me in ten days or so."

"How is Mad, bad and dangerous to know?"

She chuckled. "Same old, same old. Ready to dive into her career playing hotshot reporter, fighting city hall, exposing corruption and never letting a man get the upper hand."

"The Reid sisters—toughest girls of Blue Lake Elementary."

"And don't you forget it."

"How could I? You two both acted as my beards at one time or another in high school. I couldn't have made it without you."

"Aww, you're such a romantic. How could we resist? You know Madison and I have both always been totally hot for you."

The eyeballs were probably popping out of the heads of the guys behind her now. They were likely envisioning wild threesomes and naughty hook-ups. Huh. Other than the threesome part, she was right there with them. Two would be quite enough for the hook-up that had been on her mind all week.

"Ooh, kinky. Gonna be *that* kind of wife, huh?"

"Don't push it," she muttered under her breath.

She settled into the corner, feeling her tension drift away. Talking to Tommy was like talking to a therapist. But she didn't want to talk to him about Oliver. Mainly because she knew her friend—he'd encourage her to jump the other man's bones or live to regret it later.

She already knew she was going to regret it later. That didn't mean she could do it now. First, because he wasn't the bone-jumping type; he was the type you lost your heart, body and soul to and lived the rest of your days pining for.

He also wasn't interested. Well, he *was* interested; he just wasn't going to act on that interest. So she couldn't, either.

"Sounds like you're really not going to have much time for booty calling your way across North America, much less Europe."

"No. I'm not." She held her breath, wondering if there had been any change, if the urgency had died down. Not wanting him to think she was backing out on him, she didn't ask.

Finally, he said, "Did you catch TMZ last night?"

"No, Grandpa only gets basic cable. Why?"

"Let's just say it's getting a little more uncomfortable down here. I guess me being seen around town without a woman—namely you—on my arm is making those engagement rumors die down. And others spike back up."

Was he asking if he could announce their engagement? Oh, she hoped not. She wasn't ready for that. She hadn't even had a chance to explain it to her family, though she knew they would understand. Tommy had spent just about every summer in her backyard when they were kids. They knew who he was and loved him almost as much as she did. They wouldn't necessarily approve, but they would understand she was marrying him out of loyalty, love and friendship. Still, she wanted to tell them herself before any stupid tabloid got hold of it.

"Why don't you stay home more often then?"

"I'm in demand, hot stuff. Gotta see and be seen."

God, she was not looking forward to being part of that. Except the red-carpet Oscar stuff. That should be an experience. Of course, it would be better if she were walking that carpet as a nominee, rather than the wife of one, but beggars couldn't be choosers. Considering she still hadn't nailed down her next project—she'd done the sketches she was asked for and sent them in, but hadn't heard anything yet—she doubted an Oscar nomination for best costume design would be coming her way very soon.

"Well, gotta go, babe. There's a party with my name on it."

"Be careful."

"I will."

Then, again because she sensed the guys in the next booth were listening, she added, "I love you."

"You know, once you're wearing my ring, guys won't be hitting on you all the time."

"That goes both ways."

"Bite your tongue!"

"Bye, Tommy."

"Bye. Love you, sugarplum."

She disconnected the call, glanced at the time and realized it was now nine. Probably not late enough for Oliver to be in bed, but late enough that she'd look weird and pathetic showing up at his door and thus wouldn't be tempted to find an excuse to knock on it. So she figured it was safe to call it a night.

She lifted her hand to call for the check, but before she could catch the young waitress's eye, her vision was blocked by a big jean-and-T-shirt-clad body. A body she'd know anywhere.

Eyeball to crotch with that familiar body, she swallowed hard and slowly lifted her gaze.

"Can I join you?" Oliver's tone was almost concilia-tory, as if he regretted the way he'd ended things last night.

She swallowed hard. Why on earth had he now sought her out when he'd been trying so hard to avoid her?

"Candace?"

"Aren't you afraid I'm not wearing any underwear, or that I'll ask you for one little kiss?" she couldn't help ask-ing.

Behind her, somebody started coughing. She ignored him.

"I guess I deserved that," he said, not cracking a smile.

There was no way to refuse him, and she gestured to-ward the empty seat across from her. She heard grumblings from the baseball team and could only imagine what they thought. She'd shot them down, then had a romantic phone conversation and now invited a gorgeous man to take a seat. They probably thought she was a bored housewife on the prowl, cheating on her poor spouse.

"What are you doing here?" she asked after he sat down.

"Your grandfather asked me to check on you."

Her brow shot up. "You two think I need babysitting?"

His scowl deepened, and he nodded toward the table full of guys behind her. "When I came in and looked over, one of those bozos was right above you, just waiting for you to move enough so he'd have a clear line of sight down your shirt."

She jerked her head around and looked over her shoul-der. The amateur ballplayers all immediately ducked their heads together, as if realizing they'd been caught out.

"So you came storming over to defend my honor?"

That was rich, considering he was the only man who'd

come even close to sullying it lately. And oh, had she liked being sullied.

"No. They're men, they're out drinking beer and you're beautiful. Of course they're gonna look."

The *beautiful* part echoed in her ears.

His jaw tensed, and he crossed his arms over his chest and raised his voice slightly. "But if any of them even thinks about touching you, he'll be drinking his beer through a straw."

She should resent this he-man protector stuff. But instead, she found herself feeling all warm and soft at the realization that he felt protective of her. Mainly because it meant he somehow felt possessive of her.

He could have possessed you yesterday—twice—and twice he turned you down.

Right. She straightened in her seat, determined not to relax her guard around him, or let him know she was still smarting over what had happened. She was determined to forget all about yesterday, pretend she'd dreamed the whole thing. Well, except the orgasm. She wanted to remember that. She wanted to hug and hold that memory because, as far as she could remember, it was the only time her head had completely blown off her shoulders and then settled back into place.

The waitress sauntered over, lazy and laid-back as she'd been all evening. But when she reached the table, she did a double take and offered Oliver a much bigger smile than she'd offered Candace. "Hey, there, Mr. McKean. Nice to see you again!"

The woman practically simpered. Ugh.

"You want the usual?" the woman asked.

"Sure."

She was back with his beer in record time. "Can I get you something else? Anything at all?"

Candace gripped her hands together under the table,

determined not to react. It wasn't easy, especially when the woman responded to Oliver's request for a menu by leaning over him to grab a paper one standing between two condiment bottles on the back of the table. Her ample breasts rubbed his shoulders. He didn't appear to mind.

Once the waitress had walked away, after telling him to think about what he *wanted,* Candace said, "Gee, who's going to defend *your* honor?"

His jaw may have softened a bit. "You offering?"

"You didn't look like you needed—or wanted—any help."

"If I didn't know better, I'd say you sound jealous."

"How fortunate that you know better."

She reached into her purse, tucking her phone back inside. Before he'd shown up, she'd been planning to pull out some cash, pay her bill and leave. Now that he was here, though, she found herself wanting to stay.

"Have you eaten?" he asked.

"Yes."

"Okay, let me order, then I'll walk you to your car."

And leave him here to be the blue plate special for the big-boobed waitress? Not a chance.

"I'm fine," she replied sweetly. "I was thinking about ordering dessert." She grabbed another menu, skimmed over the offerings and decided on her very favorite: a dish of ice cream. Simple, easy, nonsuggestive, delicious vanilla ice cream.

After they'd ordered, they spoke briefly about her grandfather, and his reaction to their find in his wine cellar. The old man had been ecstatic, and had immediately started making plans for what he would do with the money. Most of his ideas had to do with helping out his family—her included—and for a moment, Candace had allowed herself to think she would not have to marry for money. Then she remembered. She wasn't really marrying for money. She was marrying for friendship. And no amount of money could ever replace Tommy in her life.

However she felt about Oliver as a man—and potential lover—she had to give him credit: he was a conscientious employee, though she suspected the relationship between the two men had moved beyond professional to personal. Grandpa liked him…that was quite obvious, and the feeling appeared to be reciprocated.

She was a little surprised by their conversation. Once they'd turned the focus away from them—the sexual tension that was so thick between them she was surprised she could see him across the table—she found Oliver very easy to talk to.

They chatted about the wine, and the results of the phone calls Candace had made today to an expert in the region. He had given her the number of an auction house in San Francisco, saying if she really did have the bottles she'd mentioned, they'd be begging for the chance to sell them. If not rich, Buddy was at least going to be a lot more comfortable soon.

The waitress returned with Oliver's hamburger a short time later, and brought Candace's ice cream. She waited until the woman had left to pick up the spoon and help herself to a small amount. Lifting it to her lips, she almost cooed, seeing the tiny black flecks of vanilla bean. This was her favorite treat. Not terribly decadent or exciting, but she had always had a thing for plain vanilla.

"You gonna marry that stuff or eat it?"

Startled, she almost dropped the spoon. She'd apparently been oohing and aahing over it before she'd even brought a spoonful to her lips. And, for a change, there had been absolutely nothing deliberate about it. She wasn't trying to tease him, taunt him or make him regret walking away from her yesterday. She just liked ice cream.

"I don't usually eat dessert."

"Don't let me stop you."

She inserted the spoon into her mouth and sighed in pleasure, closing her eyes as the creamy sweetness hit her tongue and made her taste buds burst to life. "How can something so plain and simple taste so incredibly good?"

The question had been a rhetorical one, but Oliver looked like he was giving it serious thought. Very serious. He appeared contemplative and stared at her, hard. Some devil within her made her dip the spoon into the dish and draw more toward her mouth, knowing he was watching, rapt and attentive.

"Mmm." She licked every drop, loving the tingle as the cold refreshment slid over her tongue and down her throat.

Okay, so now she was being deliberately provocative. But he so totally deserved it.

He grabbed his burger and started to eat it, not looking toward her again. Which made eating the ice cream a little less fun, though no less delicious.

She knew she shouldn't mess with him, shouldn't play with fire, but he'd been sending her mixed signals since the moment they'd met.

Takes one to know one.

True.

She scooped more, making another sound of satisfaction.

"You're such a brat."

She smiled. "I don't know what you're talking about." She licked the spoon clean, wiggling with delight.

"Would you stop it?" he asked after she'd swallowed.

"Stop what?"

"Stop licking that spoon like you're thinking about sex."

"I am thinking about sex," she admitted, licking again. She saw no reason to be coy and wasn't about to let him off the hook. "I've been thinking about it since last night. How could I not?"

He leaned over the table, coming closer, making every-thing around them disappear. "You're playing with fire."

"Funny, I don't feel like I'm getting burned. In fact, it's quite chilly."

He took another bite of his burger, chewing the thing like he had to wrangle it into submission. When she began to help herself to another spoonful of her dessert, he cast her a warning look. "Time for either a subject change or a table change. Your choice."

Meaning he would get up and leave her here alone if she didn't stop tormenting him? How cute was that? She honestly hadn't realized he would be that affected by her engaging in a little food foreplay. But she didn't want him changing tables. Not when the waitress might very well decide to take a break and plop down on his lap.

"Okay, subject change. Grandpa mentioned that you had a connection to the estate. *Your* great-grandfather was the silent movie star who built it?" That had surprised her, especially given Oliver's apparent disdain for the movie business.

"Yeah." He looked relieved she'd done as he asked. "A million years ago. I never knew him."

"Have you ever seen any of his movies?"

"Sure. My great-grandfather bought a bunch of them when his studio went bankrupt. My father has a box of them. We sometimes had family nights watching them when I was growing up."

"How very Norma Desmond," she murmured.

He nodded, getting the *Sunset Boulevard* reference.

"When he found out I was living here, he mailed me a few so I could show them to Buddy. I haven't had a chance to do it yet."

"What a fascinating era it must have been. So much more mysterious and glamorous than today, given the 24/7 coverage of every gruesome detail of a famous person's life." She knew her voice contained a hint of bitterness, on Tommy's behalf, but he didn't question her on it.

"They sure knew how to party, from the sound of it."

"I'd love to see one of those films."

He reached for his beer. "They're on big reels. A pain to operate, but they certainly make for an authentic experience. Buddy borrowed a projector from somebody, but we never got around to showing them."

Meaning he couldn't just give her a disk to pop into her laptop. He'd have to come in and set up a whole viewing room. Stay and operate the machine. Spend time with her, watching it. Like one of his family movie nights growing up, only it would just be the two of them.

"We can watch one some evening if you're bored."

This was sounding a little like a movie date, and she suddenly wondered if he would live to regret having her change the subject. She could eat all kinds of ice cream while watching a movie. And if he dared to offer her *two* kisses, she might finally get that multiple orgasm she'd been craving.

"I'd love that," she murmured. "It might make you feel like you're at home. Speaking of which, where does your family live now?"

"San Diego. I was born and raised there."

"Big family?"

"Parents, two sisters, one brother-in-law, one niece."

"All in Southern California?"

"Yes."

"So why aren't you there with them?"

"I was close, in Orange County, until four months ago."

Finally she was getting somewhere. "What on earth made you come up here?" she couldn't help asking. "I'd normally guess one of the three biggies—romance, legal trouble or job. But you appear to be single and don't look like the law-breaking type."

"I am. And I'm not."

She went over the answer in her mind, realizing he was admitting he was single—hallelujah—and an honest guy.

"Okay. So, number three. Job? I don't mean to offend you, but it seems to me your field isn't necessarily one that would require you to move so far away."

He sipped his beer again, not meeting her eye. She didn't push, sensing he was trying to reach a decision about how much to say. Finally, with a sigh, as if he realized she wasn't going to back off and would be around long enough to wear him down if she chose to, he admitted, "I was with the district attorney's office in L.A. until earlier this year."

"With…wait, you mean you're a *lawyer?*"

She shouldn't have been surprised, considering she'd already seen evidence of his intelligence, his memory and his darned interrogation skills. But it was just so strange to think of a big Los Angeles attorney moving up here to work as a laborer for her grandfather.

"It's a long story."

She merely stared.

"I don't want to get into it."

"Come on, you've got to give me more than, *I was a lawyer, quit and came up here to plant grapes.*" She suddenly remembered what he'd said the night they met, about feeling cleaner digging in the dirt here than he had in his previous life. Then she thought about the kinds of cases he must have been involved in. Los Angeles was a glitzy haven to starry-eyed actors and actresses. But anyone who actually lived there knew it could be incredibly seedy. Ugly, violent, with crimes and murders happening often enough to immunize its residents to the shock of them, unless they involved a movie star.

"One crappy case too many?" she speculated.

"Yes," he replied, staring straight into her eyes, looking a little surprised she'd understood so easily.

"I can see why you'd want to come here, then, if you needed a change. Better hard manual labor than a mental breakdown."

A smile appeared. "I don't know that I was near that point, but I was definitely feeling on the verge of a moral one."

"Oh?" Now he had her really curious.

He idly rubbed the tip of his finger on the rim of his beer mug. "You might not believe it, but criminal law is one hell of a competitive place."

"Well of course I believe it. I read John Grisham."

"Multiply that by a hundred and you might have an idea of how brutal the atmosphere can be, especially in a place like Hollywood, with the money and the star factor added in. There's a winner-take-all attitude, a score-points-on-the-other-guy mentality. It's not about guilt or innocence, not about finding the truth, not even always about justice. More than anything it's about winning."

That surprised her. She'd always been one of those idealists who believed in the justice system. But it sounded like Oliver no longer did.

"Oh, my God," she whispered, suddenly remembering some of the news coverage she'd seen last winter, about corruption uncovered in the district attorney's office. She didn't remember seeing Oliver's picture, or hearing his name, but she hadn't really been paying attention, and the timing certainly made sense. "Were you the whistle-blower?"

He stared into her eyes, not looking surprised she'd remembered the story. She didn't recall any of the details; she just knew the media had had a field day with the previous D.A., whose own employee had accused him of judicial misconduct, including hiding evidence of innocence in a high-profile murder case.

"Yeah," he said, lifting his mug and downing his beer.

"You were involved in that case where the kid in the gang was accused of murdering the pregnant mother?"

"It was my case. I was all set to go to trial when I found proof that he hadn't done it."

"And your boss buried it," she murmured, remembering more.

"Tried to." He leaned back, dropping his napkin onto his plate. "The kid was a punk, but it was mostly swagger. Maybe the close call will make him clean up his act." He frowned. "Or he could get worse and end up killing somebody after all."

"But he didn't kill that woman?"

"No, he didn't. I'd let myself go along with some of the crap you have to do to score convictions. Did stuff I'm not proud of. But I couldn't be a part of convicting an innocent young man of murder, no matter what he might do in the future."

Stepping forward and doing the right thing had been noble and admirable. But it had also probably cost him his job.

"Were you blackballed?"

"Blackballed, dumped by the woman I'd been seeing, shunned by people I'd thought were friends," he said with a harsh laugh.

"That's awful," she muttered, focused more on the dumping than anything else. How could any woman do that to this gorgeous, amazing man?

He went on. "I can never go back to any D.A.'s office in California, and I'm not ready to switch sides just yet."

"Defense attorney, you mean?"

"Right. I'm too jaded, too quick to see the bad side of humanity to start defending people I automatically assume are guilty. So for now, I dig, I shovel, I fertilize, I test pH, I till, I haul, I study. And I drink wine."

"I think that last one's my favorite."

This time, his laugh wasn't angry…it was soft and genuine.

Candace sat there and let the masculine sound wash over her. She'd seen him angry and tense, seen him sexy and aroused, seen him concerned. This was the first moment, though, that she truly believed she was seeing the real man, with his guard completely down. Seeing the Oliver he had been before his world had fallen apart last fall. She liked this man. Liked him a lot.

And oh, God, did she ever wish she had met him before she'd agreed to marry her best friend.

7

OLIVER WASN'T CERTAIN what had caused that warm, tender look to appear in Candace's lovely eyes, but he figured it was bad news. He liked it better—felt safer—when she was snapping at him, taunting him, even flirting with him. This softness, this sweetness, this emotion he saw in her now, was way outside of his comfort zone.

He should have kept his fat trap shut. He should never have told her anything about himself—his past, his regrets, his shame. Because now, he greatly feared, he'd opened up a window through which she could climb, going around his instinctive defenses.

So let her.

Huh. Maybe he should. He still wasn't ready for a relationship, still hated the idea of messing around with Buddy's granddaughter while the old man was laid up. But he had to admit, he found Candace incredibly easy to talk to. She had heart and brains to go with that boatload of sex appeal, which made her a triple threat. He couldn't deny he was tempted to take what she'd offered yesterday morning and last night. Maybe hooking up with someone who would be leaving in a week or so was exactly the right way to get back in the game of life.

Unfortunately, now that he'd realized he liked her as much as he wanted her, hooking up seemed less appetizing than it had before. He sensed it would satisfy him physically, but would just make the emotional strings that much harder to untangle. And emotions were still not his strong point.

"Will you excuse me a minute? I need to run to the ladies' room," she said.

He pushed his plate to the edge of the table so the overly flirtatious waitress, who'd come on to him every single time he walked into this joint, could pick it up. "Sure. I'll ask for the check."

She reached into her purse.

He waved a hand. "Forget it. It's on me."

"No way. You don't bring down the big bucks anymore."

He lifted a brow in challenge, remembering she'd said she was between jobs right now. "At least I'm employed."

"Good point. But I think I can spring for one hamburger."

Frankly, it was worth every penny to pay for her meal, if only for the pleasure of watching her eat that cursed ice cream.

He watched her walk away, again noting the changes in her wardrobe since she'd stopped wearing her sister's more loose, casual ensembles in favor of stylish, extremely colorful and bright stuff. Her jeans were fire-engine red. She wore them with spike-heeled black ankle boots, and a silky blouse that fell off one shoulder. Every guy in the place watched her go, Oliver included.

He would bet every other guy in the place would give his left nut to have kissed her, and touched her the way he'd touched her twenty-four hours ago.

You're a brainless bastard to have walked out on her like that.

If he had the day to do over again, he sensed yesterday

would have ended up very differently. He only wondered if it was too late to change things.

After she'd left, Oliver signaled for the waitress, cutting her off when she tried to engage in small talk. It had been fine that she'd flirted when Candace was around to see and get a little tight-lipped, but now that she was gone, he couldn't be bothered to play along. He hadn't been interested in this woman, or any of the others he'd met since coming here four months ago. Only one interested him.

So what are you going to do about it?

He honestly didn't know. But the more he got to know Candace, the more he wanted to do something.

"Hey, dude, you better watch it. She's toxic."

Startled, he looked up to see one of the jocks from the next table leaning over the back of his booth. He gave Oliver a look of manly commiseration that looked a little fake, as if he enjoyed spreading tales. "She's messing around on you."

"What?"

"Your girl. I heard her on the phone before you got here. She was all into whoever she was talking to. Just sayin', you should watch your back, man."

His muscles contracting, he realized he should tell the guy to go screw himself, that he and Candace weren't a couple and if she had been on the phone with anyone else, that was her business. Not his.

Instead, he simply ignored the jock, tossed some bills on the table and got up. No, he had no business questioning who Candace talked to. But she'd sure made it sound like she was single, and she'd certainly acted that way yesterday during their erotic encounters.

Could she really have a lover somewhere? Was she the type who got bored easily and was simply killing time with Oliver while she was stuck up here in Sonoma?

The thought bothered him more than he cared to admit.

So much so that he couldn't even force a tight smile when she got back and walked over to him.

She spied the bills on the table. "I told you I'd pay for mine."

"Forget it," he insisted, his tone brusque to match his attitude. "Are you ready to go? Because I'm leaving."

He didn't plan to walk out and leave her here, not now that he knew just how closely the table full of men had been watching her. But he didn't need her to know that.

"Sure," she said, blinking in surprise at his here's-your-hat-what's-your-hurry attitude.

He didn't enlighten her. Telling her what the nosy softball player at the next table had said would only open up a conversation he really didn't want to have. The only reason he'd need to know if she was available was if he intended to sleep with her.

He didn't.

Right?

They walked outside to the parking lot. While they'd been inside, the early signs of a storm had blown in. This area didn't get a whole lot of rain, and what it got usually came in the winter. But sometimes the spring brought wicked storms and it looked like they would have one tonight. The air was wildly alive, with gusts that had the trees bouncing and a whistling sound coming from under the eaves of the building.

Instead of tightening her jacket, ducking against the weather and racing to her car, Candace tilted her head back, smiled and closed her eyes. She apparently liked the feel of the wind battering her body. Liking it, too, he understood. There was something freeing about being in a climate so variable and elemental. L.A. and San Diego were pretty standard all year round—sunny, warm, beautiful. In the winter and spring months he'd been up here, he'd realized you couldn't really count on anything. You never knew when the winds would change and the air would crackle with electric excitement.

"I love this," she said, raising her voice to be heard.

"I can tell."

The gusts kept catching wispy strands of her honey-brown hair, blowing them across her face. She didn't even try tucking them behind her ears or restraining the long curls. The longer they stood outside, the more primal and tangled it became. She was beautiful, sultry, exotic...he had a sudden image of being back at the estate with her, outside, naked, letting the wind batter them as they came together in an explosion as powerful as a spring storm.

Unable to take it anymore, he looked away, not wanting to be utterly entranced by the wild, erotic picture she presented, all windblown and sexy, with her lips moist and parted in exhilaration as she breathed in the cool night air.

"It's going to break over us pretty soon," he said. "And it won't be a fun drive once it starts pouring. We should go."

Her shoulders slumped. "All right."

When they reached her rental car, she said, "It seems like a good night to stay inside. Maybe I could pay you back for dinner by picking up some candy and popcorn for our home movie night?"

He frowned. "It's late." It wasn't that late, maybe ten o'clock. Ten minutes ago he might have leaped at the chance. But the fact that he didn't know enough about her had been hammered home by the jock inside.

"Tomorrow maybe?"

"I don't know if I'll have time for that before you leave."

Disappointment flashed across her face. "Oh."

Part of him wanted to take it back, especially seeing the flash of hurt in her eyes. But it was better this way. Better that he put the walls firmly in place again. She'd be gone in a week, returning to her life and her...whoever the guy on the phone had been. Buddy would be home.

Oliver would descend back into his self-imposed purgatory. Everything would be as it should. Hell, maybe once he'd gotten his shit together, he'd go back to L.A. and look her up. Find out if she was single or not. But who knew when that would be?

"Well, thanks for dinner," she said as she got into her car. She wasn't meeting his eyes. Embarrassed? Angry? He wasn't sure.

Muttering, "You're welcome," he pushed the door shut. He strode to his own truck, not turning around as she revved up her car's engine, threw it in gear and tore out of the parking lot like she had a dragon on her tail.

Okay, so she was angry.

Hell.

It's better this way, he reminded himself.

Somehow, though, he didn't feel better. In fact, he felt like crap. Crappy enough that, rather than heading right for the Sonoma Highway and home, he stopped at a liquor store and bought a six-pack. Not just because he had the feeling he could use a second beer, but because he didn't want to get back to the estate until he knew she would be safely tucked inside Buddy's house.

But after his stop, as he began driving home, leaving the highway and hitting some of the twisty back roads, he couldn't get the image of her standing there, enjoying the wind in her face, out of his mind. Especially because that wind threatened to take the steering wheel out of his hands a couple of times. And now it had started to rain.

"Shit. You should have followed her home."

Candace wasn't used to driving in this area, with hilly roads full of dangerous switchbacks and steep drop-offs. The bad weather made it even worse. If he hadn't been such an ass, he could have made sure she was safe, and he practically held his breath until he got to the estate and saw her rental car in front of the main house.

He parked his truck outside the cottage, breathing a deep sigh of relief that she'd made it, too. Replaying their conversation back at the bar, he knew he'd behaved badly. So much for the smooth gentleman he'd always been praised as being in his old life. He'd been a total dick to Candace half the time. He'd been like a kid who knew he couldn't play with the toy he most wanted, so he'd pretended he didn't want it at all.

Tonight, he'd reacted like a prosecutor instead of like a man who was getting to know an honest, refreshing, bright and sexy woman. He hadn't given her the benefit of the doubt. Was he so jaded, so used to being lied to and manipulated that he no longer had the capacity to give someone a chance?

He owed her an apology. And if all the lights hadn't been off in the main house—the place utterly pitch-black in the windy night—he would have gone over and offered it up, even though he'd have had to run through the driving rain. But the building was obviously shut down. She'd come home, turned off every light and gone to bed, probably sending him a silent message to stay away from her.

"Message received," he said as he hurried to the door of his cottage, getting soaked along the way, and pulled out his key.

Buddy always laughed at him for locking the door since they were out in the middle of nowhere, but the big-city habit was too ingrained. He found himself wondering, though, if he'd really been out of it when he'd left earlier this evening for the hospital. Because the knob twisted easily in his hand. He must have forgotten to lock it.

Letting himself in, he reached for the switch on the wall and flipped it up. Nothing.

"Oh, God," he mumbled, suddenly realizing why the world was so dark. The power was notoriously unreliable in high winds, and his was probably out.

He waited for his eyes to adjust, before making his way across the big room that dominated the main floor of the cottage. It served as both living room and kitchen, the two separated by a stone fireplace that opened on either side. It was a great feature and he'd used it and nothing else to heat the place during the winter. Looked like it was going to come in handy tonight, too, both for heat and for illumination.

Before he moved to light it, he thought about Candace. She was alone in that huge house. That huge drafty house with its spiders, crickets, cracked window casings and frigid tile floors. No lights, no heat, no hot water—which was pretty well par for the course—and he'd bet the phones were out.

"Better go check on her," he mumbled.

Grabbing the coat he'd just placed on the hook, he began to put it on. But he hadn't even gotten one arm in a sleeve when he heard a soft, feminine voice coming from the sofa on the other side of the room.

"You don't have to check on her. She's right here."

CANDACE HAD ONLY been waiting for Oliver for a few minutes—since just after she'd gotten back, realized the power was out and decided his cozy cottage with the fireplace would be a better place to ride out the storm. But that had been long enough for her to decide she'd made a mistake.

Sitting here in the dark, in his space, had been more disturbing than comforting. The whole place smelled like him—all musky, spicy and hot. Utterly masculine. Her body reacted to the scent even before her mind could put it together and figure out it wasn't just the cold making her nipples hard.

She also worried how he would react to finding her there, in the dark, and what he would make of her presence. He was a private person; it had taken him days to even admit to her that he was really an attorney. He probably wouldn't take kindly to her using Buddy's keys to let herself in and make herself at home. She suddenly felt a little like Goldilocks. Add a broken chair and a few bowls of porridge and she might come face-to-face with an angry bear.

She'd decided to leave, to brave the cold and the darkness in the main house, when she heard him pull up outside. Her chance to escape was gone. She had to stay and brazen it out.

"Candace?"

"It sure isn't Goldilocks," she muttered.

He hung his coat back up and approached, moving carefully in the darkness. She'd been here longer; her eyes had adjusted, so she could easily see him moving toward her. His hair was wet, dark strands sticking to his unsmiling face.

"How did you get in?"

"I'm sorry. I used Buddy's key. I know it was rude."

"And illegal."

Twisting her hands in front of her, she rose from the couch. "I was freaked out. That place is spooky enough when it's daylight. I kept picturing spiders lurking in every corner."

"Not the ghost of Fatty Arbuckle stalking you?"

"Oh, great, thanks. That makes me feel tons better!"

"I'm surprised you know who I was referring to."

"Hello, movie biz, remember? Was he one of your great-grandpa's cronies?"

"They did a few films together," he said.

Very cool.

"Let me brighten things up a little in here."

He headed for the kitchen. She heard him fumble with something, and a moment later, a soft light spotlighted his handsome face. He came back carrying a thick candle, which he placed on the coffee table.

"So, do you want me to leave?"

He hesitated, then shook his head. "It's coming down in buckets. You'd be soaked to the skin with no way to warm up."

True. "I can stay?"

"Yes. Sit down. I'll light a fire."

"That would be wonderful."

She curled up on the couch again, watching him. Fortunately he'd had logs and kindling already set in the fireplace, and they sparked quickly. Within minutes, the small space was benefiting from the heat created by the blaze, and the room was enveloped in a lovely golden glow.

She took the opportunity to look around a bit, knowing he'd only been here a few months, but sensing he'd taken steps to make the place his own. There were some nonfiction books on the mantel, along with a few thrillers. No pictures on the walls, but a couple of framed family type snapshots stood on the end table. Some colorful pillows were tossed on the furniture, and the thick rug in front of the hearth looked new and cozy.

She'd definitely seen worse bachelor pads.

"Better?"

"Much, thank you."

He fell silent again, and she felt that tension between them that had appeared in the restaurant, after she'd gone to the ladies' room. Compared to his friendliness before she'd left, she couldn't help thinking something had happened. As she'd driven home, she'd half wondered if he'd made some assignation with the waitress and just wanted to be rid of her. She couldn't deny she'd held her breath waiting to hear him come home, and was pleased he had, even if it had meant she was trapped and busted as a home invader.

He finally broke the silence. "I think I owe you an apology."

"Oh?"

He sat on the floor, near the fireplace, on that thick rug. His long jeans-clad legs were stretched in front of him, booted feet casually crossed. The jeans pulled tight on those powerful thighs. She again noted how built he was, obviously not from any L.A. gym lifestyle but from his physically demanding job.

"Yeah. Earlier tonight, at the bar, one of the guys in the next booth told me you'd been on the phone before I arrived, having a very intimate conversation."

She laughed. "Of course I was—intentionally! My best friend called, and I was trying really hard to make it sound like he was my boyfriend, so they would stop pestering me."

He dropped his head back, shaking it and mumbling something under his breath. Something that sounded like, *idiot*.

Well, yeah, he had been. Being all macho-aloof instead of asking her about it had been the typical male reaction.

"Is that why you were such a jerk in the parking lot?"

He straightened to look at her. "I'm sorry."

"Were you angry about it?"

"Not angry. Jealous as hell," he admitted.

That sent warm shivers of excitement rushing through her. There was no reason for Oliver to have been jealous if he didn't want her for himself.

"I know it's none of my business, but you said you didn't have a boyfriend...."

"I don't," she insisted. "No boyfriend, no husband, no lover."

Just a fiancé.

The thought stabbed into her head like a brain freeze, shocking and painful. She was so used to not being involved with anyone, it was hard to remember that now, she technically was.

Oh, hell, what a mess.

She knew she should just tell him the situation, be honest and let him know what was happening. But in order to do that, she'd have to tell him why she'd agreed to a sexless marriage, and why it was okay for her to cheat on her fiancé.

She couldn't out Tommy to somebody he didn't know. Nobody had that right. Especially because, even if she didn't reveal the name of her future husband, once the press got hold of her engagement and marriage, Oliver would realize who she'd been talking about. It wasn't like he was some foreign, overseas stranger who would never give her another thought. He lived right in California, worked for her grandfather. His family lived in San Diego, and he probably still had plenty of work ties to L.A. No, he wasn't the type who would run tattling to the press the minute he heard the news, but what if he accidentally said something to the wrong person? Tommy could be hurt— badly—because of her. She just couldn't risk it.

Telling him the truth was out. But lying was just against her nature.

Was there a happy medium? Could she walk the tightrope and take what she wanted more than anything in the world—a wild affair with Oliver—without jeopardizing her best friend's reputation?

Oliver watched her from the floor, his dark eyes catching glimmers of firelight, reflecting them. He cast a long deliberate stare over her, gazing from her face, down her throat, to the single bare shoulder revealed by her blouse. She'd been wearing a raincoat when she came in, but hadn't wanted to get his couch wet. At least, that's what she'd told herself. Actually, the thought of him looking at her, like this, hadn't been a small part of the reason she'd taken the coat off.

Something was happening between them. Heat—quiet but intense—flared. But the problem bore repeating: what a mess.

"This has been pretty inevitable, hasn't it?" he asked, his tone simple, to the point. As if he'd given up resisting something they had both known was going to happen.

"Yes, I think so."

He wanted her. That was obvious. He'd been fighting it, as had she. But it seemed they'd both had enough of playing games. The attraction between them had been thick from the moment they'd met. They were always headed to this moment. Always.

Find the happy medium, an inner voice urged.

She couldn't let it go that one last step toward becoming this amazing man's lover until she'd clarified a couple of things. No, she couldn't reveal Tommy's secret, but she had to be as honest as she could be. "You need to know something."

He didn't seem to be paying attention. Instead he got on his knees, crawling closer to the edge of the couch. His glittering eyes were narrowed, his lips parted, his hair was damp and hanging in his face. He looked earthy, primal and…hungry.

"Oliver…"

"Unless you need to tell me you're a virgin or a nun, I don't think there's anything else I absolutely have to know right now."

She couldn't help laughing a little at his vehemence. "What if I needed to tell you I was gay?"

He moved closer, dropping his hand on her calf. "Then I'd tell you you're a liar."

She swallowed hard, feeling the heat of his palm through her jeans. He squeezed lightly.

Quivering in reaction, she managed to insist, "I really do need to make something clear."

He hesitated. Her heart ached as she thought of doing anything to sabotage what she sensed could be one of the most sensual, erotic nights of her life, but she had to at least try to make things as open as possible.

"Whatever happens can't go beyond this week."

He smiled a little, looking relieved. Okay, maybe he had just wanted a one-night, or one-week, stand. Which shouldn't have bothered her, since a week was all she had. But her insides twisted, anyway.

Stop overanalyzing. Maybe he's just relieved you didn't say you were transgendered.

She forced herself to go on. "I meant it when I said I don't have a lover or a boyfriend, but that doesn't mean I'm free. I have made a serious commitment and I intend to keep my word. Once I leave here next week, when Grandpa gets home, this is completely over."

He eyed her intently. "You want to tell me what the commitment is?"

"I could try, but it wouldn't be easy for me to say too much without breaking someone else's confidence," she said, hoping that wouldn't be a deal-breaker.

"Understood," he said with a nod. She already knew he valued integrity and wasn't totally surprised he hadn't insisted she spill everything.

"You're an adult, you want me and you're not married. As long as all three of those things are true, then, honestly, right at this moment, I don't give a damn about anything else."

He fell silent. So did she. Their stares locked.

Finally she spoke. "All those things are true."

He moved closer.

"But I do have a request to make. Can we just agree

that, if we, uh…" She could feel her cheeks warming. "If we enjoy tonight…"

His spontaneous laugh made her smile. The man did not suffer from any lack of confidence.

"If we do, and we want to spend the rest of the week together, that's great," she explained. "After that week though, it's never mentioned again, never referred to. You don't contact me…. I don't contact you?"

"No strings? Absolutely no regrets?"

"Exactly."

He didn't jump for joy the way most men probably would have at hearing a woman admit she wanted a no-strings sexual affair with him. "You're serious?"

"Very."

He didn't answer for a moment, considering. Then, at last, he slowly nodded. "My life's too crazy now to even consider getting tangled in any strings. If that's really the way you want to play it, that's the way it'll be."

Another long stare. A silent assent.

Then an exchange of slow, sultry smiles.

They'd made a bargain. They would be lovers.

She had a week. And she intended to enjoy every minute of it.

8

ONCE THE WORDS had been said, the deal struck, Candace let all her questions, doubts and worries fade away. She might not have a long-term future with Oliver, and her life might be taking her in directions she could never have imagined, but for now, for tonight at least, she intended to enjoy herself with a man who made her whole body come alive.

"I have a bed upstairs in the loft," Oliver murmured, sliding his hand down her calf.

"I like it right here," she said, not willing to waste the time moving, not when she was finally going to get what she'd so desperately wanted.

His approving nod said he agreed. When he reached into his pocket and withdrew a condom, she knew he'd been anticipating this moment. Considering she'd picked up a box at the drug store and had a few tucked into her purse, she couldn't pretend to take offense. She could only be grateful.

The man was gloriously handsome at any time of day, in any lighting. But when he tugged at his shirt and pulled it up and over his head, tossing it to the floor, she had to admit he did amazing things for firelight.

His body was perfectly shaped. The shoulders so broad,

the chest beautifully sculpted. Months of hard, physical labor had obviously eradicated any sign of the L.A. lawyer and turned him into a muscular god, with incredibly defined abs, a lean waist and slim hips. A light swirl of hair encircled his nipples, trailing down into a thin line that disappeared into the waistband of his jeans.

She licked her lips, wanting to see where that happy trail led. But after kicking off his shoes, he stopped, leaving his jeans in place.

She pouted. "Keep going. You definitely don't have to stop on my account."

"We'll get there. But fair's fair. You're still fully dressed."

"You can fix that for me."

"I'd be happy to."

He tugged the boots off her feet, then gently palmed and massaged her arches. When his fingers slipped up under her pant legs, the brush of skin on skin made her internal temperature soar. An hour ago she'd been freezing. Now she knew a spark had just ignited and she was going up in flames.

Her skinny jeans were tight, and he couldn't move his hand nearly high enough to satisfy her, so she stretched out and began to wriggle, reaching for her waistband.

"No. Let me," he insisted.

Still kneeling on the floor, he touched his way up her limbs, slowly, deliberately. By the time those talented fingers reached the tops of her thighs, she was groaning. She couldn't begin to imagine what it would be like when he finally got her undressed. Fortunately, she knew she wouldn't have to wait long to find out.

"Please, hurry," she whispered when he traipsed his knuckles up the strip of fabric covering the zipper.

"You're not the patient sort, are you?"

"If you go negative-two miles an hour I might just have

to kill you," she admitted, whimpering when he reached for the button and unfastened her jeans.

"We have all night," he insisted, not sounding the least bit prodded to speed up. "I've been thinking about this—dreaming about it—since the minute we met. There's no way in hell I'm rushing through it."

"Ditto," she admitted. Then, being honest, she added, "The thinking and the dreaming part, I mean. I'm all about rushing."

Fast and hard. Deep and wild. She was dying to be filled by him, possessed, pounded into and taken.

"Sorry, beautiful. It's not happening."

He slid the zipper down slowly. She could practically hear the teeth separating, the faint hiss competing with the roar of the wind outside, the crackling of the fire and the pounding of her blood in her veins.

When he'd finished unzipping her, she lifted her hips, shimmying to help him as he pulled the pants down, peeling them off and baring her legs. To her disappointment, he didn't slide his hands down the front of her groin, didn't take the skimpy panties with the jeans. But she really hadn't expected him to. Aside from what he'd just admitted, Oliver had already proven himself to be a very patient man. He was going to take his time, go slow, wring every ounce of pleasure out of each and every experience they shared.

"I will, too," she told herself, whispering it aloud. "I can do this."

"You will and can what?"

"I'll go slow," she promised. Then he traced the tip of his finger along the elastic edge of her panties and she whimpered. "Oh, God, yes, please, rip them off. Take me!"

His chuckle was pure evil. "That's not going slow." He slid his finger below the elastic, scraping it into the soft tuft of curls nesting at the top of her sex, then away again.

"I said slow, not in slow motion," she groaned, her hips thrusting up as a nameless but very familiar need took over.

"We're just getting started," he insisted, moving his hands to the bottom hem of her blouse.

Okay, that detour she could allow. Her breasts were aching, her nipples pointy and so sensitized her own shirt was giving her a thrill. His mouth and hands would likely send her out of her mind.

"God, you're beautiful. It killed me not to be able to look down at you last night when I touched your breasts," he whispered as he pushed the blouse up, revealing her tummy and her midriff. "Stay still. Let me explore you."

Being explored sounded good. Very good. She could be the wilds of undiscovered America and he could go all Lewis and Clark over every hill, valley and stream. She just hoped those hills were her breasts, the valley her pelvis and the stream the flood of creamy desire filling her sex.

He lowered his face so he could press a kiss on her hip bone. She felt the warmth of his breath on her skin, so close to her panty line, and instinctively rose to offer him more, praying he was eschewing the hills and valleys and going for the stream.

He moved in the other direction, though, kissing his way up the indentation of her pelvis, to her belly button.

She let out a groan that was half pleasure, half frustration. Ignoring her, he continued to push her blouse up, moving his mouth after it. Inch by inch, he explored her body, licking into each hollow between every rib, testing her, tasting her, breathing her in. It was wonderful, erotic…and frustrating. She was whimpering and twisting below him, wanting him to hurry up, but not ever wanting this to end.

He reached her bra, which opened with a front clasp. She held her breath, tensing as he touched the fastener with his thumb and finger, and deftly flicked it open, revealing her curves for his most delicious attention. He paused for a moment, staring, as if memorizing every line and dip. Her nipples were tight buds, pink and pointy, obviously begging for some attention.

But when he again began to trace his mouth over her, he focused on her sternum, kissing his way right up between her sensitive breasts, his smooth cheeks brushing against the sides but making no effort to suck away some of her tension. Nor did his teasing hand offer any relief, as he simply continued those light, delicate strokes over her belly, her pelvis and her upper thighs, never giving her what she really needed.

"Oh, God," she groaned, every inch of her burning. Her senses were so deliciously heightened the pleasure was almost pain. She'd never felt anything like it, never been so totally keyed up and ready.

Shudders coursed through her body, her muscles tensing, every inch of her aware and anxious. But he didn't give her any relief. He was entirely focused on what he was doing. He seemed to love the curve of her collarbone, which he sampled and scraped his teeth across. He found something delightfully kissable in the hollow of her throat. Here he licked. There he pressed his face and breathed her in. Here and there, there and here.

It was wonderful. Erotic. The anticipation was beyond anything she'd ever experienced.

But she was dying. Just dying. Because every tender caress he placed on one part of her body only sent more currents of hot, electric desire to her core. Her clit was so hard it ached, her sex was throbbing, all her nerve endings seemed to have bunched between her thighs.

Maybe because she'd only ever been with guys her own age, and those in the movie business, who were always on a schedule, she'd never had a lover take so much time, be so deliberate in every caress. Oliver seemed to savor every part of her he uncovered. He appeared determined to pay full, glorious attention to every inch of her body, leaving the choicest bits for last.

Her tummy and throat and, oh, the nape of her neck, adored him for it.

Her choicest bits were screaming for his attention.

"Shh," he ordered.

"I didn't say anything," she groaned.

"Your thoughts are very loud, Candace." He lifted his head to look at her, a smile of pure wickedness on his face. "I know what you want."

"Well, mind reader, if I've been so obvious, why…"

"Oh, you've been very obvious," he insisted with a low, sultry laugh. "And I'm looking forward to meeting your every demand." He bent to slide his lips over her jaw, moving up until he reached her ear and traced the lobe with the tip of his tongue. "But I'd like to at least kiss you before I slide my tongue into your pussy and lick you until you don't remember what planet you're on."

Bam. Explosion.

"Oh, God!"

She climaxed, just like that, from those words, from the weight of his hand on her thigh and the slide of his mouth on her cheek. Her whole body quaked, hot bolts of pleasure rocketing through her. This wasn't a slow, pulsing wave; it was a tsunami, hitting her hard in every direction. As he'd insisted he wanted to, Oliver moved his mouth over hers, catching her gasps of pleasure with his lips, taking them in and swallowing them down.

When she finally regained a brain cell, she realized Oliver had somehow managed to tug her tiny panties off her hips and push them out of the way. They were tangled around her legs, and she kicked and bucked to get free of them. He helped, drawing them all the way off her.

His wickedly erotic words still echoed in her ears, and she held her breath, wondering if he would now go back to some of those choice bits for more attention. When he began to kiss his way down her body, she suspected that's exactly what he intended.

"Oh, yes," she groaned.

He ignored her, his mouth moving down between her breasts. But this time, thankfully, he detoured and pressed hot, openmouthed kisses on her breast. She was whimpering by the time that wonderful mouth moved to cover her nipple and cried out when he sucked it. He caught her other one in his fingers, teasing and tweaking, plumping her breast in his hand while continuing to suckle her into incoherence.

Not until he'd paid equal attention to her other rock-hard nipple did he continue his downward journey over her body. He licked a line straight down, tasting her inch by inch. He nibbled her belly, nipped at her hip bone, his lips grazing the hollow above her groin. His face brushed against the curls concealing her sex and she couldn't stop her hips from thrusting up in welcome.

He turned her to face him, then tugged one leg over his shoulder, opening her to his hungry gaze.

"Oliver," she whimpered as embarrassment warred with utter lust. The look on his face was so covetous, so admiring, she decided to go with the lust.

"You are absolutely mouthwatering." He traced his fingertip over her clit, then down, separating the lips of her sex, opening her for his most intimate perusal. "So pink and shiny. I love how wet you are."

She gulped. No lover had ever examined her so frankly, or spoken so bluntly. That thick note of hunger in his voice said he meant every word he said. This man knew how to use language, all right—he seduced her with every word he said. She'd bet he was wicked in the courtroom. And more wicked in the bedroom.

"This is so pretty," he mused as he thumbed her clit, rolling it around. He slipped a finger into her channel, drawing a low gasp from her. "And so is this. I can't decide which I want to taste more."

He was apparently the decisive sort. Because not ten seconds had passed before he moved his head between her thighs and went down.

When he buried his face in her sex and began to devour her, she saw stars. She clutched him, twining her fingers in his hair as he lifted her other leg and draped it over his shoulder. Her limbs were practically wrapped around his neck, but he didn't seem interested in going anywhere else, so she left them there and focused on the incredible sensation of his mouth against her plump, swollen lips.

He devoured her, licking into her, making love to her with his tongue. She was gasping as he moved up to her clit and gently sucked and stroked. Back and forth he went until she was arching, twisting, helpless against her body's intense reaction.

This time, when she came in a heated rush, he didn't stop what he was doing. He went right on pleasuring her, focusing on her clit while he slid his fingers deep into her and worked some magic on a spot high inside. Tears formed in her eyes, and she was whimpering as another orgasm washed over her.

Now he finally seemed satisfied. He gently lowered her legs and kissed his way back up her body. Still dazed, she only regained her senses when she realized he was pulling away to stand up and unfasten his jeans.

This was worth her full, utmost attention.

She caught her lip between her teeth and watched him, feeling like a kid on Christmas morning who was finally going to get to open her biggest present.

"Wow," she whispered when he peeled away his boxer briefs.

Because big didn't quite describe him. His cock could be described with three of her favorite adjectives: *long, thick* and *rock-hard.* It jutted out, proud and male and hot. That river between her legs threatened to turn into an ocean just at the sight of him.

"I've been walking around like this since the night you slammed me with the frying pan."

"Feel free to get even by slamming me with that," she whispered.

He chuckled softly, but he soon stopped laughing. Because Candace wasn't satisfied with just looking. She had to touch him, feel all that silk-encased steel.

She sat up straight. Scooting to the very edge of the couch, she parted her thighs to make room for his legs and leaned close to his naked body. Close enough to cast warm breaths of air over him, her lips hovering an inch from all that luscious maleness. But she didn't go further, not quite yet. She wanted him as out of his mind with desire as she'd been.

Groaning, he twined his hands in her hair. Candace knew she was tormenting him, but knowing from very recent experience that anticipation was wonderful, she didn't give him what he wanted. Instead, she reached up and traced her fingers over his cock, from the top down the long back, to the sacs beneath. She cupped them gently, hearing his gasp and feeling his hands tighten in her hair. The position was incredibly intimate. He was as physically vulnerable as a man could make himself, and she was conscious of the trust that must require. Obviously, given how men loved to be blown, the benefits had to outweigh the risk. And this time, she was finding herself truly looking forward to something she'd usually viewed as an item to check off a list during foreplay.

Not with him. Him she wanted to taste. Oliver she wanted to please.

She continued to breathe deeply, evenly, loving the musky scent of man that filled her nostrils. Wrapping her hand around as much of him as she could hold, she stroked him, up and down, squeezing lightly, knowing by the way his pulse pounded in his groin that his heart was racing.

Needing to smooth the glide, she lifted her hand and traced her fingers across the top of his cock, moistening them with the arousal seeping from the tip. Curious, she drew a finger to her mouth and licked the moisture from it.

"Jesus!"

She heard pure desperation in his voice. Casting a look up through her bangs and seeing Oliver's hungry expression, she knew she'd pushed him to his limits, and finally licked her lips and moved in for a deeper taste. He was definitely too big for her to take him all the way, but she did her best, taking the bulbous tip into her mouth and sucking gently.

"Oh, God, yeah," he groaned, pumping the tiniest bit, as if a slave to his body's demands.

She didn't mind. He tasted delicious—warm, a little salty, ever-so-smooth. The act was incredibly intimate, and she loved hearing his groans of pleasure as she sucked him as far as she could, laving him so he could glide more easily.

He didn't allow it to go on too long, not nearly as long as he'd pleasured her. Within a few minutes, he'd gently pushed her away.

"I want in."

The blunt demand made her shiver with excitement. He reached for her, drawing her to her feet, and she wasn't quite sure where they were going. When he lifted one of her legs so she could rest her foot on the arm of the couch, she got the picture.

He paused to tear open the condom packet and slide it

on—it was a wonder the thing fit. When he was sheathed, he drew her into his arms, covering her mouth and kissing her deeply. His erection was a powerful ridge between their bodies, and she arched toward it, needing him desperately.

"Please, Oliver," she insisted.

He gave her what she wanted, tilting her toward him and nudging into her curls. She was slick with want, her body opening in welcome. He eased into her, bringing ecstasy with him. Candace began to breathe in shallow little gasps as he filled her, inch by delicious inch. He was so thick, hard and hot that she felt every bit of him as he possessed her.

As if he realized that her whole body was melting, he grabbed her by the hips and lifted her. She wrapped her legs around his waist, allowing herself to sink fully onto him. As he impaled her, she threw her head back and let out a low, guttural cry of pleasure.

He began to thrust slowly, sinking deep, then drawing away. The man's strength surprised her. He seemed completely comfortable bearing her weight as they gave and took. She answered every stroke, clenching him deep inside, knowing by his shudders that he felt and enjoyed every squeeze.

Soon, the frenzy built. He drove faster; she cried louder. She clung to his shoulders, and he backed her against the wall. The leverage made things deeper, hotter, and he drove into her again and again, losing himself to the passion.

She was lost to it, too. Lost to everything but this moment, this man, this act, and giving all she had to bring them both to the pinnacle of delight. When she reached that peak, climaxing yet again, she held on tight and let him drive deep to attain his own.

WAKING UP THE next morning and seeing his bedside clock flashing, Oliver realized the power had come back on at some point during the night. Honestly, it wouldn't have mattered if it had remained off. He and Candace had created plenty of heat on their own, both down in front of the fireplace, and again later in this bed.

This small bed.

He had never been more aware of its size until now, when he felt her curled up against him, one slim leg entwined with his, her arm draped across his waist, her head on his shoulder.

He liked small beds, he decided.

He liked them a lot.

And he especially liked waking up to find her in bed with him, twined around him like she needed to touch as much of him as she could while she slept.

The light sifting in through the window said the storm had passed and the day appeared sunny and bright. There were a million things he could work on, but he had the feeling he was going to want to skip them in favor of making love to this beautiful woman again.

He had her for one week and one week only. He had no idea why those had been her terms, or what the secret was that she hadn't wanted to share. Last night, in the heat of the moment, he hadn't given a damn. Now though, he couldn't deny he was curious. But not curious enough to push her and risk losing out on what time he had left with her.

It was going to be a week he would never forget. And one she would never forget. He'd make absolutely certain of that.

"Mmm...good morning," she murmured.

He glanced down to see her looking up at him, yawning and blinking against the bright sunlight.

"Hi."

She curled her arm tighter, tucking her leg a little more intimately, and cuddled close. "How did you sleep?"

"Like a man who'd run a marathon," he admitted. "Something zapped all my strength last night."

"I think that was me." She might have been a cat for the satisfied purr in her tone.

"I told you the night we met that you should come with a warning label."

"What would it say?"

"Caution: combustible female. Approach only when wearing protective gear."

She giggled against his chest and traced a lazy hand down his stomach. "You wore protective gear last night."

True, though he wished he hadn't had to. The very idea of being buried inside her, skin to skin, was incredibly appealing. Unfortunately, he might never get that chance. Their relationship was very new, and short-term, and that kind of trust and intimacy usually didn't happen right away.

"What are you thinking?"

He had to be honest, so he told her the truth.

She quivered delicately and he saw a warm flush suffuse her cheeks. "Mind reader."

"Really?"

"Yes. I'm all for being responsible, but the truth is, I'm on the pill and I thought about throwing those condoms into the fireplace last night."

"It was probably best for us to talk about it first. I'd never put you at risk—you know that, right? I'm as healthy as a horse."

"After last night, didn't I prove I trust you?"

Oh, she definitely had, lowering her guard and surrendering herself to him in every way a woman could. Of course, he'd done the same. It was the most intimate he had ever been with anyone, which made the idea of him only having her for another week all the more untenable.

No strings. No emotions. That was the deal. And really, it was for the best.

Somehow, though, it was getting harder to remember that.

"And for what it's worth, I haven't been around the block a whole lot myself. In fact, before last night, it had been over a year since I was with anyone."

"Have men in Los Angeles gone blind, deaf and lost their sense of smell, taste and touch since I was away?"

She giggled, the sound cute and unusual for her. "Well, I don't usually go around asking guys to sniff me, and when I tell them to bite me, it's not a genuine invitation."

He couldn't resist sliding down and nibbling her neck.

"So you're saying?" he asked as he moved lower to kiss her chest, delighting in those perky, pouty nipples that cried out for attention.

She groaned and wrapped her legs around him. "I'm saying I want you inside me. Right now. Unless that's a problem for you."

It wasn't.

He immediately moved between her parted thighs and tested her readiness with his fully engorged cock. She was wet and warm, soft and yielding. So ready.

"Absolutely not a problem," he muttered as he buried himself to the hilt.

The sensation was blissful, all sweet heat and moisture, and he closed his eyes, giving in to the pleasure. Then they began to rock together, bathed in the morning light, connected in every way possible.

And not for the first time, he began to wonder how on earth he was ever going to let her go.

9

OVER THE NEXT couple of days, Candace found herself falling into a routine. She would get up early, and spend the morning with Grandpa, cheering him on with his rehab. Then she would come back to the house, have lunch with Oliver, have sex with Oliver, have orgasms with Oliver, do a little drawing, then go back to have dinner with Grandpa. Often Oliver accompanied her for dinner, though they left the sex and the orgasms at home.

She couldn't remember a time when she'd been happier. Oh, she was still very worried about her grandfather, and was now busy dealing with her newest assignment. The studio had called, saying they loved her sketches and wanted her for the project. She knew as well as anyone that this could be the film that got her some major attention. Aside from that, she was also busy talking to appraisers and auctioneers about the wine collection. And surrounding all that business and activity, a happy glow of personal contentment swirled around her just about every minute of the day.

She and Oliver did more than just have the most amazing sex. They cooked together, walked together, laughed together. She'd gotten him to open up a little more about his savaged career, and even got him to admit that, with his change in lifestyle, he probably could afford to put out a shingle and take on only the clients he truly believed were innocent.

Only one thing could pierce her glow of contentment: thinking about what awaited her back in L.A.

"Hey, chickie, whatcha doing?" Tommy asked when she'd answered the phone late one afternoon.

She hadn't told him about Oliver. The only person she'd even hinted to about her relationship with him was Madison, to whom she talked every other day or so. Her sister had been her other half since birth. They had the kind of bond few people ever experienced with a sibling. Madison knew how to keep a secret, so they usually told each other everything. But even Madison didn't know the whole story. Candace had kept some things from her, the most intimate things. She'd protected the relationship, wanting to keep it private for as long as it lasted. But the fact that it couldn't last much longer was crushing her.

"I'm shopping," she admitted. "I've got to buy a new dress."

"For?"

"There's a big winery owner's ball tomorrow night," she said, still wondering if she'd made the right decision in saying she would attend with Oliver.

Their relationship so far had been mostly about sex. Drinking wine, talking about Grandpa and him teaching her what he'd learned so far about the wine business had taken up some time, too. But other than that one dinner/dessert they'd shared at Wilhelm's, they'd never actually gone on a date. So last night, when her grandfather had told them he wanted the two of them to go to the event, since he had already RSVP'd for himself and Oliver, her first instinct was to refuse. Then she'd met Oliver's eye from across the hospital room and had seen the gleam of interest there.

She couldn't deny being curious. She'd gotten to know him as a working man. This formal, black-tie event might be her only chance to catch a glimpse of the man Oliver had been before his life imploded. Not that she didn't adore the man who'd taught her things about her body she'd never even known, but she wanted to learn as much about him as she could, while she could. She wanted to discover all his facets and imprint them on her memory, to tide her over for the long and lonely years that stretched ahead.

It was getting harder to think about those years, harder to envision the life she'd chosen for herself. Even the sound of Tommy's voice, which usually made her happy, twisted the knife in the wound. For a few days, she'd been able to pretend she was at the start of a relationship that could change her life.

Maybe it still would. Maybe she'd change from a normal, happy woman to a heartbroken, never-able-to-love-again sad case.

Love? What the hell are you thinking, girl?

"Sounds fancy."

She was still too busy tripping over the word *love* in her mind to respond.

"Where is it?" he asked.

She finally shook her head, forcing away thoughts she wasn't ready to deal with, and replied, "At a hotel in San Francisco."

"Nice. I love that city."

A faint smile tugged at her lips. "I can't imagine why."

"Do you think anyone would notice if I walked in the parade? I could blend in with the crowd."

"Maybe…if you covered yourself with gold body paint from head to toe and wore a rubber gorilla mask on your face."

"Party pooper."

She shrugged as she walked around the square in Sonoma, eyeing the windows of various boutiques. "Have you been behaving?"

"Define behaving."

"Staying out of the news?"

"Babe, I'm always in the news. I can't take a piss in a restaurant bathroom without some jackass trying to snap a picture he can sell to the tabs."

"That really sucks, Tommy," she said, hearing the note of sad resignation he couldn't disguise.

"Yeah, poor, poor me," he said, his dark mood lifting quickly, as always. "Remind me of that next time I get a contract for a ten-mill picture."

"Will do."

"Considering half of it will be yours, I'm sure you will!"

Right. His millions would be her millions. Somehow, that had meant something to her once upon a time. It just didn't now.

"Hey, have you heard from the studio?"

One bit of bright news. "Yes. I got the job."

"Congrats, girlfriend!"

"Thanks. They sent me the script and I'm starting on some prelims."

"Excellent. We should celebrate."

"We will. When I get back."

"When's that going to be again?"

She swallowed hard, knowing she had to say the words aloud—not just for his sake, but for hers.

"I'm coming home in a few days. Grandpa gets out of the rehab facility on Sunday. The last time I talked to Mad, she was booking a ticket to come out and spend some time with him. She should be here sometime this weekend."

"So there's nothing keeping you there?"

No. Nothing keeping her.

Nothing at all.

She wished she could talk to Tommy. Other than her sister, he was the one to whom she could always spill her darkest secrets and woes. And since her sister lived clear on the other side of the country, and they seldom saw each other, it was Tommy who she usually relied on.

But she couldn't talk to him about this. Couldn't admit anything about her amazing relationship with Oliver. It was too personal, too vulnerable, and she had to concede, too heartbreaking. Telling him would mean revealing her feelings—she could never keep those from him. If she revealed how she really felt, she would be putting Tom in a hell of a position.

Would he urge her to follow her heart, tell her he'd deal with the fallout?

Maybe.

Or maybe he'd panic and beg her not to bail on him.

Either way, she'd end up feeling like the worst friend in the world. Because she'd promised. Agreeing to marry him was not the kind of promise she could go back on, not when so much was riding on it for him. If she didn't follow through, his career could be over, and so could their friendship. So no matter how deeply she feared she was falling for Oliver McKean, her old friend had to come before her new lover.

Even if hers was the only heart in their strange triangle that ended up getting broken.

HEARING A CAR pull up that evening, Oliver walked to the front room of Buddy's house and gazed out the window. Candace had just returned from town, and as she got out, she pulled a plastic-wrapped bundle on a hanger with her. Her shopping trip had apparently been a success.

He still couldn't believe he'd agreed to escort her to the ball. The whole hobnob-with-the-wealthy-set had never been a big part of his life, though he'd attended a few events when he was with the D.A.'s office. But he sure hadn't hauled his tux with him when he'd moved; the thing was moldering in a storage unit along with most of his suits and a mountain of law books. He'd had to stop by a rental place to order one, which was always a pain in the ass. In fact, the whole thing was a bad idea all around.

But when Buddy had suggested it, he simply hadn't been able to resist. He wanted to take Candace out, to have her on his arm, at least once. Wanted to show her a great time that didn't include them being in bed.

Well, it would probably end up with them in bed. In fact, considering he'd booked a room at the hotel, he was counting on it ending up there. Still, the point remained. He didn't want her just for the phenomenal sex. He liked being with her, and wanted her to know it.

Why, he had no idea.

Because you don't want her to leave, jackass.

Oh. Yeah. That.

Oliver had set up a special evening for them and looked forward to seeing her reaction when she walked in the door. Candace had appeared happy since the moment they'd become lovers, but every so often a shadow would appear. Her lush mouth would pull down, her brow would furrow with worry, and he knew she was stressing over something. He had a feeling it was because she was hearing the ticking of the clock. Frankly, he was stressing over it, too.

When he'd agreed to her one-week-only terms, he hadn't been thinking about much beyond getting her naked. Saying goodbye hadn't sounded so painful if it meant a week of mind-altering sex. But now that he'd become addicted to that mind-altering sex, and, he greatly feared, the woman with whom he was having it, her imminent departure weighed on him heavily.

So ask her to stay. Or to at least keep the lines of communication open when she leaves.

The thought had definitely occurred to him. He just wasn't sure he was ready to broach the subject with her. He didn't want her to go, but he also didn't want to spoil the last few days of the week she'd allotted them by pushing for more before she was ready.

She reached the porch, and he opened the door before she could even grasp the knob.

"Hi."

The furrow and the frown disappeared, as did the faintly slumped shoulders that hinted she bore some heavy weight. He would like to help her with that, but whenever their conversations turned too personal, she changed the subject by dropping an item of clothing.

Somehow, that always worked.

She draped what looked like a glittery, siren-red dress—God help him—over the railing at the bottom of the stairs. "Hi, yourself."

Stepping into his arms, she lifted her face for a kiss, and he welcomed her. It felt as right as everything else about them, this easy, coming-home embrace, as if they'd always walked into each other's arms at the end of a day.

"Success?" he asked.

She nodded. "A little out of my price range, but some of those boutiques are amazing. I think you're going to like my pretty new outfit."

The way she said it made it sound like the thing was sweet and innocent. He knew, however, judging by that color and the scantiness of the material, that it would be anything but.

"You're messing with me, right?"

"Oh, absolutely. You're going to love my wicked new take-me-now dress."

He could hardly wait. But considering he'd made other

plans for this evening, wanting to show her they could be more to each other than just incredibly erotic sex partners, he figured that would have to wait.

"Did you eat?"

"Nope."

"Good." He took her arm and steered her toward the living room, which he'd set up for tonight's surprise.

When she saw the large, old-fashioned movie projector, and the screen he'd erected against the far wall, she clapped her hands together. "Movie night?"

"You got it."

Smiling broadly, she walked over to the couch, then saw the feast he'd spread out on the coffee table just beyond it. He had never taken her to a movie, so he'd had to guess what her favorite candy would be. Covering all the bases had seemed like a good idea at the time.

"Hot dogs, nachos, popcorn...oh, my God. Dots? You bought me Dots? They're my absolute favorite," she gushed, hurrying over and plucking that box from among all the other junk food he'd piled onto the table. "If there's a wedding ring in this box, I'll say yes on the spot."

She was laughing, her eyes sparkling, but the moment the words left her mouth, she winced and bit her bottom lip. Obviously sheepish, she mumbled, "Sorry, I was just..."

"I know," he said, waving off her explanations. To be honest, he didn't want to discuss that topic any more than she did. Not because he was upset she'd mentioned it, but because the idea wasn't as immediately horrifying as he'd have thought a few weeks ago. No, he was in no way ready to get married. But since meeting Candace, he no longer considered *marriage* to be a dirty word.

He couldn't help wondering if costume designers could telecommute. How strange would it be if it turned out that he'd come up to Sonoma to find out what he wanted from the rest of his life and discovered what he wanted lived back in L.A.?

"So, what are we watching?" she asked as she kicked off her shoes and plopped onto the couch. "One of your great-grandfather's hits?"

"I don't know if it was a hit," he said, eyeing the metal case in which the movie reel had been packed. He walked over to the projector, through which he'd already threaded the film, and flipped it on. Dimming the lights, he explained, "I haven't seen this one before myself. Judging by the title, *Master of the Heated Sands,* it's either about a sheikh in a desert or a pimp in Miami."

She snickered, opened a box of her favorite candy and popped three of the juicy, colorful little treats into her mouth. "Num num," she murmured as she chewed, her grin as wide as a kid's.

He'd never developed a taste for gummy candy, but he couldn't deny he suddenly wondered how the confection would taste when devoured off Candace Reid's tongue.

"What?" she asked, obviously catching him in his stare as he returned to the couch and sat down next to her.

"I'm suddenly developing a sweet tooth."

She clutched the box to her chest. "Mine."

He snorted a laugh. "You weren't watching *Barney* the day they went over that whole sharing thing, huh?"

"Are you kidding? I was forced to share from the minute I drew breath. Madison and I had to split everything fifty-fifty."

"Your sister?" She'd mentioned Madison, who would be coming in from the east coast this weekend, always speaking fondly of her only sibling.

"Yep. Believe me, I never had a thing to call my own."

"Close in age, huh?"

Her grin was infectious. "Uh, yeah. You could definitely say that."

Before she could elaborate, the movie began to play. The image flickered on the screen, grainy and gray, and the credits began to roll.

"Where's the music?" she asked, looking confused. "Didn't they always have that really dramatic music underscoring everything?"

"The music wasn't imprinted on the movie any more than dialogue could be—hence the term *silent picture*."

She smacked her palm against her own forehead. "Duh."

"Hey, don't be too hard on yourself. I asked exactly the same question the first time I watched one of these with my family."

"Whenever I see clips from these old movies, there's always music. Where'd it come from?"

"The written score always accompanied the reels when they were sent out to the big movie houses." He reached for the bucket of popcorn. "In-house organists would play along as the movie ran."

"Live?"

"Yes. I've seen some pictures from some of my great-grandfather's movie openings. There were huge, elaborate organs."

"Guess the musicians had to be fast studies."

"I suspect a lot of it sounded alike.It was the cue to the audience about how they were supposed to feel."

"Have you ever seen any of those YouTube videos people make with clips of horror movies set to the soundtrack from a comedy? Or vice versa? The music definitely makes the moment."

"So, should I hum?" he asked with a grin.

"Are you any good?"

"I'm told I have the perfect voice for singing in the shower. Or on a deserted island."

Laughing, she curled up against him on the couch, watching as the credits finished and the action started. He draped an arm over her, amazed at how natural this was, how laid-back and comfortable. He found her so easy to talk to. There was no pretension with her, no subtext that he'd often experienced with other women, when they'd say one thing but mean another.

Candace was nothing like that. She was honest—refreshingly so—and utterly open.

Except about her secret.

Yeah. Except about that.

Forcing himself not to think about it, he focused on the screen, immediately recognizing his ancestor, who rode in on a beautiful Arabian horse.

"Not exactly politically correct," he said, noting the heavy makeup.

"Shh."

"Why do I have to shh when there's nothing to hear?"

She elbowed him in the ribs. "I'm reading."

"And you need to hear to do that?"

"Yes, so I can create the voices in my head."

She sounded a little testy, and he couldn't resist baiting her. "Hearing voices in your head…do that a lot, do you?"

She sat up and glared at him. "Shut up or I'm going for the pots and pans."

He held up a self-protective hand before making a zipping motion over his lips.

Leaning over and brushing a quick kiss on his lips, she settled back against him, her arm around his waist, her head tucked against his shoulder. She fit perfectly against him and this little scene of domestic tranquility seemed somehow right, even though it was against everything he'd expected for himself in recent months.

As they watched the story unfold, he found himself getting immersed in it. Something about watching without the music made it more dramatic. It was easier to focus on the images, the way the actors emoted. The plot was easy to follow, and probably typical of the era. Handsome sheikh rescues beautiful blonde American woman from the dangers of the desert and whisks her off to his sensuous silk-swathed palace. Their people try to tear them apart, but in the end, true love triumphs over all.

Once the film ended, Candace murmured, "It's just like that line from *Sunset Boulevard*. They didn't need words, they had faces."

"I think you're right."

"Your great-granddad was a handsome dude."

"He was apparently quite the rogue."

"Like grandfather like grandson?"

He grunted and slipped his arm out from under her so he could go turn off the projector.

"Come on, Oliver, spill," she said, leaning over the arm of the couch to watch him. "Did you leave a trail of broken hearts throughout Hollywood when you moved up here?"

"Hardly." He swallowed visibly. "Just the one."

The teasing light faded from her eyes. "You mentioned that at the bar. She left you because of the scandal?"

"Yes. She bailed right around the time the newspapers started sucking my blood."

He flipped the projector off, not bothering to turn on the floor lamp in the corner. It was cozy in here, with enough illumination spilling in from the nearby kitchen to cast warm streaks of light on her beautiful face.

He hadn't necessarily intended to have this conversation, but figured it had probably been inevitable. So he admitted, "We worked together. When I started making waves in our little office pool, she swam for the shallow end and left me there, treading water."

Looking indignant on his behalf, she sat up and crossed her arms over her chest. "Bitch."

"Maybe. She was ambitious and didn't want to go down with a sinking ship."

"Then she obviously didn't care very much about you. She could have, at the very least, thrown you a life preserver."

Nobody had. None of his colleagues, anyway. Nobody he worked with had wanted to come anywhere near him once he'd made himself a marked man by going up against the powerful D.A. Yes, eventually the media, the public and the judicial system had started calling him a rare man with integrity. A hero. But behind closed doors, he had been vilified. He was finished in Orange County, and he knew it. Unless, as Candace had suggested, he kept on living simply and started taking some jobs on his own. He couldn't deny he'd been thinking about it since she'd suggested it. His experience as a prosecutor had made him view most defendants as guilty, but he knew in his soul that some were not. It was just a matter of finding them.

Candace rose to her feet, crossed to him and put her hand on his chest. "I'm sorry you had to go through that, Oliver. But can I also say I'm glad it brought you here? I honestly hate to think of what my life would be like right now if you hadn't been here waiting for me when I arrived."

He put his hands on her hips and drew her close, pressing a soft kiss on her mouth. She wrapped her arms around his neck and kissed him more deeply, parting her lips, sliding that delicious tongue out to play with his. God, how he loved kissing this woman. Loved the way she molded against his body, every curve of her fitting into some hollow in his.

After a long moment, she said, "Want to head over to your place?"

By unspoken agreement, they'd confined their lovemaking to the cottage, as if neither of them wanted to take advantage of Buddy by making love in his house. "Yeah."

"Give me a couple of minutes," she said with an impish smile. She walked toward the stairs. "I want to throw a few things in a bag."

He didn't think she meant luggage since his place was all of a hundred yards from here. He could only hope she meant she wanted to pack something sinfully sultry...or wickedly erotic.

"Am I going to like what you're packing?"

"You're going to love what I'm packing," she promised with a saucy wink. Then she turned and hurried up the stairs.

Figuring he'd have a few minutes, Oliver carefully took apart the old projector. He placed the components back in the case, and collapsed the screen. Buddy had kept the things in a small storage room adjoining the kitchen, so he carried them back there, carefully setting the antique equipment in a corner where it wouldn't be tripped on. Afterward, he cleaned up the food and their drinks and carried the leftovers to the kitchen, finding places for them in the cabinets.

The Dots he kept. He tucked the half-empty box into his pocket, envisioning a few places he'd like to put them... just so he could pull them back out with his teeth and his tongue.

Before the night was over, he might end up liking gummy candy after all.

With that thought in mind, he was smiling as he walked back toward the front of the house. Candace was standing at the bottom of the stairs, her back to him, looking up. She'd changed her clothes and had slipped into something a little more comfortable. Not a sexy nightie, unfortunately, just a loose-fitting pair of jeans and a sweatshirt. He couldn't stop a tiny stab of disappointment that she wasn't wearing leather and screw-me heels, but figured it was chilly out and she'd have more to strip off in front of him when they got to his bedroom.

"I can't wait to get these off you," he murmured, coming up behind her and sliding an arm around her waist.

She gasped, obviously startled. Oliver held her tighter, spreading his hand across her belly, pulling her hard against him so her curvy butt pressed against his rapidly hardening cock, and bent to nibble on her neck. "You make me crazy, Candace. All day long, I think about nothing but getting you naked and wet."

Rather than lifting her arm over her shoulder and encircling his neck, or tilting her head to give him more access, she cleared her throat and slowly turned around to face him. His hands dropped lower, cupping her backside, and he looked down at her.

Then he blinked, wondering what was wrong. Something was…off. She wore a look of amused speculation that he couldn't remember ever seeing before and her lips were curled up in a tiny, jaded smile that was half sneer. Candace's grin was usually far more sexy—or, occasionally, sweet. Never jaded. Not Candace.

Tilting his head in confusion, he stared at her, slowly drawing in a breath. Because the truth finally landed in his befuddled brain.

"Son of a bitch," he whispered. "You're not Candace."

10

WHEN SHE HEARD Oliver speak, Candace thought for a moment he'd called out to her from downstairs. She strode to the top of the staircase and glanced down, expecting to find him looking up at her.

Instead, she saw the man she was falling for, with his hands on her sister's ass.

"Whoa!" she called, charging down the stairs, taking them a couple at a time as she descended.

Oliver, his mouth agape, stared at her, then at Madison, then back at her. He dropped his hands and took a quick step back, almost tripping over his own feet.

"Twins? You're twins?"

Realizing what had happened—that her lover had mistaken her sister for her and obviously copped a feel—Candace felt her flash of jealousy disappear. She bit down on her lips to prevent a giggle, knowing Oliver was incredibly embarrassed.

Madison stuck her hand out, as if he hadn't just been gripping her butt, which had always been just a wee bit curvier than Candace's. "I'm Madison Reid. It's nice to meet you. You're Oliver, I presume?"

He didn't take her hand, continuing to stare back and

forth between them, as most people did when they first realized they were seeing double.

Finally shaking off her shocked amusement, Candace threw her arms around her twin's shoulders. "What are you doing here? I didn't expect you until at least tomorrow."

"I caught an earlier flight."

Madison squeezed her tight, and they held each other for a long minute. Neither seemed willing to let go first.

Ever since Candace had moved out to L.A. to try to break into movie costuming, missing Madison had been the hardest thing to deal with. Oh, of course she missed her parents and her friends, but she and her twin had a special bond. The only person who'd ever come close to coming between them was Tommy, and that was only until Madison had clued in to the fact that he was gay and wasn't someone they ever had to compete over.

Before the move, they hadn't ever been apart for longer than a few weeks, since they'd both gone to colleges in Central Florida and shared an apartment throughout. Mad had been Candace's best friend since the day they were born, and until this moment, when tears started pouring out of her eyes, she honestly hadn't realized how long they'd been apart. It had been months since she'd flown to New York to help Mad move into her new place after she'd landed her first big-city reporting job.

"I've missed you so much," her sister whispered.

"Right back at you."

She heard sniffling—not her own—and realized she wasn't the only one who'd turned on the waterworks. Finally, knowing Oliver had to be standing there, gaping, wondering when somebody was going to explain, she let Mad go and took a step back. They both wiped their eyes, probably looking like a pair of saps.

"Uh...does somebody want to tell me what's going on?" Oliver still looked a little stunned.

Candace walked over and took his arm. "Didn't I ever tell you that Madison and I are identical twins?"

"I think I would have remembered." He didn't sound happy. "How do you not mention something like that? And I can't believe Buddy didn't."

She shrugged, a little sheepish. "I guess it never occurred to him. When we were younger, we were both pretty adamant about not being thought of as just the Reid twins. We wanted to always be known as individuals."

"Right," Madison interjected. "Individuals who had each other's back no matter what, switched places all the time and sat in on each other's classes for the subjects one or the other of us didn't like. But everybody had to call us by our given names, not, 'the twins.'"

Candace exchanged a smile with her sister, both of them obviously remembering their stubborn insistence during childhood on being unique people, not part of a duo. Of course, they'd been inseparable anyway. Oh, how she'd missed her.

"I really wish I'd known," Oliver said. When he rubbed his hands over his eyes and shook his head, she realized he was more embarrassed than anything else. He confirmed it. "I was an ass. I'm sorry, Madison, I truly thought you were Candace."

Her sister, who prided herself on chewing men up and spitting them out, both romantically and in the cutthroat world of journalism in which she'd immersed herself, offered him a wide smile. "Are you kidding? I loved every second of it."

Wondering just how much she'd missed, Candace shot a pointed stare at her sister that silently said, *Back off. He's mine.*

Madison put her hands up, palms out in a conciliatory gesture, but ruined it when she wagged her eyebrows up and down. "Candace wasn't quite as descriptive about you as she might have been."

Wishing her twin hadn't mentioned the fact that she'd been talking about him, she changed the subject. "Come on in, sit down, relax. Do you want something—coffee? A glass of wine?"

"Is it from a fifty-thousand-dollar bottle?"

Candace grinned. She'd filled her sister in on the treasure in the basement. "Sorry, no. We figured we'd better leave everything else that's down there for the appraiser. I have horrible visions of accidentally misreading something and breaking open a bottle that would pay off the mortgage on this place."

"Ah well," Mad said, waving a hand. "I guess I'll make do with cheap swill for tonight."

"I'll see if I can find something up to your New York City tastes," she replied with a chuckle.

Mad followed them into the living room and plopped down on a recliner, flipping the handle to lift the footrest. She kicked off her comfortable shoes and flexed her feet, making herself at home.

Candace went to the bar, grabbed a bottle she'd picked up at a nearby store and popped it open. Oliver, meanwhile, sat on the couch, trying unsuccessfully to hide the fact that he was looking back and forth between them, trying to find differences that were hard even for family members to spot. Candace's second piercing in one ear, a freckle on her left hand, the tiny scar on Madison's chin, which she'd split open in nursery school—those, and their vastly different wardrobes, were all that really told them apart now that Mad had given up her redhead experiment and gone back to her natural color.

"You doing okay?" she asked Oliver after she'd given Madison her wine. She touched his shoulder lightly. "I'm really sorry I didn't say anything. I meant to."

"It's all right," he said. "As long as I'm not going to get charged with groping a stranger."

Her brow went up. "Groping?" She cast an arch look at her sister. "Just how long did you let him think you were me?"

Mad smiled sweetly. "Long enough to be impressed, little sister."

Little by virtue of being born twenty-seven minutes after her twin.

Candace sat down and dropped a possessive hand on Oliver's leg. He covered it with his own, squeezing her fingers, and she knew his embarrassment was fading.

As she sipped her wine, Madison asked a million questions, mostly about Buddy. She was just as fond of their grandfather as Candace and was looking forward to seeing him tomorrow. Deciding his heart probably wasn't up to any pranks right now, she agreed not to sneak into Candace's closet and try any identity swaps.

"So when is he going to be able to come home?"

"The day after tomorrow," Candace replied.

"I'm sure he's looking forward to it." Madison dropped her gaze, eyeing the ruby liquid in her glass. "Are you, uh, still planning on leaving as soon as he's released?"

Her stomach lurched. That had been the plan all along. Mad had promised to come visit her in L.A. once Grandpa was back on his feet, since she knew Candace had already been here for almost two weeks.

She had to do it, knowing real life was waiting for her. But oh, God, she did *not* want to go. She wasn't ready to end this wonderful interlude. The time she'd spent here, her days with her grandfather, as well as the long heated nights with her lover, had been the happiest she could remember for a very long time. She loved the climate, loved the country, loved being involved in the excitement of her grandfather's collection.

She loved Oliver.

That realization had been creeping up on her a little more every day, but she hadn't allowed herself to really believe it until now. While her first inclination was to continue to shove the very idea away, pretend it had never occurred to her, she knew she wasn't that good at denial.

Somewhere between her first night here, when she'd attacked him with a pot and fifteen minutes ago, when she'd seen him holding her sister, she had lost her heart to him. All her mixed-up feelings toward the man had cemented into pure and simple love.

"Yeah, Candace," Oliver asked, his tone serious and his stare intense. "Are you leaving?"

She swallowed, but since her mouth had gone so dry, it didn't help. "I, uh…I'm not sure yet."

He nodded slowly, then cast a glance between her and Madison. "Listen, it sounds like you two haven't seen each other for a while. I'll get out of here so you can catch up."

"You don't have to…" she protested.

"Don't go on my account!" added Madison.

He stood anyway. "Tomorrow's going to be a long day." He cast a glance toward Madison. "Candace and I were supposed to go to a winery owner's event down in the city tomorrow evening. Why don't you take my spot?"

That was the courteous offer to make and she wasn't surprised he'd extended it. But her heart twisted anyway. She'd been so looking forward to an evening out with him, being on his arm, dancing with him. Spending the night in an opulent hotel room where they didn't have to share a small, lumpy bed or sneak out of Buddy's house like she was a teenager getting it on with her high school football player boyfriend.

Especially if it was to be the last night they'd have together.

The last night ever.

Tears formed in her eyes again. She blinked them away, willing him not to notice.

"Not a chance!" Madison replied with a visible grimace. "I've been working fourteen-hour days lately. I'm so burned-out I think I'll do nothing but sleep and visit the old guy for at least a week."

"It really isn't..."

"Forget it," Mad said, cutting him off. "I'm not being nice—ask Candace. I don't do nice. I'm just being honest. I really don't want to go."

True. Mad didn't play nice for niceness's sake. She was blunt and honest. Still, seeing the twinkle in her sister's eye, and knowing Madison had to realize by the way she'd been talking about him that Candace was crazy about Oliver, she couldn't help thinking that this time, her sister's crusty heart was speaking for her.

"If you're sure," Oliver said. He turned to Candace. "So will you be ready to leave by three o'clock tomorrow?"

Spoken as if he didn't think he'd see her tonight. Ha. She had a key to his cottage and she wasn't afraid to use it. She'd proved that to him already.

But, figuring she'd surprise him later by showing up in his bed without a stitch, she merely smiled. "Of course."

Bidding Madison good-night, he left the house. They were silent for a few minutes, then without saying a word, her sister got up, went to the bar and poured two glasses of wine. She came back, handed one to Candace and sat beside her on the couch.

"You're in love with him."

Candace could only nod.

"I think he's in love with you, too." She chuckled. "He's definitely in lust. Whoa, girl, that man has some plans for you. He's totally delish, by the way."

"I know."

She didn't go on, feeling that deep well of sadness rise

up within her. Because yes, she suspected Oliver had developed feelings for her. But no, she was not going to have the happily ever after her twin seemed to be envisioning.

It was silly, really. Most women would be envious, thinking she'd be blissfully happy when her engagement to one of the most eligible bachelors alive was announced. In truth, her heart would be shattered, knowing she'd given up her only chance at happiness with the lawyer-turned-groundskeeper who had made her entire world come alive.

"So why are you miserable?" Mad asked, sensing her mood. Her mouth twisted into a frown. "Has he done something to hurt you? Jesus, he's not married is he!"

"No, of course not."

"Then what is it?"

She sighed deeply. "I can't keep him."

Her sister snorted. "Of course you can."

"I have to get back to my life in L.A."

"Bullshit. You can work from here."

"It's not the job," she admitted. "I've made a commitment and I can't back out on it."

Madison leaned forward, dropping her elbows onto her knees. "There's no commitment in the world that's more important than figuring out if this guy is the love of your life."

"Yes, there is." She sighed heavily, glad to be able to reveal her secret to someone. Madison would understand, of that she had no doubt. "I'm engaged."

Her sister spit out her mouthful of wine. It dribbled down her chin, landing on her sweatshirt. She grabbed Candace's left hand, noted the absence of a ring and gaped. "What the hell are you talking about?"

"It's true," she insisted. "I've made a promise. I'm going to marry Tommy."

THE NEXT AFTERNOON, Oliver walked up to the main house, knocking on the door for the first time in as long as he could remember so he didn't make any more identity mistakes. Candace answered right away, holding a small suitcase in her hand. She looked beautiful, as always, wearing slim-fitting tan slacks and a bright pink blouse, the color of cotton candy, cut low over those delicious curves. His mouth watered with the need to taste her, because oh, did she ever melt on his tongue.

Judging by the way her nipples pebbled beneath the fabric, she'd seen his expression and read his thoughts. Those dusky points were prominent against the material, and he wondered if she'd eschewed a bra. Candace was generously built, with breasts that invited lots of deep sucking, which he knew she loved. The thought that she was bare beneath her clothes would torment him throughout the whole drive into the city.

His pants tightened across his groin. He couldn't even look at her without wanting her. If they weren't on a timetable, he'd have her on the couch and be between her thighs, cock-deep in heaven, within ninety seconds.

She'd left his place maybe seven hours ago, after a long night filled with eroticism. But seeing her now, he wanted her all over again. He didn't think he could ever possibly get tired of making love to this woman. For all the years that he'd scoffed at friends who'd fallen victim to the love-and-marriage trap, he suddenly repented. Because the very idea that she might leave tomorrow, that this might all be over, had him ready to offer her just about anything if only she'd stay.

Hell, he'd even follow her. And considering his loathing of Southern California right now, that was probably the biggest sacrifice he could offer, the most sincere declaration he could make of his feelings for her.

Love. That's what he felt for her. He'd never experienced it before, with any woman, but Candace Reid had crept into his heart and planted a flag, claiming it as her own.

Unable to resist, he slid a hand into her thick, beautiful hair, and drew her close for a kiss. He didn't for a second worry that he was kissing the wrong woman. Now that he knew there were two of them, he allowed his senses and his instincts to tell him this was his lover. His woman. He'd never mistake anyone else for her again.

They kissed for a long, sultry moment, before finally drawing apart. Candace was pink-cheeked, her lips parted and her breaths shallow.

"Hello to you, too," she murmured.

"I've missed you."

She didn't demur or wave that off with an it-was-only-seven-hours comment. Instead, she simply nodded. "I know."

They stared at one another, exchanged a slow smile, then he reached for her bag. "Ready to go?" he asked, knowing he'd be hard and hungry for her the entire forty-minute drive to the hotel.

"Yes."

"Where's your sister?"

"She stayed with Grandpa. The two of them are old backgammon enemies. She brought his board and I doubt either of them will be willing to quit until they've played a half-dozen games."

He would definitely have bowed out if her sister had wanted to attend tonight's function, but Oliver couldn't deny he was glad Madison had declined his offer. No, he didn't give a damn about some fancy party, during which the big wineries would pat themselves on the back. But getting away with Candace for a night sounded like pure heaven.

They made the drive in her rental car. The old farm truck he used was not exactly formal ball material, and he couldn't imagine driving it up to the valet stand and handing over the keys. Since her car was a convertible, they put the top down for the drive. It was breezy, but there wasn't a cloud in the sky. A perfect day. She seemed to delight in it. Her long hair whipped behind her and she closed her eyes, obviously savoring the feel of the sun on her face.

Of course, when they hit the city, that changed. Downtown San Francisco was, even on a Saturday afternoon, a busy mass of humanity, and traffic was a bitch. They didn't arrive at the hotel until late afternoon and weren't ensconced in their room until after five.

She whistled as they entered and spied the plush room, the huge bed and the great view of the bay out the window. "Nice. You sure you can afford this, groundskeeper?"

"I've got a few dollars tucked away," he said, reaching for her and drawing her into his arms.

She twined hers around his neck. "Seriously. You didn't need to pay for all of this. I'll pitch in."

Laughing, he refused the offer. "Do you really think I'm working for your grandfather because I need the money? For that matter, do you really think I've ever actually cashed one of the checks he's given me?"

Her mouth fell open. "He's not paying you? Good grief, Oliver, you work like a maniac!"

"I don't think he's figured it out yet. I don't need the money, sweetheart. I needed the escape. Needed a place to stay, and hard work to do, so I could figure things out."

She stepped out of his arms, taking his hand and pulling him toward the bed. Unfortunately, rather than stripping naked and leaping onto him, she sat down, patting the space beside her for him to sit, as well.

Oh. Great. They were going to talk.

"And have you?" she asked. "Figured things out, I mean?"

"I'm getting there."

She lifted her hand and cupped his jaw. "Are you going to be all right, Oliver?"

He turned her palm toward his mouth and kissed it. "I am. I promise."

There was only one thing that could derail him from being all right, something over which he had no control. But he couldn't push her, couldn't force her. Hell, right now, he couldn't even bring himself to ask her, not if it meant spoiling the last full day they would have together. By this time tomorrow, her grandfather would be home and Candace would be packing to leave for Los Angeles.

Maybe he could convince her not to go. But maybe he couldn't. Which meant today might be all he had, all he would ever have of her, for the rest of his days.

"What do you…"

"Later," he insisted, pressing his mouth to hers for a deep, hungry kiss. She twined her hands in his hair. Oliver continued to kiss her, breathing her in, memorizing her scent and her taste and the way he felt at this moment. God, did he ever hope he wouldn't have to bank these memories for a long time, and that she wasn't really going to walk away from him tomorrow. Whatever this promise was that she'd made, surely she could get out of it. No way could she feel about him the way he suspected she did and not stay here and fight for a real relationship.

When the kiss ended, she persisted. "I want to know what you're thinking."

"Shh," he insisted, kissing his way to her wrist. He flicked his tongue out on the pulse point, then continued moving up her arm, pushing her sleeve as he went. "Enough talking."

"Mmm," she said as he abandoned her arm and moved to her neck, nuzzling the hollow. "You don't play fair."

"Lawyer."

"But…"

"No buts. We have to be at that ball in two hours, and I intend to spend the next one-hundred-and-five minutes giving you many, many orgasms. After that, you'll have exactly fifteen minutes to wipe my cum off your thighs and get into your dress."

"Oh, my God," she groaned, her voice thick with hunger.

Candace always got off on his more blunt expressions of need for her, growing even more inflamed when he whispered in her ear the kinds of words a polite man usually didn't say to a nice woman. She loved it, always growing wetter, wilder, when he talked about how much he loved eating her pussy and the fantasies he had about her gorgeous ass. They'd even gotten into a conversation about the most forbidden word in the female lexicon, and he knew she now looked at it in a whole new way, knowing if he ever used that word, it would be because he was out of his mind with need for her. What was once offensive had become incredibly erotic to her.

"Any more arguments?" he growled as he nipped her earlobe, dropping a hand to her thigh.

She gasped. "No arguments."

"Good. Now take off your clothes, Candace," he ordered as he nibbled her collarbone.

"Why don't you make me," she said, her tone sultry, provocative. She was daring him, egging him on, testing the boundaries.

He stared at her, narrowing his eyes, giving her a moment's warning. Then he reached for the front of her blouse, grabbed two handfuls and yanked.

Buttons flew. She gasped. Two gorgeous, perfect, pink-tipped breasts spilled out.

As he'd suspected, no bra.

All was right with the world.

"I'll buy you a new one," he said as he pushed her back onto the bed, bending for a taste of one succulent nipple.

"To hell with the blouse." She cooed as he sucked one

breast while tweaking and toying with the other. They were made for pleasure, big and sensitive, and as he played with them, he wondered if every other man in the world was as hopelessly addicted to sucking the breasts of the woman he loved.

Twining her hands in his hair, she rose toward his mouth, holding him where she wanted him, whimpering with pleasure as he suckled her. Her hips were rising in tiny thrusts, as if every pull of his mouth sent sparks of heat surging to her groin.

After he'd paid lavish attention to those beauties, he kissed his way down her belly to the seam of her pants. Unbuttoning them, he pulled them off her, taking her shoes and panties, too, until she was naked, spread out like a feast for the devouring.

He stood up beside the bed, slowly stripping off his shirt, his hands shaking with need. He never took his eyes off her. Candace lay there, writhing, stretching, running her hand over her own body, from her breasts down to that perfect little tuft of curls between her thighs.

"Touch yourself," he ordered her as he unfastened his pants.

She did, slipping a long, slender finger deeper into her crevice to stroke the tiny nub of flesh that perched at the top.

"Like this?"

"Oh, yeah. I definitely like that."

She laughed softly. "I do, too," she admitted, her voice filled with feminine power. She knew what she did to him, knew he went a little crazy every time they made love.

He shoved the rest of his clothes off, smiling with male satisfaction as she stared avidly at his erect cock. She licked her lips, whimpering, her body twisting even more restlessly as her need overtook her.

He didn't reach for her yet. Reaching for his cock, he

stroked it, knowing he could bring himself to climax by just standing here watching her.

But he wouldn't. Because that wouldn't even come close to the sensation of coming inside her body.

"How do you want me, Oliver? What's your fantasy?"

His mouth went dry as he pictured all the ways he'd had her, and the ways he hadn't. He could make love to her every day for a month and find something new to try, some new place on her lush body to explore with his hands and his mouth.

But one thing immediately came to mind.

"Turn over," he told her, his tone silky.

"With pleasure."

She smiled up at him, her eyes gleaming with anticipation, and did as he'd asked. Oliver groaned at the sight of those pale, round globes, his hands tingling with the need to squeeze and stroke them.

"Have I ever told you how much I love your ass?"

"I don't believe so."

"Ever since that morning when you walked up the stairs, shaking it at me, all I've been able to think about was getting you on your hands and knees and slamming into you from behind."

She didn't hesitate, rising onto her knees, her bottom perched up invitingly. When he caught sight of that glistening pink slit, he forgot everything else. Nothing mattered except the need to get inside her and pump wildly, to imprint himself on her, body and soul.

"Come and take me," she ordered. "Take me and come."

He knelt on the bed behind her, nestling his cock between her cheeks, sliding up and down to wet it with the cream seeping from her sex. She was whimpering, pushing against him, silently begging for more. Unable to resist a moment longer, he nudged her legs farther apart and moved his cock to her slick opening.

"Yes. Now, please!"

He didn't need any further urging. Giving in to her demands, and his own body's, he thrust into her. Sensation battered him, and he was left stunned at how good the angle felt, how much deeper he got, and how fucking erotic it was to look down and see his cock buried balls-deep in her body.

He grabbed her hips, pulling out, thrusting back. Candace met his strokes, groaning, begging, going mad.

It was wild. Hot. Incredibly pleasurable. When he bent over her to cover her back, and reached around so he could toy with her clit, she came with a loud cry.

He almost followed her, but something made him stop. Yeah, he loved this. Yes, he knew it would go down as one of his favorite things in the entire world.

But he wanted to see her face. Wanted to memorize how she looked when racked with pleasure and totally lost to everything but him.

So without saying anything, he pulled out of her, gently turned her over and settled back between her thighs. She reached for him, encircling his neck, smiling as she pulled him down for a long, slow kiss.

"Amazing," she whispered against his lips when the kiss ended.

"Yeah. We are."

She tightened her hold on him, wrapping her legs around his hips as he slid back into her. Their bodies melted together, each of them giving and taking by turns. He lost all sense of time and place, sure only of one thing.

He couldn't lose her. He'd do whatever it took to keep her in his life forever.

_11_

OLIVER HAD TAKEN pity on her and given her thirty minutes to get dressed rather than fifteen. Other than that, though, he kept his word, giving her more orgasms in an hour and a half than she'd thought humanly possible. As they rode the elevator down to the ballroom where this evening's event was being held, Candace had to shift back and forth on her feet, incredibly aware of how tender and well used she felt.

He apparently noticed. Stepping close, he slid an arm around her waist and ducked his head toward hers. "Are you okay?"

"Perfect," she whispered back, conscious of the other people on the elevator, another couple—middle-aged and well dressed—and a duo who looked like a mother and daughter. Neither of whom could take their eyes off Oliver, who did things to a tux that James Bond would envy.

Good heavens, the man was handsome. Not just hot and sexy, but so amazingly handsome he turned heads—male and female. Tonight she thought he could outshine Tommy, routinely called one of the top ten sexiest men in the world.

Tommy.

Hell.

She hadn't thought much about him today. Nor had she

answered when he'd tried calling a little while ago. She'd been busy, using all of her thirty minutes to clean up, fix her hair and makeup and get dressed. She would call him tomorrow, once she'd willed herself to pack up and head home. Tonight, she didn't want to think about anyone or anything but Oliver.

When they reached the ballroom, Oliver removed two tickets from his breast pocket and handed them to the person at the door. The minute they walked in, a congenial older gentleman with a barrel chest and very little hair walked over and greeted them. When he heard who she was, he enquired after her grandfather.

"I heard he was laid up—some kind of accident?"

"Yes, I'm afraid so. But he's recovering nicely. He's supposed to come home from the hospital tomorrow."

The man nodded absently, then moved on to what she suspected was his real topic of conversation. "Say, I've been hearing some stories. Something about a fabulous secret collection of antique vintages?"

The Northern California wine community was a small one. She was not at all surprised rumors were already being bandied around. Considering these growers and vintners were also wine drinkers, she would bet most of them would be attending the auction once it was set and advertised.

But not wanting to reveal too much, she merely shrugged and pasted on a vapid smile. "I don't know about that. Actually, I'm afraid I don't know anything about wine at all," she said, forcing a giggle. "Just that I like to drink it!"

"Oh, yes, of course." He patted her hand, condescension dripping from him, and wished her a nice evening.

As they walked away, she heard Oliver's deep chuckle. "Well played."

"Hey, no point in getting the vultures circling until Grandpa gets home and decides what he wants to do. If word spreads too much, we're going to have to start locking the door to the house."

"Buddy would never stand for that."

As they walked across the already-crowded room, Candace looked around, noting the decorations. Vines that looked quite real climbed and wove around some freestanding arbors, while beneath couples danced and chatted. The softly lit chandeliers cast a gentle glow over the well-dressed attendees, and laughter and wine were in abundance.

Oliver smiled pleasantly at several people who said hello. Although he wasn't technically one of them, he'd apparently met and impressed Buddy's colleagues and neighbors. In fact, one of them, a beautifully gowned, attractive woman in her fifties, approached them before they got halfway across the room.

She leaned in close to Oliver, not looking like the typical partygoer interested in exchanging gossip and feigning ennui. "You're Mr. McKean, aren't you?"

He nodded. "Yes. I'm sorry, have we met?"

"I'm Doris Gladstone." She stuck out her hand. "I work with Ben Harmon."

He dropped her hand. "Oh."

"Hear me out."

"I'd rather not."

This was getting more and more interesting. Oliver obviously knew who this Ben Harmon was, and didn't want to talk to his associate.

Candace stepped the tiniest bit closer, wishing the nearby string quartet would quiet down so she could eavesdrop more easily.

"Look, I know the whole story," the woman said. "Everybody knows. You might have made some enemies in the southern part of this state, but I promise you, everywhere else, people are well aware that you did the right thing and got royally screwed for it."

The truth dawned. Oliver hadn't said anything about his past following him up here. But it obviously had. Hearing the way the woman was speaking, it wasn't hard to gauge her respect for him, nor her interest in engaging him in shoptalk. Since Oliver almost never talked about his old life, she found herself intensely curious, wondering what he'd been like in that other world. Had he been as sexy, as thoughtful, as sweet? Had he exhibited flashes of that sardonic wit? Had he been a wildly erotic lover to lots of women?

She swallowed, not wanting to consider that. Knowing how fast-paced life in Los Angeles could be, and how shallow some of the wealthy set was, she had to wonder if he'd ever been the flavor of the week for some socialite who'd heard about the rising hotshot of the D.A.'s office.

"Ben is still dying for you to come in and talk to us. It's a small practice, with just the office in Napa, but we're both horribly overworked and we think you'd be a great fit."

Tension poured off him, and his hand tightened on Candace's waist. She imagined he didn't even realize it.

"I don't do that anymore."

"You don't prosecute," the older woman said. "But come on, you wouldn't have made it in the L.A. district attorney's office for four years, much less with a nearly perfect conviction record, if criminal law wasn't in your blood."

His jaw was growing stiffer, his hand tighter, and Candace feared this Doris Gladstone person was pushing too hard. She wanted Oliver to think about what the woman was saying, but, like most men, he wouldn't want to be forced into it.

She caught the other woman's eye and narrowed her eyes, warning her off with a small, negative shake of the head.

The attractive blonde got the message. Smiling brightly, she said, "Well, anyway, I won't bother you and your lovely friend. I just wanted to reiterate what Ben told you. We'd love to talk to you." Ignoring his silence, she reached into her purse and drew out a business card. She held it out and for a moment, Oliver just stared at it. When Candace nudged him, though, and he realized how rude he was being, he took it and dropped it into his side pocket.

"Guess I should get back to my husband. We have a small place. He produced a thousand bottles last year and now thinks he's ready to go up against Mondavi."

Smiling pleasantly, she walked away. A few other people stood nearby, all engaged in loud conversation, but Candace kept her voice down anyway.

"They want you to come work with them?"

"It's been mentioned."

"But you declined?"

"Her partner didn't offer me a job or anything. Just asked me to lunch one day and broached the subject."

"You're not even tempted?"

He swiped a hand through his thick, dark hair and shook his head. "I don't know, honestly. I just don't want to think about it tonight."

"Understood," she said, meaning it. The subject was closed for now, and she would respect his wishes by dropping it.

Smiling his thanks, he turned toward a corner. "How about a drink? Red, white or an appallingly sweet combination of the two?"

"Let's go with red, and see if anything measures up to that bottle we shared from Grandpa's cellar."

He twined his fingers with hers and squeezed, obviously appreciating that she'd let the subject change. Oliver had come up here to think about what he wanted to do with his life, including whether that life included a career in law.

For four months, he'd buried himself in hard work and had allowed himself to believe he had no supporters, nowhere else to turn. So seeing that wasn't true was probably good for him. An occasional nudge was probably in order. But any more than that was out of line. He would have to decide for himself what his future should be.

Whatever it is, it won't include you.

She had to forcibly control a wince of sadness that thought caused. She'd done a pretty good job of avoiding reality all day, well, for the past several days. But now that it was bearing down on her, each tick of the clock bringing her closer to the moment when she would have to say goodbye, the pain within her was sharpening.

Tomorrow is soon enough. You've got tonight. Make it a night worth remembering.

Forcing a smile to her lips, determined not to let him see her sadness and question it, she let him lead her to the nearest bar. There were several set up in the room, each offering glasses of the various vintages being feted tonight. They let themselves be drawn into a brief tasting, and Candace managed to hide another wince, this one caused by some pretty crappy wine. Fortunately, another bar had much better offerings, and she accepted a full pour.

Carrying their glasses, they worked their way around the room, meeting many people who knew her grandfather, or at least had heard of him. Almost all of them brought up the subject of the rare collection Buddy Frye had reportedly found, and she changed that subject every single time.

"Good grief, these people are like bloodhounds," she said after she and Oliver ducked another busybody, who'd actually followed them across the dance floor, weaving between swaying couples. They'd evaded him by slipping into a private corner beneath a cozy arbor, a tiny oasis in the crowded ballroom.

"Want to dance?" he whispered.

She didn't want to go back out into the crowd. But apparently that hadn't been his intention. Before she could assent, he slid an arm around her waist and caught her hand, drawing her close to his body. They began to sway to the music, moving in a small circle within the arbor, oblivious to the other people who wandered in and out.

She didn't know what she expected, but it wasn't that he could dance, or that she would be so swept away by the music that she almost forgot where they were. Though surrounded by hundreds, she felt like they were entirely alone, swaying to the soft strains coming from the talented musicians, and to the gentle gurgle of water from a nearby fountain. He bent his head close to hers, brushing his lips against her temple, breathing her in, holding her as if he would never let her go.

Oh, God, she wished he didn't have to.

The moment was so beautiful, and the thought so distressing, that she suddenly felt tears well in her eyes. "Will you excuse me?" she said, abruptly stepping out of his arms. "I need to visit the ladies' room."

He raised a curious brow, his expression skeptical, but she smiled broadly and spun around, hurrying away from him before he could offer to escort her. Smiling at a few people who offered friendly greetings, she didn't pause but moved through the ballroom as quickly as she could, practically bursting out of it into the hotel corridor. She sniffed a couple of times and wiped away her tears with the tips of her fingers, looking around frantically for the nearest facilities.

She'd just spied a restroom across the hall and a few doors up when she heard something that made her freeze in utter shock.

"There she is! My gorgeous bride-to-be. Hey, honey, are you surprised?"

The walls seemed to spin around her as she slowly

turned on her heel, knowing that voice, hearing the words, but not really able to process anything.

"Tommy?" she whispered, seeing her friend approaching from the main lobby.

He was here? Not just in San Francisco, but in this very hotel? More importantly—he was claiming her as his fiancée? Now, in public, when the man she loved was waiting for her in the next room?

Immobilized by shock, she watched him approach, seeing the familiar grin, the bright blond hair, the dazzling blue eyes glued to her face. As he drew closer, she noted a tiny frown appear between those eyes. Tommy always recognized her moods and realized she was not exactly overjoyed to see him.

Nor was she thrilled about who was following him.

A person holding a microphone. Another holding a very large camera.

No. Oh, please no.

But she knew it was true. He'd brought a camera crew here to "surprise" her. He'd gone public with their engagement.

"Didn't I tell you she was gorgeous?" Tommy said as he slipped his arms around her waist and lowered his mouth to hers for a friendly kiss. Thank God he didn't try to make it a passionate one or she might have instinctively shoved him away.

"What are you doing?" she whispered.

"Crisis mode, babe," he said under his breath. Then he raised his voice, wanting others to overhear. "I'm surprising you because I've missed you so damn much. I couldn't stay in L.A. one more day without you."

Her smile pasted on, she managed to bite out a few words in a low, angry voice. "I'm going to kill you."

His arm tightened around her waist as he leaned close, as if nuzzling her neck. "Hell's breaking loose, babe. When

I ran into these media types in the lobby—they're here covering this event, I guess—I figured the time was right to let the world know our happy news."

"I can't believe you didn't warn me."

"I've been trying to call you for hours!"

She couldn't argue that, realizing she'd turned her phone off, not wanting any interruptions to spoil their special night.

Glancing over his shoulder at their growing audience, Tommy went on, his voice a little louder, intentionally so. "You left town so quickly to come to your grandfather's hospital bed that I hadn't even had time to make our engagement official."

With that, he reached into his pocket and drew out a ring with the most enormous, gaudy, ostentatious diamond she had ever seen. On either side of it were rows of tiny rubies—her birthstone.

Tommy must have seen her grimace because he chuckled. "Figured we might as well go all out with it."

Her brain wasn't functioning, and she couldn't figure out what to say. Her hand lay limply in his as he lifted it and slid the ten-pound rock onto her ring finger.

"There, now you're fully dressed," he said, leaning down to rub noses with her.

She clenched her fists in his leather jacket—no black tie for the sexy movie star—and whispered, "Get me out of here. Now, Tommy, I mean it."

"Five minutes. Then we split."

But, she suddenly realized, she didn't even have five minutes. Because word of the superstar's arrival had apparently spread, and people were coming from all over the hotel to gawk at them. Sure, San Francisco had its share of celebrities, but Tommy was the "it" guy of Hollywood right now, having starred in two blockbusters in the past eighteen months. Directors courted him, women threw panties at him, men clapped him on the shoulder. Of course people would come and stare. Including a few from the ballroom.

Panic rose within her. She had to get out of here, had to escape and find a quiet place to sit down and figure out how to handle this nightmare. What on earth was she going to say to Oliver? Yes, of course he would someday find out she was marrying Tommy. But oh, God, she did not want it to be like this. Not tonight, on what had been, up until a few minutes ago, one of the most magical she had ever experienced.

Suddenly, she spied a face in the shifting crowd. Her worst fears were coming true. Her heart thudded in her chest and sweat broke out on her brow. This couldn't be happening!

But it was. As fans drew closer, asking Tommy for autographs, she saw Oliver's face in the crowd. He stood about twenty feet away, his attention glued on her, his face expressionless. How long he'd been standing there, she had no idea. Considering Tommy was hugging her to his side like she was his prized possession, she could only imagine what he was thinking.

The worst.

"No," she whispered.

Tommy, probably thinking she was nervous about the growing hysteria of his largely female fan riot, dropped a possessive arm over her shoulder and hugged her tightly against his side. "Hey, folks, don't freak out my fiancée, okay? I don't want to scare her off before I get her down the aisle."

The words caused a stir in the hallway, and every whispering person in the hallway gaped at her, most of the women eyeing her with jealousy, the men assessing her looks.

And then there was Oliver. She watched as shock

washed over him, his dark eyes widening, his mouth moving, though she couldn't hear a word he said. Of course, she really didn't need to. Because, as the truth of the situation hit him—at least, the truth as he saw it—he drew himself up stiffly and thrust out his jaw. His shoulders squared, his eyes cold, he nodded briefly in her direction. Then he turned and walked away, heading for the lobby and, she imagined, the exit.

"Tommy, let go," she insisted, knowing she had to go after Oliver and try to explain.

"It's okay, honey, we'll get up to our room soon," Tommy said, overplaying the part of horny lover. She would bet he'd rather be chatting up the superhot waiter who was hovering near the banquet room door.

Just as she was ready to pound on his chest and scream at him to let her go, she saw another familiar face. It was Madison. She stood in the lobby and was jumping up and down, waving her arms over her head, trying to be seen above the crowd.

Her sister. Her twin. That was just who she needed.

"I, uh, need to use the facilities," she said to Tommy, knowing her face was red with frustration and anger. Hopefully his adoring fans would think she was blushing over the behavior of her flirtatious fiancé, or at least because she'd had to make a public issue out of needing to use the damn john.

He finally let her go, but pressed a quick kiss on her lips before she could escape. "Hurry back sweet cheeks."

She growled at him, and for the first time since he'd arrived, he finally looked her fully in the face and realized she was absolutely furious. And positively devastated.

"Babe?"

"I'll deal with you later," she snapped, pushing her way through the throng, who continued to converge on Tommy, gushing over his films. Nobody paid her much attention, and she slipped away, hugging the wall, until she reached the lobby.

She didn't see Oliver anywhere. But she did see her twin's head as Madison ducked down another hallway. She followed her, rounding a corner as Mad disappeared into what turned out to be a ladies' room.

Hurrying in after her, she bumped into her sister, who'd been waiting anxiously by the door.

"Oh, God, Madison!"

"I know, I know," she said, grabbing Candace and hugging her.

"How? When…"

"I was at the center and went to the cafeteria to get Grandpa some ice cream. When I came back, he said Tommy had called, looking for you because you weren't answering your cell. He had just landed at the airport and wanted to know where you were."

Of course Grandpa would tell him. He'd known Tommy since they were kids and probably thought his surprise would be a wonderful one for Candace.

"As soon as he told me, I started trying to call you."

"I forgot to turn my phone back on," she admitted.

"Where's Oliver? Did he…"

"Yes. He saw. He turned around and left." She sniffed, trying to hold in a sob as she imagined how he was feeling. "He'll probably never speak to me again."

Madison stepped back, gripping Candace's shoulders, looking into her face, her expression serious. "Is that for the best, do you think? I mean, if you're going to really go through with it and marry Tommy, maybe you should just let him go."

"No!" The very idea was abhorrent. Yes, she'd intended to leave, to remind him of their agreement, fly back to Los Angeles and move on with her life. But at no time had she envisioned him being so publicly slapped in the face with the decisions she'd made before she'd ever met him.

He deserved an apology, and as much of an explanation as she could give him. He also deserved the right to tell her off, even if she had kept the truth from him out of loyalty to her oldest friend.

She understood now, though, that her loyalties were more torn than ever. She loved Oliver. If she were free, she would want to make a life with him. She wouldn't choose marriage to a movie star, with all the money, fame and glamour it included, over Oliver. Not a chance.

But Tommy? Her lifelong friend? The one to whom she'd given her word?

"Oh, God, Mad, what am I going to do?"

Her sister scrunched her brow, then nodded. "Take off your dress."

Her jaw unhinged. "What?"

"Come on, hurry up. Somebody might come in." She pushed Candace toward the stalls, shoving her inside one. "Get out of it. We'll switch clothes. I'll go back and play adoring fiancée while you get out of here and find Oliver."

"Are you serious?"

"Of course I'm serious. Hell, it'll be an adventure. I can't stand reporters—it'll be fun putting one over on them."

Candace simply stared.

"I know, I know," her sister said, waving an airy hand. "I'm a reporter. That doesn't mean I necessarily like myself. I think I chose the wrong field."

"Nice time to decide that, Ms. Columbia Master's Degree."

"You want me to change my mind?"

"Oh, hell, no!"

Thankful there was a way out of this, at least for right

now, she immediately leaped on her sister's offer. It wasn't, after all, the first time the two of them had traded places.

"Thank you so much," she said, yanking down her zipper and flinging the dress over the wall of the stall.

Madison, who'd shoved off her jeans and shirt, took the dress, doing a double take. "Whoa, Candy, that's some serious underwear you've got on there."

She looked down, seeing the incredibly sexy set of lingerie she'd bought especially to wear under tonight's dress. A red bra with cutouts over her nipples, and a skimpy thong. She'd envisioned Oliver being the only one seeing her in them for the few minutes it would take to rip them off. Right now, though, she was too anxious to be embarrassed.

"Where do you think he went?" Madison asked as she yanked the dress on over her head and struggled to smooth it over her slightly larger butt.

"The keys to the rental car are in my purse," she said, buttoning the jeans. "So he either got a cab or walked."

"Walked, I'll bet. Men like to go walk out their frustration over this kind of stuff. It seems like the guy thing to do."

She had no idea whether that was true or not, but was ready to take any help she could get. She'd try walking, and was very glad she had her sister's flat shoes in which to do it.

Yanking her hair into a ponytail and wetting a paper towel to wipe away some of the heavy makeup from her face, she shoved her purse toward Madison. "Lipstick. Eye shadow. Now."

Her sister went to work, applying cosmetics with a heavy hand, a look that was most unusual for her. Candace took the pins she'd pulled from her own hair and used them to twist her sister's into a quick updo, hoping nobody would notice it was a lot less intricate than Candace's had been.

When they were finished, they stood side by side and looked in the mirror. Madison looked so close to the way Candace had earlier tonight—she had no doubt most people would be fooled.

Her sister took her hand and squeezed.

"It'll be okay."

"How?" she whispered, not seeing a happy ending here. Maybe she could find Oliver. Maybe he'd stand still and listen to her enough so she could apologize. Maybe he'd even forgive her.

But that didn't change the fact that they couldn't be together.

_12_

As Oliver stalked out of the hotel, needing to get away and deal with the truth, he vacillated between anger and devastation. His emotions churned one way, then the next. One minute he wanted to punch something, the next, he was tempted to go back to the hotel, haul her into his arms and ask her why in hell she was marrying a pretty boy movie star who could never make her happy.

"Married," he muttered out loud, drawing a curious look from a passing couple, dressed for clubbing, who looked like every other couple he'd passed. Saturday night in San Fran was when all the hipsters came out, and he felt entirely out of place. Although, not as out of place as he would feel in Candace's world, now that she was engaged to one of the sexiest men alive.

Bastard.

When he'd first walked out of the ballroom to look for her, having grown concerned when she didn't come back right away, since she'd looked on the verge of tears when she left, he hadn't believed his eyes. Seeing Candace there, standing in the embrace of another man, he'd had a sudden certainty that he was seeing Madison. Not Candace. Not his Candace.

But the dress was the same. The hairstyle. The pale face, trembling lips, damp eyes.

It was her. He'd known that even before she'd met his stare and silently pleaded for understanding he wasn't sure he'd ever be able to offer.

The farther away from the hotel he walked, the more he tried to understand.

That she was really engaged seemed beyond doubt. She'd let that guy slide that big ugly ring on her hand. She hadn't laughed it off as a joke or shoved him away. In fact, the two of them looked pretty comfortable and cozy together, and he had to wonder how long they'd known each other.

Probably longer than the two weeks she'd been here. But damned if he'd let anyone tell him he didn't love her more than anyone else could. She'd become a part of him. He couldn't fall asleep if she wasn't in his arms, and was edgy every day until he heard her voice. She was the one he wanted to talk to about his plans for the future—maybe going back to work in a local law office, maybe getting married and having a family. Those things had seemed impossible—and he hadn't really wanted them—until she'd crept into his life and turned it completely upside down.

She's marrying someone else. She always planned to, and you know it. She warned you.

Yeah, she had. That first night when he'd made love to her, she'd laid down her conditions, stated her terms. He tried to remember exactly what she'd said, though his brain had been foggy with lust and he'd had a hard time thinking of anything except how much he wanted to be inside her.

She'd made a promise to someone, he remembered that much. A commitment. One that meant she and Oliver could have no more than one week, and would have to part ways, no questions asked, not seeing each other again.

He'd sort of believed she meant it. But a part of him really hadn't. And once they'd started sleeping together, once the physical connection had wrapped them up in such strong emotional bonds, he'd had an even harder time with the idea.

He should have pressed her when she'd offered to try to explain. Maybe then he wouldn't have been so blindsided when she turned out to have a fiancé.

She hadn't lied. She'd answered him truthfully when he'd laid out his three deal-breaking conditions. She'd wanted him, she was an adult and she wasn't married.

Just engaged to a freaking movie star.

"Oliver, please wait!"

He froze, spinning around and seeing a woman hurrying after him. His heart leaped as he thought for a moment it was Candace, that she'd walked away from the crazy promise she'd made to marry a man she didn't love, and had come after him. But he noted her clothes, and realized that was impossible.

"I'm not in the mood, Madison," he told her, striding away before she got to within ten feet.

"Oliver, wait, it's me."

He stopped again. This time, when he turned around, he studied her more closely, noting the full lips so recently well kissed, the faint circles under her eyes and streaks on her cheeks that said she'd been crying.

"Candace?"

She nodded and came closer, stopping about three feet away.

He clenched his hands by his sides, not reaching out for her, though he very much wanted to.

"Can we please talk?"

He looked around, seeing a few bars, but also a small coffee shop that was still open. He gestured toward it, and she nodded in agreement, walking with him across the street.

They didn't speak while they walked, and the tension built. Oliver wanted to ask her what had happened, what her coming after him meant and how the hell she'd gotten hooked up with Thomas Shane. But he didn't know where to start, and she didn't break the silence.

Not until they were sitting across from each other at a small booth, waiting for the waitress to return with their coffee did she attempt an explanation.

"I'm so sorry," she whispered.

"Excuse me?"

She was looking down at her own hands, which she kept twisting together on the table, and cleared her throat. "I'm so sorry you had to see that."

He was about launch into a barrage of questions when he realized what he was not seeing on that hand.

The ring. That big ugly ring.

His heart flipped in his chest. Had she ended it? Broken off with the golden boy?

"I didn't mean for that to happen. I had no idea Tommy was coming up here or I would never have put you in that position. Or myself, for that matter." She rolled her eyes, disgusted. "He's a publicity hound."

"How the hell could you even think about marrying someone like that?"

She opened her mouth to answer, but before she could, the waitress returned with two steaming cups of coffee. She chatted a little, offering them dessert, but they both declined, waiting for her to leave.

Once she had, they both sat silently for a minute, stirring their coffee, searching for words.

Eventually, Candace began to explain.

"I've known Tommy since I was a toddler. He and Mad have been my two best friends my entire life."

He blinked in surprise, but didn't interfere.

"Tommy and I had a lot in common. We were both artistic and emotional and very theatrical, while Mad was the calm, blunt one who evened us out and kept us steady. We made a good trio, spent our entire childhoods together. Every school year, every summer break, every birthday party, Tommy was with us."

He didn't doubt anything she said, having heard that the breakout star had come from Florida, just as Candace had. He had never really thought about the young lives of the rich and shameless, but it sounded like Shane's had been pretty normal.

"So what happened when you grew up?"

"I studied design in college, he went into theater. Madison decided to move to New York to go to grad school, so we thought we'd give our starry-eyed dreams a shot and moved to L.A."

"You lived together?"

She nodded.

He clenched his teeth so tightly his jaw flexed. He had to busy himself lifting his coffee cup to his mouth, sipping it though it remained very hot, just to avoid saying something he shouldn't. She'd said they hadn't been lovers, yet they'd lived together? Was it even possible for a woman as beautiful and sexy as Candace to live with a man and not tempt him into bed?

"It's not what you're thinking," she insisted. "We weren't lovers, Oliver. I never lied to you. Tommy and I have never had a physical relationship, and we never will. I think of him as a brother. Period."

A hint of relief washed through him. It didn't last long.

"Brothers and sisters don't usually exchange wedding vows," he objected, unable to keep his anger as tightly controlled as he'd like.

"There are other reasons to get married, aside from romantic passion."

"Not any better ones," he snapped.

She sagged back in her seat, sighing deeply. "I know."

"Then why?" A thought occurred to him. "Is it because he's rich and famous?"

"Yes, although not in the way you might imagine. I don't know if I can make you understand...."

"Try."

She nibbled her trembling bottom lip, casting her eyes away, still twisting those hands. Her anguish as she tried to figure out how to explain something he already found unfathomable made his chest tighten, and he nearly reached out and covered her hands with his, wanting to stop that desperate, heartbroken clenching.

He didn't. She might have taken the ring off, but she still hadn't said whether she'd broken this sham engagement.

"As you said, Tommy is a star. He's under a microscope, his every move dissected, every part of his life spied upon and discussed." She shook her head sadly. "He doesn't deserve it. He's a good guy, one of the best, and his world is coming apart because people can't mind their own damned business."

"If he's such a good guy, why did he put on that ridiculous performance back there? Why did he back you into a corner and talk you into marrying him when you're not in love with each other?"

"I was single. I hadn't been seeing anyone in a long time.... We're best friends. I never envisioned...never thought I would..."

"Fall for someone else?"

A stark nod.

It was the closest she'd come to admitting she had feelings for him. He waited for her to say more, but she didn't.

"This doesn't make any sense," he mumbled, still unable to follow everything. "Shane is the bachelor of the damn year—he could have any woman he wants. Why the hell does he have to have you?"

"He needs me. I...I understand him."

"What's that mean?"

She dropped her gaze, not meeting his eye.

Oliver continued to mull it over, until a thought began to form in his brain. It was small at first, a crazy possibility. But he focused on it, developed it. And while it shocked him, given the fact that he'd caught a couple of Thomas Shane's movies and seen him in person, he finally had to ask, "Is he gay?"

She bit her lip even harder, refusing to say a word.

Oh, Christ. Now everything made sense.

He leaned his head back against the booth, looking up at the ceiling, wondering how things had ever gotten this screwed up.

Her lifelong best friend had asked her to help him hide his sexuality from the press and the public who would rip him apart over it.

That's why she'd said yes. That's why she'd told Oliver they could have only one week and he could never try to contact her afterward. That's why she wouldn't explain what her secret commitment was all about.

She was displaying all the character traits he most admired in a person—the ones he'd seen so little of during his years as a prosecutor. Loyalty, compassion, integrity.

Yet, right now, with his heart pounding over the fact that he really might lose her to a guy who could never make her body sing—and didn't even want to—he wanted her to give up all those things. Break her promise, betray her friend, come away with him.

If she loves you, that's exactly what she should do.

Maybe. But the choice had to be hers. He couldn't ask

it of her, couldn't make things any more difficult than
they already were.

He only owed her one thing: honesty about his feelings.

"What are you thinking?" she whispered.

He wrapped his hands around his coffee cup, realizing they were shaking when a little of the lukewarm liquid sloshed out.

"Tell me. Please."

Unable to resist, knowing it might not matter, knowing it might even hurt her, he still went ahead and told her the only thing he could. The truth.

"I love you, Candace."

She sucked in an audible breath.

"I don't mean to hurt you, or make this any worse than it already is. But I love you." He reached for one of her hands, catching it in his and holding tight, knowing he would soon have to let it go for good.

"Oliver, I…"

"You don't have to say anything. I just thought you should know. Believe me, I want to fight for you, keep you, but I know I can't. You've got to do what your heart tells you is right, and I can't be the one who makes you betray a friend or go back on your word." One more tight squeeze, then he released her fingers. "So I have to let you go."

Tears were spilling from her eyes and running down her cheeks, and he wanted more than anything to take her in his arms and comfort her, kiss the tears away, assure her everything would be all right.

He didn't, though. Everything wouldn't be all right. He didn't know if things would ever be all right for either of them again.

Knowing he needed to go now before he changed his mind and kissed her until she admitted she could never really leave him, he slid out of the booth and stood.

"Goodbye, Candace," he said.

Stiffening his resolve, he headed for the door. But right before he exited, he heard her murmur his name.

"Oliver?"

He turned back and looked at her.

"I love you, too."

Their stares met and locked, a thousand more words hung in the silence, questions asked and answered, promises offered and lost. All the might-have-beens held in that one long, steady stare.

Until he looked away, opened the door and walked out into the night.

CANDACE SAT AT the table at the all-night café until her coffee was cold and her tears had dried. The kindly waitress had brought her some tissues, patted her on her shoulder and then left her alone. She spent the next hour sitting there, going over everything that had happened, marveling at how her life had changed so very much in just a few short weeks.

And wondering what she was going to do about it.

Finally, seeing it was almost midnight and knowing her sister would be worried, she pulled her phone out of her purse and texted Madison, telling her where she was.

Her sister wrote back immediately. On my way.

She hadn't asked her twin to come, but of course she'd known she would.

She just hadn't known she wouldn't be coming alone. When Madison walked into the café, with Tommy hot on her heels, Candace threw herself back in the booth and groaned. She just wasn't up for a dramatic scene.

"Oh, honey, are you okay?" Mad asked, sitting beside her and pulling her in for a hug.

"I don't know," she admitted.

"Jeez, Candy, why the hell didn't you tell me what was going on?" Tommy took the seat across from her, frowning. "You know I never would have showed up here to-night and made that scene if I'd had any idea you were with some dude."

"He's not some dude," she retorted.

"You really are in love with him," Tommy said, sounding stunned.

She couldn't speak; she could only nod.

"Madison said you were, but I didn't believe her."

"I can hardly believe it myself," she admitted. "But it's true. I'm crazy about him. He's brilliant and fun and wonderful." Sniffling, she added, "So wonderful that after he told me he loved me, he gave me up rather than ask me to break my promise to you!"

Tommy's mouth fell open. "Seriously?"

She nodded.

"Oh, Candace, he really is a keeper," her sister said, gently smoothing her hair back from her tear-streaked face.

"Yeah." A humorless laugh spilled from her mouth. "And I just threw him back."

"I'm so sorry," Tommy said.

She looked at him, her dear friend, seeing in that handsome face the funny little boy who'd liked to do puzzles with her for hours every day. She would do just about anything for him.

Anything but rip her heart out of her chest and let it be completely shredded.

She couldn't lose Oliver. She just couldn't.

It was on her lips, a plea for Tommy to understand and let her change her mind. She loved him…he was family, but if she didn't give her relationship with Oliver a chance, she knew she would regret it until the end of her days.

"Tommy, I…"

"Oh, hell, I'll do it," her sister said, cutting her off mid-sentence.

They both stared at Madison, who was rolling her eyes

and crossing her arms over her chest, which looked a bit more impressive than Candace's had in the glittery red dress.

"You'll do what?" Candace asked.

"I'll take your place with Tommy."

Her heart thumped. "What did you say?"

Tommy's eyes widened. "Huh?"

"I said I'll be this big jerk's fiancée. I'll move in with him and play the part to the hilt."

"You can't be serious," Candace said. "What about your job? Your new apartment?"

Her sister shrugged. "Actually, I've been shifting gears a little. I thought I'd try my hand at screen writing. What better place to be than at all the best parties with all the right people?"

Stunned, Candace tried to wrap her mind around the whole thing. "But who will believe it?"

Waving her left hand, still weighted down by that ring Tommy had slipped on Candace's hand earlier, Madison said, "He never did introduce me—or you—by name, right? Nobody will know any different. Heck, since I've known him just as long as you have, we could say we were childhood sweethearts or something." Then she stared at her potential bridegroom. "By the way, this is an engagement. Not a marriage. I'll wear your ring for a year and play adoring wife-to-be. That should take the heat off until you straighten your shit out."

Tommy's sparkling eyes said he was seriously considering the offer. Then he confirmed it, saying, "Two years."

She pursed her lips. Mad was nothing if not a negotiator.

"Eighteen months. We break up Christmas of next year."

He grinned. "The tabloids will love it. I'll be all heartbroken and tragic. The Academy will ask me to present."

"If they do, we're getting back together," Madison warned. "And you're so buying me a Vera Wang gown."

"Done!"

Tommy stuck his hand out toward Mad. She took it, they shook and sealed the deal.

Candace's thoughts were reeling. Had that really just happened? Had her sister truly just agreed to take her place in Tommy's life, leaving Candace free to pursue the man of her dreams? Had the offer really come in the nick of time, so she hadn't been forced to hurt Tommy by telling him she wanted out of the deal?

She looked at her sister. Mad looked back, a sweet, tender expression replacing her usual blunt, take-no-prisoners one.

"Thank you," she whispered as the truth of it finally sank in. More excited by the second, she threw her arms around her sister, then reached across the table and dragged Tommy into a group hug. "Thank you both!"

They squeezed for a moment, until Tommy said, "Okay, now get out of here and let me make googly eyes at my wife-to-be. I'll bet some paparazzi asshole followed us from the hotel and is taking pictures from across the street."

Madison concurred. Tossing her a set of keys, she said, "My rental car's at the curb. Mr. Hollywood will get me back to the hotel safely." She reached up and touched Candace's cheek. "Go claim your man."

That was the best suggestion Candace had heard all night. And she immediately stood up and strode out of the restaurant, determined to do just that.

She didn't waste time going back to the hotel, knowing Oliver wouldn't have gone there. She would bet money he had called a cab and paid a fortune for it to take him back to Sonoma. That's where she headed, hoping her instincts were right.

During the entire forty-minute drive, she clutched the steering wheel, tense and anxious, trying to find the words to make things right, wondering how he would react when he saw her. She had so much she wanted to tell him, so many things to explain, secrets to share, wishes and dreams to whisper. She just hoped he didn't slam the door in her face when she showed up at his cottage.

Arriving at the estate, which was dark and silent, she drove up the long, windy driveway, glad Madison's rental car was a hybrid with a very quiet engine. She didn't want to give Oliver too much warning so that he could put his defenses too firmly in place.

She parked in front of the house, slipped from the car and hurried to the cottage. Reaching for the knob, she thought twice, knowing if this was the beginning of the rest of their lives, she needed to start on the right foot.

She knocked.

This wouldn't be about coercion, letting herself in, seducing him—although she hoped she'd get that chance later. She wanted him to let her in, to give her a chance.

Just one chance to win him.

A light flipped on and she released the breath she'd been holding. She'd guessed correctly.

The door slowly opened, and he saw her there. His eyes widened a tiny bit, but his mouth remained set in a firm line. No smile tugged at it, no welcoming glimmer of happiness. He merely waited. Watching, assessing. But she'd bet the wheels were churning away in his mind as he tried to figure out what she was doing at his door.

"May I come in?"

Stepping out of the way, he gestured for her to enter, still not speaking.

"I thought I'd find you here."

He finally spoke. "Why did you come?"

"To claim you."

That surprised a flinch out of him. "Huh?"

Though she desperately wanted to slide her arms around

his neck and pull him down for a warm kiss that would do a better job of explaining why she was here, she knew she had to give him the gift he'd given her earlier—utter and complete honesty.

"I love you, Oliver."

He nodded slowly. "You said that earlier."

"Yes. But I didn't say that I want to be with you, for as long as you'll have me. I want to stay here and build a life with you. To help you figure out what you want to do with your life."

He looked stunned.

"Maybe you'll want to go back into law, or maybe you won't. Maybe you'll want to stay here and help Grandpa turn this into a premiere winery. You can grow grapes, I can draw costumes and we'll drink wine and live."

He stepped closer, not reaching for her, but looking more hopeful by the second. "What about your engagement?"

"It's over."

His relief was visible. Because she'd known he hadn't wanted her doing anything purely for his sake, she explained the whole story, telling him about her sister's plans to stay in L.A., which, frankly, made her very happy on many levels.

"But you didn't ask her to?"

"No, I swear. I was just about to tell Tommy we needed to find another solution because I couldn't give you up. But before I said anything, Madison jumped in and offered to be the phony fiancée for a while."

She wasn't entirely sure Madison had been serious about the screenplay-writing thing. It was possible, though. Her sister had recently hinted that she wasn't happy with her job, despite how hard she'd worked toward a career in journalism. Mad had always loved to write, and had thought hard-hitting news articles would be her forte. She'd also been great at creative writing, so perhaps this idea of hers hadn't been just a throwaway offer meant to make Candace not feel so guilty. Maybe she really wanted this shot at a new career. Candace certainly hoped so anyway.

"So she's not giving up her dreams so you can have yours?"

"No, I really don't think she was."

They fell silent, staring at one another. She saw him processing everything, that keen mind evaluating all that had happened…what she'd said, what she'd done, what it meant.

"I love you," she repeated, holding nothing back, her voice thick with emotion.

He took a step closer. Then another, until he stood a foot away, close enough for her to feel the warmth of his body. Far enough away for her to miss it.

"Say something," she said.

His perfect mouth widened little by little, until that sexy grin appeared, stopping her heart and chasing away all her misgivings.

"Something."

Laughter spilled from her mouth. "Jerk."

He didn't torment her anymore, didn't hesitate. He reached for her, wrapping his arms around her and drawing her hard against his body. His mouth covered hers, lips parting, in a kiss that seemed like a very long time coming, though they'd only been apart for a few hours. With that kiss, she told him again and again how she felt, and knew he was saying the same thing.

Eventually, he picked her up in his arms and carried her to the steps. Carrying her up them, he began to whisper the sweetest things—promises, dreams, hopes for the future.

All she'd ever hoped for. All she'd ever wanted.

"I love you, Candace. I want you with me always. I want to go to bed with you every night and wake up with you every morning. And I promise I'll do everything I can to make you happy."

This time the wetness in her eyes was brought on by pure joy. She knew he meant what he said, knew she could trust him with everything—her heart, her body, her life.

He was her present and her future.

Her everything.

And she was his.

The Hollywood Insider: She's Landed The Big ...

We ___ it's official. Superman! Thomas Shane had an-
noun___ his engagement to his club hostess girlfriend,
a pri___te, reclusive journalist from New Jersey who
has r___ntly moved with him into ___ oceanfront
home. A certain Ms. Reed is sporting an enormous
ring th___ ___ennifer Aniston would covet, and has
quickly settled into life on the West Coast.

The happy couple has been seen romancing all
over town, with cozy dinner dates in exclusive restaurants, and late nights dancing at all the hot spots.
Sources say these two put off some major heat—
theirs is obviously a real love match.

Shane's future wife is also rumored to be writing a screenplay adaptation of a recent blockbuster,
with an eye toward her future husband landing the
leading role. Sounds like the birth of another Hollywood supercouple!

Don't you just love happily-ever-afters?

* * * * *

NO STRINGS...
JANELLE DENISON

Janelle Denison is a *USA TODAY* bestselling author of over fifty sensual contemporary romance novels who has written for Mills & Boon® Blaze®, Kensington Brava, Berkley and St Martin's Press. She is a two-time recipient of the National Reader's Choice award and has also been nominated for the prestigious RITA® Award. Originally a California native, she now calls Oregon home. She resides in the Portland area with her husband and daughters and can't imagine a more beautiful place to live. When not writing, she can be found exploring the great Northwest, from the gorgeous beaches to the amazing waterfalls and lush mountains. To learn more about Janelle and her upcoming releases, you can visit her at www.janelledenison.com, friend her on Facebook at www.facebook.com/janelledenisonfanpage or chat with her at her blog at www.plotmonkeys.com.

To Don
Thank you for the best twenty-six years of my life!

1

"Don't look now, but Aiden just walked in." That statement was followed up with a long, lingering sigh of adoration.

Waiting in line to order her morning coffee, Chloe Reiss smiled at her coworker Holly, who was standing in front of her, facing the line of people behind them. Her friend had a dreamy, wistful look on her face, one that was common among most of the women who set eyes on Aiden Landry, and especially for the ones who worked with him at Perry & Associates. The man was gorgeous, sexy and charming—a lethal combination any female with a healthy libido was quick to appreciate.

Including Chloe. Because she'd never be able to touch *that,* looking was all she had the luxury of doing. She and Aiden worked for the same ad agency and had been required to sign a strict "no dating co-workers" agreement as part of their employment as advertising executives. She understood the need for such a rule, especially in a career where creativity, drive and focus was key. Dating was a huge distraction, and more times than not, it ended in a messy breakup that made working together difficult and awkward, if not impossible.

But Chloe had to admit that the firm's policy was both a blessing and a curse. A blessing, because it kept her from doing something incredibly foolish— like giving in to the heated attraction between her and Aiden and doing all kinds of wicked things with him. A curse, because it kept her from experiencing what she was certain would be the most phenomenal sex she'd ever had. As it was, a little harmless flirtation would be all that they'd ever indulge in, but there were definitely times she wished she could straddle the line between business and pleasure with Aiden.

She and Holly took a step forward in the line, and Chloe casually glanced over her shoulder. Piercing blue eyes met hers, as if Aiden had been waiting for her to turn around. The slow, purely male smile easing up the corner of his mouth gave her a jolt of instantaneous awareness, stronger than any shot of caffeine ever could. In return, she waggled her fingers at him in a playful morning greeting before returning her attention to Holly.

"Coffee is on me this morning," Chloe said as they stepped up to the barista. The day was off to a fine start.

Holly asked for a Chai tea, and Chloe ordered a skinny vanilla latte for herself and a cappuccino with one packet of sugar for Aiden. Two years of them working together as account executives for Perry & Associates had given her some insight into the man's vices. She knew how he liked his morning java, and because coworkers often met up after hours at the Executive Bar located on the ground floor of the high rise where they worked, she also knew his alcoholic beverage of choice was Glenlivit Scotch neat.

After paying for the drinks, she and Holly picked up their orders at the other end of the counter.

"Thanks for the tea," Holly said, and shifted anxiously on her feet. "I hate to bolt on you, but I have a marketing report that's due on Leland's desk first thing this morning. You know he'll start bellowing if it's not in his chubby little hands at eight o'clock sharp."

Chloe grinned at Holly's apt description of her marketing supervisor. "Go ahead. I'll talk to you later."

Holly took off for the bank of elevators located in the lobby outside of the coffee shop, and Chloe headed toward Aiden, two cups of brew in her hands. Still waiting in line, he watched her approach, a dark, curious brow raised as she neared. The man was model gorgeous, with chiseled features and a sensual mouth. His pitch-black hair, cut into a neat, short style, combined with those devastatingly sapphire blue eyes, was one helluva potent combination that never failed to make her a little breathless when all that hotness was directed at her—as it was right now.

In Chloe's estimation, Aiden was total male perfection, and then some. Tall, lean and built like a
Greek God, he wore the expensive cut of his tailored
suit with flawless ease and effortless sophistication.
The times he took off his jacket, usually by the end
of the workday, was always an added visual treat for
Chloe, because those crisp white dress shirts he fa-
vored showcased his broad shoulders and hinted at
the athletically honed body beneath. And when he
rolled up the sleeves and exposed those strong forearms...well, she wasn't a girl prone to swooning, but
there was just something incredibly arousing about
a man with arms and hands that spoke of inherent
power and strength that did it for her in a major way.

And Aiden Landry had a pair of big, strong hands,
and nice long, capable fingers. The kind she imagined could give a woman all kinds of erotic pleasure.
Unfortunately, she'd never find out for real. Instead,
she'd just have to be satisfied with the fantasies she
spun in her head.

Reaching Aiden, she handed him the tall paper
cup of espresso and cream, topped with a generous
dollop of foam. "I've got you covered this morning.
Cappuccino with one packet of sugar."

"Thanks." He smiled his gratitude as he stepped
out of the coffee line and fell into step beside Chloe
as they headed for the building's elevators. "Looks
like I owe you one."

She cast him a sidelong glance filled with teasing
intent. "You know I like to keep it that way."

Amusement glimmered in his eyes. "What? Me, owing you?"

She took a drink of her latte and nodded. "You never know when an outstanding favor might come in handy."

He chuckled, the deep, smooth sound stroking across her senses like an intimate caress. "Yeah, you like having me indebted to you, don't you?"

"Oh, absolutely," she agreed, enjoying their flirtatious banter. It gave her an extra pep in her step, and released all kinds of feel-good endorphins inside her. "You know what they say. Keep your friends close, and your work rival even closer."

The corner of his mouth quirked with a playful grin. "Are you saying you like having me on a short leash?"

"The shorter, the better." They were joking, of course, as they'd done for the past two years. But oh, the images that flooded her mind, of him wearing nothing but a leather studded collar and her tugging on a chrome chain leash like he was her personal plaything, willing to obey her every command, was a heady fantasy, indeed.

They arrived at the elevators, and since it was close to eight o'clock in the morning, there was a mad rush for those who had a time clock to punch. The Boston high rise, located in the financial district, boasted forty-two floors and was comprised of a few hundred companies and firms, which made for a congested elevator ride in the morning and at quitting time. Since she and Aiden weren't in any big hurry, they sipped their coffees and gradually shuffled their way forward.

"Are you ready for your presentation for Organic Kitty this morning?" he asked, referring to the pitches she'd been working on for the past month.

She always had a little flutter of nerves the morning of any client meeting, and this one was no exception, especially since she was going it solo, which was happening more and more lately as she built her own client base. She felt confident about her overall campaign and was certain she'd meet, or exceed, all of the client's expectations.

"I was up until two this morning putting the final touches on the proposal, and I'm pretty damn happy about it," she told him.

"You know I'll be at the meeting." He sipped his cappuccino, his eyes crinkling slightly at the corners as he grinned mischievously. "For moral support, of course."

"Of course," she replied drolly, and rolled her eyes, not buying his "moral support" statement for a minute. And he knew it, too.

Perry & Associates had a lax policy about allowing other employees to sit in on presentations, as a learning experience and to keep abreast of what the agency was doing, so long as there were no disruptions. But for someone as experienced as Aiden, his strategy was more about keeping himself informed on what the competition was doing. Chloe was just as guilty of doing it to his presentations, too.

But while there had been some incidences of back-stabbing with other employees, she and Aiden had never stooped to that level. Over the years, they'd developed a mutual respect for one another and their work, probably because they'd started out on the same marketing team that had required them to work together on various projects. They'd learned early on to trust one another with their ideas and campaigns, but now, with each of them building their own client base, there was a level of competition between them that kept them both striving to one up the other.

And ultimately, they both had their eye on the next rung in the corporate ad agency ladder. Word had gotten out that Perry was looking to promote someone within the firm to a senior executive position within the next few months, and that person would be given their own team to manage. It was a huge coup, and one that Chloe had every intention of achieving. She'd worked extremely hard establishing herself as a qualified leader within the firm, and she'd like to think she deserved the promotion.

But first things first. She and Aiden were both being considered individually to lead a huge upcoming campaign for the St. Raphael Resort, an exclusive matchmaking retreat that catered to singles looking to find love—a multi-million dollar campaign that came with a generous, five-figure bonus and would elevate their standing within the firm, as well as in the advertising industry. If Chloe nailed today's presentation for Organic Kitty, she was fairly optimistic that she'd be assigned the St. Raphael Resort account. From there, it was a logical leap to the senior executive position.

She smiled to herself as they waited for the next available elevator, enjoying those visions of grandeur dancing in her head. As much as she liked Aiden, as a person and a coworker, her own competitive streak drove her to succeed—on her own, and without relying on anyone else to get her there.

With the morning crowd finally thinned out, the next elevator enabled them to step on board without feeling crushed. She and Aiden ended up in the back. Standing so close to him, she could feel the heat of his body. And God, he always smelled so damned delicious, like sandalwood and fresh, clean citrus. Whatever his cologne, it was like breathing in a tempting aphrodisiac that never failed to arouse her womanly senses.

After stopping on various floors to let other people out, they finally arrived at the thirty-second floor, which opened directly into the reception area of Perry & Associates.

"Break a leg today, Chloe," Aiden said, winking at her.

She laughed at his choice of words. "Don't you wish."

They parted ways, and as soon as Aiden was out of

sight, her thoughts returned to the Organic Kitty presentation and how she intended to win over the client.

Aiden sat at the back of the conference room, along with a few other colleagues, silently watching as Chloe worked her magic in wooing the higher-ups at Organic Kitty with her stellar campaign. She'd focused on giving the company a much needed boost to their consumer visibility through new branding and a catchy slogan. Her voice was strong and engaging as she spoke, and her PowerPoint slides showcased a multitude of innovative advertising ideas, clever marketing and social media strategies focused toward elevating the Kitty brand, as well as attracting new buyers.

The clients were riveted by her persuasive and appealing presentation. Aiden was riveted by the woman herself. As always, she was confident, commanding and in control, traits he found sexy as hell. Today she was wearing a conservative, but feminine skirted suit in navy blue, a professional choice for her meeting with clients. The cream silk blouse layered beneath the tailored jacket hinted at a softer, more sensual side, as did the peek of lace from the camisole she wore.

His gaze traveled down the length of her body, to the fitted skirt that hugged the curve of her hips and rounded bottom and ended just below the knee. From there, she had a fantastic pair of long, slender legs that most of the men in the firm took the time to notice as she walked by, probably because of the four inch heels she always opted to wear—the kind that made guys think of sex and sin, and doing both with her while she kept them on.

Yeah, he was definitely guilty of utilizing that fantasy a time or two, and now was *not* the time or place to let his thoughts wander in that direction. Shifting subtly in his seat, he glanced back up at her pretty face. Her rich, dark brown hair was pulled back into a sleek, sophisticated ponytail, and her bright hazel eyes were more green than brown at the moment. Her enthusiastic expression matched the same infectious energy infusing her voice and body language, adding a nice little punch to her very compelling sales pitch. It was clear to anyone who watched Chloe that she was incredibly passionate about her work, as well as the advertising campaign she'd created for Organic Kitty.

While Aiden was highly attracted to Chloe on several different levels, her utter focus, control and drive when it came to advancing in the corporate world reminded him of his ex-wife and how her ambition had eventually destroyed their marriage, and his trust. Paige had refused to allow anything to get in the way of her success as a defense attorney, not even an unplanned pregnancy that she'd made clear she never wanted. A pregnancy she'd terminated without any discussion or input from him.

The end result of what she'd done in order to pursue her professional goals still cut Aiden deeper than a knife and had shattered his illusions of love and commitment, and the sanctuary of marriage. After their bitter divorce three years ago, he'd vowed that he'd never get seriously involved with another career-minded woman again. No, the next time he put a ring on someone's finger, he'd be damned sure she was on the same page as him when it came to the importance of family.

Career-wise, Aiden recognized that Chloe and Paige had a lot in common. But while his wife had been cold and calculating, Chloe was the complete opposite. Chloe was undoubtedly driven to succeed, but having worked with her for the past two years, he also knew she was warm, genuine and friendly. Most important, she respected her colleagues and had a great reputation in the industry—two exceptional qualities that were hard to find in such a cutthroat business.

But damned if he wasn't overwhelmingly attracted to her, despite the many reasons why he shouldn't want her. He'd be a liar if he said all that confidence and sass of hers didn't do it for him in a major way. Sexually, he liked a woman a little on the aggressive side, a woman who knew what she liked and wasn't afraid to challenge him in the bedroom. Judging by their seductive flirtations and Chloe's determined attitude when it came to getting what she wanted, Aiden highly suspected she was *exactly* that kind of woman.

Not that he'd ever have the pleasure of discovering for himself what kind of lover she was. Resisting Chloe and the tempting awareness between them was paramount, not only because of the no dating policy the company enforced, but because Aiden was fairly certain she was seeing someone—some guy he'd seen her with a few times down at the Executive Bar after work. Besides, even if she wasn't dating someone else, Aiden wasn't about to risk a career opportunity that was so close to being within his grasp by having an office affair that ended up damaging his future plans to start up his own ad agency.

Right now, his sole focus was on acquiring the multi-million dollar St. Raphael Resort account, because the substantial bonus that was being dangled as an incentive was exactly what he needed to fund his new venture. It was between himself and Chloe as to who would be assigned to St. Raphael, and considering the exceptional job she was doing on the Organic Kitty campaign today, there was no doubt in Aiden's mind that the competition for the resort account was going to be fierce. Making the choice between him and his office rival for the job was going to be very difficult indeed.

Chloe wrapped up her PowerPoint spiel, and it was evident that the client loved her ideas and was eager to implement them. Perry, the owner and CEO of the firm, had been present during the sales pitch, and he appeared equally pleased with her campaign. Right on the spot, Organic Kitty agreed to sign on with Perry & Associates, and Chloe's surprise and delight made Aiden smile. He knew how amazing it felt to close a deal. The adrenaline rush of victory and the high of success was *almost* as good as sex.

With the presentation over, he stood up to leave the conference room, and on his way out he gently grabbed Chloe's arm to get her attention for a moment. She glanced up at him, her hazel eyes bright with exhilaration, and her face flushed with the sheer joy of success. Her pink, glossy lips were curved into a delightful smile, and damn if he didn't want to kiss that luscious mouth and discover if she tasted as good as he imagined she would.

He cleared his throat and released his hold on her arm. "Nice job, Reiss," he told her, meaning it. "I don't even like cats and you made me want to buy their product."

She laughed at his attempt at humor. "Then I've done my job."

"Very well, it seems." He briefly looked over at the happy client who was busy shaking Perry's hand while gushing about the campaign, then back at Chloe. "Congratulations on the new account."

Her gaze warmed with appreciation. "Thanks, Aiden."

That was another thing he liked about Chloe. Despite her creative talent and advertising savvy, she displayed absolutely no conceit or arrogance over her newest triumph, as many of their coworkers did. She didn't feel the need to flaunt or brag about her acquisitions, and to Aiden, that spoke to her confidence and determination when it came to pleasing her client.

Her success today was a nice feather in her cap and put her another notch closer to a promotion and taking on bigger accounts, but Aiden wasn't too worried. There was no denying that Chloe was good at her job, but he'd like to think that he was better. The proof would come as soon as he was awarded the St. Rafael account.

"How about I buy you a drink later, after work, to celebrate?" he offered.

She nodded, and smiled. "Yeah, I'd like that."

Knowing she and Perry had contract details to go over with the client, Aiden left the conference room and went to his office to return some phone calls and to work on a few accounts that needed his attention. He skipped going out for lunch, and instead bought a roast beef sandwich from the lunch cart to eat while he answered emails and edited copy for a client's upcoming media blitz.

At three-fifteen in the afternoon, the phone on his desk buzzed and Perry's personal secretary, Lena, spoke through the intercom. "Aiden, Mr. Perry would like to see you in his office regarding the St. Raphael account, please."

A jolt of excitement surged through Aiden. *This was it,* he thought, tamping down the crazy urge to execute an elated fist pump in the air. Despite Chloe's fantastic campaign today, Perry was going to entrust *him* with one of the firm's biggest clients—and as soon as he blew away St. Raphael with a kick-ass campaign, that five-figure bonus would be all his. *Yes!*

"I'll be right there, Lena," he said, his voice much calmer than he felt inside.

After disconnecting the call, he stood and put his suit jacket back on to look as professional as possible, straightened his tie and started toward Perry's suite of executive offices. On the way, he caught sight of Chloe across the way, heading in the same direction. Her smile faded, as did his, as they both came to a stop at the double glass doors that led to Perry's domain.

"Wait a second," he said, unable to stop the unease settling in his stomach like lead. "Where are *you* going?"

"To see Perry." She looked equally wary, as if seeing him there had taken her by surprise, as well. "And you?"

"The same." *Shit.* This situation didn't bode well. Not at all. "Did he want to talk to you about the St. Raphael account, too?"

A slight frown creased her brow. "Yes."

Aiden had no idea what was up, because they were each qualified and experienced enough to handle the account on their own. Chloe was coming off the high of her Organic Kitty presentation earlier today, which was no doubt fresh in Perry's mind and could possibly give her an added edge. But honestly, there was no telling what the CEO had planned, or why he'd summoned them both. Unless he intended to give one of them the account, and let the other one down easy, all in one fell swoop.

It wouldn't be the first time something like that had happened in his career—and he hated that he was in that position now.

He exhaled a deep breath, refusing to let Chloe see him sweat because he hadn't lost the account yet—and wouldn't let it slip through his fingers if he had his way. Pushing open the glass door, he gave her an easygoing smile and waved a hand inside the executive offices. "After you."

2

CHLOE SAT DOWN in one of the plush seats in front of Richard Perry's large glass-topped desk, and Aiden settled into the chair next to hers, while their boss regarded them both with an unreadable expression.

A nearly tangible tension vibrated in the air between her and Aiden. There was so much at stake, for the both of them, and she reminded herself that confidence, sprinkled with a large dose of fortitude, was the key to getting what she wanted. That way of thinking had served her well for most of her adult life, and certainly during her career as an advertising executive.

If she didn't count her horrible lapse in judgment with her ex-fiancé, Neil, four years ago that had nearly cost her everything, personally and professionally, and made her realize that she wasn't so different from her mother after all. That despite the goals she'd set for herself and her vow to never let a man control her life and decisions, she'd failed miserably. Her screwed-up relationship with Neil made it abundantly clear that her judgment when it came to men sucked.

But *unlike* her mother, she refused to make the same mistake twice. Dropping her guard and allowing herself to get involved with a man on an emotional level was no longer an option for her. Now she put all her time and energy into her career, which fulfilled her in all the ways that mattered—except one. But for those times when she had a sexual itch to scratch, well, that's where friends with benefits came in handy. It was an arrangement that worked well for all involved, but mostly, for her. No mess, no fuss, and nothing to interfere with her main pursuit of climbing the corporate ladder straight to the top.

And right now, there was only one thing standing in the way of her stepping up another rung and getting the St. Raphael account—Aiden Landry, the man who'd also been called to Perry's office. But she'd just proven her worth to Perry that morning, and hopefully her ability to completely overhaul a company's advertising and marketing plan was still fresh in his mind and would provide her an advantage over Aiden.

That was her hope, anyways, but she had to admit it was a bit unsettling to be sitting right next to her biggest competition in the firm, a guy who wanted this account just as badly as she did. Only one of them would get the job, and a quick glance at Aiden told her that he had that confident look about him, too—backed by an impressive amount of determination.

Refusing to be the least bit intimidated, she gathered her composure, crossed her legs, clasped her hands in her lap and waited for their boss, a distinguished-looking man in his early sixties, to address them.

"I'm sure you're wondering why you're both here," Richard Perry said a moment later as he glanced from Aiden, to her, direct and businesslike. "And I'm not going to drag this out any longer than necessary. Bottom line, the partners and I couldn't decide which one of you deserved the St. Raphael account more. You're both incredibly innovative and have outstanding success rates with your current accounts. Since there is so much riding on this campaign, in this instance we've decided that two creative minds will give the firm a better advantage, than one."

Chloe was so taken aback by Richard's announcement that she didn't know what to say. All the hopes she'd harbored in regards to her career and a big promotion dwindled in that moment.

Aiden didn't seem thrilled about the new arrangement, either, not when they'd been expecting a solo mission. "So, we'll be working *together* on the St. Raphael account?" he asked, a cautious note to his voice.

"No, you'll be working separately, in *lead* positions," Richard clarified as he reclined in his leather chair, looking completely at ease even though he'd just delivered a one-two punch to her and Aiden. "You'll each be assigned your own marketing team to help you with your campaign, and you'll each give the client a full presentation, along with a complete advertising and promotional package geared toward developing the resort's matchmaking brand. They're open to restructuring their activities at the resort to make the social interaction between couples more appealing, and they'd like to see ways to increase their profit margin, while still giving their targeted consumer a great overall experience."

Oh, wow. The project was huge and complex, and clearly Perry wanted to see which one of them could better deal with the stress and mental challenge of such an enormous task—the same kind of pressures that would face a senior executive. Chloe was more than capable of handling the assignment, and although the man sitting next to her was equally qualified, she wasn't going to let that fact mess with her head.

Richard steepled his fingers in front of him, and continued, "I think it will be interesting to have two separate campaigns for this particular client, one from a female perspective, and one from a male perspective. But you both also need to be aware that there is another ad agency that will be vying for the resort's account, which makes it all the more important that the two of you come up with some kind of unique marketing twist to your presentations to edge out the rival company. Two separate campaigns from each of you gives our firm twice the advantage, however, only one of you will be awarded the account, based on which, if any, campaign the client chooses."

So, in essence, she and Aiden were being dealt a double whammy. Not only were they in competition with each other, they also had the added competition of another agency soliciting the account, as well.

Curious to know what Aiden thought of this new twist, Chloe cast him a quick, sidelong glance. The man was good at hiding his emotions. His poker face gave her no indication of how he was feeling about the two of them being directly pitted against one another, and she supposed he was smart not to give her any kind of advantage, just as she had no intention of letting her own frustration show.

"In order to create the best presentation and campaign possible, you've both been invited to St. Raphael to experience the resort's amenities and atmosphere for yourselves," Richard said as he reached for a butterscotch drop in the crystal bowl on his desk—his favorite type of hard candy he usually grazed on in the afternoon as a sweet treat. He unwrapped the confection and slipped it into his mouth, sucking on the candy for a few seconds before speaking again.

"Fully immersing yourself in the experience will give you a better idea of what works, what doesn't and what the resort needs to change or elevate in terms of quality, service and overall customer satisfaction."

Aiden rubbed a hand along his tense jaw. "So, you want us to go through the matchmaking process along with everyone else registered at the resort?" he asked their boss.

"Just go through the motions, Landry," Perry said with a casual wave of his hand. "You're not there to find the love of your life, but you can't create an effective campaign without knowing what you're up against. In this case, there are millions of dollars on the line. The other firm's executives will be there, as well, so I trust that you both can handle the situation and what you're required to do?"

Perry's request was more of a subtle challenge than a question, and Chloe wasn't about to voice her own aversion to mingling with other desperate singles and risk being replaced by another hungry ad executive who'd kill to have the opportunity she was being given. This wouldn't be the first time she'd stepped into the dirty trenches to get the job done, and if she had to endure organized activities, fend off unwanted advances and make small talk with men who'd been deemed compatible for her, well, then, she was willing to suffer for her career.

"Absolutely, Mr. Perry," she said in a tone as unwavering as her commitment to the firm, and the campaign.

Aiden's reply was just as resolute. "Yes, sir."

"Good." Richard gave a curt nod, pleased to have them both on board. "You'll be leaving a week from Monday, so make sure you have all your other accounts covered before you go. Good luck to both of you."

With that, Perry let them go, and she and Aiden walked in silence back toward the outer offices. As soon as they stepped through the double glass doors, Chloe came to a stop and so did Aiden, both of them still processing everything that had just happened back in Richard's office.

Aiden gave his head a hard shake. "I didn't see *that* coming," he muttered.

"Me, either," she agreed. She'd anticipated that one of them would have been celebrating right now, preferably her. Instead, there was another firm involved and she and Aiden were now adversaries of sorts, each one of them motivated to do whatever might be necessary to create the winning campaign and outshine the other, while spending a week together at a matchmaking resort.

While they'd always had a great working relationship, they'd never been set against one another, and she hated to think that their drive and ambition to secure this client, and the generous bonus, might ruin their friendly rapport.

She glanced up at Aiden, meeting his vivid gaze, momentarily struck by how mesmerizing those blue orbs could be. "Promise me something?" she blurted out, before she could think better of what she was about to ask. Or why it was so important to her. It just *was*.

"Sure," he said, taking her request very seriously.

Exhaling a deep breath, she put her concerns out in the open before she changed her mind. "Promise me when everything is said and done, if one of us ultimately gets the St. Raphael account, it won't change our working relationship. Or our friendship," she added, because she definitely considered him that, too.

He tipped his head, a reassuring smile on his lips. "You should know by now that I don't operate that way, or hold professional grudges."

She knew that to be true, but his words relieved her, anyway. "I don't, either," she said, and allowed a sassy grin to surface, as well as her competitive nature. "But I hate to see a grown man cry, and I'm sure you'll be reduced to tears when I'm awarded the campaign."

Aiden chuckled, clearly amused with her prediction. "Chloe, Chloe, Chloe," he chided in a deep voice as smooth as aged whiskey, and just as intoxicating. "Just for the record, I have absolutely *no* intention of losing, to the other firm, or to you."

Now this, a direct challenge, she could handle. "We could spend the rest of the night arguing over that, but let's make this short and simple. May the best woman win." She extended her hand toward him.

His much larger hand engulfed hers in a sensual warmth that traveled all the way up her arm, and he leaned in close, his eyes dancing with his own brand of wit and daring. "With the emphasis on *man,* though I'm sure it'll be a fight to the finish."

She withdrew her hand from his, doing her best to ignore the heat and awareness his touch had so effortlessly aroused in her. "Oh, yeah, you can count on that."

Game on.

"SO, WHAT BRINGS YOU to my neck of the woods?" Sam Landry, Aiden's younger brother by two years, eyed him curiously across the scarred wooden table where they were seated at McGann's Pub in downtown Boston. "Don't you usually spend your Friday evenings at that fancy Executive Bar where you work, schmoozing with colleagues?"

Aiden grinned at Sam's exaggerated description as he lifted his cold bottle of Guinness to his lips for a drink, enjoying the taste of the dark, rich stout. His brother, a P.I., never missed an opportunity to rib Aiden about his white-collar profession, especially since it was such a departure from the proud family tradition.

Their grandfather had been a decorated cop for the Boston Police Department, then their father, Jack, followed by Sam—until his brother had been shot on the job and the injury had forced him to reevaluate his career and future. Even though Sam no longer worked for BPD, he was still entrenched in the business as a private investigator who often used his past connections with the force to help him in the current cases he worked on.

Everyone had assumed that Aiden would carry the same torch for justice and head off to the police academy once he graduated college. Instead, he'd shocked everyone when he made the decision to major in advertising and marketing over criminal justice his junior year. The big difference between him and Sam was that Aiden loved the creative aspect of his career, while his brother preferred the constant movement of chasing bad guys and the unexpected twists that came with detective work.

While Aiden's parents had always been supportive about his choice of job and his accomplishments, he knew he'd initially disappointed his father by venturing outside the realm of law enforcement. And being the so-called black sheep who'd strayed from family expectations, it made him an easy target for his brother's good-natured needling, which he'd grown used to.

Aiden set his bottle of beer back on the table and shot Sam a halfhearted look of irritation. "Do you always have to give me shit because I sometimes prefer a good beer over aged Scotch and want to visit with you?"

"Yeah, I do, because it doesn't happen often," his brother answered, his gaze flickering with amusement. "I gotta get my licks in where I can."

Aiden just shook his head, because despite their differences in personality and profession, and his brother's penchant for busting his chops, he and Sam had always been close. Aiden, being the firstborn, was far more serious than his carefree, easygoing sibling, but there was no denying that beyond the bond of being brothers, they were also best friends. And now, with their parents retired and living in Florida, he appreciated his relationship with Sam even more.

The truth was, after today's shake-up at the office, Aiden just wanted to relax and unwind, without the added pressure of smiling and laughing with colleagues when he wasn't in the mood. He'd even promised Chloe a drink to celebrate her new account with Organic Kitty, but he'd have to make it up to her another time. She was another distraction he didn't want to deal with tonight, not when he was still trying to process the fact that they'd gone from being coworkers to rivals vying for the same account.

"Whatever is bugging you, get it off your chest already," Sam said, pulling him out of his thoughts. "That brooding look is going to scare off the women. Oh, wait, your uptight business suit already did that." He smirked.

Aiden laughed, giving his brother the reaction he'd been angling for. True, he stood out in a place where the dress code was jeans and T-shirt casual, which was all Sam ever wore. "Then it's a good thing I'm not here to pick up women."

"Yeah, well, you're cramping my style," Sam grumbled, and gazed longingly at two pretty females sitting a few tables away who were giving Sam an equally interested look. Leaning forward in his seat, Aiden braced his arms on the table, figuring it might help to talk to Sam about what had happened today at the office, as he'd suggested. "Actually, I have some news I need to get off my chest. Do you remember me telling you about the big account I was hoping to get?"

Sam thought for a moment, then asked, "The one for that singles, matchmaking resort?"

Aiden nodded. "Yeah, that's the one."

"Are we here to celebrate?" Sam asked hopefully, already tipping his beer for a premature toast.

"No, not yet." Aiden released a heavy sigh. "I found out today that not only is another ad firm vying for the job, but Perry decided to assign Chloe and I to the account. Not to work together, but to come up with separate campaigns for the resort. He wants a male and female perspective. Whoever's campaign the client chooses will be awarded the account."

Sam's eyes widened in surprise. "So you have to compete directly *against* Chloe for the account?"

"Yep." His troubled tone echoed the way he felt about the entire situation.

Over the past two years of working at Perry & Associates, Aiden had spoken about Chloe numerous times to Sam, saying how much he respected her as a colleague. His brother had also met and talked to—or rather *flirted* with—Chloe the one and only time Sam had stopped by the Executive Bar to have a drink with Aiden, so Sam was familiar enough with their working relationship to know just how bothered Aiden was that the two of them were now adversaries. However, Aiden had promised Chloe that he wouldn't let this campaign ruin their friendship, and he was determined to make sure he held true to their pact.

"I'm sorry, bro." Sam gave a sympathetic shake of his head. "That plain sucks."

"Tell me about it." Aiden finished off his beer, and if he didn't have to get in a car and drive, he would have ordered a double scotch. He certainly needed one.

They sat in silence for a few minutes, the Friday night crowd in McGann's growing louder as the bar filled up with patrons. Women walked by in skimpy outfits, giving both him and his brother a lingering glance that made it clear they were more than interested in a good time, but Aiden wasn't. When he glanced across the table at Sam, there was no mistaking the sly grin on his lips and the mischievous look in his eyes.

Aiden narrowed his gaze, wondering what his brother found so amusing. "What?"

"You're not going to let a *girl* win, are you?" Sam asked, an all too familiar taunting note to his voice. It was the same one he'd used to goad Aiden into doing things he shouldn't, all throughout their childhood.

"Hell, no." Aiden considered himself a gentleman, but this was a competition between two coworkers, and all bets were off. Girl or no, his kick-ass campaign was going to earn him the St. Raphael account.

"Good." Despite Sam's succinct tone, his lips were still twitching with mirth. "I don't want you to go all soft because your competition is smoking hot and lust is clouding your feeble brain."

Aiden blinked in shock at his brother. "Excuse me?" What the hell did Sam know about his attraction to Chloe?

"Oh, come on, Aiden," Sam said with a laugh as he tipped his chair back on its hind legs. "I'm not deaf, dumb or blind. I only saw the two of you together once, at that highbrow bar of yours, and the chemistry between the two of you was pretty damn obvious."

Aiden shrugged off his brother's claim. "It's just a friendly flirtation."

Sam lifted a dubious brow. "Except for the way you stared at her ass when she walked away from our table. I can guarantee that the thoughts in your head involving that sweet backside of hers were indecent and downright kinky."

He shrugged and didn't even try to deny the truth. "She's got a great ass. So sue me for appreciating all its finer qualities."

A wide grin curved Sam's mouth. "Good to know your libido isn't dead. I was starting to worry."

"My sex drive is fine, thank you very much." But Aiden had to admit he hadn't seen much action lately, by his own choice. His main focus was his job, and ultimately grabbing the brass ring of opening his own ad agency in the near future. And in order to achieve that goal, he had to win the account.

"So how long are you going to resist the attraction between you and Chloe?" Sam asked, as persistent and pushy as ever. "I got the impression if you made a move, she could be easily persuaded."

For Sam, being with a woman was that simple. Not so much for Aiden. "We're both professionals, working for the same ad agency, and we're not going to risk our careers for sex."

Sam rolled his eyes dramatically. "Jesus, Aiden, who says you have to risk anything? It's just feel-good *sex,* not a lifetime commitment. Besides, the risk of getting caught could give the affair an added element of excitement."

That's exactly how *Sam* operated...getting laid was all about having a good time without any strings attached. It hadn't always been that way, and while Aiden understood his brother's perspective on sex and women and keeping his emotions out of the equation, Aiden's views were much different, despite his ex-wife's betrayal. He'd never been the love 'em and leave 'em type, and that hadn't changed after his divorce. If anything, he'd become more discriminating when it came to women and relationships. And yeah, sex, too.

"Don't you ever want something more than just a string of one-night stands?" Aiden asked his brother.

Sam gaped at him, as if he'd spoken blasphemy.

"You're kidding me, right? We both thought we had something *more,* and look how well that turned out for us."

Not well at all. "Okay, point taken," Aiden said. Being burned by a woman had left Sam jaded and uneasy about trusting again. But even though Aiden's marriage had been less than ideal, he liked to believe that there was a woman out there for him. But he knew that Chloe wasn't that woman. She was too career-oriented to be anything more than a passing affair. And even *that* wasn't an option for him.

"Hey, Sam," a soft feminine voice called out, pulling Aiden out of his thoughts.

One of the women that had been sitting a few tables away now stood in front of them, gazing down at Sam with a sultry smile on her lips while her fingers lightly touched his shoulder. She was young and pretty, and wore a tight-fitting dress that accentuated all her best assets. She had Sam's full attention.

"Denise and I were wondering if you and your friend wanted to join us?" She bit her lip seductively as she glanced briefly at Aiden, then back at Sam again. "We can pull up an extra chair or two, if you'd like."

"I'd love to, Carol," Sam looked at Aiden, his raised brow silently asking if he was going to accompany them.

This was Sam's scene, not Aiden's. He shook his head and tried to appear regretful. "Thanks for the invite, but I need to get going."

"Okay," Carol said, not at all disappointed, since clearly it was Sam she wanted. "We'll save a seat for you, Sam." She sashayed back to her table, a deliberate sway to her hips—all for Sam's benefit, which he openly enjoyed.

Aiden chuckled and stood up, along with his brother. "Looks like someone's getting lucky tonight."

"Jealous?" Sam grinned.

Pulling out his wallet, Aiden tossed enough cash on the table to cover their drinks and leave a decent tip. "Not at all," he said, meaning it. "By the way, just so you know, I'll be leaving next Monday for the Bahamas, where the St. Raphael resort is located."

"Is Chloe going, too?"

"Yes, we're both going." He tucked his wallet back into his pocket, and knowing exactly what his brother was thinking, Aiden attempted to cut him off at the pass. "It's a *business* trip, Sam."

"Which also presents the perfect opportunity for the two of you to take advantage of your attraction, in a place where no one would ever be the wiser." Sam waggled his brows suggestively.

"Not gonna happen."

Sam released an exasperated sigh. "You know what your problem is? You're way too uptight. And you've been that way since your divorce."

"I'm not uptight. I'm careful and discreet."

"Like I said. You're *uptight*." Sam slapped him on the back in brotherly camaraderie. "Loosen up and live a little, bro. You might be surprised how much fun you can have when you're not being so damned serious."

With that bit of advice, his brother walked away, leaving Aiden to ponder the wisdom of Sam's comments. Or the lack thereof.

3

THE FOLLOWING MONDAY at seven in the morning, Chloe was seated next to Aiden on a plane heading to Nassau in the Bahamas. From there, they'd take a small puddle jumper to the island of St. Raphael where the private, secluded resort was located. They were scheduled to arrive at the hotel by early afternoon. Once the jet leveled out, the pilot announced that it was now okay to move about the cabin and turn on approved electronic devices, and promised that the refreshment cart would be making its way down the aisle shortly.

Chloe frequently took business trips for work and was used to sitting by the window in the cramped quarters of coach, usually next to a stranger who kept to themselves for the duration of the flight. But the moment Aiden plopped his big body into the chair beside hers and their knees and elbows bumped as they buckled their lap belts, she knew their intimate seating arrangements would wreak havoc with every one of her five senses for the next few hours.

So far, her prediction proved to be true. Sitting next to the window, her body was hyper aware of his broad shoulder brushing against her arm and the way his leg occasionally grazed her thigh when he shifted in his seat to find a comfortable position that would accommodate his long legs. At least he'd settled down for takeoff, and as she cast a sidelong glance at him, she found herself envious of his ability to completely relax when the surface of her skin buzzed with sensual awareness.

His head was resting against the back of his seat, and though his eyes were closed, she wasn't sure if he was sleeping or not. But even like this, he was hotter than any man had a right to be with his early morning tousled hair, the sweep of his ridiculously long, dark lashes against his cheeks, and those full lips that were made to give a woman all kinds of forbidden pleasures. Even his casual attire made him look sexy and confidently male.

She'd never seen him in anything but a business suit, and she had to admit that he looked damn fine in a dark blue short-sleeved knit shirt that complimented his toned physique, and a pair of well-worn jeans that lovingly clung to his muscular thighs and other interesting body parts that piqued her interest. And why did he always have to smell so damned good? His expensive cologne was subtle, but the warm, sandalwood scent, mixed with his own male pheromones, never failed to tap into her desires and make her ache deep inside.

At the office, she was constantly near Aiden, but with work as her top priority she was able to keep her attraction to him in check. Or walk away when that heady pull between them became too overwhelming. But right here, right now, there was no putting distance between herself and Aiden, so she was just going to have to suck it up and deal.

Lord, it was going to be a long flight.

Desperately needing some kind of distraction, she reached down and pulled a folder from the computer bag she'd stowed beneath the chair in front of her. Releasing the fold-down tray, she set the file on top and immersed herself in work. Specifically, the research she'd already compiled on the St. Raphael resort and its current branding, mission statement and operating procedures.

Unlike a singles resort, where the main draw was drinking and partying in a girls/guys gone wild style, and hooking up with the opposite sex was a free-for-all, St. Raphael offered a unique and modern-day spin to matching compatible couples while offering fun, interactive activities in a romantic atmosphere. While the concept didn't interest Chloe on a personal level, from an advertising angle it was an executive's dream. There were so many interesting aspects to build a campaign on, like developing a catchy slogan to pull in consumers, beautiful pictures to capture their imagination, and the lure of finding love and a happily ever after.

She and Aiden had already filled out the required questionnaire that the resort used to match up couples, and the two of them were scheduled to attend events and various activities to mix and mingle and "make a connection." It was the only way for them to evaluate the process in order to present the client with a cohesive advertising campaign for the resort. Perry had even hired a local professional photographer to be on hand to capture any shots she or Aiden needed to elevate their presentation.

There was no way Chloe could forget that this was a business trip with a huge incentive on the line. But she also knew in order to really absorb everything the resort had to offer, she had to open herself up to the fun, seductive aspect of the island retreat so she could better translate the experience into her campaign.

And that included relaxing around Aiden, too. They weren't at the office, and there was absolutely no harm in a little flirtation between them, which they already indulged in, anyway. And if her seductive teasing threw him off his game a bit, well, it would be his own fault for letting their attraction get the best of him.

"We're not even at the resort yet, and you're already working?"

The low, chiding voice came from Aiden, who was no longer dozing. She glanced at him, meeting his dark, velvet blue gaze, still heavy-lidded from his brief nap. "I started a portfolio for notes and ideas for my campaign as soon as Perry announced we'd each be doing a presentation. Do you know what the name St. Raphael stands for?" she asked, testing his knowledge of the resort.

A slow, lazy smile curved those sinful lips of his. "St. Raphael is the patron saint of love and lovers, which is very appropriate for a matchmaking resort."

The husky way he said the word *lovers* sent a warm shiver through her. Yeah, flirting with him was very natural and easy and always reciprocated with genuine interest. "I'm impressed. You've obviously done your homework, too." She would have been more shocked if he hadn't.

"I always do," he murmured. "Speaking of homework, how crazy was that matchmaking questionnaire we had to fill out?" he asked with an incredulous shake of his head.

The required survey had been a long, tedious process that had covered every end of the spectrum of a person's life, from personality, career aspirations, religion, finances, pet peeves, family values and even sexual compatibility. That last part had been her favorite section of the test. As she'd answered each question, her mind had strayed to Aiden, wondering if his responses had matched hers. Was he more gentle and romantic in the bedroom, or did he prefer the aggression of unleashed passion? Was he open to role-playing and fulfilling fantasies if his partner was willing? And how important was foreplay to him?

Oh, yeah, she'd definitely had fun with those questions. The other more personal ones, not so much, but she'd been honest with her replies in order to see how the whole matchmaking process worked.

"The quiz was pretty intensive," she agreed, and since he was in a chatty mood she slipped her work folder back into her computer case. "I felt like I was back in college taking a final exam. Except the subject was my life. I know the questionnaire is necessary, but it all seems so...desperate and forced."

He absently rubbed his palms along his jean-clad thighs, considering her reply for a moment. "How so?"

Since he looked genuinely curious to hear her opinion, she gave it to him. "I'm not a big fan of professional matchmaking," she said honestly. "I'd rather let nature take it's course instead of my interest in someone being dictated by the answers on a quiz." After how badly her last relationship ended, for her, basic chemistry was the way to go, without any messy emotions to lead her astray. And it gave *her* more control over how long an affair lasted.

"Which also has its pros and cons," he refuted smoothly, not the least bit bothered by the rattle of the plane as it hit an air pocket. "The problem with letting the relationship develop naturally and being lured in by the initial physical attraction is that you only see what's on the surface and you don't really know the person beyond the basic likes and dislikes."

She tipped her head to the side, always enjoying a good debate with Aiden, knowing that the deeper they got into this conversation, the more her point would be revealed. When he believed strongly in something, his fierce passion, drive and intelligence was always a delightful sight to behold. "And you think a matchmaking quiz would change that?"

"I think the test might reveal some potential problems between couples that might not be there in the beginning, but could cause issues and conflict once the initial glow wears off. Or even after marriage."

Something in his gaze hardened with that last sentence. Aiden was always so charming and easygoing, that the darker emotion she saw flicker in his eyes startled her.

"I think it's important to know if you have a similar outlook on politics as someone you're seriously dating," Aiden went on, as if choosing his words carefully. "Or if your views on finances are the same. Or what kind of priority having kids and a family is in comparison to career aspirations."

"I see your point, but I also think the results could be skewed, depending on the answers the other person provides," she disputed lightly. She knew Aiden was divorced, and wondered if his argument was based on his own personal experience. "I highly doubt that someone is going to openly state on the application that they're a controlling jerk, or that they have severe OCD tendencies or if they have an internet porn addiction."

He grinned at that, his demeanor relaxing once again. "Okay, I'm not saying it's a perfect system, but statistics do show that taking a compatibility test does work and can identify issues between couples *before* things get serious. And that's not a bad thing."

Chloe doubted that a quiz would have alerted her to Neil's dominating behavior and his explosive temper when things didn't go his way. No, it wasn't until he'd put an engagement ring on her finger that she'd started to see the true personality he'd kept under wraps while they'd been dating. "Well, it's a good thing that I'm not looking for anything serious, anytime soon," she said, pulling herself back from those dark thoughts.

A slight frown marred his brows. "What about the guy you've been seeing?"

She hadn't been seriously involved with anyone in years, and had no idea what had given him the impression she was seeing anyone, let alone seriously. "What are you talking about?"

"That guy I've seen you with at the Executive Bar," he explained, and then she understood. "I just assumed the two of you were dating."

"Ummm, no." An occasional hookup didn't equate to dating. Steve, the guy Aiden was referring to, had been nothing more than a friend with benefits. Neither of them had been interested in a complicated relationship, until Steve had met Jenna and he'd fallen hard for the other woman. That had put an end to their booty calls, and Chloe hadn't been with anyone since.

"I'm not seeing anyone," she said, deciding to keep her reply simple and straightforward. And now that the question was out there in the open, she was curious to know if he was dating anyone. "How about you?"

"Nope." He shook his head. "I've been so focused on work that I haven't had time for a relationship."

A relationship, no. But what about sex, she wondered, just as the refreshment cart came to a stop by their seats. She couldn't imagine a sexy, virile man like Aiden abstaining for long stretches of time. But as she hadn't volunteered that information, she couldn't ask him, either.

The pretty female flight attendant turned their way. "Would either of you like something to drink?" she asked, her gaze lingering appreciatively on Aiden.

Aiden didn't seem to notice the attention as he glanced at Chloe with an impish smile. "I believe I still owe you a drink to celebrate the Organic Kitty contract," he said, sounding truly apologetic for not showing up at the Executive Bar like he'd promised. "Can I make it up to you now?"

"It's kinda early for alcohol," she said, her tone wry.

"Coffee then?"

She nodded. "Sure." She could use a shot of caffeine since she'd been out of the house early to catch their flight.

Aiden asked for two coffees, hers with cream and sugar, and just sugar for his. The attendant filled the order, placed the paper cups on their trays along with a warm cinnamon roll for a morning snack, then moved on to the next row.

"I think you're getting off way too easy for standing me up," she said, motioning to the *free* coffee she was sipping. "I waited for two hours that evening and you never showed. The least you could have done was text me to let me know you weren't coming."

His grimace reflected a genuine amount of contrition. "I really am sorry about that. I was just so thrown by Perry's decision to pit us against each other, I needed time to process it all."

"I get it," she said as she pulled off a piece of her cinnamon roll and popped it into her mouth. "Honestly, I felt the same way."

"But I'm fine now," he reassured her with a grin while biting into his own breakfast pastry. "In fact, I'm looking forward to the challenge."

"That's good, because you're going *down*, Landry," she said with a playful, flirtatious growl that sounded very suggestive, even to her own ears. Her innocent comment had twisted into a sexual innuendo that hung in the air between them like a challenge of its own.

"Mmm, we'll see about that," he murmured.

His eyes had turned dark and hot, and something

deep inside Chloe quivered with awareness. After what seemed like an endless amount of time, he finally glanced away, took a drink of his coffee and devoured the rest of his cinnamon roll before she'd even finished half of hers.

Not quite ready to let the slow burn between them fade away, she decided to embrace her new go-with-it attitude and have a little fun with Aiden. "So, back to that questionnaire we filled out. How important is sexual compatibility to you in a relationship?"

Aiden's bemused expression told her that he had no qualms discussing the intimate details of his sexual preferences with her, and it was that playful, comfortable attitude she enjoyed so much about him. They could pretty much talk about anything and it never felt awkward.

"On a scale of one to ten, I'd rate it a nine. I have a healthy sexual appetite and I'd like my partner to match that. You?"

She'd always pegged him for a man who went the distance, in *everything* he did. Including sex, it seemed, and that enticing thought had her nipples tightening against the confines of her lace bra. "Oh, definitely a nine for me, too," she murmured, even knowing they were playing with fire with this particular conversation.

"And what about foreplay?" he asked before she could formulate another question, so effortlessly turning the tables so that *she* was now sitting in the hot seat. And clearly, he liked having the upper hand.

There was no mistaking the wicked grin curving his lips, or the shameless look in his eyes that dared her to be just as bold and brazen. She'd never shied away from a little risk and adventure, and this discussion was much too entertaining to pass up.

"Well, that all depends on the situation," she said as she took another small bite of her cinnamon pastry and oh-so-slowly sucked the sweet icing off her index finger, which he watched with avid heat and interest. "I love being caressed and stroked and having a man's hands and mouth all over my body, and vice versa. I could indulge in foreplay for hours before the main act, if there's time and we both want to take it slow and tease one another."

Just the thought of Aiden's fingers and lips skimming intimate places made her pulse race a bit faster. "However, there's something to be said for a hard, fast quickie, when you're already so hot for each other that touching isn't even necessary to climax."

"Agreed," he said, the gruff, husky pitch of his voice brimming with a low, heady thrum of arousal.

She swallowed hard. He'd subtly shifted closer, his upper body now turned toward her seat. Their gazes were locked, his intense stare so hot and dark and hypnotic it seemed to singe right through her.

The sizzling arc of energy between them was palpable, and in the depth of Aiden's gaze she glimpsed all the forbidden places he could take her, the carnal pleasure he could give her, and knew an affair with a man like him would be like riding a runaway roller coaster that ended in a wild free fall.

Her stomach fluttered, the sensation spiraling south, and Chloe knew she ought to put an end to their provocative banter—they were sitting in an airplane, for God's sake—but she was much too intrigued by his responses, and very curious to know more.

"Biggest fantasy?" she asked, the question rushing past her lips in a breathy whisper before she thought better of it.

"Watching a woman pleasuring herself." His tone was soft and bone-meltingly seductive, the kind of voice she imagined he'd use when coaxing a woman to do his biding. "You?"

Chloe crossed one leg over the other, because there was a sudden throbbing, insistent ache between her thighs that was getting increasingly more difficult to ignore. "Being taken by a man. Aggressively. Passionately." A part of her was shocked that she'd truly revealed her biggest turn-on, instead of opting for a more watered down reply. But the lust reflecting in Aiden's gaze made her honesty all the more worth it.

The truth was, after her last serious relationship she had a difficult time relinquishing any kind of control, even when it came to sex. She knew her previous partners had found her intimidating in the bedroom, and she had to admit that her direct approach to sex helped to keep their affair from getting emotionally complicated. But secretly, the thought of a man being confident and aggressive enough to take charge of her pleasure was a fantasy that made her weak in the knees.

His gaze dropped to her mouth, adding to the chaotic hunger taking up residence within her. "You have icing on your bottom lip," he murmured.

The muscles in her stomach tightened, and she swiped her tongue across the plump surface, tasting the remnants of cinnamon and vanilla. He tracked the movement with his gaze and gave his head a slight shake.

"No, right *here.*" Lifting his hand, he skimmed his thumb just below the corner of her mouth, the same time she licked the exact spot.

Her tongue accidentally touched the pad of his finger, and he sucked in a harsh breath but didn't move his hand away from her face. Instead, his fingers slowly slid around to the nape of her neck and his thumb pressed gently against her jawline, holding her steady in his grasp. She watched and waited, utterly spellbound by the fascination and desire etching his gorgeous features and illuminating the brilliant blue of his eyes.

Their attraction was certainly nothing new, but this blatant hunger, well, this was exciting and potent and irresistible on so many levels. Her gaze dropped to his mouth, and her lips parted of their own accord, while her heart began a heavy, wild beat in her chest.

Had she ever wanted a kiss so badly? Not that she

could ever remember. But it was *Aiden's* kiss she craved, to the extent that nothing else mattered but feeling the heat and pressure of his mouth on hers.

He must have felt the same way, because he uttered a coarse, resigned, *"screw it,"* and gave in to the same temptation she was battling.

His lips claimed hers, as confident and persuasive as the man himself. Without preamble, his tongue slipped inside her mouth with a direct challenge, one she accepted just as eagerly. Long fingers tangled in her hair as he angled her head to the side and took her to a deeper, darker place, where two years of verbal foreplay and daring flirtations culminated into an explosive kiss that was nothing short of incendiary.

Chloe certainly felt as though she was about to go up in flames, and she moaned in the back of her throat as her body melted from all the heat they'd generated. A needful ache spiraled straight between her thighs. For all the times she'd fantasized about kissing Aiden, she had to admit that reality was far more erotic and twice as exhilarating.

With her head held in place by his big, strong hand, he controlled everything about the kiss—the rhythm, the depth, the thrust and parry of tongues—providing her with a glimpse of what a dominant lover he could be, how he'd wield that same power over her body, given the chance. The arousing thought made her purr like a cat being stroked in all the right places…until the plane hit a patch of turbulence, jarring them both back to the present.

He quickly pulled his mouth from hers and swore beneath his breath, as if belatedly realizing what he'd done and how it might affect their working relationship. She stared into his enigmatic blue eyes, just as stunned by her own reckless behavior, but she couldn't deny that his kiss had rocked her world in a major way.

She licked her bottom lip, tasting the remnants of Aiden in her mouth—a dark, delicious flavor she knew could become highly addictive, if she let it. "Why did you do that?" she asked, because he'd clearly been the one to instigate the kiss.

He withdrew his fingers from her hair and settled back into his own seat, though his gaze never left hers. "Because I have impulse control issues?" he offered as an excuse, a playful half smile curving his lips.

"Liar," she accused softly. The man was controlled at all times, and she shivered as she recalled how he'd oh-so-skillfully, and much too easily, commanded her during that intimate lip-lock.

He released a long breath and shook his head. "Honestly, it just happened. And I'd *really* be lying if I said I was sorry."

Surprisingly, she had no regrets, either. "I get it. We've been flirting with one another for the past two years, and since we're being so candid, I have to admit I've always wondered what it would be like to kiss you." Okay, she'd imagined more than just *that,* but she wasn't about to confess all the down and dirty things she'd thought about doing with him. "It's nice to know that the attraction is mutual."

"No kidding." He scrubbed a hand along his jaw and groaned. "Shit. This is bad."

"You started it," she said, and laughed, trying to make light of the situation.

He gave her an impish grin. "Yeah, and we both know it would be career suicide to see where that spontaneous kiss might take us."

It was a statement they both were very familiar with. A company edict that had served as a reminder of why there were certain personal lines they'd never crossed...until now.

"Don't worry, Aiden," she reassured him with a pat on his knee. "I don't kiss and tell, so no one at the office will ever find out."

However, having just shattered the one sacred, fundamental rule that had once stood between them, Chloe wondered how they were going to revert back to professional colleagues. Especially when their brief encounter had left her wanting much, much more.

$$\underline{4}$$

HOURS AFTER ARRIVING at the St. Raphael resort, Aiden was still wondering what the hell he'd been thinking to kiss Chloe on the plane.

The truth was, he hadn't been thinking, not with the head on his shoulders, anyways. If his brain had been functioning properly, it would have brought him to a screeching halt the moment she'd accidentally licked his finger as he'd wiped away the icing from the corner of her mouth. But years of wanting to take a bite of forbidden fruit had beckoned to him, and giving in to the temptation that was Chloe Reiss had been incredibly easy to do—especially when she'd done absolutely nothing to stop him.

That kiss had changed everything between them, because now he possessed carnal knowledge of just how sinful and decadent Chloe tasted. Now, when he glanced at her, he saw more than just an attractive business associate. Instead, he found himself looking at a hot, lush, passionate woman who made him all too aware of how long it had been since he'd indulged in steamy, mind-bending sex for nothing more than the sake of pure pleasure and satisfaction. And there was no doubt in Aiden's mind that he and Chloe had merely ignited a spark that would burn them both up in flames if one of them dared to strike that match.

Putting his attraction to Chloe out of his mind should have been easy enough to accomplish, considering they'd both shifted right into work mode after checking into the hotel. And for a few hours, anyways, he'd managed to keep his thoughts on gathering information for his campaign.

He and Chloe had spent the entire afternoon with a resort representative who'd given them a private tour of the island and amenities, and answered any questions they had about the planned curriculum. The island itself was tropical and mystical, a true paradise getaway designed for relaxation and romance. The resort's hotel was a sprawling masterpiece set along an endless white sand beach, with lagoons and waterfalls amidst a lush landscape of foliage and fragrant, exotic flowers.

They met their photographer, Ricardo, who would be taking random pictures of the resort and activities for them to use for their presentations. The man would also be on hand to do private sessions if either one of them wanted specific shots and would also provide professional models to use during the photography session.

At the end of the tour, Aiden and Chloe were given the same orientation package as all the other registrants, which included a schedule of activities, a daily itinerary and all the enhanced services the resort had to offer singles looking to make a love connection.

He'd spent the rest of the afternoon outlining a basic PowerPoint presentation based on the information he'd gleaned about the resort, as did Chloe. Tonight was the initial meet-and-greet mixer, a cocktail reception designed to kick-start the next five days of fun, sun and matchmaking events. While he needed to attend the festivities in order to evaluate the resort's quality of service and assess their current marketing strategies, Aiden wasn't looking forward to mingling with a bunch of women who were searching for a committed relationship.

Fashionably late, he walked into the large, spacious ballroom that had been set up with an elaborate buffet and an open bar. Fun reggae music native to the island played in the background for those wanting to take advantage of the dance floor.

Already, groups were forming based on the color-coded silicone wristband everyone was required to wear—a simple and effective system that let other participants know that anyone with a matching wristband was in their pool of compatible picks, based on the questionnaire they'd filled out prior to arriving on the island. Once a couple made a connection, they could then exchange their initial bracelets for matching red ones that signaled to others that they were paired off and no longer available.

First things first. He needed a drink, and he headed to the bar and ordered a Glenlivit Scotch neat. Just as he walked away, he caught sight of Chloe, surrounded by three men who wore the same bright yellow band encircling her wrist. Aiden's neon green wristband was a much needed reminder that while he and Chloe might share a hot sexual chemistry, there was the proof that they weren't compatible on other levels.

That should have been enough to put a huge damper on his desire for Chloe, but as he well knew, sometimes wanting someone had nothing to do with sharing the same ideas and values. Sometimes it was just all about pure lust and passion. And those were two things he and Chloe had in common, as they'd proved with that kiss they'd shared.

She laughed at something one of the men said, her eyes alight with amusement as she responded with a retort that had the guys chuckling, too. The spikey-haired blond dude to her left placed a possessive hand low on her back and leaned close to whisper something in her ear that made her raise a flirtatious brow.

Aiden read her lips as she said, "you're so bad," and felt a strange burning sensation in the pit of his stomach, along with the urge to join their group and stake a claim he had no right to.

He frowned to himself. Jealousy was not a feeling he was familiar with, and he wasn't happy that Chloe was the one to rouse the emotion.

Shit. He took a deep drink of his scotch, hoping the alcohol would help soothe his irritation.

"I see you're wearing a green wristband, too."

The soft, feminine voice pulled Aiden from his unpleasant thoughts and forced him to shift mental gears. Grateful for the diversion, he smiled at the petite brunette who'd approached him, noticing that her bracelet did match his. She was wearing a simple white blouse and navy blue skirt, along with a pair of flats—a very conservative choice when he compared it to the more formfitting bandage-style red dress and killer black heels Chloe had worn tonight.

This woman was plain but pretty, with kind blue eyes and a nervous smile, and he quickly tried to put her at ease.

"Hi. I'm Aiden," he said, and extended his hand toward her in greeting.

Her hand slipped into his, soft and delicate, lacking the kind of confidence he was used to in a handshake. "I'm Joy. It's nice to meet you, Aiden."

"Likewise," he replied.

She shifted anxiously on her feet, her discomfort obvious. "I'm finding this mixer so overwhelming, so I'm glad that everyone is wearing a color-coded wristband, which makes it easier to find someone who I'm compatible with, like you."

Her assumption that they were a perfect match when she didn't even know him was unnerving. Deciding she could use a bit of alcohol to loosen up, he guided her toward the bar.

"Can I get you something to drink?"

"Umm, sure." She thought for a minute. "I'll take a Roy Rogers."

He bit back a groan at her choice of mocktail— cola mixed with grenadine syrup and garnished with a maraschino cherry. He ordered her beverage, handed her the drink, and when he gravitated toward the buffet, she followed him. She was quiet and shy, and in order to fill up the awkward silence between them, he tried to keep the conversation flowing.

"So, Joy, where do you live?" he asked as he scooped some pasta salad onto his plate.

"In a small town just outside of Cincinnati, Ohio."

He was a big city kind of guy and couldn't imagine being confined to a small community. He added a chicken breast drenched in a savory sauce onto his dish, along with a warm roll and butter. "And what do you do for work?"

She selected some raw vegetables and cubes of cheese, her appetite not nearly as hearty as his own. "I'm a first grade teacher."

Interesting, and very fitting, he thought. "So you like kids?"

"I love kids." Her voice reflected her enthusiasm. "I can't wait to get married and have a big family of my own. The sooner, the better. How about you?"

She returned the question with way too much eagerness and hope in her gaze, and warning bells went off in his head. Yes, he wanted those things, too, but the way she was looking at him, as if he'd make the perfect baby daddy, sparked a bit of panic deep inside Aiden.

For the next hour, Joy stuck by his side, and he learned more about her than he ever wanted to. She loved to cook and bake, she sewed her own clothes and enjoyed gardening. She admitted to being a homebody, and had all those traditional, domestic qualities Aiden thought he wanted in a future wife.

This was the type of woman who'd been deemed a match based on the compatibility questionnaire he'd filled out, Aiden realized. On paper, she fit what he believed were non-negotiable requirements for the next woman he allowed himself to get serious with. But in reality, there was no doubt in his mind that she was way too passive and would bore the hell out of him if he had to spend more than a few hours in her company.

It was a very sobering thought.

When another guy with a green wristband started talking to Joy, Aiden used the interruption to quietly slip away and continue mingling. Unfortunately, he found himself bombarded by a steady stream of women with the same matching bracelets, and similar traits to Joy.

He smiled and nodded as the women talked and vied for his attention, but as his gaze spotted Chloe standing a few feet away, surrounded by her own male fan club, she was the one who captured his interest. He wasn't surprised to see that men with all different colored wristbands had flocked to her. Not only was she beautiful and alluring, but she was charming, intelligent and had a great sense of humor. What guy wouldn't be drawn to such a vibrant personality?

"Do you have a time frame of when you want to be married and start a family?"

The personal question from one of the women made him feel as though he was starting to suffocate, and he didn't know how much more of this charade he could take.

The problem was, he really wasn't here to find a spouse, and it wasn't fair to all these ladies to even pretend that he was. He didn't want to be continually pursued by women who believed they were a match when he had no intentions of following through, and he saw that as a potential problem as the week went on.

His reasons for being at St. Raphael were to assess the resort's current program so he could create a strong marketing campaign, and he knew he could accomplish that without all this other pretense. He had an idea in mind, and if he could get Chloe to agree, then they'd both be better able to concentrate on the business side of this trip.

Without answering the woman's question, he politely excused himself from the group and walked straight to Chloe. He came up beside her, touched her arm, and she glanced at him in surprise.

"Care to dance?" He grinned at her, hoping like hell she took pity on him.

She didn't even hesitate with her reply. "I'd love to."

He guided her toward the dance floor just as a lively reggae tune gave way to a slower melody. Stealing Chloe away earned him some serious glares from her avid suitors, but Aiden didn't care. The relief on her face told him that she appreciated the break—so maybe she wasn't cut out for this whole matchmaking scenario, either.

There were only a few other couples enjoying the music, leaving them plenty of room on the dance floor. Pulling Chloe into his embrace, Aiden tucked one of her hands in his and wrapped his other arm around her waist, bringing their bodies flush. The scent of her perfume—exotic, floral and seductive—instantly inundated his senses. She was like a femme fatale, and he desperately wanted to bury his face in her neck and inhale the intoxicating fragrance lingering on her skin.

He'd never had the pleasure of having her pressed so intimately against him, and he was instantly conscious of how perfectly her soft curves complemented his harder, masculine frame—not to mention how well the snug bodice of her dress displayed the provocative swell of her breasts.

Desire stirred deep and low, and when he met her gaze, there was no mistaking the same level of heated awareness glimmering in her hazel eyes. Absently, he stroked his palm down her spine and let his hand come to rest just above her toned bottom.

"Do you see those two men standing over there by the bar?" Chloe asked as she casually draped one of her arms around his neck.

Aiden glanced in the direction she'd indicated and frowned, something he seemed to be doing a lot of tonight when it came to her. "You mean the guys that are staring at you like hungry vultures?" He all but growled the question.

She lifted a brow, amusement glimmering in her eyes, but didn't call him on his possessive behavior. "They're staring at me because they're sizing up their competition. Those two men are from the other rival ad agency Perry told us about."

"Really?" he asked, surprised by the certainty in her voice. "How do you know that?"

"The dark-haired guy is wearing a yellow wristband like mine and he started talking to me when I first arrived," she said. "He introduced himself as Brad, and I thought he was just another single guy making the rounds. He asked me what I did for a living, so I told him I was an ad executive, and his whole demeanor changed because he must have realized who I was. He said he worked for an ad agency, too, and came right out and asked if I was here for the St. Raphael account."

Ahh, now he knew why the duo was keeping an eye on her. "I take it you told them yes?"

"I'm not going to lie about it," she said and

shrugged, seemingly unthreatened by their rival's presence. "I'd rather it be out in the open so we're sure to keep our distance."

He preferred to know who their opponent was, too, so he and Chloe could watch their backs and keep any advertising strategies to themselves. "At least now we won't be constantly wondering who the competition is."

"Exactly. I'm sure they feel the same way."

Undoubtedly. "By the way, thanks for saving me from having to deal with all those women," he said, nodding back toward were he'd left the group of la-dies to dance with Chloe. They were all still clus-tered together—probably plotting their revenge for the way he'd abandoned them.

She followed his gaze. "They look nice enough, and they're all wearing the same colored wristband as yours. Surely you all have plenty in common based on the questionnaire you filled out."

He caught the sly smile on her lips and knew she was teasing him about their earlier conversation.

Now he had a better understanding of what she meant when she said that the survey was desperate and forced and how she preferred to let a relation-ship develop organically. But he still believed a quiz could help eliminate potential conflicts between two people before they invested too much time and emo-tion into the relationship.

He shrugged nonchalantly. "I don't know that those women and I had a lot in common, so much as their biological clocks are ticking and they're anxious to get married and have babies."

She tipped her head to the side, her body relaxing completely against his. "There must have been *something* in your answers that matched you up to those particular women. Maybe *your* biological clock is ticking?"

He smiled, as always enjoying her sense of humor. "I don't feel a sense of urgency about it, but sure, I want to get married again someday and have a family. Don't you?"

"Not anytime soon," she said with an adamant shake of her head that caused her loose hair to cascade over her bare shoulders. "I've got too many career goals I want to achieve, and that kind of focus demands all my time and energy. I'm not willing to give up my aspirations for a relationship that would demand way more than I'm willing to give."

Okay, yeah, he already knew that about Chloe. Her words reinforced once again why they were wearing different colored bracelets. "What about your lap dogs?" he teased, referring to the men who'd huddled around her, and were still watching her from across the room, waiting for an opportunity to claim her once she was free again. "Any potential suitors in the group?"

"Good Lord, no." She looked appalled by the mere suggestion. "You know I don't take all this matchmaking stuff seriously. It's fun and interesting, and I'm making mental notes for my campaign, but there will be no love match for me. I suppose I'd have a good time hanging out with a couple of those guys for the next few days, but that's about it."

That ridiculous bite of jealousy reared its ugly head again and before he could stop himself he splayed his hand at the base of her spine and pulled her lower body tighter against his. "Don't you feel bad about leading them on?"

"I'm just flirting and having fun," she said, something that was an inherent part of her personality. "I didn't say or do anything that would give any of those guys any indication that I'm interested in them on a one-on-one basis."

"Yet that's what everyone at this resort is here for," he pointed out.

"True." She sighed, a small frown creasing her brows. "I guess I'll have to be very careful about the things I say and do."

The song that was playing blended into another slow tune as more couples joined them on the dance floor. Aiden was grateful for yet another low-key ballad because he wasn't ready to let Chloe go just yet.

"Actually, I feel the same way," he said, and knew what he was about to propose would easily solve the issue, if she agreed. "I know tonight's initial meet and greet was important to both of us to see how everyone is matched up, but I'd really like to just concentrate on the business aspect of being at the resort. Since you seem to be in a similar mindset, I have a proposition to offer that would benefit both of us."

"Really?" she murmured, her eyes alight with sensual interest as her fingers threaded through the hair at the nape of his neck. "You have my undivided attention."

Her tone was ripe with innuendo. Clearly, Chloe's mind had gone the playful, naughty route, enticing a grin from him. "It's nothing indecent."

She feigned a guileless pout. "Too bad."

Chloe had always been a shameless flirt and a tease, but after that kiss, everything between them now smoldered with an underlying heat and hunger. He was keenly aware of everything about her, making it impossible to ignore the erotic slide of her thighs against his, the heady scent lingering on her skin, and the delectable lips he wanted to taste again.

Hell, who did he think he was kidding? The impulse to claim her mouth for another deep, drugging kiss was just the tip of the iceberg. He had a list of all sorts of wicked things he wanted to do to her, with her. But mostly, he wanted to be that man to tap into her secret fantasy, to assert a bit of aggression and coax her to completely surrender to the darker side of pleasure.

"So, what's this proposition of yours?" she asked curiously.

He exhaled a deep breath, which did absolutely nothing to lessen the sexual tension coursing through his body. He was certain nothing short of a cold shower would help at this point. "Since neither one of us is interested in being pursued this week, what do you think about trading in our current wristbands for matching red ones?"

She raised a perfectly arched brow as she contemplated his suggestion. "You want us to be a couple?"

"In wristband only," he clarified, though the longer he remained pressed up against her, the more his unruly body clamored for the real deal. "If we're both wearing a red bracelet, which lets everyone know that we've found a match and are no longer interested in mingling, then we can give one hundred percent of our attention to what we need to do for our respective presentations. We can attend events together, or separately, without having to worry about other people thinking we're still single."

"That's a great idea," she said enthusiastically. "It'll eliminate the problem of having to turn down overtures from men I really have no interest in."

"Then let's do it."

"Right now?" She widened her eyes in scandalized shock as she deliberately chose to put a playful, suggestive twist on his words. "Here? In front of everyone?"

He chuckled. "Yeah, what can I say. Beneath this stuffy suit and tie, I'm really an exhibitionist."

"Hmm. You and I might be compatible after all." Her gaze sparkled with laughter. "Now let's go switch out these wristbands."

5

CHLOE MET AIDEN for a late morning brunch in the dining room, where they enjoyed an elaborate spread of food ranging from health-conscious dishes to rich, gourmet cuisine. There was something for everyone, and so far she was impressed with the resort's selection of meal options, and the service, too.

She finished off her banana fosters crepe, and the efficient waitstaff promptly cleared her plate and refilled her cup with fresh, steaming coffee before she could even ask. She stirred cream and sugar into the brew and glanced across the table at Aiden, who'd just taken the last bite of his fully loaded omelet.

Today they were wearing matching red wristbands, indicating they were a couple, and so far, the ruse was working. None of the other singles approached them, which allowed both her and Aiden to just relax and do what they'd come to St. Raphael to accomplish.

"What are you in the mood to do today?" she asked him.

A wicked grin tipped up one corner of his mouth. "Is that a trick question?"

No, it wasn't, but after that heated kiss on the plane and feeling his hard, masculine body moving rhythmically against hers as they'd danced last night, she could think of a dozen different things she'd rather do with him than the various ice-breaker activities the resort had to offer. But those more erotic, get-naked-and-burn-up-the-sheets-together type games weren't an option for them, despite how much she wished otherwise.

"I was talking about what's on the list of organized activities scheduled for the afternoon and evening," she said, passing him the single sheet of paper listing the day's events. "Is there anything in particular you'd like to check out?"

He leaned back in his chair and looked over their options. "There's certainly a lot to choose from."

She agreed. The activity director had covered the gamut of recreational offerings, from the basic getting-to-know-you trivia contests to the more lively, physically interactive games for those who enjoyed a bit more adventure and uninhibited fun. Each event was rated from mild to wild, so there was no confusing the level of sexual content in each activity.

Aiden glanced at his wristwatch. "Looks like there's a golf tournament starting in half an hour."

She rolled her eyes and shook her head. "Forget about it. Golf is one of the most boring sports *ever*."

"How about the wet and wild T-shirt competition?" he suggested, and waggled his brows at her way too lasciviously.

He was such a *guy*. "Only if you'll agree to learn the cha-cha with me," she replied just as audaciously.

He visibly cringed at her suggestion, though the laughter in his eyes gave him away. "Okay, I guess *neither* of those things will be happening."

There were a few activities on the list that no longer applied to them since they were now a couple. There was no need for the speed dating event, or any of the other singles mixers, so Chloe figured they might as well choose something fun and entertaining.

After taking a sip of her coffee, she tossed out the one idea that appealed to her the most. "I was thinking that the risqué charades could be kind of amusing to watch, but that's not for another two hours."

"That would give us some time to walk around the resort and check things out now that everything is in full swing."

She nodded. "That's a good idea. I also want to talk to Ricardo about setting up a time frame tomorrow for him to take certain pictures for my presentation."

"I need to do the same thing." He placed his napkin on his empty plate and stood, looking extremely handsome in a casual gray polo and khaki cargo shorts. The man pulled off the executive look as well as a more casual style with equal aplomb. "Shall we?"

She joined him, and together they walked out of the hotel to the pool and lounge area. The sun was shining, making it a beautiful, cloudless day, perfect for outdoor activities. The area was quickly filling up with singles and couples, and laughter rang out as a nearby drinking game at the underground pool bar turned a bit rowdy. Other men and women were heading down a pathway that led to the beach to enjoy a swim in the ocean, or participate in the on-going volleyball game on the sand.

Waiters carrying trays of fruity rum drinks aptly named "Love Potion" seemed to be everywhere. Chloe grabbed one for herself and Aiden as they watched a Ping-Pong tournament for a while before moving on to the game of bikini Twister that had them at times cringing and chuckling out loud as nearly naked, oil-slicked bodies vied for space on the overly large Twister mat. Each turn of the spinner had the men and women switching into very interesting and compromising positions that Chloe couldn't imagine executing in a public place.

"I'd love to see the greenhouse they have here on the island," Chloe said, ready for something a bit more low-key and quiet. "Want to join me?"

He gave a nonchalant shrug. "Sure. We still have a little bit of time to kill before charades."

Chloe swapped out her empty glass for a refill of the fruity cocktail, then followed the signs pointing the way toward the botanical garden. The sounds of calypso music faded the farther away they walked from the hotel, while the lush green foliage and bright flowers and shrubbery increased. Most of the plants along the way were labeled with their name, origin and description. The intoxicating scent of jasmine hung in the air, seductive and alluring… as if pulling Chloe toward a magical place.

She sipped on her drink as the narrow pathway eventually gave way to a smaller, more intimate area, with a gazebo and greenhouse filled with beautiful, vivid flowers. Intrigued, Chloe gravitated toward the glass-enclosed nursery, and Aiden followed. As soon as they stepped inside, they were wrapped in humidity and the perfumed scent of flowers.

With no one else around, it was quiet and peaceful, and stunningly beautiful. Chloe wasn't one to stop and smell the roses, so to speak, but she was completely in awe of all the beauty surrounding her. She and Aiden walked along the rows of floral displays, taking in the dozens of exotic blooms in brilliant hues, and more species of orchids than she realized existed—all labeled with names and descriptions.

Drawn to a unique cluster of fuchsia flowers that looked like a cross between a lily and an orchid, she studied the blossoms, fascinated by the way the inside folds looked similar to a woman's vulva, with a small nub resembling a clitoris, while the thick stamen gave the impression of a very large, erect penis.

"This one looks like a combination of female and male genitalia," she murmured in amusement, her thoughts tumbling out of her mouth thanks to the alcohol loosening her tongue.

Aiden moved closer to get a better look, the warmth of his body and the brush of his arm against hers causing her nipples to tighten in awareness. Everything inside this greenhouse—the steamy humidity, the drugging scent in the air, the erotic flowers—made her think of sex.

"The flower definitely has a lot of similarities," he agreed, his voice low and huskier than normal, as if he, too, was affected by the sensual atmosphere.

Drawn to the bright pink flower, Chloe reached out to caress the protruding yellow stamen—even though she knew better than to touch something so fragile.

"Hello, you two," a soft female voice said from behind them, causing Chloe to snap out of her weird trance and snatch her hand back before she could make contact with the fuzzy stalk.

Startled by the fact that they weren't alone as she'd originally thought, both she and Aiden turned around to face the person who'd spoken—an older woman, probably in her sixties, with dark brown skin, warm brown eyes and a kind, welcoming smile. She was wearing a colorful caftan dress with billowing sleeves and her hair was wrapped atop her head in multiple braids entwined with colorful strips of fabric.

"We didn't realize someone else was here," Aiden said.

"I'm the greenhouse caretaker," the other woman explained, spreading her arms wide to encompass the area, her voice filled with pride. "My name is Hattie, but here on the island, they call me the matchmaker."

"To tie in to the theme here at the resort?" Chloe guessed, curious to know the woman's angle.

Something mystical twinkled in the older woman's eyes. "Some would say so, but while the resort has managed to find a way to modernize a love connection between two people, I still prefer to do things the old-fashioned way."

Chloe wasn't sure what the woman meant by that, but before she or Aiden could ask, Hattie spoke once again.

"It's nice to have some visitors. With the resort offering so many activities, not many travel down this path to the greenhouse," she said, her gaze seemingly scrutinizing the two of them with a discerning amount of insight. "Usually just the couples with a romantic soul."

Chloe resisted the urge to roll her eyes. She didn't want to offend the woman. But she couldn't help but wonder if Hattie was feeding them a line, to make it seem as though the greenhouse possessed some sort of mysterious, enchanting properties. Then again, hadn't Chloe just been mesmerized by that erotic flower she'd nearly touched?

Hattie glanced at the matching red bands on their wrists, a knowing smile curving the corner of her lips. "I love seeing when two people find their soul mate early on in the week."

Realizing that the woman thought she and Aiden were a real couple, Chloe shook her head. "Oh, we're not together that way," she quickly clarified. "The bracelets are just a distraction. We're one of the ad agencies here to work on a marketing campaign for the resort. This is just a pretense so we don't have to mingle like everyone else."

Hattie moved to a row of plants on a long table and tested the soil with her fingers before plucking away a few wilting leaves. "Trust me, the two of you were meant for one another."

Hattie's statement couldn't have been further from the truth, but there was a calm certainty in her voice that made Chloe's heart skip a weird beat.

Aiden shifted besides Chloe. "How do you know that the two of us are...uh, soul mates?" he asked.

Chloe frowned at him and his question. Had he really gotten sucked into the woman's claim that she had the ability to predict a couple's compatibility? The man was far more intelligent than that, but he appeared truly interested in the woman's reply.

"The easiest answer is your pheromones," she said with a shrug. "I can't give away all my secrets, but I come from a very long line of matchmakers, and I'm rarely, if ever, wrong about my predictions."

"So, when couples happen into your greenhouse, you can just sense their compatibility?" he asked, a skeptical note in his voice.

"Yes, I just know," she said with the conviction of a woman who was confident in her abilities. "But everyone always seems to want some sort of tangible proof in order to believe my claim. This very unique hybrid flower, which is native to this island, provides that." She indicated the bright pink flower that Chloe had nearly touched. "I call it the flower of love. I like to think it represents love and passion, because that's the results it produces."

"What does it do?" Chloe asked, curious despite her very practical nature.

Hattie smiled. "When a couple touches the stamen at the same time, it changes color. Sometimes it's two different colors, which indicates incompatibility. But when the color is the same, well, that's when the true magic of love happens. Would the two of you like to give it a try?"

Chloe's heart was suddenly beating hard and fast in her chest, and she wasn't sure why. She was torn between wanting to scoff at such nonsense, yet she was tempted to see how the whole color-change thing worked. And did she really want to know the results she and Aiden produced?

Aiden made the decision for them. "What the hell," he said unexpectedly. "Let's do it."

Alrighty then. Chloe exhaled a deep breath, and reached toward the flower the same time that Aiden did. With her thumb and forefinger, she lightly grasped the stamen, right below where Aiden touched. Beneath the pad of their fingers, a deep, dark purple hue saturated the delicate stalk.

"Ahhh," Hattie said, her voice infused with satisfaction and excitement. "Desire, lust and love. I was right. The two of you are extremely compatible."

Chloe quickly pulled her hand back, while Aidan did so more casually. She couldn't dispute the desire simmering between them, but the other emotion Hattie spoke of, well, that she *could* argue. "We're not in love."

Hattie tipped her head to the side, her brown eyes gentle yet insistent. "But you have the potential to be, if you open yourselves up to it."

As they walked back to the resort a few minutes later, Chloe cast a glance at Aiden, who'd been oddly quiet since the older woman's spiel. "So, what do you think of Hattie the Matchmaker and her claims?"

"Do I believe she just knows that two people belong together, with or without that flower trick?" He shook his head, clearly a man who thought in pragmatic terms. "No, I don't. However, I think I just found my marketing angle for my campaign."

"Really?" No wonder Aiden had asked so many questions, and had so willingly gone along with all of Hattie's antics. "So, you're going to spin the fact that St. Raphael has an actual, old-fashioned match-maker on the island?"

"Absolutely." He gave her a smug smile. "And I'm going to make it work in a way that's going to in-crease the resort's exposure and gives them an added edge over their competition." He grabbed her hand and picked up their pace along the walkway. "Come on, we need to hustle or we're going to be late for the risqué charades."

Liking the feel of her hand enclosed in his, Chloe tried not to read too much into the gesture, though it did make her feel a little warm and mushy inside. Or maybe that light, pleasant buzz she was experi-encing was a result of that second love potion drink. As she looked at Aiden's face, she could see that his mental gears were already churning out ideas for his presentation, and she had to admit that using Hattie and her traditional methods of matchmaking, be-yond standard compatibility quizzes, would provide a unique twist to Aiden's campaign.

He'd just verbally staked a claim to Hattie and her matchmaking knowledge—which they've done plenty of times in the past to make sure the other person didn't latch on to the same idea, too. Now Chloe just had to find a bigger and better hook for her own presentation. She had something in mind, but wasn't quite ready to share her concept just yet.

Back inside the hotel, they entered the room for the charades just as the men and women were in the process of dividing into teams. Chloe intended to sit on the sidelines and just enjoy the show, but when one of the teams came up short a couple, she and Aiden were recruited to play. With a little alcohol in her system, it didn't take long for her to put the incident at the greenhouse out of her mind, loosen up and get into the spirit of the game...and the competition.

Each couple drew a phrase from a large glass bowl, and a timer was set for three minutes. Back and forth the teams battled for supremacy, playacting the expression or sentence they'd been given, which ranged from a couple having sex on a sandy beach, skinny dipping in the ocean, impatient newlyweds on their wedding night, to a couple playing nurse and doctor.

More rum cocktails were served, and inhibitions were shed as everyone got into character to execute their scenes. The sketches were at times bawdy and X-rated, and hilarious to watch unfold as different guesses were shouted out. Chloe's sides ached from so much laughter.

She and Aiden managed to avoid being chosen until the very end of the game, when it came down to a win-or-lose tiebreaker for their group. Since they were the only couple who hadn't performed, it was up to them to score the last point in order for their team to win.

"Bring it on!" someone on their team cheered as Chloe and Aiden stepped up to the small staging area.

Chloe flashed Aiden a sassy smile. "You know I

don't like to lose at anything, so you'd better bring your A-game."

"You're such an overachiever," he teased as he reached into the glass bowl and randomly withdrew one of the crumpled pieces of paper.

She rubbed her hands together. "Failure is not an option for me."

He unfolded the paper, silently read their phrase and grinned like a tempting rogue. "Are you sure you're ready for this?"

Judging by the sinful look on his face, Chloe was certain he'd selected one of the more daring expressions—but then again, this *was* risqué charades so she'd expected something outrageous. "You know I love a good challenge."

"Well, then, here you go." He revealed the act they had to execute.

Making out in the backseat of a car.

Getting their team to guess "backseat of a car" was a fairly easy process and took less than thirty seconds of their time. After that Chloe and Aiden embraced in order to playact the first part of the parody. Their bodies entwined and Aiden ran his flattened palms up and down her back while she threaded her fingers through his hair in an attempt to look like frenzied teenagers in the throes of passion. The only thing *not* touching were their lips. Chloe was pretty certain that Aiden was trying to avoid a repeat performance of yesterday's kiss.

Unfortunately, everyone on their team shouted out

words that were close to the phrase, but not an exact match. There was groping, feeling up, hugging and heavy petting, but no "making out."

"You have one minute left," someone yelled.

With time running out, and the lingering effects of the love potion drink coursing through Chloe's system and bolstering her courage, she decided to give their onlookers the real deal. No way was she going to let them lose this one last point because she hadn't given all she had to beat the competition. Not if she could help it.

Sliding her fingers around to the back of Aiden's head, she pulled his mouth down to hers. The moment their lips touched, everything around Chloe faded away, except for her desire for this man who tempted her like no other. There was no hesitation on his part, either, just a mutual hunger that promised all sorts of wanton pleasure.

Despite having an audience, there was nothing sweet or chaste about this kiss. With a rumbling groan she felt, more than heard from Aiden, his tongue touched and tangled with hers, sweeping deep inside her mouth to dominate and possess. His hands got into the action, too, skimming along the outside of her thighs and grabbing her ass to simulate the phrase that no one had guessed yet.

Excitement sent Chloe's pulse racing and had her body melting into a pool of lust and need. Kissing Aiden was akin to the most delicious kind of foreplay, providing a hot tease of what other carnal delights his mouth and tongue were capable of giving.

Lost in pure unadulterated sensation, she was having a difficult time remembering that they were playing charades, that this was all pretend for the sake of a game. Her attraction to Aiden was real and undeniable, and in that wild moment of abandon, she wasn't sure she wanted to resist him any longer.

Her decision was absolute craziness, she knew. The risks involved were enormous, but being here on this secluded island, where no one knew who they were, was to their benefit, as well. Far away from work, prying eyes, and rules and restrictions, they had the perfect opportunity to finally indulge in what they both wanted—each other—without the worry of being caught. A quickie affair to diminish all the sexual tension burning between them. They could return to Boston and the firm with a clear head, completely focused on their respective campaigns.

Outside of her current sensual universe, she heard cheers and catcalls because of their avid embrace, and finally, through all the commotion, someone shouted out the correct phrase, "making out in the backseat of a car," giving their team the last point they needed to win the entire game.

She pulled back and ended the kiss, and for a long moment they stared at one another, breathless and aroused, while their team celebrated their success around them.

"I'm beginning to think that maybe you really

are an exhibitionist," she said, referring to the comment he'd made to her last night on the dance floor. "You quite enjoyed that kiss and certainly didn't hold back."

He didn't deny her allegation as he slowly released her, so that their bodies were no longer intimately entangled. "I'll admit, you have a good game strategy, Reiss."

She flashed him a daring grin full of sass. "Who said that kiss was a game?"

With that, she walked away from him. She could feel Aiden staring after her, pondering her parting remark, and knew she'd just given him a whole lot to think about—which is exactly what she'd intended. Because tonight, at dinner, she was going to turn up the heat and let him decide if he was interested in taking the bait.

6

AIDEN ESCORTED CHLOE toward the large ballroom hosting one of tonight's dining options, excruciatingly aware of her, in every way. It wasn't so much what she was wearing, though the chocolate-brown dress definitely drew his attention. The top portion fell off of one shoulder, revealing an alluring expanse of creamy skin, and the fitted skirt showcased her toned ass and ended just above her knee, accentuating her long, slender legs. Her four-inch heels were the strappy kind that wrapped around her ankles and screamed *fuck me, please*.

The thought of doing just that made him hot and hard.

She'd worn her hair piled up on her head, giving her a slightly tousled look and exposed the elegant line of her throat. An assortment of gold bangles encircled her wrist and a pair of shiny gold hoops dangled from her ears. Her green-gold eyes were full of mystery, like a siren experienced in luring a man to commit all sorts of carnal sins.

But what was making it difficult to function was the air of confidence she moved with. It made him wonder what she was up to, though he definitely had a clue. Especially after the subtle challenge she'd issued that afternoon that had him seriously considering crossing some very strict personal and professional boundaries with her.

Normally, he wrestled with his conscience when it came to wanting Chloe, but right now the only voice in his head was his brother Sam's, telling Aiden to stop overanalyzing things, that giving in to his desire for Chloe was all about feel-good sex, not a lifetime commitment.

Maybe, just maybe, for once his brother was right.

Tonight, they'd been given the choice between attending a Murder Mystery Fete, or a Truth or Dare Soiree—both events had been designed to create more social interaction between couples and singles. Since neither one of them were mystery buffs, they'd both decided on the latter, and as they stepped into a ballroom decorated in red and black tones, with sheer draping and candles flickering everywhere, a bubbly hostess greeted them.

"Welcome to the Truth or Dare Soiree. I see the two of you are a couple," the young woman said as she glanced at their matching red wristbands. "That gives you two options tonight. Would you like a group table to share with other couples, or a private table for two?"

Aiden knew there was security in large numbers, which the group table would provide, but he didn't want to go the safe route with Chloe tonight. Between all the sexual tension that had thrummed between them in the greenhouse, and later at the risqué charades, he was more than ready to kick things between them up a notch or two.

"We'll take one of the private tables."

The approving smile that Chloe gave Aiden told him he'd made the right decision. They followed the hostess to one of the secluded tables at the back of the room. Instead of taking the chair across from Chloe, he settled into the seat next to hers. Beneath the table, their thighs brushed, and neither one of them moved or shied away from the intimate contact.

"Here is a list of meal options," the hostess said, handing them each a menu before she indicated a tray with a few items on it. "As for the truth-or-dare part of tonight's dinner, it's a very simple game that will require you both to answer a truth, or accept a dare, depending on what the roll of the die reveals."

On the tray was a red cube stamped with the words *Truth* and *Dare* on each of the six sides. Next to that were four tall silver cylinders holding long wooden sticks. Each cylinder was marked TRUTH or DARE, along with the "mild" or "wild" option in each category.

"Once you roll the die, your partner will pick one

of the wooden sticks from the corresponding container," the hostess went on to explain. "They will
then read aloud the truth or dare printed on the stick,
and the other person must either answer the question
or complete the task. Most important, have fun!"

"Thank you," Chloe said, and picked up her menu
to peruse the meal options.

Aiden followed her lead, and when the waiter arrived at their table, he ordered the rib-eye steak and
potatoes, and Chloe opted for the grilled salmon and
rice pilaf. When they were offered either wine or
champagne, he went for the cabernet, while Chloe
asked for an iced tea, citing that she'd consumed
way too many love potions cocktails that afternoon.

Once the waiter was gone and they were alone
again, Chloe eyed the red die on the tray, a very
vixenlike smile curving her mouth. "So, shall we
play?" she asked him.

He took a drink of his cabernet and quirked a
brow at her. "Are you sure you want to?"

She leaned a bit closer, amusement shimmering
in her gaze. "What, are you afraid of having to give
up deep, dark secrets?"

"I have no problem sharing truths," he replied.
The loose top portion of her dress slipped a bit lower
on her arm, distracting him a moment with the urge
to trail his fingers along that smooth, tanned skin, all
the way up to the side of her neck. "I'm just thinking
of what dares might be in store for us."

"I can handle *any* dare thrown my way," she said boldly. "How about you?"

"Oh, absolutely." He waved a hand toward the game items. "By all means, ladies first."

She rolled the single red die, and the word *Truth* remained faceup. Deciding to go easy on Chloe for the first round, Aiden selected a wooden stick from the "mild" category.

He read the question out loud. "What is the reason why your last *serious* relationship ended?" Recalling their vague conversation on the plane about the guy she'd been dating, he acted on a hunch. "And I don't think that guy I saw you with at the Executive Bar counts."

Her body language stiffened slightly, enough to tell Aiden that she'd been about to go the easy and superficial route with her reply. "Why not?"

He met her gaze and held it directly, not at all put off by the defensive tone of her voice. "Because I get the impression that he was more of a temporary thing, than someone you'd been committed to."

She glanced away, and when she hesitated, he knew he'd assumed correctly. She absently bit the corner of her lip and he was struck at how vulnerable she looked in that moment, an emotion he never would have equated with the strong, always self-assured Chloe, had he not witnessed it himself.

Clearly, she didn't want to discuss her last serious relationship. But Aiden was suddenly intrigued and wanted to find out what had happened that had made her so guarded, and how her past experience had shaped her current views on relationships, as his own divorce had.

"Spill the truth, Reiss," he said, adding just enough of a challenge to his voice that he knew she'd never back down from. "That's the name of this game."

Schooling her features into an indifferent expression, she shrugged her bared shoulder. "I broke up with Neil because he was a real asshole."

Aiden smirked. Okay, that was succinct, he thought, more curious than ever. But being an asshole translated to many things, and she'd just avoided the truth of the matter with a vague reply. "You're cheating," he murmured as he swirled his red wine in his glass. "And I've never pegged you for someone who would skirt any issue."

That bit of prompting made her chin jut out stubbornly, and he waited patiently to see which direction she decided to take this conversation—avoid it completely, or give him a glimpse of something personal, and clearly, painful for her.

"Obviously, Neil isn't someone I like to talk about. If I could, I'd erase the eighteen months we were together." She paused, as if deciding what she wanted to reveal, then spoke again. "I met him my junior year in college, and everything was fine our first year together, until we got engaged, and then he... changed."

Aiden was very familiar with how people could

change, how someone *he'd* trusted so implicitly could betray him so completely and leave him with devastating regrets that would haunt him for the rest of his life. He never, ever, wanted to be blindsided like that again.

So yeah, he understood that kind of deception, and was surprised that he and Chloe shared a very similar past. The revelation was unexpected, and made him feel a strange, emotional bond with her.

The waiter came by with their dinner salads, and once he was gone Aiden returned to their conversation. "How did he change?" he asked gently.

"At first, it was all very subtle and I didn't even realize what he was doing," she said as she pushed her lettuce leaves around on her plate before taking a small bite. "But little by little, he started controlling every aspect of my life. Since we were engaged, it seemed logical to me that we open joint checking and savings accounts together. He monitored everything, which I didn't have a problem with until he started criticizing me for spending even a penny more over *his* budget, even if it was basic necessities that I needed. Yet he never had to account for anything. He obsessively checked my texts and emails, and accused me of sneaking around on him when he had no evidence. He caused problems at the ad agency where I was working, and alienated all my friends so I had no one left but him."

The pain in Chloe's gaze spoke volumes. "Neil also developed an explosive temper I'd never seen before. He was so certain I was having an affair with one of the guys at the office, that one night when I stayed late with Simon to finish up a campaign for the next day, Neil came to the office and physically assaulted the poor guy in front of my coworkers. A few days later, I was conveniently laid off."

Her mouth flattened into a thin, bitter line. "In short, he turned into an asshole. And I was so gullible and stupid I didn't even see it coming until after he cost me my job at the agency."

Instinctively, Aiden reached out and placed his hand over hers, giving it a comforting squeeze. "That doesn't make you stupid, Chloe. Just trusting."

"No, *stupid*," she reiterated adamantly. "My mother has a history of hooking up with these same types of men, the kind that charm their way in, then take over everything. I saw it growing up, over and over again, and I swore I'd never let any man have that much control over my life... It's kind of ironic though, the first guy I get really serious about ends up being a jerk who could have been handpicked by my mother."

Finished with his salad, Aiden pushed his dish aside. "Where has your dad been in all this?"

A hint of sadness passed over her features. "He died in a motorcycle accident before I was born. I never had the chance to know him."

"I'm sorry," Aiden said, blown away by everything she'd just shared. "At least you found out about

Neil's tendencies before you married him." Aiden hadn't been that fortunate.

She stared at him as the waiter cleared their salad plates and set down their dinner dishes. Her expression turned contemplating, and he knew she was analyzing him now that she'd just laid herself bare emotionally.

"Why did you get divorced?" she asked as she picked up a piece of her salmon with her fork.

He took a bite of his steak. His rib eye was just the way he liked it—seared on the outside and medium rare inside. While he appreciated that Chloe had played the game fairly and had answered her question honestly, he didn't want to add his own depressing story about his marriage and divorce to tonight's conversation. And luckily, he had a legitimate excuse not to.

"I plead the fifth," he said, and grinned at her. "The question about serious relationships was *yours* to answer, not mine."

She wrinkled her cute little nose at him. "You suck, Landry."

A teasing glimmer returned to her eyes and he chuckled. "Yeah, I do suck," he said, purposely using the playful innuendo to lighten up their exchange. "Are you sure you want to have *that* discussion?"

"I'm sure it would be a far more enjoyable conversation than the one we just had," she grumbled beneath her breath.

So, she was still holding a little bit of a grudge

that she'd gotten the short end of the stick—so to speak—even though the very personal question had been selected randomly. "Isn't that what this match-making resort, and these games we're playing, are all about?" he asked, looking at the experience as the advertising executive he was. "Meeting someone you're compatible with and having deep, meaningful discussions that dig deeper than all that superficial stuff that doesn't matter when it comes to develop-ing a long-term relationship?"

She arched a brow and pointed her fork at him. "If you'll remember correctly, we weren't originally wearing matching wristbands. So technically, you and I aren't compatible, no matter what Hattie and that silly flower indicated today. So it really wasn't necessary for me to give you all the details of my dysfunctional past with Neil, and my mother."

He couldn't argue her point, but he didn't regret pulling that particular question, or hearing her an-swer. Listening to her story gave him a whole new perspective on her strong-willed personality. Be-neath her driven and focused attitude was a woman who'd been emotionally manipulated by a man she'd trusted, and now she channeled all her energy and passion into the one thing she could control—her career.

Yes, he now had a greater understanding of where her motivation to succeed came from, but it didn't change the fact that her single-minded determina-tion, to the exclusion of everything else in her life, made Chloe the exact kind of woman he'd never get involved with on an emotional level.

His physical attraction to her, however, was beginning to be a whole different issue.

"I know we probably have different views on fundamental and personal matters," he said as he cut off another slice of steak, "but that hot kiss on the plane, and again this afternoon during charades, is more than enough proof that we'd be a perfect match in other ways."

A sensual, knowing smile tipped up her lips. "Well, sexual chemistry wears off, and then you're left with everything that doesn't work in a long-term relationship."

He held her gaze, deliberate and direct with his reply. "Who said anything about long-term?"

Her eyes widened ever so slightly, a little bit shocked at his blatant overture. Yeah, he went there. Put into words what they'd both been sidestepping since the day they'd started working together at Perry & Associates. He wasn't alone in this attraction, and being on this secluded tropical island, their desire for one another was at an all-time high, making the situation ripe for a hot, no-holds-barred tryst.

He'd just issued a subtle invitation, but by the end of the evening there would be no doubt in Chloe's mind exactly what he wanted—a steamy, lust-fueled night of sex with her.

With that decision made, he picked up the die and rolled for his turn. The word *Truth* remained faceup and he watched a slow, tempting smile curve the corners of her mouth. He was certain things were about to get very interesting, since *she'd* be selecting one of the wooden sticks.

Would she keep things modest as he had, or go for something more extreme?

CHLOE LOOKED FROM Aiden to the game containers on the table, quietly contemplating which category she'd choose—mild or wild. Her mind was still reeling after the very personal discussion they'd had...all because Aiden had picked a more reserved question. Considering she was still dealing with the churning in the pit of her stomach that always accompanied thoughts of her relationship with Neil, Chloe was ready to go the spontaneous and fun route to alleviate the tension of everything she'd just revealed to Aiden.

Besides, his insinuation of an affair had completely changed the tone of the game and gave the atmosphere between them a seductive vibe, and that was definitely the path in which she wanted to continue this soiree.

She waited a few seconds while their waiter whisked away their finished dinner plates, then selected a wooden stick from the wild container. She felt her face flame as she silently read the very risqué question, and knew that Aiden was definitely going to enjoy answering this one.

"If I was a type of fruit, what would I be and how would you eat me?"

Pure, unadulterated *wickedness* was the only word to describe the grin on Aiden's lips. "That's easy. You'd be a ripe, juicy peach," he said in a low, throaty sound that hypnotized her. "And you'd be so good to eat. I'd open you up with my thumbs and catch all that sweet nectar on my tongue, and suck gently on the soft center of your core until my entire mouth is filled with the taste of you."

Holy crap. The look in his eyes was so freakin' hot, and combined with that erotic description of him eating her as a peach, well, she felt breathless and thoroughly aroused. Beneath the table, she crossed her legs as a steady, throbbing sensation settled between her thighs, but the pressure only increased that agonizing need he'd just inflicted upon her. To be touched, stroked, sucked...

"Your turn," he said, as if he hadn't just filled her mind with such provocative, unforgettable, erotic images.

She reached for the die and gave it a light toss across the table. The first *Dare* presented itself, and Aiden didn't hesitate in plucking one of the sticks from the wild category. Chloe swallowed hard and prepared herself for an outrageous challenge.

Aiden smirked as he divulged the adventure he'd selected for her. "Pick up a stemmed Maraschino cherry with your lips. Feed the cherry to your partner using only your mouth, then tie the cherry stem using only your tongue. No hands allowed."

"No problem," she said, prepared to dazzle Aiden with her skills in tying a cherry stem with her tongue. Who would have thought that a silly talent she'd perfected as a teenager would come in handy one day?

He motioned to their waiter and asked for a few stemmed cherries. While the other man headed off in the direction of the bar, Chloe glanced around at all the other nearby tables. Everyone was having fun playing the truth-or-dare game. The groups of singles were laughing and cheering their teammates on, and the couples who sat alone like her and Aiden were either engrossed in a truthful conversation, or doing equally intimate dares with their partners.

The waiter returned and set a small plate with three Maraschino cherries in the middle of the table, and at the same time delivered their desserts—a slice of cheesecake drizzled with a rich-looking caramel sauce. Chloe was tempted to take a bite, but not until she finished executing her dare.

Folding her hands securely in her lap, she glanced from the dish, to Aiden. "Since I can't use my hands, you'll have to feed me one of the cherries to get me started."

More than happy to accommodate her, he picked up a cherry by the stem and dropped it into her waiting mouth. First, she had to transfer the actual cherry to Aiden, and in order to do so she needed his lips on hers.

Tucking the piece of fruit against the inside of her cheek, she crooked a beckoning finger at him. "Come closer," she cajoled sweetly, and when he did as she asked, she framed his face in her hands and brought his mouth to hers. "The cherry is for you, but first, you'll have to find it."

She could have kept things chaste and pushed the cherry immediately into his mouth, but this evening wasn't about playing it safe. Not any longer. She kissed him, her lips parting to invite him inside. His tongue glided along hers as they played hide-and-seek with the piece of fruit and she let him chase the treat until she was ready to end the playfully hot kiss. Finally, his tongue curled around the cherry and he drew it into his mouth. She clamped down on the end of the stem between her teeth, allowing him to bite off the Maraschino to enjoy.

While she went to work on the second part of her task, he chewed and swallowed the cherry, then grinned like a rogue. "Not quite as good as eating a peach," he said meaningfully.

Oh, he was so bad. A slow burn blossomed in her belly, and spread lower…to the exact part of her he associated with a ripe, juicy peach. With seductive eyes, he continued watching her as she manipulated the stem with her teeth, lips and tongue. Less than a minute later, she presented him with the cherry stem, now with a tight knot in the middle.

"Voila!" she said, proud of her accomplishment.

Amusement etched his gorgeous features. "Very impressive."

She laughed huskily and gave him something else to consider and mentally fantasize about. "My tongue is quite talented and can do all kinds of neat tricks."

"I'll just bet it can," he murmured, and rolled the die she'd nudged toward him since it was his turn, which landed on another *Dare*.

Feeling bolder and more brazen with each scene they completed, she went straight for a wild adventure. Anticipation spread throughout her entire body as she read his challenge. "Suck on your partner's finger for one full minute."

With a slow, shameless smile that ramped up her awareness of what he was about to do, he gently grabbed her wrist and pulled her hand toward him...and unexpectedly dragged the tip of her finger through the sticky caramel sauce on his dessert plate. The impulsive move startled her, but not as much as the wet heat of his mouth as he gradually pulled her index finger all...the...way...in.

Her breath hitched in her throat, then released in a low, sensual moan as he leisurely sucked the caramel off her finger, his gaze so dark and smoldering she knew what it was like to melt from the inside out. His tongue was as soft as velvet along her skin, and the scrape of his teeth added a sharp, erotic edge of pleasure that made her shift in her chair. With excruciating thoroughness, he licked his way all the way to the tip, then drew the digit deep once again.

Her eyes rolled back, and she bit her bottom lip to hold in another groan. She felt that suctioning pull on her nipples, which peaked into tight, hard pebbles against her top. And when he flicked his tongue along the sensitive skin between her fingers, it was as though he somehow had a direct link to her sex and had just stroked his tongue deep between the moist folds of flesh between her thighs. She had the vague thought that if he kept this up, she was going to end up climbing onto his lap right here and now and demand satisfaction.

Abruptly, he stopped and let go of her hand, jarring her back to reality and the fact that they were in a room full of people. But the hungry look in his eyes told her that he was just as affected as she was. The air between them was fueled with sexual tension, and she needed an orgasm so badly, she was close to begging for it.

Finished playing it safe, she decided to do exactly that. "Aiden—"

He pressed two fingers against her lips and shook his head to stop her words, clearly wanting to be the one to take the lead. "I have one final dare for you, Chloe," he said, his voice low, gruff and just aggressive enough to pique her interest. "I want you. My room. My way. All night long."

She shivered, the promise of pleasure and ecstasy implicit in his proposition. Her answer came without any hesitation whatsoever. *"Yes."*

7

As soon as they stepped into Aiden's hotel room and the door shut behind them, Chloe found herself pressed against the nearest wall with his lips claiming hers in a deep, toe-curling kiss. He skimmed his hands along her curves, palms hard, seeking and propriety. Just the way she liked it.

Reaching the hem of her dress, he pulled the material upward, and she lifted her arms so he could pull it off in one smooth motion, leaving her clad in just her bra, panties and heels. His seductive mouth came back to hers again, his need and hunger matching hers as she eagerly shoved his jacket off his shoulders and helped him out of his shirt, until she was finally able to touch his naked chest.

His skin was hot and firm, the muscles in his abdomen flexing as she dragged her palms all the way down to the waistband of his slacks. Beyond anxious to feel the thick length of his erection in her hands, she fumbled with his belt, trying desperately to release the strip of leather from the buckle so she could unzip his pants.

A rough groan rumbled in his chest, and he grasped both of her wrists and pinned her hands at the sides of her head. He abruptly ended their kiss and rested his forehead against hers, their panting breaths mingling.

"We need to slow this down," he rasped in a hoarse voice.

She rolled her hips toward his, teasing and tempting him the best she could. "Why?"

Bracing his strong thighs against hers to keep her in place, which also served to nudge the impressive ridge of his erection against her belly, he nuzzled the side of her neck with his warm, soft lips. "Because I want to savor everything about this night."

A full-bodied shiver shimmied through her. She turned her head to the side, giving his mouth better access to her throat, and anything else he wanted. She understood his need to enjoy every moment, because there would be no repeat performances once they returned to Boston and their respective campaigns. But right now, she was anxious and impatient and slow seemed…well, too damned slow.

"We can do slow later," she said, groaning as he nipped her earlobe. "You put me right to the edge of an orgasm at dinner and I'm dying for it."

He lifted his head and stared down at her, his expression both pleased and cocky. There were no lights on in his room, but the drapes were wide open and an ample amount of moonlight spilled in, illu-minating his gorgeous features and the wicked glint in his eyes.

"All in good time, Reiss," he murmured, and re-leased her hands so they fell back to her sides. "My way, remember? And we've got the rest of the night to do it a dozen other ways. But right now, I want to take my time, because there are so many things I want to do to you...improper, indecent, down-and-dirty things I've thought about since the day we met."

His arousing promise made her wetter than she already was. Oh, yeah, she wanted those things, too. With effort, she kept her palms flattened against the wall behind her, letting him do this *his way* because she knew the end result would be pure, mind-blowing pleasure for both of them.

"What kind of improper, indecent, down-and-dirty things?" she asked, eager to experience each and every one.

"Things like this..." He slipped his fingers be-neath the straps of her bra and pulled them down her arms. His mouth touched her skin, and he un-expectedly bit the curve of her neck and shoulder with his teeth.

She gasped at the light twinge of pain, enjoying his uncivilized behavior when he was a man who always came across as so refined and sophisticated in the boardroom.

"And this," he continued seductively as he un-hooked her bra, letting it fall to the floor, then filled both of his hands with her breasts. His piercing gaze held hers as he cupped and squeezed the mounds of flesh, while his thumbs brushed over her taut nipples, then lightly pinched them.

She groaned, so turned on she could barely stand.

His eyes smoldered, and his wholly satisfied smile made those secret muscles deep inside her clench in anticipation as he lowered his head and claimed her breast. His tongue swirled around her areola, his teeth rasping and teasing the rigid tip before he drew her nipple into the damp heat of his mouth and sucked hard.

There was no holding back the cry of delight that escaped her lips, or the path of fire he created as his hand trailed down her body and slipped past the elastic waistband of her panties.

"And especially *this*," he murmured against her breast, and with a skillful stroke of his fingers along her swollen, throbbing clitoris, he had her thighs quivering and her heart racing.

That quickly, her body screamed for release, but she knew he wasn't done tormenting her just yet. She closed her eyes, let her head fall back against the wall, and lost her breath when he pushed one, then two fingers, tight and hot inside her body.

His knee wedged between her thighs, coaxing them apart. "Spread your legs wider for me, sweetheart," he commanded and without hesitation she did exactly what he asked, widening her stance for him so that he was better able to thrust deeper.

In...then out. Slowly. Leisurely. His thumb circling, stroking. Again and again, while his mouth and tongue continued its sensual assault on her breasts. Her juices flowed, hot and inviting, adding a slick friction to his intimate invasion. Each enticing caress drove her out of her mind with the excruciating need to climax. Every erotic slide of his fingers made her helpless to do anything but ache for the orgasm he held just out of her reach.

His mouth came back up to her neck, his breath hot against her ear. "You're so warm, so soft and wet."

Moaning softly, she arched against his hand the best she could, craving more. "Stop teasing me."

She felt his lips curve into a smile against her cheek. "Tell me what you want, Chloe, and I'll give it to you."

The dominating edge to his voice, combined with the way he'd already mastered her body, was enough to make her beg without shame. "Please let me come," she whispered, and gasped as he finally gave her exactly what she desired.

He kissed her, his tongue sweeping into her mouth as his fingers plunged deeper, harder, faster, and the pad of his thumb rubbed that sweet, sensitive spot that sent liquid fire rushing through her veins. She clutched at his broad shoulders, her fingers digging into the taut muscles of his back in an attempt to hold on as the tension spiraled tighter and tighter inside her. Suddenly, it was all too much, and she moaned against his lips as an overwhelming climax rippled through her in strong, shuddering waves of rapture.

In the aftermath, her legs buckled, and Aiden wrapped an arm around her waist to give her the support she seemed to need. He lifted his head, that smug, cocky smile on his face, despite the fact that he was still as hard as stone against her belly. "You okay?"

She drew a steadying breath, nodded and gave him the praise he deserved. "I have to admit, *your way* isn't half bad."

He lifted an arrogant brow. "And just think, we're not even close to being done. We've only covered improper and indecent, and I'm *so* looking forward to getting down-and-dirty."

Oh, Lord, so was she.

He guided her to the bed. "Make yourself comfortable. I'll be right back."

As he disappeared into the bathroom, she slipped off her heels, shimmied out of her panties and settled against the pillows. Seconds later he returned with a few foil packets, and he tossed all but one of them onto the pillow beside her. Judging by how many condoms he'd retrieved, he obviously planned on having a very busy night with her. Not that she was complaining.

He stood at the foot of the bed, and she watched as he stripped off the rest of his clothes. He toed off his shoes and removed his socks, then unbuckled his thin leather belt. With a sexy smile on his lips, he unbuttoned and unzipped his slacks, then pushed his pants and briefs down his legs.

Completely naked, she looked her fill of him and sighed with female appreciation. If she thought he was gorgeous in a business suit at work, he was a perfect Adonis wearing nothing at all—lean, muscled and impressively endowed where it counted most. His strong, capable hands sheathed his erection, the sight of him touching his cock adding to the eroticism of the act.

He came up on the mattress, circled his fingers around her ankles and separated her feet until she was sufficiently spread for him. Settling between her legs, he dipped his head and brushed his lips along her inner thigh, making it very clear what he had in mind next.

"Let's see if you taste as good as a peach," he murmured, and used his thumbs to separate her folds so he could sweep his tongue along her sex, licking her with such thorough reverence she felt worshipped.

His fingers joined in, penetrating her aching core. He sucked on her clit as if she were as ripe and juicy as the fruit he'd indicated, then traced his tongue all along her swollen, sensitive flesh before starting the devastatingly erotic process all over again. Multiple times. Her entire body trembled and when he finally let her come, the release was more than just physical—it was beyond anything she'd ever experienced before.

Moaning softly, she reached down and threaded her fingers through his soft, silky hair, unable to recall when a man had ever taken such time and care with her, instead of racing to the main event. Even now, he was nuzzling her thigh and giving her time to catch her breath. It was an intimate act, and more than just about getting her off so he could take his own pleasure. He'd enjoyed going down on her, reveled in her response even, and for that he received extra points.

He straightened and knelt between her legs, his gaze taking a slow, leisurely journey from her thighs all the way up to her face. "That was fun," he said huskily. "And now that we've gotten 'down' out of the way, it's time to get dirty."

In a move that caught her by surprise, he rolled her over so that she was on her stomach, then grasped her hips and pulled her toward him, until she was positioned on her hand and knees, his intentions very clear.

Excitement coursed through her. Obviously, traditional, missionary sex was too tame for a sexual God like him. This position put him in control and fed into the fantasy she'd revealed to him on the plane... where she'd confessed her preference of being taken by a man, aggressively and passionately.

He caressed his palms over her bare butt and squeezed the mounds in his hands. "You have the sweetest, sexiest ass. When you wear a tight skirt at the office, I can't help but stare and fantasize about what it would be like to do this." His fingers traced the crease separating her cheeks, then stroked her inner lips, gliding through her slick heat, driving her crazy until she was on fire for him again.

"And what it would be like to do this," he said, and thrust his cock into her, his thick length stretching her in the best possible way.

They groaned in unison, and she went down on her forearms so that her back was completely arched, allowing him to slide even deeper inside her. With his hands at her waist again, he plunged into her, hard and fast, her body clutching around him hungrily, eagerly.

Another round of tension coiled low and tight in her groin, shocking her. She'd thought he'd wrung everything out of her with those two explosive orgasms, but apparently not, because she started to shake and quiver anew. She fisted the bed covers in her hands, desperate for something to anchor her in a sea of overwhelming sensation.

Behind her, Chloe felt Aiden's restraint start to unravel as he began pumping against her in earnest. His hips surged forward, driving every last inch into her, and she cried out as blissful waves of ecstasy contracted through her, and around Aiden's shaft. Seconds later, a harsh groan vibrated in his chest as he gave himself over to his own powerful orgasm.

He collapsed on top of her, bracing his forearms on either side of her head to keep his weight from crushing her. Still buried deep inside her, he pressed his face against her neck, the scent of his body and down-and-dirty sex surrounding them as their heart rates gradually slowed.

"God, you're even more incredible than I imagined," he rasped against her ear.

An exhausted, incredulous laugh escaped her. He'd just given her three amazing orgasms with utmost enthusiasm, had made her body sing in ways it never had before, and he was complimenting *her?* Unbelievable. *He* was the one who was incredible. And addictive, because now that she knew how good they were together, how was she ever going to give this, and him, up?

She immediately shook that unbidden thought from her mind, just as Aiden rolled off of her and got to his feet. He disappeared for a quick moment into the bathroom to take care of the condom and then he was back, pulling her into his arms, spooning her backside against his chest and thighs.

As nice as cuddling with him was, Chloe suddenly felt an overwhelming sense of apprehension brought on by his physical display of affection. Tonight was supposed to be about *sex,* no post-coital snuggling and getting close involved. And being held in his arms felt much too intimate. It made her feel exposed and vulnerable.

She swallowed hard. Giving her an orgasm while pinning her against the wall was just the way she liked things…aggressive and hot. But *this* was so much more than she'd bargained for with Aiden, and something warned her that falling for him, beyond this coworkers-with-benefits-for-a-few-days arrangement of theirs, wouldn't be difficult to do. And that kind of attachment was something she could never allow—personally or professionally.

Needing space, she tried to wriggle away, but he tightened his arm around her waist, oblivious to her internal distress.

"Stay put, Reiss," he said gruffly. "I'm not finished with you yet. I just need about a half an hour to recharge."

I need to go. She swallowed back the panic rising within her, and tried to keep things light and superficial until she figured out a way to leave without making a scene. "What are you, the Energizer Bunny?"

He chuckled and replied drowsily. "Apparently, with you I am."

She said nothing more, and within a few minutes she felt his body go lax and the rise and fall of his chest deepen. And even though the arm he'd secured around her loosened, her lungs seemed to burn with every breath she struggled to take.

Good Lord, she was going to hyperventilate! What the hell was wrong with her? The crazy temptation to stay the night warred with a deeper common sense. While a part of her liked the warmth and security his embrace provided—it had been much too long since a man had just curled up with her after sex—it was nothing more than a false sense of security. Besides, all this intimate, emotional crap slipping beneath the surface of her skin wasn't what their agreed upon affair was all about, and she'd do well to remember that.

She waited another few minutes, until he relaxed once again and a soft snore rumbled from his chest before she gently lifted his arm and slowly moved off the bed. Leaving the lights off, she found her clothes and slipped her dress back on, sans underwear, and picked up her shoes from the floor. Then she made her way to the door.

If he heard her slip out of the room, this time he didn't try to stop her, and she was relieved and grateful.

THE NEXT MORNING, Aiden strolled into the dining room for the complimentary brunch the resort provided for its guests, surprised to find Chloe already there. She was sitting alone at a table at the far end of the room near a window overlooking one of the tropical gardens outside, eating her breakfast while writing something in a notebook—probably notes for their campaign. That's exactly how he'd spent the past few hours, working on his own presentation and how to best use Hattie-the-matchmaker as his focal point for the campaign.

His stomach grumbled ravenously, demanding to be fed, and he headed straight for the omelet bar and put in his order, then piled his plate high with bacon, fruit and other side dishes. He filled a large glass with orange juice and added a cup of coffee to his tray, then carried his hearty meal toward Chloe's table.

He honestly wasn't sure what to expect from her this morning, not after the way she'd snuck out on him last night while he'd been dozing. The soft click of the door shutting had woken him up, and he'd instinctively known that she was gone. He'd gotten as far as tossing off the sheets and grabbing his pants to put them on so he could go after her, before realizing he'd be chasing after a woman who clearly didn't want to be pursued.

The thought was a much needed reality check that this thing between them was nothing more than a casual island fling. He had no claim to her other than just sex. But he'd be lying if he said that being with Chloe was nothing more than an itch he'd been dying to scratch for the past two years.

Oh, they'd definitely indulged in a whole lot of pleasure, had finally surrendered wholeheartedly to the lust that had burned bright and hot between them for much too long. But afterward, as he'd pulled her into his arms, he'd been filled with a contentment that wasn't all related to his physical satisfaction. It had more to do with how good and right she felt in his arms—more than any woman he'd been with since his divorce.

That realization was like a sucker punch to his stomach and definitely got his attention—because his mind had no business contemplating those thoughts with her. Ever. No matter what the island matchmaker, or the stamen of a flower, revealed.

So, while Aiden was disappointed with Chloe's stealthlike exit last night, he understood why she'd felt the need to leave. She was trying to keep some semblance of normalcy between them, to keep their affair separate from the fact that they still worked together, at an agency that frowned heavily on inter-office romances. It didn't matter that he intended to leave the company within the next few months, especially if he was the recipient of the five-figure bonus that would be awarded to the St. Raphael campaign winner. He and Chloe were opposites in all the important ways that mattered, which meant they had no future together beyond this week.

As he neared her table, she glanced up while taking a drink of her coffee, her eyes widening ever so slightly over the rim of her cup as she watched him approach. Wearing her hair in one of her sleek ponytails, she looked beautiful and fresh-faced, and he'd like to believe that the three orgasms he'd given her last night had something to do with the pink glow on her cheeks.

Yeah, he was totally going to take credit for that.

She was wearing a pair of white shorts, a pink lace tank top and sparkly flip-flops, trying to blend in with every other woman in the dining room. But to him, she stood out like an exotic fruit he wanted to taste—again and again.

Not wanting to risk a rejection until he got a feel

for her mood, he didn't bother asking if she wanted company, just set his tray down on the table and took a seat across from her. She said nothing, but the wary look in her gaze told him that she fully expected an interrogation about giving him the slip after last night's sexcapades. Lucky for her, he wasn't going to complain about it. Hell, he wasn't even going to mention the issue because it was a discussion they didn't need to have.

His plan was to keep things between them light, casual and fun. No morning-after angst necessary.

Scooping up a forkful of his omelet, he nodded toward her notebook. "Already hard at work?"

She shrugged and relaxed somewhat, her obvious relief softening her features. "I had some ideas about a catchy slogan running through my head that I wanted to get on paper before I forgot the words. I always swear I'm going to remember a brilliant idea because it's so ingenious, but if I don't write it down, it slips right through my mind."

He caught the small inkling of a smile teasing the corner of her mouth, a positive sign that things were getting back to normal between the two of them. "I hate when that happens."

She eyed the massive amount of food on his plate. "Somebody is hungry this morning."

He finished eating a piece of bacon and chased it down with a mouthful of coffee, seeing in her eyes that she was teasing him. She clearly had a knack for compartmentalizing sex and work—maybe better than he could because when he looked at her mouth, all he could think about was how he enjoyed kissing her. And not just on the lips, because she tasted sweet *everywhere*. He knew that for a fact now.

He grinned wolfishly and waggled his brows at her. "What can I say? I worked up an appetite last night."

She laughed and dropped her gaze to the slice of cantaloupe she'd picked up with her fingers, examining it more than necessary before taking a bite. She chewed, then spoke. "Speaking of last night, I think we need to establish some rules."

"Okay," he said, and waited for her to steer this conversation in whatever direction she felt necessary.

She licked the remnants of fruit juice off her fingers, making his gut clench with that familiar burn of desire for her. "I just want to be sure that we're on the same page with this temporary affair."

It was a legitimate enough request, and he simplified things for the both of them. "How about what happens at this resort, stays at this resort?" It was a clichéd line, but so appropriate to their situation. "Once we're on the plane back to Boston, we leave it all behind and chalk it up to one helluva good time together. Then we go back to the way things were. Simple, easy and uncomplicated."

Something that looked suspiciously like disappointment flashed in her eyes, then was quickly gone. "Agreed," she said with a succinct nod of her head.

Rules were good, he told himself, and the one he'd just established put things between them back into proper perspective and gave them free rein to indulge in their desires and fantasies. "So, that still gives us four more days to enjoy each other, including today," he said, even as a tiny part of him wondered if he'd be able to get enough of her in that short amount of time.

She flashed him a seductive smile full of promise. "I'm looking forward to it." Finished with the rest of her fruit, she wiped her hands on her napkin. "I have a full schedule of things I need to do today to prepare for my campaign, including meeting with the photographer and the couple he hired for us to use in our shots, but tonight we have a choice between attending a toga party or a masquerade ball. What's your pleasure?" she asked, her tone flirtatious.

"You," he said without hesitation, infusing the one word with erotic intent. "Any way I can have you."

She bit her bottom lip, her gaze flaring with reciprocal lust. "Well, since you had your way with me last night, I think it's only fair that I get my turn this evening."

Oh, hell yeah. Her invitation sent a rush of heat and anticipation through his veins, the kind that would undoubtedly have him spending most the day in a mild state of sexual frustration. "I can't wait."

"Me, either," she practically purred as she rested her chin in her hand. "So, what'll it be. Toga or masquerade?"

Since a toga party reminded him too much of his college fraternity days, he opted for something more low-key. "I vote for the masquerade party."

"Mmm. That would be my choice, as well," she said, her voice laced with approval. "It's perfect for a little mystery and seduction."

Her eyes—dark, sultry and teasing—told him that she was already thinking about all the ways to use that to her advantage.

"In the meantime, I have work to do." She stood up, grabbed her notebook and smiled at him. "I'll see you later, Landry."

He watched the sweet sway of her ass as she walked away, his incorrigible mind filling with the arousing memories of how he'd taken her last night. He groaned to himself and was grateful when she finally disappeared from his view.

He finished his breakfast and decided to use his time wisely and get some work done, too. He had a meeting with Ricardo, the photographer, after Chloe's appointment, and he wanted to find the most opportune places to stage some pictures that would best elevate his visual presentation and showcase his marketing ideas for the St. Raphael Resort.

But first, he wanted to talk to Hattie again, to see if he could figure out the best way to merge her traditional matchmaking methods with the resort's current contemporary approach. Five minutes later, he entered the humid greenhouse and found Hattie talking to another young couple, and he hung back so as not to interrupt their conversation.

Hattie was dressed in yet another cheerful caftan dress, but today she'd worn her long braids down. They were entwined with tiny red flowers, and the length of them nearly reached her waist. As soon as she saw him, her eyes lit up with pleasure, though she didn't approach him until after the other man and woman left the greenhouse.

"You came back, but where is the pretty woman you were with yesterday?" she asked, tipping her head curiously. "Did I scare her off with my bold prediction that the two of you belong together?"

He chuckled. Chloe didn't scare easily, and despite the other woman's claims, he knew the only way he and Chloe would ever be *together* was between the sheets. And as he'd discovered last night, that wasn't a bad place to be with a woman as passionate as Chloe.

"Chloe had other things she needed to do," he explained easily. "I'm here because I'd like to talk to you about your matchmaking abilities. I think the resort's advertising could really benefit by utilizing you and that hybrid flower as an added draw, to romanticize the island and give guests an extraordinary experience they can't get elsewhere. It's a great marketing angle."

Hattie's brows furrowed into a frown. "Tell me something. Do *you* believe I have the ability to know when two people are meant for one another?"

Not wanting to offend the older woman, Aiden thought carefully about his answer before he spoke. "I think your intentions are honest and real, and I think that most people want to find that one special person, which makes it easy for them to believe in your intuition. When it comes to marketing and advertising, that's all that matters."

"What made you so skeptical when it comes to love?" she asked, her tone softening as she tended to the potted plant between them.

He shrugged, not wanting to get into a discussion about his failed marriage and bitter divorce with a woman he barely knew. "I'm just practical when it comes to certain things." Like his feelings for Chloe, which did not include love or a future together. "But that doesn't mean others wouldn't benefit from your knowledge and instincts."

She considered that for a moment as she watered the plant, then met his gaze, a secretive type smile on her lips. "I'll agree to be a part of this marketing angle you want to use for your campaign, and maybe, by the time you leave the island, you'll see for yourself that my prediction about you and Chloe is true, that the two of you are meant for one another."

"Fair enough," he said, though he already knew that Hattie was going to be sorely disappointed, because despite him and Chloe being sexually compatible, that's all there would ever be between them.

8

A WHILE LATER, when Aiden met up with Ricardo at their designated time, Chloe was nowhere to be seen. Aiden discussed the shots he wanted with the photographer, and they started their session with candid pictures of the different activities the resort had to offer. He arranged shots of the professional couple having drinks at the underwater bar at the pool, then on to a more romantic setting of them in one of the upgraded bungalows away from the main hotel. Lastly, they did a fun, playful session of the couple at the beach and frolicking in the ocean.

Aiden figured in the next few days he'd have Ricardo take some pictures of Hattie for him to add to his presentation, and he planned to tape a short video interview with her, too. The more the idea of focusing on the sentimental notion of a traditional matchmaker took shape in his mind, the more enthusiastic he became about the entire concept. Aiden didn't yet know what ideas Chloe was considering for her presentation, but he was confident that he'd be giving the resort a unique and distinctive point of view that would ultimately award him the account. As far as he was concerned, he didn't have to personally believe in Hattie's intuitive nature in order to pitch a convincing and effective campaign.

A few hours passed to midafternoon, and just when Ricardo called the final session a wrap and his crew began packing up all their equipment, Aiden caught sight of Chloe making her way down the pathway to the beach, clearly intending to enjoy the rest of her day now that her work was done. She was wearing a white cover-up and flip-flops, and was carrying a canvas tote bag. She headed toward the private cabanas set up on the sand, not even noticing him standing beneath a large palm tree with Ricardo, in the opposite direction.

As he waited for Ricardo to finish talking to the models, Aiden's gaze strayed back to Chloe, who'd found a vacant cabana with two lounge chairs. She was peeling off her white frock. He nearly swallowed his tongue when she revealed the itty-bitty turquoise bikini that showcased her amazing figure. The top drew his attention to her full, pert breasts, and the tiny bottoms accentuated her slim hips and long, slender legs. She bent over to retrieve her suntan lotion from her bag, then began rubbing the silky oil along her shoulders, arms and chest, over her flat stomach, her thighs, her calves—making him wish he was with her to do the deed himself.

Once she was finished, she angled her chaise so it was in the sun, then reclined on the chair, her entire body glistening in the sunlight like a tempting offering to all mankind.

He bit back a groan of appreciation, and noticed a few other guys in the area casting surreptitious, lust-filled glances her way, too. A possessive emotion spiked through him, along with an unwanted urge to head over to Chloe to establish ownership of a woman that wasn't his—other than sexually, and for only four more days.

You are such an idiot, Landry. Annoyed with himself and his barbaric, antiquated thoughts of claiming Chloe, he scrubbed a hand along his jaw and released a tension-filled breath, which did nothing to ease his internal frustration.

"You've got your hands full with that one."

Ricardo's comment snapped Aiden out of his silent thoughts and he redirected his attention back to the photographer. "Excuse me?" he asked, unsure what the guy meant.

Ricardo grinned in an all-knowing male way. "She has a lot of drive and ambition, in a way that's going to keep a guy on his toes."

Didn't he know it. Professionally, the competition between them had always pushed him to excel, and now personally, he was beginning to feel challenged, as well. And not in a good way. "I've worked with her for two years and she definitely makes me bring my A-game to the table."

Ricardo chuckled as he removed the long lens from his camera and packed it gently in a padded bag. "I bet she does. She said the two of you are competing for this account."

"Yep." He nodded, though it was hard to forget that another ad agency also had a hat in the ring. But for Aiden, his only true competition was Chloe. "The end results should be...interesting."

"Well, good luck with the campaign. And Chloe," Ricardo said meaningfully, a man-to-man look in his eyes. "Having an exciting woman in your life to keep you from becoming complacent isn't a bad thing."

Obviously the other man had seen the way he'd looked at Chloe just a few minutes ago, but Ricardo didn't know his history when it came to women. One in particular—the one he'd chosen to marry. A woman who'd been vibrant, exciting and had provided enough challenges to always keep him guessing. A woman who'd completely destroyed a part of him with her selfish decision to put her career aspirations before anything else in her life, including their marriage vows to honor and respect one another.

Paige had completely shattered his trust, and putting that kind of faith in a woman again was a huge issue he'd carried with him since the divorce. While Paige had walked away without looking back and had gone on to climb the corporate ladder with a high-ranking firm in New York, she'd left Aiden questioning his judgment.

"Looks like a vulture is circling," Ricardo said

in amusement, his gaze trained in the direction of Chloe once again.

Aiden turned his head so quickly he came close to giving himself whiplash. Sure enough, a young guy—shirtless, buff and cocky-looking—was walking up to where Chloe was laid out like a gorgeous, glistening goddess. It was then that he noticed that she wasn't wearing her red wristband, making her free game for the single men at the resort.

Nope. Not gonna happen. She was his...at least for a few more days and nights. That was his excuse, and he was sticking to it.

"Thanks for today, Ricardo," he said, and shook the other man's hand, eager to be on his way. "I'm looking forward to seeing the proofs."

"We got some great shots," the other man said, clearly enjoying Aiden's sudden interest in getting to Chloe. "I'll get them edited and to you on a flash drive by tomorrow afternoon so you can use them for your campaign."

"That's perfect."

Finished with his own work for the afternoon, Aiden followed the pathway to Chloe's lounge chair, his irritation growing as he watched her smile at the other man as he talked to her. She said something to make him laugh, and Aiden thought he'd pop a blood vessel. *Shit.*

Trying not to grind his molars, he stepped up to Chloe's cabana, determined to send her admirer on his way as quickly as possible. The guy frowned at him, as if *Aiden* were the interloper, and not him.

Aiden assumed an assertive stance next to Chloe's chair. "She's already taken." The tone of his voice was equally brusque.

The other guy dropped his gaze to Chloe, waiting for her to confirm or deny Aiden's statement. After a moment she sighed and offered her Romeo an apologetic smile. "Yes, I'm with him."

Immediately, the man held up his hands and backed away, looking contrite. "I didn't know. She wasn't wearing a red band."

She glanced up at Aiden from her reclining chair, her expression reflecting a hint of humor. "I didn't want a tan line."

As soon as the other man was gone, a smile twitched at the corner of her lovely, sensual mouth. "What was *that* all about?" she asked.

Hands on his hips, he shrugged, trying to keep his gaze on her face, instead of leering at her gorgeous breasts, barely concealed by a scrap of bright blue fabric. "Just trying to save you from the buzzards."

She rolled her eyes. "I don't need saving. I'm not some damsel in distress who needs a white knight to rescue her."

Of course she didn't. "When I'm with someone, I don't share."

She laughed at him, the sound light and teasing. "That's a bit of a caveman mentality, don't you think?"

"Caveman?" He smirked, recalling just how she'd liked being manhandled last night. "I'll show you *caveman*."

He pulled off his shirt, then scooped her off the lounge chair and up into his arms. She squealed in surprise, and he grinned as he bounced her and shifted her quickly so that she was slung over his shoulder—caveman style.

A shocked gasp escaped her. "Are you kidding me?"

She squirmed against his shoulder, her slippery, oil-slicked body making it more difficult for him to keep her in place. He locked his arm tight across the back of her knees so she couldn't slide off him, and started down the beach to the ocean. "Does it look like I'm kidding you?"

She tried to kick her feet, all to no avail. Then she smacked his ass. Hard. "Put me down, Landry!"

"Oh, I will," he drawled as he wrapped a hand around her smooth, supple thigh and gave it an affectionate squeeze. He'd release her just as soon as she had a soft surface in which to land.

"Oooh, you are so going to pay for this!"

Considering she was laughing, her threat lacked any true animosity. "I'm sure I will, and I'm looking forward to it," he said, just as he reached the water—and continued wading in until the gentle waves lapped around the hem of his shorts.

"I'm warning you, Landry," she said, exasperation and defiance mingling in her stern tone. "Do not do this!"

"Sorry, babe," he said as he maneuvered her body so she was once again in his arms and he was grinning down at her. "But I really can't resist."

Effortlessly, he tossed her into the clear blue ocean—her arms flailing, eyes wide, and a garbled "arrghhh!" rending the air before she dropped into the water with a satisfying splash, then sank below the surface.

She came up sputtering, wet strands of hair in her face, and he couldn't restrain his deep, throaty chuckle as he started back out of the water. Damn, but that felt good.

"Oh, no you don't," she said from behind him. "You're not getting away until you get dunked, too."

The next thing he knew she'd jumped onto his back and wrapped her arms and legs around him like a monkey. And while he could have kept on walking, he decided to have some fun instead. He let her take him down to the water, just so she felt as though she'd gotten even. When he came up for air, she was trying to swim away, and he went after her for a playful game of chase—giving her a bit of leeway before he caught her in his arms once again.

This time, she came willingly, her carefree laughter making him chuckle, too. He was chest deep in the water, and she entwined her arms around his neck and secured her legs around his waist, clinging to him for support as she fisted her fingers in his damp hair and settled her mouth over his and kissed him…slowly, deeply, thoroughly.

Beneath the water, he cupped her bottom in his hands and pulled her closer, so that his growing erection rubbed between her legs. She groaned blissfully against his lips before ending the heated, lust-fueled kiss and stared into his eyes.

"God, you are so hot and sexy," she breathed. "I can't wait to do you tonight."

He raised a brow. "Do me?"

"Oh, yeah," she said with a nod, her bright green/brown eyes promising all sorts of wicked pleasure. "I'm going to *do you* in ways that are going to make you forget every other woman."

It was quite a claim, but he believed her…because right now, just being with Chloe like this, so playful, flirtatious and incredibly sexy, no other woman existed for him. He wanted her, any way he could have her. For as long as their time together allowed.

"How about a preview?" he teased, wondering if she'd be that bold and brazen, even with them submersed in the ocean.

She shook her head, the long, wet strands of her hair tickling across his bare chest. "I don't want to get kicked off the resort for public indecency."

She was so fun and uninhibited, and he loved seeing this lighthearted side of her, outside of work and all the rules and restrictions that had forced them to suppress their attraction for way too long. "Then give me a hint of what I can expect."

"It will include a lot of licking," she said, as she dipped her head and dragged her tongue along the side of his neck. "And probably some biting…" Her teeth gently nibbled along his jaw to his mouth. "And especially *sucking*."

He groaned like a dying man as she rolled his bottom lip between her teeth and applied enough of a soft, wet suction to inspire all kinds of provocative images in his head. His cock, already standing at attention, grew hard as stone, and there was no doubt in his mind that she felt every inch.

She pulled back and blinked at him guilelessly, as if she hadn't just elevated his internal temperature by ten degrees. "Is that enough of a hint for you?"

"Oh, hell yeah," he said huskily. "You had me at licking. Though biting and sucking are good, too."

She laughed. "You, Mr. Landry, are so *easy*."

He couldn't argue with that, because he was coming to realize that when it came to her, he was easily persuaded, influenced and seduced.

DRINK IN HAND, Aiden casually strolled through the crush of people at the masquerade ball, searching for Chloe in the sea of singles and couples attending the formal affair. Like most of the other men at the party, he'd worn a black suit, while the women were dressed in an array of formal cocktail dresses and elegant gowns ranging in color from basic black to bright jewel tones.

Upon entering the ballroom, everyone had been

required to choose a mask to wear for the evening, and there had been a wide selection to pick from—ones with glitter and jewels, some that looked like butterflies, and others decorated with elaborate feathers, ribbons or lace. Not one for frills, he'd opted for the simple black gentleman's mask, which concealed the upper half of his face.

Music played and a huge buffet of food and desserts were on display for guests, but the only thing Aiden was interested in was finding Chloe. Considering how difficult it was to identify the women wearing masks, he questioned the wisdom of agreeing to meet her here, instead of them coming together.

"Hey, sugar, care to dance?"

Aiden turned toward the petite brunette who'd come up to his side, her blue eyes inquiring beneath the pearl-and-sequin mask hiding her face. She appeared pretty enough, but seemed to be trying overly hard to attract a man in the skintight, strapless, bust-enhancing purple dress she was wearing that screamed *look at my breasts.*

Not even a flicker of interest passed through him, because the only woman on his mind was Chloe. Yeah, he had it bad for her. "Sorry, but I'm with someone," he told the other woman, indicating the red band on his wrist.

She sighed, her lips pursed in disappointment. "I should have known someone as hot as you would already be taken. It seems all the good ones have already been snatched up."

Aiden watched in amusement as the woman continued on her quest to find an unattached guy. Most people had paired off, but there were a few singles still mingling. He supposed not everyone would leave the resort having found someone they wanted to pursue once their time on the island was over.

He absently swirled his scotch in his glass, his gaze stopping on a woman making her way through the crowd and heading toward him. There was no doubt in his mind that it was Chloe, and his body instantly tightened in awareness. He knew that slow, sexy walk of hers that made her hips sway oh-so-sensually, and recognized the compact curves beneath the black dress she wore. A mask with colorful feathers covered most of her features, and while he couldn't see her face, the seductive smile on her lips was pure, provocative Chloe.

Clearly recognizing him, as well, she stopped in front of him and curled her fingers in the lapels of his jacket. Without preamble she tilted her head to the side and settled her mouth against his, kissing him like a woman with a purpose—to drive him out of his mind with wanting her.

He was already there.

Sliding her tongue along his one last time, she ended the mind-bending kiss, and just as mysteriously as she'd materialized, she turned back around and walked away. Seconds later, she vanished into the crush of party revelers—leaving him dazed and intrigued by her flirtatious game of hide-and-seek.

Grinning, he headed in the direction she'd just disappeared, knowing he'd spend the entire night trying to find her if that's what it took. Fortunately, his search only lasted a few minutes, until one of the waiters serving champagne handed him a small sealed envelope with his name on it.

"I was instructed to give this to you."

Recognizing the handwriting as Chloe's, Aiden accepted the note. "Thank you." Breaking the seal, he pulled out a card and read the message she'd written for him.

I want to be your fantasy come true. My room. My way.

God, she already *was* his deepest, most erotic fantasy come to life, and there was no way he could resist her invitation. Tucking the card into his jacket pocket, he removed his mask and left the masquerade ball, his final destination Chloe's hotel room. A few minutes later, he was knocking on her door, his pulse pounding in anticipation of what the night would bring.

Chloe opened the door, now dressed in a deep purple, thigh-length silky robe, her mask gone, though he was pleased to see she was still wearing her black stiletto heels. With a sultry smile, she took his hand and pulled him inside. Somehow, she'd gotten a hold of some candles, which were placed around the room, the flickering flames creating a warm, romantic glow of light. The intoxicating scent of vanilla filled the air, and soft mood-music played from her iPod on the dresser, adding to the seductive atmosphere.

"First, let's get *you* out of some of your clothes," she said, her eyes alight with promise as she pulled his suit jacket off and draped it over the back of one of the desk chairs.

While he toed off his shoes, she tugged on his tie, loosening the strip of material enough to remove it over his head, then she began unbuttoning his shirt and slipped the crisp white cotton over his shoulders and down his arms. He removed his socks, and when he started to unbuckle his thin black belt, she grabbed his wrists and stopped him.

"Leave your pants on," she said, leaning into him to gently nip at his bottom lip. "For now."

"Yes, ma'am," he murmured, letting her run tonight's show without any objection from him.

"Sit on that chair by the bed," she told him, indicating the other desk chair she'd positioned there.

Her request ramped up his curiosity another level as he walked around to the side of the bed. Withdrawing three foil packets from his slacks' pocket, he set them on the nightstand and flashed her one of his charming smiles. "I'm hoping we'll be needing these at some point tonight."

A flirtatious smile touched the corner of her mouth. "Maybe. If you're lucky."

Oh, he was feeling extremely lucky tonight. He

sat down, stretching his legs out in front of him, and clasped his hands over his stomach. He watched as she strolled back to the dresser, touched her iPod, and Kings of Leon's song, "Sex On Fire," started to play.

She slowly made her way back to him, her hips moving rhythmically, while every step she took allowed him a glimpse of creamy bare thigh peeking from the front opening of her robe. Oh-so-slowly, she tugged on the silky belt, letting the material part gradually as she performed a riveting striptease just for him. In time, she shrugged her shoulders and the robe fluttered to the floor at her feet, leaving her standing in front of him in a black lace bra, matching panties and those do-me heels.

It was all he could do to keep from grabbing her and pulling her onto his lap for a more private, intimate kind of dance.

Her fingers slid the straps of her bra down to her elbows, exposing the top swells of her breasts as she reached behind her and unhooked the closure. She straightened her arms, and the lacy fabric joined her robe on the floor, her firm, full breasts on glorious display.

He shifted in his seat as heat and arousal pumped through him, hardening his cock in a flash. The growing bulge in his pants didn't escape her notice, and when she licked her lips, he felt it all the way to his groin.

Christ, she was killing him...in the best way possible.

Closing her eyes, she lifted her arms above her head and started dancing provocatively for him—so confident, sexy and gorgeous. Candlelight flickered across her bare skin, caressing her breasts with a golden warmth as her entire body shimmied and her hips gyrated in time to the music, her every move sinuous and mesmerizing.

And then she began touching herself...

Her fingers threaded through her long, silky brown hair, then leisurely trailed along her throat. He bit back a groan as her hands cupped her breasts, lifting and playing with them, kneading the hard nipples until her lips parted with a soft gasp of pleasure that resonated through him.

Her lashes fluttered back open, and she stared at him, a wicked smile on her lips as her hands continued downward, skimming lightly, playfully, over her flat belly. Slender fingers dipped beneath the waistband of her panties, slid between her thighs and pressed inward. A deep breath shuddered out of her, leaving no doubt in his mind that those fingers were buried in the slick, wet heat of her own arousal. Right where *he* wanted to be.

Her eyes darkened with desire. "Remember that fantasy you told me about on the plane?"

As if he could forget revealing his biggest turn-on. "Watching a woman pleasure herself," he said.

She withdrew her hand and hooked her thumbs into the sides of her panties, pushing them down her legs and off, so that she was now completely naked.

Then she stepped out of her high heels and sat down on the bed directly in front of him, legs together.

God, she was gorgeous, and so damn sexy she stole his sanity and nearly obliterated his self-control. Her rich, dark hair cascaded over her shoulders to her breasts, her taut nipples peeking out through the silky strands. Her skin was flushed from her strip-tease, her eyes dilated with the kind of carnal lust that speared straight to his aching cock.

"I want to be that fantasy for you," she said huskily. "Tell me what you want me to do."

Her irresistible offer stunned him, and made him realize just how much thought she'd put into tonight's rendezvous. No other woman had ever been so uninhibited just for him, and he was glad that Chloe was going to be the one to fulfill this secret fantasy of his.

"Spread your legs and touch yourself," he said, his voice a low, growling demand. "Show me what makes you hot and wet."

"You do," she whispered as her thighs parted wide, giving him the unobstructed view he wanted.

He liked her answer, liked even more how she bit her plump bottom lip as her fingers parted her delicate pink flesh, then glided along her swollen clitoris in slow, lazy circles that caused her to shiver in delight.

"Deeper," he ordered huskily.

Her fingers, damp with her own desire, glided lower, until one penetrated her core, dipping and swirling rhythmically while her thumb continued to caress and stroke her cleft. Her breasts rose and fell, faster and deeper, matching the seductive dance of her fingers on her sex.

His body, already tense with need, was on fire for her. His dick was so hard it hurt, and it didn't help that it was confined inside his slacks. Desperately needing to ease the uncomfortable, building pressure, he unbuckled his belt, unzipped his pants and freed his erection from his boxer-briefs. His groan of relief caught Chloe's attention, and her hungry, lust-filled gaze dropped to his thick shaft.

"I want to watch you touch yourself, too," she murmured.

More than happy to oblige her request, he wrapped his fingers around his cock and began to stroke, root to tip. Slowly. Leisurely. A drop of moisture beaded on the head, and he dragged his thumb through the slick lubrication, using it to increase the friction, just enough to feel good without taking him over the edge.

Her gaze was riveted to his hand stroking his shaft, just as fascinated and aroused by the sight of him masturbating as he was with her display of eroticism.

"Oh, God, Aiden…"

Hearing the catch in her voice, and knowing she was on the verge of climaxing, he gave her that final push she seemed to need. "Let go and come for me, babe," he rasped.

Her fingers moved faster over her clitoris, her hips

jerking, her thighs trembling as her orgasm rocked through her. Tipping her head back, she closed her eyes and whimpered softly, losing herself in her own private world of ecstasy, while allowing him to be a voyeur to her pleasure.

He'd never witnessed anything so freaking hot and erotic, and his own climax surged forward, threatening to erupt. Not wanting to come until he was buried deep inside of her, he tightened his fingers around the base of his cock to keep his release at bay. More than anything he wanted to press her back on the bed and drive into her, but with effort, he held back.

It took her a few extra moments to come down from her high and regain her equilibrium, and when she did she moved off the bed and settled on her knees in front of where he was still sitting on the chair. She grabbed the sides of his pants and pulled downward, clearly wanting them off. He lifted his hips and let her undress him, until he was just as naked as she was.

Smiling like a woman who was about to blow his mind, she pressed her palms against his knees and pushed his legs apart. "This is where the licking, biting and sucking are about to happen," she said, reminding him of the promise she'd made this afternoon at the beach.

Leaning forward, she nibbled her way up the inside of his thigh, her breath damp and hot against his skin, and her teeth eliciting just enough of a sting to elevate his awareness of where she was heading. When she reached his shaft, her tongue came into play, licking a wet path all the way up to the sensitive tip. He groaned, tangling his hands in her hair, and with a devilish smile she wrapped her lips around the throbbing head and pulled him into the lush, silky heat of her mouth...all the way to the back of her throat.

Overwhelming lust pounded at him as her tongue swirled along the length of his cock, and then she sucked him, hard and deep, and he damn near exploded.

Considering how intensely aroused he was, this bit of foreplay was all he could handle without climaxing right then and there. Swearing beneath his breath, he fisted his hands in her hair and pulled her head back until she had no choice but to release him.

Eyes smoldering, she blinked up at him, surprised that he'd ended things so soon, and he quickly explained. "As tempting as your mouth is, I need to be inside you."

Need. Such a strong, emotional word. But that's what she made him feel...a desperate, undeniable demand to be a part of her that shook him to the core. And not just physically. Refusing to overanalyze things when this week was supposed to be nothing more than a fun, sexy affair, he shoved those thoughts and feelings out of his head. Right now, tonight, it was all about pleasure, and nothing more.

Unsure how she wanted to proceed, he let her

take the lead, knowing he'd do whatever she wanted because the end result would be the same no matter what—being buried deep inside her. She reached for one of the condoms on the nightstand and sheathed him. Then she stood back up, straddled his thighs, and with her hands gripping his shoulders and her gaze holding his, she slowly, gradually, sank onto his cock, the fit so tight and hot he didn't even try to stop the low, rough, possessive growl of *need* that escaped him.

He placed his hands at the small of her back as the music on her iPod changed to another feverish song, and she began moving to the heavy, driving beat in an erotic lap dance—her body grinding into his, hips gyrating, thighs clenching tight along his as she rode his shaft.

Moaning softly, she threaded her fingers into his hair, pulled his head back and settled her mouth over his, kissing him deeply, passionately, completely fusing the connection between them. Feeling her body clench around his cock, and knowing she was as close as he was to coming, he slid a hand between them and stroked her clitoris, triggering her release. He thrust upward and surrendered to the wild, intense pleasure pouring through him, while Chloe held on to him as if he were the only solid thing that still existed in a universe that had just tipped crazily on its axis.

He felt the same way and knew that no matter what they'd originally agreed upon when they'd arrived at the resort, things would never be the same between them again. And he wasn't quite sure what to do about that.

9

THE NEXT THREE days at the resort passed quickly for Chloe. The mornings and afternoons were filled with attending activities and working on her ad campaign and presentation, while her nights were spent with Aiden, fulfilling all sorts of fun fantasies and just enjoying one another. Yeah, that was definitely the best part of their time together, she thought as she cast a glance at Aiden where he sat across from her at the spacious boardroom table in one of the conference rooms that the hotel had given them to use during their stay at the resort.

Sex with Aiden was so off-the-charts hot, beyond anything she could have imagined or predicted, and just thinking of being with him made her go all warm and soft inside. Physically, they were incredibly in sync, but as the days passed, she was becoming increasingly aware of the fact that every time they were together, she became more emotionally involved, and that was something she never could have anticipated happening.

She continued to silently watch Aiden, very familiar with the slight crease of his brows that indicated he was deep in thought as he worked. His hair was tousled from being finger-combed, something he did when he was completely immersed in a project. He was wearing a casual T-shirt that clung to his broad shoulders, drawing her gaze to his toned biceps and strong forearms and how those muscles flexed as he typed a steady stream of information on his laptop.

She could sit for hours and marvel at how gorgeous and sexy he was, but that wouldn't be very productive for her, though she had accomplished quite a lot since they'd arrived earlier that afternoon. Chloe figured she deserved a break. Especially after the intense meeting they'd had with the vice president of the resort, Edward Luca, which had given them both the opportunity to ask pertinent questions about marketing strategies and objectives and get a better feel for what they envisioned for the future of the resort.

The knowledge they'd gleaned from Edward had been invaluable, but she and Aiden were still very aware of the fact that there was another ad agency on the island, and they'd had a meeting with the VP, as well. The pressure was on, because today was their last day to gather any last bits of information for their campaigns before flying back to Boston tomorrow.

She and Aiden had both used the large, flat surface of the conference table to spread out the visual presentation boards they'd created over the past few days that included the photographs that Ricardo had taken for them, along with their campaign theme and branding message that would complement their PowerPoint presentations. Chloe had yet to nail her slogan for the St. Raphael Resort; she wanted something simple yet nuanced, and while she had a few ideas in mind, nothing had yet to grab her in terms of giving the client that clear message that would resonate with their target audience.

The one thing she was extremely excited about was the flash mob concept she'd come up with that gave the entire campaign a fun, fresh and hip feel, and would showcase all of the resort's activities and focus on an entertaining matchmaking theme. The ad agency had the means to make the video a viral sensation that would sweep the internet and increase the resort's visibility, while appealing to singles looking for a fun and unique way to find romance, and ultimately, love.

Love. The one word prompted Chloe's heart to flutter wildly in her chest as she stared at Aiden, who was still deep in concentration as he typed away on his laptop computer, oblivious to anything but his campaign. Good God, had she done the unthinkable and fallen in love with Aiden? She swallowed hard in denial, but it was getting more and more difficult to dismiss the intense feelings he evoked that indicated she was perilously close to letting their brief island affair mess with her head and her emotions. And that had disaster written all over it for both of them.

They'd always been friends, and the sex between them had been nothing short of amazing, but spending the past week with him as an intimate couple had unlocked something inside of her that made her want…more. More time with Aiden, and not just between the sheets. And *that* was a huge revelation for her, considering she swore she'd never, ever, allow herself to be that vulnerable with another man again.

But there was no denying that she enjoyed being with Aiden. He made her laugh and he'd even pried some of her darkest memories out of her. She'd shared things with him she'd never intended to, let him into places she'd sealed off after her painful breakup with Neil—and that was something she'd never shared with anyone before.

But the fact remained, they were colleagues, working for a company with a strict no dating policy. She had goals for her future, and the promotion she wanted so badly was within her reach…yet a part of her wondered if she wanted it bad enough to walk away from Aiden after this week together. She gave her head a slight shake at how one-sided her thoughts were. While she and Aiden had had a great time together, he'd never given her any kind of indication that the two of them had a future beyond the resort. And even though she'd opened up about her past with him, he'd remained tight-lipped about his own divorce and what had transpired between him and his ex-wife. But he'd obviously been burned, and she was curious to know what had happened.

With a low groan, Aiden stretched his arms over his head and rolled his neck from side to side, easing the tension that had settled there. "I think I'm just about done."

"Me, too," she said, though there were a few things she needed to refine and tweak. But those could easily be done back at the office. "How did your presentation turn out?"

"Honestly, better than I'd anticipated," he said, a pleased note to his voice. "I just have a few more final touches to add, but I have to admit that Hattie is quite a convincing matchmaker."

Chloe knew he'd spent the past three days interviewing employees at the resort about the older woman's reputation, along with perusing dozens upon dozens of letters written from past guests about how accurate Hattie's predictions had been. Considering how the woman's skills directly related to the resort's main purpose of pairing up compatible singles, Hattie's expertise was hugely overlooked and underutilized. Especially from an advertising perspective.

"It's a fantastic marketing angle," she said, then took a long, cool drink from her bottled water.

"So is your flash mob concept." He leaned back in his chair and smiled indulgently. "It's very current and trendy."

"Thanks." Despite the fact that Perry had instructed them to develop individual campaigns,

Chloe appreciated that she and Aiden trusted each other enough to bounce ideas off one another to help refine their own strategies. He was incredibly creative and insightful, and she loved brainstorming with him.

"I guess it just depends on what the vice president is looking for and what appeals to him the most," she said of their individual ideas. "And we have no idea what the boys are doing, either."

They'd nicknamed the two executives with the Metro Ad Agency "the boys," even though they knew their names—Darryl and Ken. While she and Aiden had seen them around the resort, they hadn't fraternized with the enemy, and they'd been careful about keeping their own advertising concepts under wraps.

Aiden rubbed his thumb along his jaw, the brief hesitation glimmering in his gaze giving way to something more decisive. "Would you like to see my PowerPoint presentation? I'd really like to get your take on it."

Her eyes widened in surprise. Yes, they'd verbally discussed their campaigns over the past few days, but she hadn't expected him to share such an integral part of his presentation with her. It was such a huge show of trust on his part, and she was dying to see what he'd come up with.

"Yes, I'd love to."

He withdrew the small flash drive from the side of his laptop and slid it across the conference table to her. She connected the memory stick to her own computer, and within seconds the program streamed onto her monitor in a compilation of slides spotlighting some of the resort's most spectacular amenities, and featuring photographs of the tropical landscaping, gorgeous beaches and couples enjoying many of the recreational offerings.

The pictures that Ricardo had taken for Aiden conjured excitement and passion, and he'd used them in a way that was romantic and seductive. The presentation segued into a video interview with Hattie in her greenhouse. With a sparkle in her deep brown eyes, Hattie introduced herself as the island's resident matchmaker and spoke about seeing that magic spark between two people and knowing when a couple was meant to be together.

In another clip, upon Hattie's urging, a young man and woman gently grasped the stamen of that pink hybrid flower Chloe and Aiden had also touched. The stem turned a deep, dark crimson in both places, and with a satisfied smile Hattie pronounced them soul mates...if they opened up their hearts and *believed.*

Chloe believed, and that knowledge sent a crazy, unexpected surge of adrenaline rushing through her veins. She might have been doubtful about that flower and Hattie's prediction that first day in the greenhouse, but her shifting feelings for Aiden supported the older woman's claim that he could possibly be *the one* for her.

In her head, she could deny the inevitable all she

wanted, but in reality she knew it was too late. There was no stopping the emotions blossoming deep in her heart when it came to the man sitting across the table from her. It was a frightening realization, because she had no idea how he felt about her.

Aiden's presentation offered hope and romantic possibilities to singles wanting to fall in love, and the irony of Aiden's core message to his target audience wasn't lost on Chloe. He was hinging his campaign on Hattie and her matchmaking intuition, yet he clearly didn't really believe that the older woman had the ability to see a couple's fate. For him, Hattie was nothing more than an advertising tactic to romanticize the St. Raphael Resort and the island itself.

As a marketing ploy, it worked, and Chloe knew in her gut that between her flash mob idea and Aiden's more traditional approach, his packed an emotional punch that would be difficult for her to trump. Not that she wouldn't do everything in her power to sell her concept and give Aiden a fight to the finish. Being competitive was in her nature, and ultimately she wanted the St. Raphael account and the bonus that came with it.

"So, what do you think?"

Chloe didn't miss the anxious note to Aiden's voice, as if her opinion mattered to him. Glancing up from her monitor, she met his gaze and gave him the truth. "I think it's phenomenal."

The stiff set of his shoulders relaxed. "Really?"

She smiled. "Yes, really. But how is it that you and

your presentation made me believe in Hattie and the magic of this island when you have your doubts?"

"I'm creating a perception of the resort and engaging the consumer," he said with a nonchalant shrug. "That's what you and I do. I don't have to believe in the product in order to sell it. As long as it works for the resort and their matchmaking theme, that's all that matters."

His reply was logical and rational, and she couldn't argue his point. "You're right."

He stood up and began gathering the files and papers he'd spread out on his side of the conference table and tucked them into his leather attaché case. "There's a few things I need to follow up on before we leave the resort tomorrow, but we're still on for tonight, yes?"

More than anything, she wanted this last night with Aiden before their affair ended and they returned to real life. And she was feeling selfish enough not to want to share him with anyone, or anything. "Instead of attending the farewell gala, how about you come up to my room? We can order room service and have our own private party, just the two of us?"

His gaze heated, matching the slow, wicked smile on his lips as he added his laptop to his bag. "I like that idea. A lot. I'll come by around seven."

She honestly couldn't wait, and she planned to make the most of their final night together. She watched him walk out of the conference room, already planning in her mind how the evening would go.

It wasn't until she was finished working on her own campaign an hour later that she realized she still had his flash drive with his PowerPoint presentation. She tucked the small device into her briefcase to give to him later, and with the rest of her afternoon free, she decided to take advantage of the complimentary spa package the resort had extended to her when she'd first arrived.

AIDEN ARRIVED AT Chloe's room a few minutes before seven. As he stood in front of her closed door, he was struck with the somber realization that tonight was the end of their time together. Tomorrow was Sunday, and after nearly a week at the St. Raphael Resort, they were heading back to Boston and to real life…as colleagues, not lovers.

His gut twisted with a twinge of disappointment, because he knew that reverting back to being just friends and coworkers was going to be incredibly difficult to do—and it wasn't all about giving up their sexual encounters, though he was definitely going to miss that, too.

No, it had more to do with their comfortable conversations and how quickly and easily he could laugh with her. She made him feel lighter inside than he had in years…and she also made him realize all the things he wanted in his life. Marriage. A family. A wife who shared his same life goals. He wished

Chloe could be that woman, but there was no possible way.

As much as he and Chloe clicked, intellectually and physically, they had no future together. Their goals were on the opposite end of the spectrum. She was career-focused and competitive, and while he admired her drive and determination, all that ambition was a sharp reminder of just how far his ex-wife had gone to achieve her own personal success. Though he no longer believed Chloe would betray him like his ex had, their future desires were incompatible and out of sync.

He exhaled a deep breath and knocked on the door. No matter how hard he tried, he couldn't keep his past out of the equation when looking at his future. So, he'd made sure his heart and emotions were kept out of this affair. It didn't matter that the resident matchmaker had deemed them soul mates, or that a silly flower had backed up Hattie's claim, because he was pragmatic and realistic enough to know that compatibility went much deeper than just sexual chemistry.

Those thoughts quickly fled his mind as the door swung open and Chloe filled the frame, happy to see him, a soft pink flush on her cheeks and the green glow in her hazel eyes outshining the gold and brown. Her peach-colored halter-style dress exposed a lot of smooth, sun-kissed skin that tempted him to touch and caress. She'd left her hair down, falling around her shoulders in those soft, careless waves that told him she'd let her hair dry naturally, instead of blow-drying the silky strands straight. She wore minimal makeup, just a sweep of black on her lashes and a glossy shine on her lips, and he loved this "au natural" look on her.

"I hope you're hungry," she said with a welcoming smile.

Her comment, rife with unintentional innuendo, fed into the need for her that seemed to suddenly consume Aiden. "I'm famished," he murmured as he stepped into her room and kicked the door shut.

Her eyes widened as he pressed her up against the nearest wall and dropped his mouth to hers, devouring her as if he was a starving man and she, his last meal. That's certainly what tonight felt like to him, and he couldn't stop the desperate urge to gorge himself on Chloe in hopes of satisfying that overwhelming need he felt for her.

But as he deepened the kiss and her mouth softened beneath the wild, reckless onslaught of his, the longing inside of him grew stronger, making him feel as though he'd never get enough of this woman, no matter how many times he had her.

He was so lost in the heated desire coursing through him that it took him a moment to realize that Chloe had placed a hand on his chest and was giving him a gentle push to end the kiss. Reluctantly, he lifted his head and stared down at her. They were both breathing hard, and he wasn't sure what to make of her putting a stop to something that clearly could have ended with them both naked and him buried deep inside of her. He knew his thoughts were selfish and reckless, but if this was their last night together, he wanted to make sure they made the most of it.

Chloe ran her tongue along her bottom lip, then smiled up at him. "That was a nice hello, but how about we save the rest of that for dessert?" she suggested huskily. "I went ahead and ordered dinner for both of us, and it's already been delivered. It's going to get cold if we don't get started. Besides, the sun is just beginning to set and I don't want to miss that, either."

Before he could reply, she clasped his hand in hers and pulled him toward the sliding glass doors leading to her balcony, giving him a chance to gather some semblance of control and calm his raging emotions. A small table had been set up for the two of them, with a white tablecloth, silverware and crystal glasses for the bottle of wine she'd ordered. Their dinner was covered with silver domes to keep the contents warm, and they had a spectacular view of the bright orange sun as it slowly lowered itself beyond the horizon.

He sat down next to her and relaxed in his seat, inhaling the scent of jasmine—the island's signature scent. He heard calypso music playing somewhere in the distance, and guessed it was probably drifting from the farewell party. Their dinner was intimate and private, yet still allowed them to enjoy many of the resort's romantic nuances.

"I hope you like chicken primavera," she said as they both removed the cover from their dishes and set them aside.

As soon as the savory scent of creamy garlic basil sauce filled his senses, his stomach rumbled, loud enough for Chloe to hear. She laughed and he grinned.

"I guess I'm hungrier for *food* than I thought."

"Good, because I'm starving," she admitted, smoothing her cloth napkin on lap.

He reached for the bottle of wine and poured them each a glass of the chilled Pinot Grigio, a nice pairing for the pasta. They ate in silence for a few minutes, enjoying the island atmosphere just beyond the balcony, as well as the stunning sunset dipping lower and lower where the ocean met the skyline.

"So, tell me something about yourself that I don't already know," Chloe said after a while, her tone light and casual. "Something that might surprise me."

He knew she was just being conversational, but her personal question struck a chord in him, because the things she didn't know about him were private incidences in his life that he'd normally only share with someone he trusted or had a connection with.

And Chloe, he realized, was both.

He ate a bite of his pasta as he mulled over what he wanted to share with her before deciding to give her some insight into how he'd shunned family expectations to follow his own career path. "I'm the first son in three generations who bucked tradition of getting a job in law enforcement."

"Really?" Her brows lifted in genuine surprise. "I just can't imagine you as a cop. Was your family upset?"

"My mother understood because I was always the creative one with these big ideas, but my father was disappointed in my choice to major in advertising and marketing in college. My grandfather was a cop, then my dad. He was this tough military guy who just assumed that both of his boys would follow in his footsteps." Aiden absently swirled his wine in his glass. "At least my brother continued the proud family tradition, and while my father and brother still give me a hard time about being the black sheep of the family, it's all in good humor."

Her eyes glimmered with amusement, and she tipped her head curiously. "Does your brother at least enjoy being a police officer?"

"He did," Aiden said, then seeing the questions in her gaze, he explained, "A few years ago Sam was shot on the job, and the injury made him reassess what he wanted to do. Now he's a private investigator with his own business, so while he's technically self-employed, he still has some involvement with law enforcement."

She pushed her pasta and chicken around on her plate, then found a carrot and stabbed it with her fork to eat. "He seems like a nice guy."

"*Nice* is being generous," he said, though there

was a rumble of affection in his voice for his brother. "Mostly, he's a pain in the ass."

"I suppose siblings can be a pain sometimes," she said softly, and drained the rest of the wine from her glass.

He heard the wistful note in her voice, reminding him that she was an only child, with a mother who hadn't been an ideal parent. "It's your turn to tell me something I don't already know about you," he said, refilling her glass with more Pinot Grigio and topping off his own.

She leaned forward and whispered mischievously, "I love reading romance novels. The hotter and sexier they are, the better. It's like mind candy after a long day at the office."

Her sexy secret definitely intrigued him, because he would have pegged her for a straight literary fiction kind of girl. "So, you like books with hot sex and a happily-ever-afters?"

She shrugged and placed her fork on her plate, finished with her meal. "It's nice to believe that it's possible."

"You don't?"

A small smile touched her lips. "Well, considering my mother's track record, and my own with Neil, I think I'm better off making my own happiness."

Despite her past experience, he wanted to give her something to believe in. "My parents are still married after thirty-five years, so it's definitely possible."

"And you're divorced."

Her words were direct and to the point, leaving him little choice but to address her statement. "That doesn't mean I don't think I could be happy and settled with someone else who has the same goals and ideals that I do."

She relaxed back in her chair, her eyes meeting his for a moment over the rim of her wineglass as she took a drink. "Was that the problem between you and your ex-wife?" she asked, digging a little deeper. "Incompatibility?"

Aiden had managed to avoid this particular conversation with Chloe numerous times, and he was tempted to evade the discussion now. His marriage and divorce wasn't something he liked to talk about, with anyone, but she'd shared so much with him this past week, he felt compelled to do the same now. And maybe, by getting his own past out in the open it would help to serve as a reminder of why things with Chloe could never work out beyond this temporary affair.

"Paige and I actually had a lot in common," he said, trying to sound nonchalant, even though he knew this conversation was going to dredge up emotions he'd rather not relive. "On the surface, we enjoyed the same things, and had the same interests. She was a defense attorney, so we both had careers in the corporate world that required drive and ambition to succeed. But I never had a clue just how cutthroat she really was."

He rubbed a hand along his jaw, feeling a familiar tension twist through him. "Before we got married, we talked about having a family, and we both agreed we wanted kids after a year or so. But every time I brought up the subject of having a baby, she said she wasn't ready because her career was really starting to take off. I understood and backed off, but when one year turned into two and she claimed she still wasn't ready to have a baby, the issue became a huge source of contention between us."

"I could imagine," Chloe said softly, as if she truly sympathized with the situation. And him.

"The more we fought, the colder and more distant Paige became," he went on, hating this next part but forcing himself to tell her the entire story, no matter how difficult. "Then one day I came home from work and she was already in bed and claimed she wasn't feeling well, but I could tell something was off. Paige was *never* sick. Yet, she'd been fine that morning when we each went to work. I decided to go and get her some soup from a nearby deli, and since it was more convenient to drive her car than mine, I went to grab her keys from her purse and saw this piece of paper with a local hospital logo across the top. I was both curious and concerned, so I read the paperwork and discovered it was instructions for aftercare for a surgical abortion procedure she'd had that afternoon. She'd terminated our baby without ever telling me she was pregnant."

Chloe gasped, her eyes round in shock. "Aiden,

I'm so sorry," she whispered, obviously stunned and appalled by what he'd revealed.

His hand curled into a fist on the table, but he managed to tamp down the bitterness threatening to engulf him. He could recall that moment so vividly, how everything inside him had gone stone cold and yet he'd wanted so desperately to believe that there was some kind of logical explanation for what he'd discovered...for what Paige had done.

Instead, he'd been slapped with the truth of just how little she valued their marriage, and the lengths she'd gone to protect and secure her climb up the corporate ladder. She might as well have stabbed him directly in the heart with a sharp knife; the pain of her deceit had been that enormous and great.

"I confronted Paige, and she didn't even deny it," he said with a harsh laugh that made his chest hurt. "She just calmly told me that the pregnancy was a mistake and she wasn't willing to give up her job to take care of a baby she didn't want. It didn't matter to her what I might have wanted. She gave me no choice in the matter."

Chloe reached across the table and placed her hand over his fisted one, her thumb grazing across his knuckles in a soothing caress. "That was an incredibly selfish thing for her to do."

He met her gaze, seeing the compassion etching her features. He could feel her empathy for what he'd gone through, and her sensitive, supportive response played tug-of-war with his own emotions and made him see her in a different light, too. One week with Chloe, without any outside influences to dictate their feelings, and she was becoming a woman who knew him better than anyone else in recent years.

She stood up, pushed the small table out of the way, and then sat down on his lap, the move more comforting than sexual. He welcomed the tenderness she offered, which was something that had been missing in his life for much too long.

She pressed her warm palm against his cheek, so sweet and caring. "I can't begin to imagine how difficult it was for you to find out about the abortion after the fact. You deserved better than that."

He shook his head, a part of him still mired in the past. "How could I be so wrong about someone—someone I actually married?" It was a question he knew he'd never have the answer to, but it haunted him, nonetheless. "How could the one person I trusted so unconditionally betray me in a way I never thought possible, all because her career was more important than our marriage?"

"You couldn't have known what she'd do, and she should have been open and honest with you, instead of stringing you along with false hopes."

Despite his own bitterness, Aiden realized just how similar their past situations were, more than he ever would have expected. How Neil had presented one persona to Chloe, then revealed another after time. The same as Paige.

She dipped her head and settled her lips on his,

the touch soft and reverent. A healing balm to his fractured soul. He accepted the kiss, wanting it, craving her in ways that went beyond pure physical desire and shook him to the core, making him think about the reasons why he believed things could never work between him and Chloe. Made him wonder how something so wrong could feel so damn right.

His confusion gave way to heated passion as their mouths fused more deeply, and that wild desperation rose within him again. An impatience to have her, to lose himself so completely in her lush body that only the two of them existed, and nothing else. The need to make this one final night together last as long as possible.

Abruptly, he stood up with her in his arms and carried her back into the hotel room. Next to the bed, he set her down on her feet, still kissing her, his hands sliding around to the nape of her neck to untie the bow holding up the top panels of her halter dress. The fabric fell away, and he immediately filled his hands with her breasts, groaning into her mouth as her nipples puckered tight and hard against his palms.

She moaned, too, her fingers slipping beneath his T-shirt to stroke his bare skin, to skim her thumbs across his own rigid nipples while she nibbled on his bottom lip. He pushed the rest of her dress over her hips and let it fall to the floor. She tugged his shirt over his head and tossed it aside.

More languid kisses and sultry caresses ensued as

they finished undressing one another, much too leisurely for his liking. But every time he tried to speed
things up a few notches, she deliberately slowed him
down, making him excruciatingly aware of the fact
that tonight was going to be much, much different
than all the other nights before.

It was so unlike Chloe to want to take her time—
she who always wanted to be in control, to have the
upper hand, who opted for hard and fast over soft and
slow and thorough. But as he followed her down onto
the bed, donned a condom, then moved over her, he
couldn't help but note the subtle change in the back
of his mind and knew exactly what this joining was.

They were making love.

Tonight, there was no hiding behind forbidden
fantasies, wild seductions or frenzied, reckless mat-
ing. The emotion between them was palpable, and it
made him feel raw and exposed. Made his heart feel
wide-open and vulnerable.

Fairly certain that he'd fallen in love with her,
he swallowed hard and tried to maintain his composure. With her soft, giving body pinned beneath
his, the hard length of his cock nestled between her
spread thighs and his hands framing her face, he
saw the longing in her gaze and knew with absolute
certainty that their no strings affair had suddenly
become very complicated. Despite the revelation,
he lacked the willpower necessary to stop whatever
was happening between them, regardless of his own
fears and misgivings. He wasn't sure he even wanted

to, because he didn't know how he was going to live without this, without *her* in his life.

As if sensing his emotional turmoil, she wrapped her slender legs around his waist and urged his hips forward, distracting him with the slick heat of her desire drenching the sensitive head of his dick.

She arched beneath him, restlessly rubbing her breasts against his chest. "Take me, Aiden," she whispered.

Temptation and heaven beckoned, and with a long, grinding flex of his hips he slid all the way home... impossibly, deliciously deep. A perfect fit, she clasped him tight, and as he withdrew then pushed back in, those internal muscles contracted and her soft moan became a whimper of need.

He breathed her name before he claimed her mouth, taking the kiss deeper with a purposeful slide of his tongue. His hips began pumping and grinding against hers, filling her, over and over. He took her with mindless greed, with heat and passion and selfish demand, and knew by the way her body strained against the onslaught of his that he was giving her as much pleasure as he was taking.

She turned wild beneath him, her hips rising to meet each of his heavy, driving thrusts. Her hands gripped his muscled back, holding on to him as she started quivering around his cock, the exquisite sensation more than he could bear. The rolling waves of her release milked his shaft, and he could no longer hold back.

His orgasm slammed into him, exploding out of control, and he came so long and hard he saw stars. And in that moment, he surrendered everything to her…possibly even his heart and soul.

10

AIDEN WOKE JUST before five in the morning, still in Chloe's bed, his body spooning the back of hers and his arm wrapped around her waist. The realization that he was still there when he should have been long gone jolted him to full consciousness.

After their first night together, as if by unspoken agreement, neither one of them had stayed the entire night in the other's bed...and now he understood why. Because sharing this kind of intimacy was a dangerous thing and made their relationship feel *real,* when their affair was only supposed to be a temporary fling.

But last night he hadn't been able to get enough of Chloe, and every time he started to go, she would lure him right back in with a seductive kiss, a whispered promise or an erotic caress...until they were both too exhausted to do anything but fall into a deep, sated sleep together.

Which brought him back around to his current

predicament. He couldn't resist Chloe, that much was clear. But his desire for her went beyond the physical. Everything about her felt good and right, in ways he never would have imagined. She exhilarated him, challenged him in ways he enjoyed, and made him want to open himself up to the possibility of more. With her. Despite her drive and ambition and need to climb the corporate ladder.

Because he was falling in love with her.

The thought terrified him, and it was that tangle of fear currently tightening his chest that had him itching to get out while the getting was still good.

He couldn't stay. He had to leave. Not just Chloe, but the island, too. There were so many conflicting feelings battling within him, and he wasn't ready to face Chloe until he sorted things out in his own head. And the only way he could do that was to put distance between them. He had decisions he needed to make, and none of them were easy. But he just couldn't think straight when he was around her.

Ignoring the dull ache in his chest, he eased away from the delicious warmth of her body. She let out a soft sigh and snuggled into the warm spot he'd left behind, giving him the opportunity to move off the bed. Careful not to awaken her, he quietly got dressed, knowing he was taking the coward's way out, but unable to change what he needed to do...for his own self-preservation.

They were supposed to leave the island today, anyways. He was just taking the very early morning flight out, instead of waiting around for the late afternoon one they'd initially booked. He had everything he needed for his campaign, so there was no reason to stay, and he'd be long gone before she realized what he'd done.

Finding the standard hotel notepad and pen on her nightstand, he wrote her a quick note letting her know he'd flown out early, and that he'd see her back in the office on Monday morning. Then, with one last longing look at her, he silently slipped out of her room and hoped like hell he wasn't walking away from the best thing that had ever happened to him.

CHLOE WASN'T SURPRISED to wake up alone, but as she reread the vague, impersonal note that Aiden had left for her to find, a huge knot of hurt and disappointment twisted inside her stomach. He'd decided to leave the island earlier than their scheduled afternoon flight, and considering it was after eight in the morning, he was likely already gone.

She set the piece of paper back on the nightstand and dragged her fingers through her disheveled hair, reminding herself that no promises had been made between them other than to indulge in a hot affair during their time at the resort.

And today definitely marked *the end,* no matter how much she wished otherwise.

A foolish part of her had hoped that after last night's discussion about his ex-wife, she and Aiden had forged an intimate bond that went deeper than just appeasing their lust for one another. And the way he'd made love to her after sharing something so painful, there had been no denying the emotion and need pouring from him.

Last night had been so different from all the other times they'd been together. When she finally fell asleep, curled up against Aiden, safe and secure in his arms, she'd truly believed that something significant had changed between them. That despite their differences and the standing no dating policy at the firm, that they could quietly continue seeing each other outside of work and find out if what they'd started here on the island translated into a real-world relationship.

But she realized it was all wishful thinking on her part. If Aiden's actions were any indication, he had no desire to continue *anything* with her...and that realization hurt more than she wanted to admit.

She pulled in a deep breath, and the lingering scent of Aiden filled her senses. Refusing to sit in her room for the rest of the morning wallowing in what could have been, she decided she needed to get out, to breathe fresh air and clear her head.

She took a quick shower, changed into a lightweight sundress and sandals, and headed down to the lobby, which was filled with guests going through the check-out process, and groups of people saying farewell to the friends they'd made. There was laughter and lively conversations, as well as many couples walking hand in hand, giving credence to the fact that love matches had been made, and would hopefully flourish even long after they left the St. Raphael resort.

Feeling a twinge of jealousy for those who were heading back home in love and with the promise of a bright, fresh future with someone they'd met, Chloe quickly made her way outside, where it was a beautiful, sunny, breezy day. She walked aimlessly along various pathways, inhaling the familiar fragrance of jasmine, until she realized she'd ended up at the island greenhouses. The flowers beckoned to her, and she didn't hesitate to enter the glass enclosure.

Silence greeted Chloe, along with the perfumed scent of all the tropical flowers growing around her. She was immediately reminded of the first time she'd been in here, with Aiden, and when she caught sight of those fuchsia flowers that Hattie claimed to predict a couple's compatibility, she slowly strolled over to those potted plants and lightly stroked one of the soft, velvety petals.

"Hi there," a familiar female voice said from behind Chloe. "I wasn't expecting anyone to stop by the greenhouse today, not with everyone leaving the island."

Chloe turned around, and as soon as she met Hattie's perceptive gaze, she realized why she'd come here...even if it had been subconsciously. Because she believed Hattie's claim, that the possibility existed that she and Aiden could be soul mates—even if Aiden didn't. Chloe felt the connection in her heart, and other places she'd thought she'd closed off after the way things ended with Neil.

"I was just taking a walk around the area and ended up here," she said easily. "Did you have a busy week here in the greenhouse?"

"Actually, I did. A lot of matchmaking going on, that's for sure," she said with a throaty laugh, then she tipped her head, regarding Chloe a bit more speculatively. "Where is your man? The one so interested in my matchmaking skills, yet so skeptical about love, even when it's right in front of him?"

There Hattie went again, spouting insight about a person. But as far as Aiden was concerned, Chloe had to admit the other woman's intuition was pretty dead-on. "Aiden took the early morning flight out," she said, keeping her reply simple, when it was anything but.

Hattie gently took Chloe's hand between the two of hers, her deep brown eyes kind and tender. "He left you," she said softly, knowingly.

"Yes," Chloe whispered, hating the way her throat closed up with emotion.

"The man is a fool," Hattie said with a scowl that made Chloe chuckle, before the older woman grew serious once again. "But he's also been betrayed in the past and doesn't trust easily. You've been hurt, too. But you, at least, are open to love again."

Hattie's statement was very matter-of-fact, and Chloe no longer questioned how the woman knew such things, especially since what she'd just said was dead-on—about both her *and* Aiden. It was true that the way things ended between her and Neil had left her guarded and more intent on exerting her time and energy on her career, rather than another man. After Neil had taken control of so many aspects of her life and decisions, she'd sworn she'd never give another man that much influence over her.

But with Aiden, there was no emotional power-play between them, just an equal give and take that had turned their flirtatious friendship into something much deeper and caring. This past week with Aiden had made her realize just how much she missed being in a real relationship...one based on mutual respect, caring, great sex and the kind of faith that came in knowing that Aiden would never do anything to deliberately hurt her.

There was no question that her heart ached for Aiden and what he'd gone through with his ex-wife. They both had screwed-up pasts, things that had happened to each of them that kept them from letting someone close again. But after everything they'd shared, she trusted Aiden, and that's what ultimately mattered.

Unfortunately, those feelings weren't reciprocated.

The thought made her chest hurt. "I am open to love again, but that doesn't do me much good when the man I want isn't."

Hattie gave the back of her hand a consoling pat. "You need to give him a little push, I think," she said thoughtfully. "If you haven't told him how you feel, then you need to. Men can be very obtuse that way."

The other woman managed to make Chloe laugh, but her biggest fear was that she'd put her feelings for Aiden out in the open, and he'd reject them. But then again, when had she ever backed down from something she believed in? "No guts, no glory, huh?"

"Yes, you strike me as a woman with a lot of guts," Hattie said, her tone amused. "The worst thing in life is living with regrets. Don't let your man be one of them."

"Thank you," Chloe said, and gave Hattie a hug, because this woman had given her more useful advice in the span of fifteen minutes than her own mother ever had.

Filled with a renewed purpose, she headed back to the resort, wanting to believe that Aiden's reasons for bolting on her were *because* of the emotional impact of what had happened between them. But she wouldn't know for sure, not until she had the chance to ask him herself. Because unlike him, she needed closure to this affair, one way or another. She wanted to look into his eyes, tell him what was in her heart, and know that she'd laid herself bare, with no regrets.

As she made her way into the hotel lobby, she caught sight of Darryl and Ken, the Metro Ad Agency boys, who were talking with Edward Luca, the vice president of St. Raphael Resort. She could tell by their expressions that it wasn't a casual conversation, but rather a more intense discussion that raised her awareness and business instincts. They'd all had their time with Luca during the week to discuss the resort and potential ideas. They weren't supposed to pitch their presentations until next week, after they'd returned to their respective ad agencies to refine their campaigns.

There was just something about how insistent Ken was being with Luca that didn't sit right with Chloe. Curious to know what they were discussing, she stopped at a nearby rack of brochures about the island, and with her back to the trio she perused the selection while blatantly eavesdropping.

"We really feel we have the winning campaign for the St. Raphael Resort, and we're ready to pitch our presentation today, before we leave the island," Ken said, doing his best to convince the VP to give them an edge over the competition, without outright saying so.

It was all Chloe could do to keep her mouth shut, when she wanted to step in and argue just whose campaign was superior. She'd never be so crass in front of the vice president of the resort, but that didn't mean she wasn't going to make damn sure that she and Aiden had their shot, too.

"I have meetings with your agency, as well as Perry & Associates next week," Edward said hesitantly. "I wasn't planning on viewing anyone's campaign here on the island."

"We understand," Darryl chimed in, his tone a

bit more assertive. "But we feel that our presentation is all you need to see to make a final decision."

The man's gall and arrogance made Chloe's blood boil in her veins, and she nearly tore the brochure she held in her hands in half. Maintaining her composure took extreme effort.

"That's very presumptuous of you both," Luca said, his tone frank.

"We're just confident."

There was a distinct pause, then Edward spoke again. "All right," he said, a twinge of reluctance in his voice. "Let's set up a meeting in conference room C in half an hour, and I'll see what you've come up with."

"Excellent," Ken said in a too cocky tone. "We'll be there."

As the three of them went their separate ways, Chloe swallowed back her anger and knew she had no choice but to be present at that meeting, too. Because there was no way she was going to let those boys steal something that rightfully belonged to her or Aiden.

AFTER BOARDING A small puddle jumper plane from the island early that morning, Aiden sat in the Nassau, Bahamas, airport, waiting to catch his connecting flight to Boston. He had a little less than two hours to kill, and way too much time alone to *think*. About Chloe, and the way he'd slipped out on her this morning.

At the time, it had been a defensive reaction, a way to protect himself from having to deal with the intense emotions rioting within him. True, those feelings were still present and wreaking havoc with every rational reason he tried to come up with why things would never work between him and Chloe, so why did he think that any amount of distance was going to change that?

He dragged his hands through his hair, his stomach roiling with a ton of regrets, because he could only imagine how Chloe had felt when she'd realized he'd left without so much as a goodbye, or an explanation. Just a brusque note, when she deserved better than an impersonal brush-off.

Jesus, he was such an ass, and Aiden was certain his brother Sam would heartily agree with that sentiment. If he could turn back the clock and do things differently, he would, but trapped between the island and Boston while waiting for his flight, without any cell service to the island, there was nothing he could do about his stupidity.

Knowing he had no choice but to wait and deal with Chloe and the situation until they were both back in Boston, he decided he needed to keep himself distracted, or let his thoughts drive him crazy. Deciding to use his idle time to refine his presentation, he retrieved his computer from his leather attaché. While his laptop booted up, he reached into the front pocket of his briefcase for the flash drive with his PowerPoint presentation, but it wasn't there.

Frowning, he thought back to when he last remembered having it, and his stomach churned with apprehension when he realized he'd never gotten it back from Chloe.

He didn't believe she'd deliberately kept it from him, and it wasn't as though he didn't have a backup on his laptop's hard drive, but he couldn't stop the niggle of unease coursing through him. He knew how much securing this campaign meant to her—just as much as it meant to him, and he wanted to trust her but...

He shook his head of those negative, cynical thoughts before they could completely form. She'd never do that to him. Then again, hadn't he thought the same of his ex-wife?

No. He wasn't going to go there. He had to believe she wouldn't betray him that way. Besides, what was Chloe going to do with his presentation in a day's time? They were due in the office tomorrow morning, and he'd get the flash drive back then. No harm. No foul.

HEART PUMPING WITH adrenaline, Chloe rushed back to her hotel room, knowing she had a limited amount of time to change into something more professional than her casual sundress, and gather up what she needed to give Edward Luca the best, most cohesive presentation possible with such short notice. Most of her concept was laid out, but she still hadn't come up with a catchy tagline that the resort could use in their advertising and branding. She thought she'd have more time to figure out a slogan, but she was just going to have to wing it. It certainly wouldn't be the first time for that.

Feeling frantic because the clock was ticking, she found a simple black dress that she hadn't worn yet and hastily slipped it on, and added a pair of red pumps. The pop of color gave her a boost of confidence, yet kept her overall appearance classy and sophisticated. Quickly, she pulled her hair into a sleek ponytail, then focused on the material she needed to take with her for this very impromptu meeting.

As she fired up her laptop to make sure that her PowerPoint slides were as clean as possible, she couldn't stop the frustration making its way to the surface. God, she wished that Aiden was still here on the island, that he hadn't left on the morning flight out. Even though they had separate campaigns and ideas to offer, this was something they should be doing *together,* but he'd left her with no choice but to go it alone.

Then she remembered she still had his flash drive with his matchmaking concept on it and experienced a swell of relief. If Aiden couldn't be here, at least she'd be able to pitch his presentation, too, and that's all that mattered—that the two of them got a fair shot at the campaign.

She gathered up her laptop and retrieved Aiden's flash drive and made her way down to conference room C. The door was already closed, and she heard male voices from inside, indicating that the boys were already presenting their campaign ideas to Luca.

She paced the carpeted floor in the hallway, tension tightening across her chest. She didn't usually get nervous before a meeting, but she and Aiden each had so much riding on this deal. She didn't want to blow it for either one of them. Knowing she had to shake off her anxiety, and fast, she leaned back against the nearest wall, closed her eyes, and took the Zen approach. She inhaled deep, tranquil breaths, until a peaceful calm cleared her mind and relaxed her body.

She could do this, she told herself, feeling more in control and focused. She loved to pitch to clients, and she was damn good at it. Today would be no different.

After a short while the door opened, and Edward's voice drifted out into the hallway as he spoke, "I do have to say, your advertising and marketing ideas are solid." Chloe smiled to herself, knowing she and Aiden were still in the game.

She'd been an ad executive long enough to know when a client used a bland word like *solid* to describe a marketing approach, they were being more diplomatic than complimentary. Edward hadn't been all that impressed by what he'd seen. If he had used terms such as unique or innovative, Chloe might have had a cause for concern, but his lack of any obvious enthusiasm filled her with a much needed surge of confidence.

Darryl and Ken strolled out of the room first, both of them wearing smug expressions...until they saw her standing there in the hallway, her laptop tucked under her arm, ready to present her campaign, too. She wanted to laugh at the shocked, *oh shit* looks on their faces, but managed to maintain her composure.

"Darryl. Ken," she acknowledged politely. "Mr. Luca, I'd also like the chance to pitch our company's campaign ideas today."

Edward arched a brow, amusement in his eyes. "By all means, come inside," he said, motioning for her to enter the conference room.

She walked inside, and he closed the door securely after her, watching as she set her laptop on the table and turned it on. He was dressed casually in a pair of khaki pants and a collared shirt, and she had to admit that for a man in his late fifties he was very good-looking. His hair was still thick and dark, though there was some silver at the temples that gave him a distinguished appearance. His body was still trim, his skin tanned, and there was a charm about him that put her at ease.

"You came prepared." He sat down in a nearby chair, then tipped his head curiously. "How did you know that the other agency was presenting their campaign?"

"I overheard them speaking with you down in the lobby, being more than a little insistent about pitching their presentation to you today," she replied honestly as she prepared her PowerPoint slides. "I wasn't about to leave the island without you seeing our campaign ideas, too."

He leaned back in his seat, admiration flickering in his gaze. "I have a lot of respect for a woman with such determination and fortitude."

She accepted his praise with a smile. "Oh, I have plenty of that, Mr. Luca."

"Where is Aiden?" Edward asked. "Shouldn't he be here, as well?"

Yes, he should have been there, but she'd never throw her partner under the bus for her own personal gain. Yes, she wanted this account badly, but she just didn't operate that way. She'd cover for him the best she could. "He had to leave the island early this morning."

"I hope everything is okay?" Edward asked, clearly concerned.

"Yes, everything is fine." She didn't offer details, because they weren't necessary. Besides, she wasn't about to share the real reason why Aiden had left... *her.* "In fact, I have his presentation with me, which is a different concept than my own, so I'm all set."

Edward gave an approving nod. "Excellent. Let's see what you've come up with."

She remained standing and positioned the laptop so that it faced Edward, but she could see the screen, as well, and control the speed of the slide show as she added her commentary to the presentation. She clicked the start button, and the program began to play.

As the slides clicked from one to the other, providing Edward with visual pictures of the resort, the island, the romantic aspects and her fun, sexy flash mob concept that conveyed personality and attitude, she explained the marketing strategies she had in mind, how she could boost their consumer visibility, and finished off her presentation with a memorable hook that would leave Edward wanting more.

"This campaign is all about finding love in paradise," she said, and realized that she'd just discovered her tagline for the St. Raphael Resort. Even she was proof that it was possible, considering she'd fallen in love with Aiden, and she latched on to the slogan.

"Find Love in Paradise," she said again as the slide show ended, this time giving the words more meaning and emotion, which was easy to do, since they came from her heart. "*That's* what your guests can expect when they arrive at St. Raphael."

Edward nodded thoughtfully. "I like it. It's very current and contemporary, but still stays true to the St. Raphael goal of making sure that everyone finds love...in paradise," he said, as if testing the slogan she'd come up with. He smiled, his eyes alight with enthusiasm, and she knew she'd definitely captivated him with her ideas.

She plugged in Aiden's flash drive and switched out her slide show for his, and continued the presentation with seamless ease. "The flash mob concept is certainly more modern, but Aiden has taken a more traditional approach with his campaign. Guests are still exposed to many romantic elements, but the one thing you could use as a draw is Hattie, your island matchmaker."

He frowned in confusion. "Hattie? She's just an old woman who enjoys tending to her exotic flowers and visiting with the guests."

The man had no idea just how valuable Hattie was to him, and the resort, and Chloe planned to enlighten him. "Oh, she's much more than that, Mr. Luca. She comes from a long line of matchmakers, and she's an untapped source that could elevate this resort's reputation. Take a look at this interview Aiden did with Hattie, and imagine the element of fantasy, romance and magic she could add to your campaign and advertising."

She clicked the play button, and the interview streamed onto the computer. Edward watched the video with interest, and she could tell by the surprised look on his face that he was seeing Hattie's potential, and all the ways they could utilize her as a draw to the island and resort.

As soon as the interview ended, she wrapped up the presentation with her closing statement. "Who else in this industry has an island matchmaker? Someone who intuitively knows if two people belong together and has a very high success rate of pairing up compatible couples, and uses an exotic flower to predict a couple's fate? No one. And that gives you, and the St. Raphael resort, a competitive edge."

He nodded in agreement. "It certainly does."

She exhaled a deep breath, knowing she'd given her absolute best, to both campaigns. "So, there you go...an exciting, fun flash mob, or a traditional matchmaker. The choice is yours."

"Both concepts are unique and innovative," he said, making Chloe smile by his choice of words, which were music to her ears. "You've made it very difficult to choose just one."

"Then I've done my job well," she said as she powered down her laptop. She knew Edward wouldn't give her an answer before she left, but she was confident that she'd engaged and captivated him more than the Metro boys had.

Now it was just a matter of which campaign Edward liked better...hers, or Aiden's?

11

AIDEN HAD BEEN home from the airport for a few hours and had just finished his last load of laundry when his cell phone rang. He glanced at the display, surprised to see his boss's cell number, especially since it was Sunday evening and Aiden was due back in the office in the morning.

He connected the call and answered. "Hey, Perry."

"Aiden," the older man said. "I just got a call from Edward Luca, the VP of the St. Raphael Resort. He told me that you had to leave the island early this morning. Is everything okay?"

Aiden inwardly cringed. Perry sounded more concerned than upset that he'd taken an earlier flight out, instead of the scheduled afternoon one, but Aiden wasn't about to tell his boss the real reason why. "I had everything I needed for my campaign, and I had a family situation that needed my attention." The little white lie was better than the truth...that he'd fallen in love with Chloe and didn't know how to handle his feelings for her. God, he was pathetic.

"Well, I just heard from Luca," Perry informed him enthusiastically. "Chloe pitched this brilliant concept this morning that would utilize a traditional matchmaker they have on the island. Luca loved the concept and is going with it!"

Perry went on, but the sudden ringing in Aiden's ears prevented him from hearing anything else. His stomach churned, making him ill, and his head began to spin. Angry thoughts flashed through his mind, fast and furious. Chloe had pitched without him and behind his back? And Jesus, she'd actually used his concept to win over Luca and secure the account? Used it as her own idea and took credit for something he'd created?

He pinched the bridge of his nose with his fingers, trying to see things another way, to think maybe he was wrong. But Perry himself had said, *Chloe pitched a brilliant concept using a traditional island matchmaker.* There was no other explanation.

How could a woman he thought he knew so well, a woman he'd trusted in so many ways, do something so unforgiveable? And how stupid was he for believing she was any different than Paige when it came to her career when he'd known all along how important climbing the corporate ladder was to Chloe?

After everything they'd shared, her betrayal cut deeper and sharper than a knife, and left him reeling with disbelief…yet there was no denying what Perry had just told him.

He shook his head hard, and forced himself to focus on what Perry was saying.

"…I haven't had the chance to talk to Chloe yet," his boss continued. "Luca told me that she missed the afternoon flight out because she'd been doing the presentation. He flew her out by private commuter plane, but chances are she missed her connecting flight in Nassau. I'll just see the two of you in the office in the morning."

"Uh, yeah, sure," Aiden said, because he didn't know what else to say. Besides, he was still trying to process the fact that Chloe had double-crossed him.

He disconnected the call and tossed his cell phone onto the counter. Frustration roiled through him. With no way to confront Chloe when she wasn't back in Boston yet, his anger simmered all night long. By the time he arrived at the office in the morning, he was like a lit fuse waiting to explode.

AFTER ONLY A few hours of sleep in her own bed, Chloe's alarm clock startled her awake. It took everything in her not to hit the snooze button and go back to sleep. Instead she dragged her tired body into the shower. Exhausted or not after her flight snafu yesterday that had finally gotten her back to Boston after midnight, she was expected in the office this morning.

She hadn't had a chance to call Aiden, or talk to

Perry about her spontaneous meeting yesterday with Edward Luca, and she needed to let them both know that she'd already pitched their ideas, and why. She still felt it had been the right thing to do, because there was no way she wanted the Metro boys to have any kind of leverage over her or Aiden.

A hot shower helped to clear her head, but she couldn't shake the fatigue and jet lag weighing her down. She figured it would probably take a day or so for her body to readjust. Dressed in a leopard print A-line skirt, a black silk blouse and black heels, she grabbed her computer case and headed out the door. On the way to work, she picked up a large skinny vanilla latte with an extra shot of espresso, and made it to her office with minutes to spare, even after stopping to say a quick hello to Holly.

She'd just sat down and turned on her computer when she glanced up and saw Aiden heading toward her office, looking as gorgeous as ever in a charcoal-gray suit that fit his broad shoulders and lean frame to perfection. Memories of their time together, the intimate ones where they'd both been stripped bare, emotionally and physically, swamped her. There was no doubt that her feelings for this man had changed drastically during their time on the island, but she still had no idea where she stood with him, and she had to admit, it was a very vulnerable place to be.

His stride was purposeful, his body language tense, but it was the dark, angry look on his face that took her completely off guard. He entered her office, bringing with him a wave of foreboding that sent a chill up her spine...even though she didn't know *why*.

"Hi," she said, and smiled at him, trying to act normal, as if their time on the island hadn't changed anything between them when it came to working together. After all, that had been their promise—that what happened at the resort, stayed at the resort.

He didn't return her greeting, or her smile. Instead, he braced his hands on the opposite side of her desk and leaned toward her, his expression furious. "Are you seriously going to sit there and act as though you didn't screw me over?"

She jerked back, stunned by the bitterness dripping from his voice and the contempt in his gaze—as well as his abrasive, confusing question. "Excuse me?"

"Don't play stupid with me," he said, his voice a low, savage snarl. "You know exactly what I'm talking about. According to Perry, you pitched my goddamned matchmaking concept and won the St. Raphael account."

Two things hit Chloe at once—the startling fact that Aiden already knew about her meeting with Edward Luca, and that Luca had already chosen Aiden's campaign. On the heels of that knowledge came the more painful realization that Aiden had jumped to the automatic conclusion that she'd passed off his presentation as her own to *steal* the account from him.

A crushing pressure banded around her chest. She was devastated that he could so easily think the worst of her, that he honestly believed she'd betrayed him without giving her any opportunity to explain or defend herself against his harsh accusation.

A muscle in his jaw clenched, and his gaze narrowed. "Don't you have anything to say for yourself?"

She pushed aside the pain enveloping her heart, and let her own anger surface. "Why should I?" she said with a shrug that seemed to piss him off even more, but she didn't care. "You think you have it all figured out."

He opened his mouth to say something, but a brusque knock on her office door, and the sound of Perry's voice, stopped him before he could reply.

"Hey, you two," Perry said in a cheerful tone, oblivious to the heated conversation he'd just interrupted. "I need to see both of you in my office right away."

Perry moved on, and Aiden glared at her. "I guess we'll settle this in Perry's office." He pushed off her desk and stalked down the hallway toward the executive rooms.

Chloe slowly stood up, realizing her legs were shaking as she followed Aiden from a distance. The emotions swirling through her ranged from devastation and hurt to indignation. But it was the latter that she focused on as she took a seat beside Aiden in Perry's office.

Their boss looked from Aiden, to her, and frowned, finally sensing the animosity radiating off of Aiden. "Everything okay between you two?"

"No," Aiden said immediately. "Just to be clear, the matchmaking concept that Luca wants for his campaign was *my* idea, not Chloe's."

Perry looked taken aback by Aiden's very pointed claim. "When I called you last night, I never said it was Chloe's idea," Perry said carefully. "What I said was that Chloe pitched a matchmaking concept, Luca loved the idea, and is going with it."

Aiden still didn't look convinced, and it killed Chloe that he thought she was capable of doing something so deceitful, that after two years of working with her and spending a very intimate week together, he didn't trust her to have his back. The conversation they'd had about his ex-wife came back to her, how the one woman who should have been the most loyal to Aiden had betrayed him and their marriage for the sake of career.

She understood that he'd been burned badly in the past, but the fact that Aiden had lumped her into the same category as his ex-wife wrecked her in ways that made her wonder if she'd ever recover. Chloe was the first to admit that she was competitive when it came to her job, but she wasn't devious, under-handed or unscrupulous. She'd certainly never steal a concept or idea from a coworker to win an account.

Somehow, she managed to keep her own temper

in check and addressed Perry. "I'd like to explain exactly what happened yesterday."

Perry waved a hand in the air. "By all means, please do," he said, obviously anxious to clear up the misunderstanding.

"Yesterday, I overheard the boys with the Metro Ad Agency, who were being very persistent about pitching to Luca before they left the island, even though Edward told them he had meetings with both agencies this week," Chloe said, her tone calm and professional, despite the upheaval going on inside her. "Darryl assured him that their presentation was all Edward would need to see to make a final decision, so Luca gave them a meeting time. I decided to show up, too, because I wasn't about to let another agency pull one over on us."

The corner of Perry's mouth quirked up in a smile, as if he admired her gumption as much as Edward had.

"I had Aiden's flash drive with his presentation on it, because he'd shown me his campaign the day before and I forgot to give the drive back to him. But thank God I had it because I was not only able to pitch my own concept, but Aiden's, too, *separately,*" she added, making sure that Aiden understood she'd presented his campaign with just as much dedication as her own.

Finally, she glanced at Aiden. She should have been gratified by the stunned look on his too handsome face as he realized what she'd done *for* him, but the moment lacked any enjoyment because her heart just felt utterly broken.

"And it appears I did a damned good job on your behalf, since obviously Luca liked your idea the best. *You* and your concept won the account, not me," she said, her tone cool. "Congratulations."

"Chloe—"

She'd never know what Aiden had been about to say as she stood up, refusing to acknowledge him.

"What's going on with you two?" Perry asked.

Clearly, their boss suspected something had happened between them on the island. But what did any of that matter when she and Aiden were now adversaries? She'd not only lost Aiden as her lover, but as her friend. And that only compounded her devastation.

"If you'll excuse me, I'd like to get back to my office," she said, and walked out before her forced calm gave way to the full-blown anger still simmering inside her and she gave Aiden a real piece of her mind.

She strode into her office and sat down at her desk, watching as Aiden passed her office on the way to his. She tried to concentrate on answering the emails she'd gotten during her absence, but her mind wouldn't let her focus—on work, anyway— and she knew there was something she had to do to begin to put this whole mess with Aiden behind her. She wasn't sure if that was even possible, but she had to try. The hurt and resentment swirling inside her was only going to grow and get worse if she didn't confront Aiden and get everything out in the open between them.

With determination and a whole lot of irritation driving her, she headed over to Aiden's office and closed the door, because this was something she didn't want the entire floor overhearing. Aiden glanced up, his features etched with misery and contrition. But for her it was too little, too late.

"Chloe—"

She heard the apologetic note to his voice, and refused to let it soften or waylay her. "No, you don't get to talk," she said, quickly cutting him off. "You had your chance and you chose to be an ass and make all kinds of wrong assumptions. Now it's my turn to get a few things off my chest."

He sat back in his chair, quiet and wary.

She braced her hands on the opposite side of his desk, just as he'd done in her office earlier. "I could have just pitched my own concept and never mentioned yours, but I don't operate that way. We've always worked together, as partners, sharing ideas and concepts, and trusting one another. I've always been honest and real with you, and I've given you absolutely no reason to think I'd *ever* betray you."

Emotion clogged her throat, making her realize that this conversation had just turned very personal. Now that the floodgates were open, she couldn't stop the flow of words, or the overwhelming hurt she felt. "*You* left the island, Aiden. You left *me*. Without any kind of explanation. Like what we shared didn't matter to you at all. Not just the sex, but the intimate conversations we had, the way I trusted you with things that had happened in my past. You made me care again when I swore I didn't have it in me, and even worse, I fell in love with you."

The declaration tumbled out, and his eyes widened in shock, then clouded with regret, though he didn't respond—and she didn't want him to, anyway.

"It doesn't matter, though, does it?" she said, hating the pain and sadness in her voice. "Because when it comes right down to it, you don't trust me. You think I'm so focused on my career that I'd do whatever it takes to make it to the top, even steal an idea from my own colleague. From *you*. You want to believe that we're opposites and not compatible in any other way but in the bedroom, but you couldn't be more wrong. We have a lot in common, Aiden, if you'd just seen past the scars that your ex-wife left you with, instead of dwelling on them. I love my job, but I'd never be so underhanded. And just for the record, I'd never sacrifice a baby for the sake of my career. I'm the kind of woman who believes she can have a marriage, family and a profession, so do *not* lump me into the same category as your ex."

He shifted in his seat, his gaze darkening with anguish, and she knew her words had struck a very sore spot for him. Tears choked her, and before the moisture could fill her eyes and she completely lost her composure she turned around and left his office.

She heard him curse, but he didn't come after

her, and honestly, she was glad because she was so close to falling apart. Back in her office, she picked up her phone and dialed Perry's extension. Her call went to his voice mail, and she took advantage of that fact and left him a message, telling him she was exhausted and taking a few days off and would be in touch. With Aiden winning the St. Raphael account, it wasn't as though she was needed at the office.

All she wanted was to be alone with her misery. She needed time and space to figure out what her next move was going to be, because one thing was certain. She could no longer work with Aiden, because seeing him day after day, loving him the way she did, would absolutely destroy her.

She'd have to resign from the firm, she realized, as she tossed a few things into her briefcase so she could work from home. She had a great résumé and it wasn't as though it was the first time she'd started over with a new company. But she knew better than to make a rash decision in the heat of anger, not that she expected to change her mind—or calm down anytime soon.

She stilled when she caught sight of the piece of paper and the tagline for the resort she'd come up with on the spur of the moment and had written down after her presentation with Edward Luca, so she wouldn't forget it.

As if she ever could.

Find Love in Paradise. The laugh that escaped

Chloe held no humor at all. She might have found love in paradise, but her current reality was a nightmare.

AIDEN MET HIS brother Sam's inquisitive gaze from across the table at McGann's Pub, swallowed his pride, and confessed just how badly he'd botched things with the one woman who meant more to him than he ever could have imagined. "I screwed up with Chloe. Big-time." And the worst of it was, he didn't know if he'd be able to repair the damage he'd done.

He'd just finished telling Sam about what had happened between him and Chloe at the resort—from their agreed upon affair, to falling for her, to how he'd thought the worst of Chloe and her intentions when it came to pitching his campaign to Luca. He'd been miserable all day, wanting to apologize and make things right, but considering she'd taken the next few days off of work, Aiden knew she had nothing left to say to him, and no doubt wouldn't listen to him, either. She'd made that abundantly clear in his office that morning.

Not that he could blame her for blasting him with her indignation, which he fully deserved. His behavior, and the conclusions he'd jumped to, were inexcusable, even if they'd been a knee-jerk reaction based on his past. In reality, that made his assumption even worse, because Chloe was nothing like Paige when it came to honesty, integrity and her sense of loyalty. Those were characteristics that mattered to him, and over the past two years of working with Chloe, she'd proved time and again that she was a woman who lived by those traits.

She was right in telling him that she hadn't had to pitch his presentation to Luca, that she could have just promoted her own campaign and not even mention his. Yet she'd delivered his concept with enough persuasion to sell his idea to the vice president of the resort. She was the type of woman he'd always be able to trust to have his back, and he was sick to his stomach to think that he'd destroyed something so precious and rare.

Sam leaned forward in his seat, arms braced on the table and a cold bottle of Guinness in his hand. "Well, the first step to making amends with Chloe is admitting that you're wrong," Sam offered with a hint of humor, trying to make light of a dark situation. "And as difficult as I know that is for you to do, you just confessed that you screwed up."

Aiden raised a brow at his brother, not all that impressed with his worldly advice, but curious to hear what he'd suggest next. "And the second step?"

"Groveling. Lots of it." Sam grinned, as if he'd done his share and was an expert. "Women love that shit."

Aiden shook his head. "That might work with your playmates, but I don't think groveling is going to cut it with Chloe."

"Then just take the direct approach and man up,"

Sam said simply. "You owe her an apology and it's up to you to make her listen to it."

"Kind of hard to do when she won't even listen to me."

"You hurt her, so of course she's going to be standoffish and defensive." Sam took a drink of his beer, paused for a moment, then slanted him a curious look. "Do you care about Chloe?"

"Of course I do," Aiden said, his tone adamant.

"Do you want a *real* relationship with her?"

His brother's question brought up yet another huge obstacle standing in his way. "Yes. But even if Chloe forgives me, having any kind of real, open relationship with her is a whole other complication."

Sam frowned. "How so?"

Aiden swirled the amber liquid in his own bottle of beer. "Everyone at the agency is required to sign a strict no dating policy." It was a common practice in most high-profile firms, because of potential legal issues, conflict of interest and distractions at work. "An office relationship is grounds for termination of employment."

"Awww, shit," Sam muttered, sympathizing with Aiden's dilemma. "That sucks."

The rule definitely put Aiden at a disadvantage, because even if Chloe forgave him and wanted an open relationship, he wasn't willing to risk Chloe losing *her* job. He'd always planned to leave the firm to start up his own ad agency, was nearly there financially thanks to the bonus he'd gotten winning the

St. Raphael account, but this was Chloe's career, and she didn't deserve to be terminated. It was a catch-22 situation, and Aiden needed to figure out a way to not only get Chloe back, but keep their employment intact.

"Do you love her?"

Sam's quiet question made Aiden's heart beat faster. No matter how complicated, there was no denying that he did love Chloe. On the island, during their last night together, he'd known that she was the one he wanted to spend his life with, but he'd been so damned afraid to embrace the emotion and believe he could have a future with her. And then everything had unraveled from there, and he'd let those fears overrule rational thought.

A huge mistake he wanted to rectify.

"Yeah, I love her," he said gruffly.

Sam grinned. "Then do whatever it takes to make it happen, bro. Personally and professionally. I like Chloe and I think she's good for you. You two seem very compatible."

Aiden groaned at his brother's choice of word, since he and Chloe had just spent the past week debating the different aspects of compatibility. They'd each filled out a questionnaire that had deemed them opposites, yet a traditional matchmaker and her mystical flower had determined that they were soul mates. He could believe the results of those quizzes they'd taken, or he could take a chance on what Chloe made him feel. How he loved being with her, laughing with her, having deep, intimate discussions with her that bonded them emotionally.

Ironically, he chose to believe Hattie.

Chloe loved him, and knowing how she truly felt gave Aiden the hope that he still had a chance with her, to make things right and to let her know he wanted a future, and everything that came with it, with her.

Now he just had to figure out a way to have Chloe in his life, without jeopardizing her job.

_12_

AIDEN SPENT MOST of the night tossing and turning, but by the time he arrived at work the following morning, he'd come up with a possible solution to his situation. It was a risky proposition, and it all depended on how lenient Perry was willing to be with Aiden's suggestion, but if his boss didn't agree, Aiden was ready and willing to walk out the door before he'd ever allow Chloe to lose her job.

Aiden was just reaching for the phone on his desk to call and request a meeting with Perry, when his intercom buzzed and Perry's personal secretary, Lena, spoke first. "Aiden, Mr. Perry would like to see you in his office immediately."

Lena rarely used the word _immediately,_ which put an urgent spin to the request. Whatever was on Perry's mind, the other man wanted to address it posthaste, and that could either mean good news, or bad.

Aiden was prepared for either.

"I'll be right there," he said, and within a few minutes he was sitting across from Perry, who appeared calm, composed and very unreadable. Aiden had no idea what to expect.

Perry leaned forward in his chair and clasped his hands together on his desk, all business. "I just got off the phone with Edward Luca, and there's been a change in the campaign and what he wants."

"Okay," Aiden said hesitantly, wondering if Luca had instead decided on Chloe's flash mob concept, or worse, had elected to go with the Metro Ad Agency. A contract hadn't been signed, so the other man wasn't committed to any firm yet and could easily opt to go with a different idea or company.

"Now that he's had time to really think about your concept, and Chloe's, he's decided that he would like to incorporate elements of Chloe's presentation into the campaign, as well," Perry said, his expression remaining serious even though he was imparting some very exciting news. "It seems he likes the idea of using a flash mob as a viral marketing tool, with the focus being on the island matchmaker. He wants to mesh both concepts, and I agree that it could be a very effective campaign."

"That's fantastic," Aiden said, meaning it.

"I'm honestly glad you feel that way, because I wasn't sure you'd be okay sharing the account with Chloe. It would mean splitting the bonus with her, and working closely together for the next few months," Perry said pointedly. "And after what happened in my office yesterday between the two of you,

I have to wonder if that's going to be possible. Care to tell me what, exactly, happened on the island between yourself and Chloe?"

Perry's direct gaze met Aiden's, waiting for him to answer the question. Perry wasn't a stupid man, and probably had a good idea what had transpired on the island. Not just the misunderstanding of her pitching his presentation, but on a more personal level. And Aiden wasn't going to lie about it. This is where he intended to fight for Chloe, and prayed that it all worked out in the end.

He exhaled a deep breath. "Chloe and I broke the no dating policy," he admitted, trying to be as diplomatic as possible with his reply. "And I plan to continue seeing her outside of the office, if she'll accept my apology after yesterday's misunderstanding."

Perry's brows furrowed into a deep frown. "I figured something like that happened between you two, and now we have a situation where the tension has the potential to affect and hurt each of your efforts on the campaign." Perry's lips pursed, and anger flashed in his gaze. "This is exactly why the no dating policy exists. You do understand that this is grounds for termination, don't you? Not just for you, but Chloe, as well? I'm now in the position where I have to fire two of my best executives."

Aiden knew there was a firm stance on the no dating rule, because an intimate relationship with a colleague did tend to affect their working relationship. He'd seen it happen before, in other firms and even this office, and knew that there would be no exception for him and Chloe. One of them would have to leave, and Aiden planned for that person to be him.

"I have a compromise I'd like to offer," he said, because he cared for Chloe, loved her and wanted every aspect of a relationship with her to work. And that meant securing what was so important to her—her job and career. "I'm offering up my resignation, effective in three months, when the campaign for the St. Raphael account has been finalized. At that point, I'd like the entire account to become Chloe's, and *I'll* leave the firm."

Perry stared at him in shock. "You'd sacrifice your job for Chloe's, just like that?"

Aiden nodded, knowing he'd sacrifice a helluva lot more for the woman he'd fallen in love with and wanted in his life—every single day. "That's how much she means to me."

Perry considered his proposition for a moment, then spoke. "I think we could make that work."

Relief poured through Aiden, and he stood, feeling triumphant. "I'd like to get the agreement in writing, sir."

"Fair enough."

Perry stood and the two of them shook hands. "I have to say, I hate like hell losing you, but I have no doubt you'll be just fine."

"I know I will be," Aiden said with certainty. He might be starting his own firm sooner than he'd anticipated, but his decision felt good and right. And with Chloe by his side, supporting him, he knew he'd succeed.

Now, he just had to go and get the girl.

AFTER WORK, Aiden drove directly to Chloe's apartment, admittedly nervous about how this evening might end. He'd like to believe she'd forgive him, but the possibility existed that she wouldn't want to have anything to do with him or his apology.

He refused to even consider the latter.

He knocked on her door and heard footsteps nearing on the other side, then they stopped. Silence ensued. He knew she was looking through the peephole, and enough time passed that he was fairly certain she was going to completely ignore him.

"Open the door, Chloe," he said gently. "I need to talk to you."

No reply. He blew out a frustrated stream of breath and dragged his fingers through his hair. The stubborn woman was going to make him suffer—rightly so—but he could be just as determined.

"There's a lot I have to say, and I'm not going anywhere until I do," he persisted. "If I have to say it from this side of the door, I will, but I'd rather not have your neighbors listening in to the conversation."

Finally, the lock turned and the door opened, with Chloe standing on the other side. She wore a pair of sweatpants and a tank top. She wore no makeup and her hair was in a ponytail. He thought she was the most beautiful woman he'd ever seen—except for the irritable scowl on her face.

"Can I come in?" he asked.

Still not saying a word—though the apprehension in her body language spoke volumes—she stepped aside and let him enter. He'd never been inside her apartment before, and the living area was decorated in deep purples and forest-green. The room was warm, vibrant and inviting—like the woman herself when she wasn't so angry with him.

He turned to face Chloe, who was standing too far away for his liking, but he understood why the distance was there. He'd put it between them, and he hated himself for doing so.

She continued to stare at him, silent, not making any of this easy on him. "I owe you an apology for ever doubting that you'd do anything to hurt me," he said, the words heartfelt.

Her chin lifted an imperious inch. "Yes, you do."

She still wasn't softening, wasn't falling into his arms like he'd imagined. His gut tightened, but he hadn't thought it would be that easy. "I was an idiot, and I'm so sorry, Chloe. For ever believing that you are anything less than someone I can trust unconditionally. I'm sorry for leaving you alone on the island, instead of staying and talking things through with you."

She folded her arms over her chest. "Okay."

Okay? That's all he got...just *okay?*

Her tone was flat and emotionless, and it scared

the hell out of Aiden, made him fear that he was too late to repair any damage he'd done. He swallowed back the huge knot of uncertainty lodged in his throat and tried again. "Will you forgive me?"

"Why should I?" she said with a shrug of her shoulder.

He groaned. She was killing him with her cool indifference, and Aiden was forced to admit that his brother was right. He was going to have to grovel. Pull out the big guns to shake a real, emotional response from her.

"Why should you forgive me?" he asked, slowly stepping toward her. "Because I love you."

She gasped and took a step back, her eyes widening in shock.

Satisfied that he now had her full attention, he continued to move closer. "I'm so sorry that I let my past affect things between the two of us, because you are *nothing* like Paige. I was an idiot, and it wasn't until I'd lost you that I fully realized what holding on to the hurt from that betrayal was costing me. A future with you."

He stopped in front of her. "I know for a fact that you love me," he said, his gaze holding hers as he continued to list all the reasons why she *had* to accept his apology. "Because I want to be with you. Because I want to marry you and create a family together."

She shook her head furiously. "You can't just

come in here and say those kind of things to me, Aiden. Not unless you absolutely mean every word."

God, he loved her fire, her spirit. "I do mean every single word." He took her shaking hands in his, holding them tight. "There's always been something between the two of us. For two years we've worked together and denied our attraction, but a strong friendship developed. And then, on the island, being with you and seeing who you really are away from the office, well, it wasn't hard to fall in love with you. Even Hattie knew before I did," he said with a crooked smile. "I resisted, because of what happened with Paige, but there is no doubt in my mind that I love you, that I want to do whatever it takes to make it work between us."

"Oh, Aiden—" Her voice cracked with emotion, cutting off her words, and moisture shimmered in her eyes.

He panicked, his heart jolting in his chest. "Please tell me that those are tears of happiness."

"They are," she said, and laughed. "Oh, God, they are."

She wrapped her arms around his neck and kissed him, and the emotions that poured through Aiden were stronger than anything he'd ever felt before. He wholeheartedly embraced the feelings, and welcomed the need and desire she evoked in him.

The kiss deepened, the heat and passion between them escalating. Her moan of surrender was his undoing, making him desperate to be inside of her again, to feel that connection, and by mutual agreement they made their way to her bedroom. She was just as frantic as they tugged and pulled their clothes off, until they were both naked and he pressed her down onto the soft mattress. Framing her beautiful face in his hands, he lowered his head and took her mouth the same way he took her body...slowly, deeply, sensuously, until they were both unable to do anything but give in to the inevitable pleasure they created together.

Completely spent and ridiculously happy, Chloe snuggled against Aiden's side and rested her head on his shoulder, feeling more content than she could ever remember. Forgiving Aiden was easy, because she understood why he'd jumped to the conclusions he had, even if it had been a painful experience for her to go through. And, he'd groveled with such conviction and sincerity, which had gone a long way in proving to her that he was a man who could admit when he was wrong.

She sighed and smiled to herself as he lazily stroked a warm hand along her hip and trailed his fingers along the dip of her waist. She was in love, Aiden loved her, and her world couldn't be more perfect...until she remembered the one thing that could tear them apart.

A surge of panic rippled through her, and she lifted her head and stared down at Aiden, who looked up at her with slumberous, sexy eyes. "What are we going to do about work?" she asked. "If anyone finds out that you and I are in a relationship…"

"Perry already knows. I told him about us."

"You did?" Aiden looked so calm and unconcerned, while Chloe couldn't stop the dread swirling in her stomach. "Are we both fired?" She wasn't giving up Aiden, but she would have rather quit the firm, rather than have a termination on her employment record.

"Nobody's fired, and you still have a job," he said, smiling at her. "In fact, Luca called Perry and wants to incorporate both our concepts for his campaign, and so I made a deal with Perry. I'm going to stay for the next three months to help you finalize the St. Raphael campaign, and then I'm resigning from the firm and the account becomes yours, along with half of the bonus."

Her jaw dropped open. "What? You can't do that!"

"I can and I did," he assured her. "It was either that, or one or both of us would be fired. I wasn't going to risk you losing your job."

She swallowed hard, realizing what he'd done for her, what he'd sacrificed. "But what about you?"

"I'm good. Honest." He lifted his hand and tenderly caressed her cheek. "I've been planning on starting up my own ad agency for a while now. This just pushes up the time frame a bit faster. And guess what?"

Humor danced in his eyes, making her smile and curious to know what amused him. "What?"

"If you ever want to come to work for me, which I'm hoping you will at some point in the future, you won't have to worry about a no dating policy." A sinful grin curved his lips. "In fact, I'll have to insist that you sleep with the boss."

She laughed, knowing she'd be taking advantage of that special perk. "You've got yourself a deal."

* * * * *

MIDNIGHT SPECIAL
TAWNY WEBER

Tawny Weber has been writing sassy, sexy romances for the Mills & Boon® Blaze® line since her first book hit the shelves in 2007. A fan of Johnny Depp, cupcakes and colour coordinating, Tawny spends a lot of her time shopping for cute shoes, scrapbooking and hanging out on Facebook. Come by and visit her on the web at www.tawnyweber.com.

To everyone who asked for Hunter's story

Prologue

HE COULD HAVE BEEN WRAPPED around a sexy redhead, letting her use his body to fulfill any number of her kinkiest desires. He could be playing pirate and the captive wench at that very moment, stripping off his eye patch while singing "Love Machine."

But, *no*.

FBI Special Agent in Charge Hunter had figured he'd wrap up the last hour of the day by picking up a low-level criminal reputed to be fencing hot art. Find the guy, work a little intimidation, figure out who he was schlepping bronze nudes for. Easy as one-two-three, done in plenty of time to grab a shower before his date.

Except the dumb-ass fence must've had something hot going down, because after finally tracking him down in that skeezy bar in Hoboken ten minutes ago, the guy had taken one look at Hunter's face, run to his rusty Tempo and peeled out.

Adrenaline racing, he'd chased the idiot over the bridge back into Manhattan. Now, his hands gripping the steering wheel, Hunter stayed glued to the guy's bumper. He eyed the speedometer. One-twenty heading into a residential district. Probably not a good idea.

As chill as if he were on a Sunday drive, he mentally mapped the area, then pressed down a little harder on the gas so his front fender was level with the Ford's rear tires. He feinted to the right, as if he was going to ram the guy. He grinned at the wild-eyed stare in the rearview mirror, quickly followed by a look of desperation. The dumbass cranked the wheel, taking the first right on two tires.

Hunter smirked, easing back on the gas and letting dumb-ass think he was getting away instead of falling into a trap.

"Special Agent Hunter, in pursuit of suspect in Ford Tempo." He reeled off the license number and their current location. "Requesting backup at Pier 57. ETA, three minutes."

Just then, the Ford lost control. The guy bounced his fender off three cars, and then he got stupid. Hunter saw the Ford's rear glass shatter just in time to duck before the bullet came through his own windshield.

Son of a bitch. This was going to screw up his ETA. To say nothing of his date.

Pissed now, he set his jaw, wrenched hard on the steering wheel and used the momentum of the car ricocheting off the curb to slam into the back end of the other car.

Hunter hated being late.

He didn't bother pulling his own gun. He just rammed into the back of the idiot's car. The damned thing exploded. Hunter flinched as the flames lit the night sky, not sure if he was glad or not when the dumb-ass rolled out of the car just before it went kaboom.

The impact of the blast sent his own ride spinning.

He flipped three times, each one sending his brandnew, government-issue vehicle bouncing like a beach ball across the pavement. The seat belt cut viciously across his chest before the air bag deployed with the impact of a fist to the face. Hunter's head snapped back, his ears ringing like the Liberty Bell.

Freaking A.

As his car slid to a stop, his head kept on spinning like the tires that were whirling in the air. With a growl, Hunter decided that, yeah, he was glad the idiot had been thrown clear. Now he could kick his ass.

Climbing out through the window, he grimaced as his palms met a carpet of broken glass. Pain ripped through his head. Muscles, clenched tight during his little loop-de-loop, seized up painfully.

"Sir?"

Knees drawn up, the back of his head resting against his wrecked car, Hunter opened one eye.

"Ferris." Figured. The beat cop was Hunter's age, but gleamed like a bright new penny. Bright, hopeful and so damned young.

"Are you okay?"

"I'm breathing, aren't I?" As long as the air was hitting his lungs, Hunter was on the job and doing fine. "You get my guy?"

"Layton is rounding him up now. An ambulance is on its way."

"He needs an ambulance?" Hunter opened both eyes now, squinting across the dock to the other squad car, the cop and the puny idiot who didn't know how to drive.

"The ambulance is for you."

Hunter sneered. Then, figuring it'd have more impact if he wasn't sitting on his ass, he pushed to his feet and shook his head. He regretted the move when the sky did a slow three-sixty. "I'm fine."

"Uh-huh. Sir, I gotta say, I've worked with a handful of feds over the years. Most of them, they're total paper pushers. But you?" Ferris shook his head, giving Hunter a doleful once-over. "This is the second time in as many weeks I've answered a call with you on the other end. Running out of exploding buildings, high-speed car chases... You might want to sit behind your desk once in a while. Push those papers. Give your body time to recover."

"Desks are for wimps," he said with a dismissive smirk. Desk jockeys meandered up the ladder. Hunter planned to vault his way up. Eight years on the job and he was a special agent in charge. So far, he was doing pretty damned good, about two years ahead of where his old man had been at his age. Not surprising, since his father had wasted time and energy on marriage and a kid. Of course, as the kid in question, Hunter figured the old man's choice had worked out fine. But losing his wife when his kid was six had unquestionably put yet another crimp in the career climb. So, while Hunter was more than willing to follow his father's footsteps as far as his career was concerned, that was as far as it went.

No wife.

No kid.

Just the job.

It'd be nice to quit getting blown up or set on fire, though.

He lifted his hand to the wet patch on his cheek, noted the blood and sighed. Yeah. A break wouldn't be a bad thing.

"Aren't you, like, a boss?" Ferris matched his steps to Hunter's limping stride as they made their way toward the EMTs. "You don't *have* to have the crap trashed out of you on a regular basis, right? You could opt out once in a while."

Well, that was one way of looking at it. Hunter glanced down, saw his new jeans were ripped at the knee, and cussed a mental streak. Dammit. The deputy director wasn't gonna spring to pay for two pairs of pants in a single month. And the shoes were toast, too.

Behind them, a huge explosion was followed by a gust of fiery air. Bits of metal flew through the air, followed by the sound of the firefighters rushing to contain the conflagration.

There went his car.

"Holy shit." Ferris turned to watch the blaze.

Hunter didn't bother looking back.

Not that he'd admit it to anyone, but suddenly the idea of cozying up to a desk for a few days was sounding pretty damned good right this second.

1

A SMART WOMAN KNEW WHAT she wanted, and how to get it.

Marni Clare considered herself damned smart.

Every step she'd taken up the career ladder had been weighed, calculated and carefully thought through. From starting her first newspaper in second grade, to choosing to work as a reporter at smaller papers instead of larger for a chance to build a stronger criminal-reporting portfolio. Right up to her move last year to shift from papers to *Optimum,* a renowned national magazine that'd give her a stronger gravitas.

Everything she wanted always boiled down to her career. And what she wanted right now was information on a patient who'd been admitted here a week ago. The huge explosion of a derelict warehouse owned by reputed mobster and current FBI prisoner Charles Burns had been all over the news.

What hadn't been on the news, but Marni had managed to ferret out using her super-reporter insider info, was that someone had been injured, requiring an ambulance ride to this very emergency room.

She wanted to know who that someone was. Everyone was focused on Burns. On the trial, on the odds of a conviction. Marni had the feeling that whatever had gone down in that explosion, whoever had been involved, was the bigger story, though.

And she wanted it.

But sneaking patient information out of a very ethical nurse wasn't an easy task. It required stealth. A gift with reading people. A little bit of finesse.

And, of course, a bribe.

"I brought you cupcakes. Your favorite, chocolate with raspberry frosting," Marni said, setting a cute little purple basket on the counter and giving her cousin a bright smile.

"You brought me cupcakes?" Sammi Clare-Warren gave Marni a suspicious look. "Why?"

"Why would I bring my favorite cousin cupcakes?"

"You're up to something," Sammi declared knowingly. Still, she did slide the basket closer and sniff at the cupcakes. She gave a hungry little sound, as if she was sniffing at pure temptation, then pushed them back and gave her cousin a narrow look. "What do you want?"

Marni debated. She could tell the truth, that Meghan, Sammi's sister, said her twin had come home eight days ago raving about the drool-worthy, too-sexy-for-words FBI guy who'd been admitted to Emergency after a building exploded.

Or she could just throw herself out now, muttering a lecture on the sanctity of patient privacy and abuse of family ties.

"Wait…" Sammi gleefully drew the word out like she'd just discovered where Marni kept her secret stash of girly toys. "I know why you're here."

"Do you?" Marni wasn't sure if she should pull on an abashed look or go for guilty. It was hard to tell what Sammi suspected.

"You're hoping to meet someone." Sammi's grin was

pure triumph. And now that she'd divined her cousin's ne-
farious scheme, she pulled the basket of cupcakes across
the counter.

"Seriously? You think I'm trolling the emergency room
for a date?" What was wrong with her family? Did they
not know her, not at all?

"Why else would you be here at nine o'clock on a Friday night?"

Marni pushed her hand through her hair. Oh, now that
was just pathetic. Just because she was the only one of her
thirteen cousins still uncommitted didn't mean she was
looking to change that status. Especially not like this. She
didn't figure it conceited to acknowledge that she was a
good-looking, intelligent, fun woman. If she wanted a guy,
there were plenty of better places than this to find one.
But she didn't want a guy. She wanted a career. A fabulous, famous, reporting-on-big stories career.

Which she'd told her family over and over and *over*.

"You think I'm here looking for, what?" She gestured
to encompass the sterile, run-down room. "An old man
with pneumonia and a fat inheritance he's looking to be-
queath? Or a single, male accident victim with a good-
paying job that doesn't live with his mother?"

Sammi peered around the glass partition toward the
waiting room, as if checking to see if either of those potential dates had come in. Then she squinted at Marni.

"You make it sound like the only guys we get in here
are all messed up."

"That's because other than the doctors, whom you've
already deemed not worth setting me up with—" *thank
God* "—the only guys you get in here *are* all messed up."

Choosing the cupcake with the most frosting, Sammi
peeled back the paper liner and took a big bite.

"Then why are you here looking for a date?" she asked around her mouthful of chocolate.

Marni buried her face in her hands and groaned.

"Hey, some of those messed-up guys are pretty good-looking. There's a car accident victim in room five right now even you would drool over. He has that smoldering, sexy thing going on. And muscles. Talk about hot. His shoulders are to die for."

Sammi sighed so deep, she sent the papers on her nursing station fluttering. Marni wasn't sure any man was worth that much oxygen. Not even the one she was after.

Then again, what she wanted from him had nothing to do with the size of his…shoulders. And everything to do with the Charles Burns case. Indicted on SEC fraud and money laundering, the wealthy CEO was on his way to trial. After his dockside warehouse had exploded last week, rumors had started flying that the feds were going to bring new charges.

If she could get a handle on what they were, even an inkling about what had gone down with that explosion, she could write the article of her life. The one that would launch her out of the questionable fluff as the senior editor of Style and Entertainment and into the nitty-gritty of real reporting. Investigative reporting.

Marni gave a mental shiver of delight.

All she needed was a break. And that break was standing in front of her, licking frosting off her knuckles.

"You've had *one* sexy guy in here in the entire month, yet you think this is the place I should look for eligible bachelors?"

"You're the one who came in here looking for a guy." Touché.

"If I wanted a guy—" which she wasn't saying she did "—I wouldn't want one who was sick. I want a guy who's healthy. One who's strong, with a brilliant mind and an intense personality. Sexy and fit, with a body that you can tell he takes care of. Running, swimming, I'm not picky. As long as he's got a sweet ass and some solid biceps. Oh, and washboard abs. There's nothing sexier than a guy with a flat stomach in tight jeans and a T-shirt."

Whew. Marni almost had to fan herself over that image. Not that she wanted a guy. She really didn't. But the fantasy was pretty sweet to entertain, all the same.

"We get guys like that," Sammi assured her. "The hottie that's in here right now? He's all of that and more. I mean, not too many guys can look gorgeous after almost being blown to pieces. But this guy is hot, and not just because his hair was singed."

"Hair straightener gone wrong?" Marni joked with watchful eyes.

"Building gone boom."

Bingo.

"So what's his name?"

A name would tell her if he was really with the FBI. Marni's pulse raced. A name might, with the right research, even tell her what the case was that'd resulted in an exploding building.

"I nicknamed him tall, dark and sexy." Sammi shrugged. "But really, I just know him as 'ruptured inner ear and broken rib.'"

Tall, dark and sexy? What good did that do her?

Well, Marni considered, it might do her good if she was open to getting naked and wild with a guy. But hot sex was on page two of her goal list, something she could get to later. After she'd reached her career goals.

"How can you stand it?" She tilted her head toward the computer. "You claim the sexiest guy you've ever seen was in here, you have his vital statistics, home address, heck, even where he works all there in the computer. You're telling me you don't peek?"

How had she cornered all of the nosiness in her entire family?

"Peeking wouldn't be ethical," Sammi said, her lips a prim bow.

"What fun is your job if you can't peek?"

"Oh, and your job is better? Why don't you get to bring home all those fashions you're always writing about?"

Because the magazine had a strict policy against their reporters accepting products, figuring any gifts would result in a story bias.

Okay, fine. Ethics were a good thing.

But they weren't going to help her get that name.

"There's tons of intrigue and excitement in Style to make up for the lack of perks. You should see how crazy it is during fashion week." Marni didn't add that most of the craziness stemmed from her chafing over always being stuck covering fluff stories. She'd been thrilled to get on with a magazine like *Optimum.* An award-winning periodical with national distribution, covering everything from politics to human interest to entertainment with a little crime and world news thrown in, too. It was a dream job. Originally hired for her gift with human-interest pieces, Marni had quickly realized that wasn't going to get her any big attention. So she'd taken the only senior editorial spot and became the head of Style. But now nobody took her seriously. She was the pretty little blonde with an eye for spotting the next hot trend and a gift for schmoozing with the hoitiest of the toity. But not a real journalist.

This story was it, she vowed. The one that'd make them see her as more than a curvy Kewpie doll with a trivial byline. But first she had to get that name.

"I guess you're right, though." Marni put a heavy pout

into her tone, adding a sigh for good measure. "The magazine really is a lousy place to meet single, heterosexual guys. So maybe you can help me out. Tell me more about the one with the singed hair. He sounds dreamy. Maybe I could meet him."

Marni wanted to cringe, to yell, *Hey, doesn't anyone know me well enough to realize that's total B.S.?* But she knew better. It didn't matter how often she claimed her career was her life, twenty-six was old-maid status in her family.

"Really?" Sammi did a little dance in place, jiggling with enough excitement to dislodge the pencil from behind her ear. "You want to meet tall, dark and sexy? He's in exam room five, and has to walk right past us when he leaves. You can check him out yourself."

Was it the FBI agent? Was he working the same case? Grilling her cousin and trying to sneak out a name was one thing. But actually seeing the guy herself, being able to follow him, maybe even meet him? *Holy cow.* Marni almost did a little dance herself right there on the faded linoleum. It took all her control not to rush down the hall, trying to find the fifth exam room.

"Nurse Clare-Warren?"

The women both turned, Sammi coming to subtle attention for the approaching doctor. "Hang back," she muttered to her cousin with a subtle shooing motion of her fingers.

Using patience she only expended on the job, Marni gave a cheerful nod and stepped aside. All the while pretending she didn't see the doctor trying to catch her eye.

This was it. Her shot. If she pulled off this article, they'd give her a slot as an investigative reporter. Working the crime beat. Digging for details, breaking the big stories. In a world where most reports in the papers and magazines were fed via carefully controlled press releases and media manipulation, she wanted to stand out. To be like the big reporters in the heyday of newspapers. The ones who squirreled out information, who were often as instrumental as cops in stopping crime. The ones who weren't afraid to expose ugliness.

She wanted to be like her aunt Robin. A Pulitzer Prize–winning reporter, she'd given the cold shoulder to traditions, diving into the men's milieu when women were still chained to the oven by their apron strings. She'd jumped right in and made their world her own. She'd interviewed global leaders, had waded into war zones and broken stories on topics as varied as criminal justice and corrupt politicians. Her career was amazing.

Exactly the path Marni wanted for herself. She just needed her break.

And this FBI case, with the exploding building, art theft and rumored mob connections, was going to give it to her. She'd write a huge story exposing the truths, the reality of how the FBI had busted a bigwig CEO, and she'd get the inside scoop on the real crimes of Charles Burns before the trial got going. Fame, fortune, accolades…they were right around the corner.

"Marni." Sammi's impatient tone interrupted Marni's daydream. "This is Dr. Green. Maybe he could show you through the E.R."

Huh?

Shaking off the dream of glory, Marni pulled her attention away from her ambitions and focused on the eager man standing next to her cousin. Forty, balding with bad plugs and a hint of garlic on his breath, he was looking at her as if she was his favorite centerfold come to life.

"Hello, it's nice to meet you," she offered formally, hoping the distant tone would clue him in to her disinterest.

"It's great to meet you," he said, shaking her hand just long enough to make her want to grab the antibacterial lotion off the nurses' station. "Nurse Clare-Warren explained that you're writing an article on our hospital?"

Again, huh?

At Marni's questioning look, Sammi shrugged, then tilted her head toward the no-personal-visitors notice taped on the file cabinet. Then she held up five fingers and tilted her head toward the exam rooms.

Ooooh. Marni offered her cousin, and the good doctor, a big smile.

"You were interested in a tour of our emergency facilities?" he queried, making it sound as though he was extending an invitation to see the backseat of his Lexus. "I'll fill you in on the details of what I do here."

Sammi was now mouthing *married* behind his back and making faces.

Figured.

Still, he could get her in closer eavesdropping range of exam room five, so she might as well take advantage of his interest. In the fake article, and in her body.

When a girl looked like Marni did, the choices were limited. Fight to be taken seriously, courting frustration and disappointment on a regular basis. Or accept that her curvaceous figure, Kewpie doll face, flaxen hair and big blue eyes were the stuff fantasies were made of, and use it to her advantage. Marni wasn't big on frustration, disappointment or losing. So she was all about the advantage.

"Sure. I'd love a tour, especially of the exam areas. That's the focus of the article," she lied. Smiling, she pulled out her ever-present notebook, making sure her elbows angled out so as to keep at least a foot between them. Noting exam rooms one and two to her left, she turned in the opposite direction.

And was pretty sure she heard her cousin giggle as she went. It was hard to tell, though, with the doctor rambling on about his qualifications. A few of them even applied to his job.

"Excuse me, Dr. Green?" An exhausted-looking guy in scrubs stepped out of one of the exam rooms and gestured for help. "A minute?"

The good doctor gave a frustrated huff, then asked Marni to wait.

Her gaze angled one door away, labeled five.

"Oh, sure." She bit her lip, then made a show of making a few notes. "I'll be fine here. I'll just get everything you said written down before I forget."

Giving the doctor a big smile, Marni stepped just a smidge to the left and let her eyes slide past the balding head to the open door of exam room five.

Her heart raced. Her pulse skipped. Her mouth went dry.

Oh, baby.

Those were definitely some sexy shoulders. Right there, above a very nice ass. The shoulders were bare, and Marni was pretty sure it was a crime that the ass was covered.

She'd never wanted anything more than her career.

Until now.

"I DON'T HAVE TIME for this crap."

Hunter glared at the doctor, then shifted the same threatening look at his boss.

"You should have thought of that before you messed yourself up again. What were you doing chasing some low-level art fence? It has nothing to do with the Burns case, dammit." Looking as frustrated as Hunter felt, Deputy Director Murray took the clipboard from the doctor's hands and flipped through the chart. As if he could change the diagnosis by reading it himself. "You should have taken the time off like I ordered."

"That was an order? I thought it was a suggestion," Hunter countered with a grin. At least, it was supposed to be a grin. But the good doctor, his hands now free of the clipboard, was poking at Hunter's ribs again like some kind of sadist. They were cracked again, dammit. He knew it, the doctor knew it, Murray knew it. Poking wasn't gonna change that fact any more than Murray glaring at the chart was going to change the diagnosis of further damage to Hunter's inner ear.

"You're supposed to be on the West Coast to testify in a week," Murray snapped, shoving the metal file at Hunter in accusation. "How are you planning to make that happen now that you're on the injured hero's no-fly list?"

"Seriously?" Hunter asked the doctor. "I can't fly at all?"

"Not unless you want to risk losing your hearing, collapsing in the air or possibly bleeding from the brain." The doctor offered a cheery smile to go with that dire prognosis before stepping out of the room and closing the door behind him.

Well, none of that sounded appealing.

Hunter's brain, still thankfully not bleeding, raced. He had to get to California for that trial.

Charles Burns was a nasty piece of work who thought he was going to skate on the current charges. He'd already won the first round by having the case tried in California, claiming that was his main residence and corporate headquarters. His defense team was the best dirty money could buy and the crooked CEO knew that the worst he'd do was a couple of years and a fistful of fines.

Unless the FBI could pull together all the pieces that had exploded in their lap last week. Pieces that would add racketeering and, if Murray had his way, attempted murder to the list of charges. Burns was so sure that he'd gotten away with murder. The creep had no idea that Hunter had rescued the victim he'd left for dead just before the building exploded. It was up to Hunter to turn a botched homicide into enough evidence to not only put Burns behind bars for life, but take down his entire operation for good.

He had an ace in the hole to make that happen. By hauling Burns's victim out of the explosion last week, before she was blown into tiny bits, he'd secured the devotion—and a huge amount of insider information—from the rumored late Mrs. Burns. In return, he'd promised that she'd stay dead.

"Beverly Burns only agreed to hand over her husband's books, files and passwords in exchange for not being brought into the trial."

Murray waved that away.

"And she's yet to hand it all over. At this point, she's offered up maybe, what? Seventy percent of what she said she would? She's holding out the rest for a cushy life of luxury in witness protection. To hell with that. I don't care if she's interested in testifying or not. We have ways of making people talk."

His eyes narrow with dislike, Hunter asked, "Don't you need a heavy accent and a flashlight when you say shit like that?"

Murray sneered. Hunter's flippant remarks were just one more thing the deputy director didn't like about the man he saw as his subordinate.

"Look, I want this guy put away. We have a witness who can guarantee that. Just because you're all comfy cozy with criminals doesn't mean we should coddle her at the expense of the case."

"Comfy cozy?"

"Black Oak, California," Murray shot back. "Three known criminal elements, and you let them go. Hell, you were best man at one of their weddings last year, weren't you?"

"Caleb Black was DEA and is now the sheriff of Black Oak. Hardly a criminal element."

"And the rest of his family?"

"Well, I did walk Danita down the aisle when she married Gabriel. But I wasn't best man at that one, even though Danita's FBI, too. Maya married an FBI agent as well and I caught the bouquet at their wedding. Is that too cozy?" Hunter made a show of shaking his head in disgust. "Yeah, they're all major criminal elements, all right. Good thing each is assigned their own personal law-enforcement babysitter."

"You think it's funny?"

Yeah, pretty much. Murray was one of those guys who operated in black-and-white. Us and them. Good and bad. Hunter saw life in shades of gray.

He didn't say that, though. Instead, he pointed out, "You're just pissed that you'd have arrested the wrong person."

"I'd have arrested a criminal."

"Tobias Black wasn't behind the crimes in question. Arresting him would have been a grave miscarriage of justice. Just as it will be if you force Beverly Burns to testify against her husband, jettisoning the illusion that she died in that explosion. If Burns knows she's alive, he'll have her killed. He knows she's alive and cooperating with the feds, he'll have her killed faster. She won't make it to the trial."

"She's under FBI protection. She'll make it to testify."

Hunter just stared. Unspoken, but clear, was the truth

that if she testified against her husband, her life expectancy would thereafter be on par with that of a fruit fly.

"This is my case." Ignoring the pained scream from his rib, Hunter got to his feet and gave Murray a look of cold determination. "I've already cleared the plan through all appropriate channels."

"I spoke with the director myself. Unless you can show you've nailed Burns without his wife's testimony, she's taking the stand. You have a week into the trial. Good luck with that." He waited a beat, then with a smile filled with malice, added, "Oh, by the way. How are you getting to California? Driving? You're gonna have a great time building a case from behind the wheel."

That Hunter's car currently resembled tin foil went unspoken. Not because the deputy director was playing nice. But because the man knew the value of leaving the worst unsaid. It lingered there, floating above them like a vile stench.

Hunter debated his options.

"Fine, I'll take a train."

"Train?"

"Sure. There has to be a train going from New York to San Francisco." Despite the fact that the room was spinning in three directions at once, Hunter shifted into intimidation mode, using his four-inch advantage to loom over his boss. "Bottom line, we're not bringing Beverly Burns into this trial. I made a promise. She gave us ample information to indict Burns on twice as many charges as we already had. Enough to shut down his entire operation. In exchange, we not only tuck her away in the hidden depths of WitSec, but make sure everyone believes she died in that explosion."

"The trial is in a week. And we're still desperately sifting through all of that *ample information*. It's not like the pieces we need are just sitting there waiting to be used to nail him to the wall."

"I know the Burns operation inside out. I'll find every single piece," Hunter vowed.

"This case hinges on you, then, doesn't it? Now there's a damned good chance this guy will walk free because you couldn't resist hotdogging it down the pier on the hood of your car."

Hunter gritted his teeth. Asshole or not, Murray was right.

"I can work the case while I'm on the train just as well as I could here in my office. I'll just take it with me."

"Those files are classified."

"I've got clearance. You need more, I'll make a couple of phone calls and get it for you."

Hunter didn't pull the connection card out very often. He didn't need to. His father's legacy at the FBI was the stuff legends were made of. The bureau chief was Hunter's godfather. And his own record wasn't just shiny, it glittered. So while he never played the prima donna, it was pretty rare that he heard the word *no*.

And he wasn't about to hear it now. Murray offered a sour smile. The man knew Hunter was going to vault right over his position on his climb up the ladder. He didn't like it, but there wasn't a damned thing he could do about it.

The doctor stepped back into the room. Face blank now, Murray turned away to make a phone call.

"Here's your prescription, filled. I wrote up a list of dos and don'ts for you to ignore, as well."

"Add the drugs to the list because I'm not taking them." Hunter grimaced as he shrugged into his shirt. Every muscle in his body was screaming.

"You don't take two of these before you go to sleep tonight, you won't be moving tomorrow." He held out the pills and list with a patient smile.

He had a job to do, one he couldn't accomplish doped up. Hunter's eyes cut to Murray's back, then he started buttoning his shirt. The tips of his fingers whimpered their protest.

He wouldn't get it done if he was laid out, either.

"Fine." He stuffed the bottle and paper in the pocket of his leather jacket just as his boss ended his call.

"I pulled some strings and found a vintage rail car heading west. New York to Chicago, Chicago to San Francisco. You've got a private sleeper car on the Midnight Special. It leaves tonight at nine forty-five. An agent will meet you in Chicago with the files, a secured laptop and luggage."

Hunter didn't gloat. Why would he? He'd known he'd win all along.

"Midnight Special?" It sounded like something offered by a discount prostitute.

"It's a restored luxury train owned by a private rail company. This is some kind of themed trip. Passengers are required to participate."

"I don't play dress up."

"You do if you want on this train."

Hunter just stared, his gaze steely and his jaw set.

"You want to find something else, feel free. You want to go now, the train leaves at nine forty-five," Murray said again, his smile just this side of gloating.

He could ignore the participation requirement once he was there. But he just had to get on that train. Hunter glanced at his watch.

"It's quarter of eight now."

"Guess you'd better hurry, then."

2

ALL MARNI COULD HEAR from the exam room were murmurs. Words like *expert witness, new information* and *vital testimony*. There had been mention of studying the case, of classified documents and secrets to protect.

It was all so juicy.

And she had the inside scoop.

The *Midnight Special*.

Her fingers flying across the screen of her phone, Marni called in her excellent research skills to find as much about the train as she could while hurrying back to the nurses' station.

Owned by an eccentric movie director, the fully restored passenger car was a dedication to opulence and luxury. Crossing the country only six times a year, each tour was dedicated to a particular theme. She squinted at the screen and winced. This one was film noir. Ah, well, at least the fashions had rocked in the forties.

She wasn't sure what excuse she'd babbled at Sammi as she raced out of the hospital. She vaguely remembered muttering something about a story, vintage clothes and sexy shoulders.

She flew across the hospital parking lot as fast as her

high heels could carry her, diving into the driver's seat of her Mini Cooper and giving a little scream of triumph.

This was it. Her big break.

She was going to follow him.

Marni glanced at the dashboard clock. Eight o'clock, a half hour to the train station and she didn't have a ticket. Thinking fast, she pressed the phone button on her steering wheel, then chose her roommate's number.

"I need a favor," she said over the top of Carrie's cheerful hello. "I'll be swinging by in about ten minutes. Can you meet me out front with a suitcase?"

The stunned silence on the other end made Marni wince.

"You want me to pack for you?" Carrie asked, sounding equal parts thrilled and terrified. As if she'd just been asked to play opposite Johnny Depp in a love scene.

Film noir meant forties crime melodrama. She'd read that the entire trip was one of those mystery events where everyone dressed up.

"Think vintage fashion, the forties era," Marni instructed her cousin. "Cocktail dresses, pencil skirts, my floral cotton dress and maybe the wool suit if you can find a wide belt. Oh, can I borrow your fedora? And don't forget to pack my black leather T-strap pumps. They're perfect."

"You want me to pack anything vintage, in less than ten minutes?"

"You can't do it?"

"Are you kidding? This is awesome. What's the deal? Where are you going? With who and for how long?"

Marni cringed, then tried to pretend that the sound of drawers and doors flinging open was reassuring.

"Put together enough for a week—no, make it two weeks, just in case there isn't laundry on the train. I'm catching the Midnight Special tonight to San Francisco and I'll miss it if I don't hurry."

"Ooh?" From the beginning of the syllable to the end, Carrie went from excited to curious to suspicious. The banging and slamming stopped. "Why? What are you doing?"

"I'm chasing a guy." Hoping that didn't sound as silly to Carrie as it did to her, Marni bit her lip.

"A man...?" The last word was offered in a juicy whisper, with just a hint of *as if* thrown in. The skepticism didn't just come from the fact that Carrie and Marni had been favorite cousins since they were babies, or that she'd heard Marni vow over and over that she wanted to be just like their aunt. It was that Carrie, like everyone else in the family, figured that Marni was just biding her time with this career until the right man came along. Oh, she could keep her job. The family considered themselves evolved enough to believe women could and should have careers outside the home. As long as the home in question included a husband and at least one darling tot. Which meant the careers had to lend themselves to taking good care of said husband and requisite tot.

Carrie had listened often enough to Marni railing against that family creed, sympathizing with her vow to someday, somehow, find the perfect guy. A sexy stud who'd be available when she wanted him, able to cater to all her sexual needs and happily slide back into obscurity when she was busy with her career.

"You found a boy toy like you're always talking about?" Carrie asked in hushed awe. "A hot, gorgeous guy who will provide your every sexual desire, know where the G-spot is and why foreplay is vital, then quietly leave you alone in the morning?"

"I wish," Marni muttered.

That was her ideal man. There to scratch that G-spot itch, dispose of ugly spiders, to be able to laugh at himself and, oh, if only, know his way around a dance floor. So, pretty much nonexistent.

But that wasn't going to get her cousin packing any faster.

"Well, maybe," she corrected more loudly. "I mean, I don't know how good he is in bed or anything. But he's got shoulders to die for, a body that won't quit and oh, baby, his butt is so nice."

Stopped at a red light, she squirmed a little in the seat of her car at the memory of the FBI guy's back. A guy like that, sexy and strong, dedicated and focused? That kind of guy was dangerous. Not because he carried a gun. But because he was the only kind of guy she could ever imagine herself giving up her dream for.

Lucky for her, she was sure he didn't have the rest of her fantasy guy requirements.

Great shoulders or not, no guy was that perfect.

Which made it easy to tell Carrie, "I'm going to chase him down and see, though. I mean, why not, right? I'm supposed to be on the great manhunt, putting every effort into pulling myself out of this shameful single life."

"You saw a guy for the first time, what? Tonight? And suddenly you're so hot for him, you're hopping a train to chase him across the country?"

Marni scrunched her nose, wondering if that sarcasm was going to ooze some ugly substance out through the car's Bluetooth speakers.

"Didn't you chase Robert to Virginia?" she countered.

Carrie had followed her army paratrooper all the way to the altar. When he'd been deployed to the Middle East a couple of months after their wedding, she'd chosen to move back to New York to be close to family, with plans for Robert to put in for a transfer to Fort Hamilton when his tour was finished.

"You're thinking marriage?"

Marni cringed.

"I never said that."

"You compared chasing this guy to my chasing Robert. That means marriage."

Maybe that'd been the wrong argument. Too late to change it now, though.

"Look, I've got to call the train station and make sure I can get a berth. Will you have my bag ready when I get there?"

"I'll be on the front stoop in five minutes," Carrie promised.

With a quick thanks, Marni gratefully ended the call.

Her gratitude, and good humor, were gone when she pulled up in front of the apartment building twelve minutes later.

"I'm late," she said through the open window. "I've got to hurry."

"I added a few extras from my closet, and borrowed some from Liza across the hall. She has better evening wear than either of us," Carrie said before she hefted two suitcases and a satchel. "I wish you had a bigger car, though. I don't think this is going to fit in your trunk."

Before Marni could lift her chin off her chest, her cousin rounded the car, pulled open the passenger seat and started hefting bags into the back.

"How could you pack so much in such a short time?" And where was she supposed to put it? Didn't trains have dinky berths?

"Hey, don't let it be said that I didn't do my part to help my cousin launch a major offensive on the Great Clare Marriage Quest."

An offensive in defeating it, maybe. If she knew the truth, though, Carrie would likely grab the bags back out of the car, then throw herself across the hood to keep Marni from leaving. So she kept that to herself.

"Thanks," she said instead. And knowing her cousin tended to worry, she added, "I'll check in tomorrow."

She only caught a glimpse of Carrie's smile before the other woman wrapped her arms around Marni's neck and whispered "good luck" in her hair. Then, with a glance at the clock on the dash, she scooted back out of the car, slammed the door and made an *onward* gesture by waving her arm forward.

Her stomach doing a crazy interpretive dance of nervous excitement, Marni grinned and waved.

This was it, time to make her dreams come true.

Thirty minutes later, she was ready to scream. Every second was tiptoeing closer to a nightmare than a dream.

"What do you mean, I can't get a berth? I called. I was told there were three available."

"Those are the overflow berths," the porter said with an apologetic smile. He gestured, moving Marni off to the side and out of the way of the ticketed passengers boarding the train. "You shouldn't have been offered one. The train is actually fully booked. I'm sorry for the mix-up."

"Can't I just get a seat instead, then?" Pretending she loved the idea of crossing the country sitting uncomfortably upright, Marni offered her sweetest smile. The one that flashed not only a dimple, but included a flutter of her lashes, as well.

The porter, a distinguished-looking gentleman in his forties, blushed. But he still shook his head and gave her a regretful look.

"I'm sorry. We're not a commuter train. There is no sleeping in the public cars."

"But—"

"Excuse me, Porter Jones, there's a passenger situation that needs your attention."

The porter and Marni both turned to the younger man, also dressed in the blue serge uniform and cap to indicate he was a part of the train crew.

"Of course. Porter Simpson, could you finish up with Ms. Clare for me please?"

"Sure," the younger man said with an enthusiastic grin. After a sharp look from his superior, he brought it down a few watts, plastering on a serious look and nodding. "I'd be happy to help."

After a warning look, Porter Jones excused himself.

"So what can I do for you?"

"According to Mr. Jones, there's nothing that can be done." Marni pushed a frustrated hand through her hair, then lifted it in a helpless gesture. "I called forty-five minutes ago, and thought I'd booked space on the train, but apparently I was wrong."

"What? No way. I took that call. You asked me to reserve you a berth, so I logged it in." He opened his vintage brass-and-leather folder to reveal a very modern computer tablet, using his finger to pull up a registration page.

"Marni Clare, right?"

At her nod, he tilted the screen toward her.

"See, here. I reserved the last berth for you. I just need your credit card to finish the booking."

"Thank you so much." Excited, Marni plucked her wallet from her clutch and slid out her credit card for him.

He ran her card through a little handheld device, then waited. He ran it again, then frowned.

"Okay, well I must have done something wrong." His face crumpled a little and he looked down the platform as if searching for help. Not seeing anyone, he gave Marni a rueful grimace. "This is my first trip. I'll figure it out, though. I mean, most of our training is in service, you know? Bookings are usually done by the senior porters."

Not sure if she should be worried or not, Marni took her credit card back. "Is this going to be a problem?"

"Nah. I mean, I put your name on the berth registration, see?" He held up the tablet and pointed. Marni noticed the small icon at the bottom of the screen labeled Apply was still lit. As if it hadn't been pushed, or the registration information hadn't been sent through. "And it has your credit card number right here so it recorded your payment information. So it's all good."

"But—"

Before she could ask him about the apply icon, the train's whistle blew loud and strong.

"All aboard," he said with a grin. Closing the tablet back in its case, he lifted her suitcases and angled his head toward the steps. "Right this way, ma'am."

But...

Her hand on the handle of her satchel, Marni hesitated. She was pretty sure he hadn't actually completed the reservation. Which meant that she might not have a berth when she got on the train.

Of course, it wasn't as though they were going to toss her out the window once they were in transit. Worst-case scenario, she spent the night in a lounge or dining car sitting up, and they'd put her off in Chicago the next day. Plenty of time for her to work the train, schmooze her way through the passenger list and see what she could find.

Even if she did get the berth, this was a gamble.

Less than twenty-four hours to find a guy who, given his injuries, would definitely be sleeping for the next eight or ten of them. She didn't know his name, his voice was a husky blur. All she had to go on was a set of gorgeous shoulders and a very nice butt. The chances of getting all of the male passengers with dark hair to strip off their shirts and turn their backs was probably on the slim side.

Still, it was a chance.

"Coming," she said with a big smile. She swung her satchel over her shoulder, tucked her purse tighter under her arm and hurried after him. Excitement swirled as she looked around, taking in all of the details. The train was a crisp red, the windows glistening like crystal against the harsh neon lights of the station. Holding the brass rail, she climbed the steps after the porter, then gave a soft gasp.

"Oh, my," she breathed. It was like stepping into the past. Lantern-style lights lined the damask-covered walls of the narrow aisle. Instead of utilitarian grays, metal and plastic, everything she could see was pure luxury. Rosewood gleamed. Brass shone. Each berth door was heavy, polished wood with a discreet brass number.

It wasn't going to be easy to find her FBI guy in this setup, she realized. When they reached the door marked seventeen, the porter stopped and, using a key from the huge ring at his waist, he opened the door.

He set her bags at the foot of the comfortable-looking full-size bed before pulling a second set of keys out of his pocket and choosing one.

Holding the two up to the light, he compared the key to the one on his ring, gave a satisfied nod, then handed it to her. He settled her suitcases into a cubby at the foot of the bunk-style bed, twisted the blinds to let in the bright station lights, then stepped over and turned on the light in the tiny bathroom.

"Breakfast is served in the dining car from six to eleven. The schedule of movie events is here," he indicated, pointing to a brochure on the little dresser. "Tomorrow I'll deliver your information packet. It will describe the rules and suggest strategies, as well as detailing your role for the Mystery Murder event."

"Thank you so much," Marni said, tucking a tip into his gloved hand. "I appreciate this, a lot."

His boyish grin flashed again before he wiped it clean and gave her a sedate nod.

"If you require anything, just call the porter's desk. It's star four on the intercom."

With that and one last look around as if completing a mental checklist of his duties, he gave her a nod and left.

"Well, then," Marni muttered to herself as she peered around the sleeper car. It was bigger than she'd expect on a train, and just as luxurious as everything else she'd seen so far. Way more luxurious than her credit card would probably like, she realized.

Were all the berths this fancy? Was there anything cheaper? Holy cow. She dropped into one of the plush club chairs and took a deep breath. The magazine was generous with her expense account. Mingling with the rich and famous of the fashion world didn't come cheap, after all. But they weren't going to reimburse her for this since she wasn't on a legitimate assignment.

Unless she broke the story.

Ambition stirred, intense and edgy in her belly. Big breaks were few and far between. This one had fallen into her lap. This was meant to happen.

The story was hers.

Excited again, Marni jumped to her feet and pulled one of the suitcases out, setting it on the crisply made berth, and flipped it open.

"Oh, Carrie." She sighed.

No wonder she'd looked so smug. She hadn't packed for Marni to travel across the country to the theme of film noir. She'd packed for Marni to manhunt her way into hot-and-sexy's bed.

All of Marni's best lingerie, silkiest underthings and most provocative clothes were tucked in here. Fitting in was one thing. Looking as if she was on the forties stroll was another.

Suddenly exhausted as the chasing-a-hot-story adrenaline drained from her body, she decided to worry about it in the morning. Right now, she just wanted sleep. With that in mind, she showered in the itsy-bitsy excuse of a bathroom, then slid into an even ittier and bittier excuse of a nightie. Her face freshly scrubbed, her hair tidily brushed, she slid the suitcase under the berth and pulled her own tablet out of her purse. Read, or sleep? Realizing she wouldn't manage to read two pages, she set the tablet aside and turned off the lights.

She cued up her tiny MP3 player to her favorite subliminal recording, "Ambition Made Real" set to relaxing music. Tucking her earbuds in, she scooted down under six-hundred-thread-count sheets and moaned in delight.

A good night's sleep filled with subconscious messaging and she'd be in prime investigative reporting mode first thing in the morning. Time to make her dreams come true.

WHAT A FREAKING NIGHTMARE.

As he got on the train, just before the departure whistle blew, Hunter cursed. Every cell in his body throbbed in painful unison, from his hair follicles to his toenails.

Hunter cursed as he made his way painfully through the train's corridor, looking for the dining car. He needed food. Food, a shot of whiskey and about thirty hours of shut-eye.

He'd settle for the food, though.

"Are you still serving meals?" he asked the tuxedo-clad host who met him at the door of the dining car. "Can I get a burger?"

"Of course, sir. Right this way."

It was a sad state of affairs that Hunter wanted to ask for a table near the door just so he didn't have to cross the room. Instead, he gritted his teeth and followed the guy. Always alert, he scoped out the other diners. A dozen people in the high-income range from the bling and quality of their clothes. Couples, except one lone woman who was looking at him as if he might be more tasty than the piece of prime rib on her plate.

Now that he had a gauge on the room, Hunter ignored them all. Including the hungry-looking brunette.

"Burger," he repeated as he dropped into a chair, his back to the wall and the room in full view. "Medium, along with whatever you put on the side. Add a bowl of that beef soup, rolls and a Cobb salad. In whatever order they cook fastest."

Rolling a car tended to make him hungry.

"And to drink?"

He debated.

Technically, he was off duty. He was also under doctor's orders to take the next twenty-four hours off and recuperate. He couldn't work the case until they reached Chicago and he got the files.

"Whiskey, neat."

While he waited, he'd go through his own notes and list a few priorities. He barely had time to pull out his notebook before his drink arrived, quickly followed by the rolls and his soup. Hunter dove into the meal with gusto, jotting down notes between bites.

Saving Beverly Burns had been a godsend. For the FBI as much as her, probably. A trophy wife with a brain, she'd made the fatal mistake of telling her husband off for having an affair. Charles Burns, figuring divorce proceedings might be headed his way, had thumped her over the head and tossed her into one of his warehouses, then set the damned thing on fire.

Hunter read over his outline of events, jotting down notes here and there as he ate. By the time he wiped the last crumb from his lips, he was comfortable with his plans for the case, full and totally exhausted.

"Can I get the bill?" he asked the waiter who was clearing his plate.

"No charge, sir. Meals are included in the cost of your trip. I just need to note down your berth number."

He hadn't seen the berth yet, hadn't even checked to see where it was. Hunter pulled out the train ticket from his pocket to check, impressed despite himself. He hadn't figured Murray for the type to book a luxury trip. The guy doubtless had no choice, though. The cattle cars were probably all full.

"I'm in seventeen."

"Very good." The man made a note before asking if Hunter wanted anything else.

"Just some sleep."

It wasn't until he stood up that Hunter realized his aches were gone. He blinked a couple times to bring the room back into focus and wondered what the hell kind of whiskey they served here.

Then he winced. Hell, the doc had poked him with a needle or two, probably some kind of painkillers. Too bad he hadn't remembered that before he'd thrown back a couple fingers of alcohol.

He wasn't impaired. Just a little foggy.

No problem. He wasn't driving, wasn't working the case. His only objective for the rest of tonight was to get some damned sleep. He'd walk a little slower to compensate for the slight haze the room had taken on. Hunter never let anything stand in his way.

Sleeping berth seventeen was easy enough to find. Not bothering with lights, he stripped naked, tossing his clothes over the back of a chair. Thankfully, Murray had had someone deliver a change of clothes to the hospital, but it was all Hunter had until his luggage was delivered, along with the case files.

Soft fingers of moonbeams peeked through the window, lighting the bed curtain enough for him to find the opening. The bed was turned down, welcoming as he sank into its comfort.

His last thought before he dived into sleep was a mild feeling of regret. He'd really been looking forward to his naked romp with the redhead. So much that he could smell that rich, floral temptation that was pure feminine delight.

Not a bad thing to go to sleep with.

3

HUNTER WASN'T SURE what woke him up.

One second, he was down so deep, even his subconscious was sawing logs. The next, he was floating on a sea of pleasure, his entire body stirring with passion more intense than anything he'd ever felt while awake.

Gotta love the dream life.

And he was loving it enough that he didn't even try to surface. Instead, even as his conscious mind nagged and poked at him to deal with…something? A problem? An issue? He didn't know. He didn't care. He was feeling way too good.

It was rare that he mixed painkillers and alcohol. He didn't know if it was the quality of the hooch or the fact that his meds had been injected, but this was all new. Instead of fuzzy and zoned, he was horny and hard.

He liked this experience a hell of a lot better, he decided as his hands curved over some sexy imaginary ass.

Might as well ride with it. A smart man knew better than to try and wake himself from an erotic dream. A smarter man took control of the dream and dived in for all he was worth.

So Hunter grabbed on to the fantasy—by the sweet

cheeks, no less—and dived in. He buried his face in the soft cloud of hair, breathing deep the floral scent. Then he slid lower, until his lips encountered warm flesh.

Soft, silky warm flesh. His mouth skimmed a slender throat with hot, openmouthed kisses. One hand still cupping a lushly curved butt, his other slid upward. Over a deliciously curving hip, along the sweet indentation of her waist covered in a slippery satin fabric, and up to the full—oh, baby so full—round flesh of her breast. For one delightful second, he simply held her. Then he brushed his thumb once over the satin-covered nipple.

It hardened with gratifying speed.

God, he loved a responsive woman.

Reveled in the instant pleasure her body offered when it reacted to his touch.

Fingers, as soft and light as a breath of air, skimmed over his shoulders, leaving a trail of pleasure everywhere they touched. So delicate, so tempting.

His body, so miserable the night before, was awash with passion. It was like floating on a sea of pure sensation, every breath, every touch feeling better than the last.

Hard, throbbing and ready to rock, his dick signaled its approval of the fantasy.

Now, this was how a guy should recover from almost being blown up.

MARNI'S HEAD SPUN with delight, falling back against the pillow as she sank deeper into the best dream of her life. Had she ever felt this good? She didn't need to do a body check to know the answer. The delight, the power of desire, they tangled and swirled through her sleep-heavy mind. She'd fallen asleep to her subliminal messaging and the gentle rocking of the train, exhausted by nerves and adrenaline.

And this, she was sure, was her body's way of thanking her for a wonderful night's sleep. By giving her a hot, juicy wake-up fantasy.

Her dream lover's lips trailed over the sensitive curve of her throat with hot, openmouthed kisses. She shivered when he buried his face in the curve of her shoulder, reaching up to comb her fingers through his hair. The strands fell like silk over her flesh.

His hand, firm, yet tender, cupped her butt, squeezing the full flesh. The other was doing magical things to her nipple, teasing and tweaking. Spiraling around, then pinching. Pleasure pooled, hot and wet, between her thighs. Marni shifted, sliding one leg up her dream lover's rougher one. The friction added an edgy delight to the already incredible feelings swirling low in her belly.

He moved lower, sliding his lips over her chest. His mouth was wet on the satin of her nightie, leaving a damp trail until he reached her aching nipple. His fingers worked the other one with skillful precision, keeping time with the swirl of his tongue, the scrape of his teeth.

Marni shifted, pulling his thigh between hers, pressing the throbbing, swollen wet heat of her clitoris against his leg, trying to relieve the building pressure.

His teeth nipped, then he pulled back to blow a puff of air over the tip of her breast.

Marni's body exploded. It was a pop of an orgasm. Quick and intense, a prelude to the banquet of delight yet to come. She shuddered, her fingers digging into his hair as she held his mouth close, wanting more.

So much more.

Her dream lover moaned.

Out loud.

So loud, so real, the sound reverberated against her nipple. It felt so good.

Except, dream lovers didn't do that.

Alarmed out of her delightful reverie, Marni forced her eyelids open.

Her dream lover was solid.

Real, even.

Black hair swirled like silk over a head—a real, live head—currently snuggled up against her breast.

"What the hell?" she gasped, both hands releasing their passionate grasp of his shoulders to shove at him. "What do you think you're doing?"

Dream lover's head shot up, his dark blue eyes snapping with emotions so intense, so violent, Marni recoiled against the wall. Terror pounded in her head as her fingers scrambled to find her nightie's straps and pull them into place. To cover her nakedness, even though her body was still clamoring for more.

As quick as the fury had flashed, his eyes mellowed. Turned calculating, assessing. Not cold. A blue that rich could never be cold. She didn't know why, but the feeling of threatened terror eased, drained away. The embarrassed shock was still there, though, along with a huge dose of what-the-hell?

She pushed again, her hands tingling as they slid over shoulders as hard as iron but smooth as silk. Whiskers shadowed a strong jaw, and midnight hair, mussed from her very own fingers, fell over sharp brows to emphasize the tiny line between them.

Her eyes skimmed lower, taking in the breadth of his shoulders, the skin golden even in the dim light filtering through the shaded window. His chest was a work of art. Her fingers itched to touch it again, to comb through that light dusting of midnight-dark hair and see if it was as smooth as it looked.

Still on tour, her gaze continued south, following the

tempting path of hair. His belly was flat, lightly dusted so the hair emphasized, rather than hid, the sexy six-pack.

Feminine curiosity, and her body's craving to know if it was as big as it felt against her thigh, tempted her eyes to wander just a little lower.

Whoa. She yanked her gaze back to his face. Strange man in her bed. Ogling him topped her stupid-things-to-do list.

"I know this train is all about luxury and indulgence, but I don't think this is the wake-up call I expected," she finally said. She'd hoped for humorous sophistication. She had to settle for a breathless squeak.

WELL, THIS WAS ONE HELL of a way to wake up.

All traces of sleep, painkillers and whiskey cleared from his head with a blink. Hunter was left with surprise and an overwhelming degree of passion.

Waking up horny was one of the perks of being a guy, like peeing standing up. But in all his years of appreciating his masculine advantages, Hunter couldn't recall waking up quite this horny.

Then again, this was the first time he'd ever had a fantasy come to life.

As still as a cat gauging its prey, Hunter inspected the woman next to him. She looked like a cross between a porcelain doll and a sex kitten.

Flaxen blond curls waved around her face, floating to pale white shoulders. Her eyes were huge, the color of a cloudless sky and surrounded by a lush fringe of dark lashes. Heavy with passion, clouded with dazed shock, they had an intelligence in their depths that warned Hunter not to underestimate her. The rounded cheeks, flushed pink, and cupid's bow mouth completed the picture of adorable confusion.

Figuring it was only fair since she'd taken her own visual tour, he shifted back a little to take in the rest of the view.

Damn.

She was as deliciously curvaceous as she felt. Perfectly rounded breasts pressed against the glistening satin of her nightgown, her skin so pale it almost glowed in the morning light. The fabric clung to her, emphasizing her tiny waist before disappearing beneath their shared blankets.

He should get up, give her some space. But he liked it here. Liked the warmth still radiating off her lush form. Liked to think his large body, his intimidating presence, were putting her on the defensive.

Except she didn't look very defensive.

Amusement danced in her pale blue eyes. Her full lips curved now, as if she knew he was trying to intimidate her and she wasn't impressed so far.

Well, then.

Time to be impressive.

"You don't make a bad wake-up call yourself. What have you got on tap for Snooze?"

She arched one perfect brow, then shifted back toward the wall. For some women, that might look like a retreat. Others, an escape. On Blondie, it just looked like she was getting a better view of the situation, so to speak.

"I'm not much of a snooze kind of gal." She slid into a sitting position, taking the blankets with her as if to emphasize her point.

Well, it seemed the fun was over.

Which meant it was time to find out what the hell was going on. That sort of figuring was his specialty, but he'd never had to use his deductive skills and analytical talents to figure out why a gorgeous woman was in his bed before.

This should be interesting.

Not caring that he was nude, Hunter tossed the blankets aside and slid from the bunk. His lips twitched at Blondie's appreciative gasp. He met her eyes, liking the heat there. This was a woman unafraid of her own passions, eager to embrace and explore life and avail herself to its sensual offerings.

And he wasn't just thinking that because she was looking at him as though he was a hot fudge sundae, topped with extra whipped cream. Or because her nipples were once again stiff peaks beneath the satin of her nightgown.

He was too busy taking in the rest of her body, exposed by the blankets he'd tossed aside, to care if she was liking what she saw. Because he was *loving* the view himself.

The tiny nightgown was a rich berry shade. The same color as her nipples? He couldn't tell through the satin, even though the wet fabric still clung to her hardened peaks.

"Do you mind?" she protested, holding one hand up as if to block the view of his dick. Hunter gauged the size of her palm, then his own impressive erection and shook his head. She was going to need a few more hands to block the sight of this baby.

"Sweetheart, you sneak into a guy's bed, you have to expect to see a few things you wouldn't catch sight of over drinks and dinner."

MARNI SHOULD BE OUTRAGED. Shocked, even.

But she was too busy visually gobbling up the delicious view.

Oh, sweet baby. What a body.

"I didn't sneak into your bed," she finally responded, her tone more absent and offhand than angry and dismissive.

"No? My bed." He pointed to the bunk, then shifted

his finger to her. "You. Since I didn't invite you in, I'd say *sneaked in* is a good term."

That cut right through Marni's foggy passion. Irritation chased back desire. Not away. There was no chance of not feeling desire when a guy as gorgeous as this one stood naked in front of her. But her brain was starting to override her body. Or, at least, trying to.

"Let's think about this," she said, sitting up straighter and offering a chilly smile. "When I arrived in this cabin last night, mine was the only luggage here. There was no sign of anyone else using the room. When I climbed into bed, it was empty. You weren't here. I'd say that makes you the one sneaking around, don't you think?"

His laugh was as appreciative as it was sardonic.

Then he turned his back toward her. She couldn't quiet her approving moan at the site of his perfect—not just great, but perfect—butt. Her gaze slowly meandered up the golden planes of his back, and since he wasn't looking, she wiped her lower lip to make sure there was no evidence of drool.

Then her eyes landed on his shoulders.

His shoulders!

Her drool dried up, the lust in her belly replaced with a different kind of excitement.

It was him.

Those were the shoulders.

Marni shifted to her knees, ignoring the blanket that fell back to the mattress, and narrowed her eyes. Then she squinted, blurring her vision a little, as if she was seeing that broad muscled wonderfulness from farther away. Like, from a hallway peering into an exam room.

She took in the hairstyle, shorter in back and longer on top. The taper of his waist and the sharply defined muscles of his back. Then her gaze returned to those shoulders.

Oh, yeah, it was him.

She'd had a little early-morning delight with the very man she'd told her cousin she was chasing down for a hot, sexy time.

Funny how those things worked out.

"Do you have your ticket?" he asked, turning to face her and buttoning his jeans at the same time. "We'll take them to the porter, see where they made a mistake."

Wincing, Marni dropped down to sit flat on the bed.

Uh-oh.

Cute porter boy hadn't given her a ticket.

Which meant he probably hadn't finished booking the berth, either.

Think fast.

"I'm not sure where my ticket is. I know I had it when I got on board," she lied, pushing her hand through her hair and heaving her most frustrated sigh. "Tell you what, why don't we get breakfast. After a cup or three of coffee, I'm sure I'll remember where it is."

Her brain scrambled from scheme to idea to plan, but none of them seemed viable. She'd come too far to lose this story now. Fate wasn't putting everything in her lap just to toss her off the train, was it? She just needed a little time. She'd come up with a plan, make contact, establish a rapport and be well on her way to getting an inside scoop on the hottest criminal case of the year.

Cool your jets there, hotshot, she reminded herself. *Gotta get past step one before celebrating a Pulitzer.*

Hadn't the senior porter said something about overflow berths? Maybe one of those was unclaimed and she could book it. In the meantime, she just had to keep from getting kicked out.

How the hell was she going to do that?

Her eyes dropped back to the bed.

Oh, no, her mind screamed.

Please, yes, her body clamored.

"We can eat after we sort this out. I'll go get the porter, see what happened," hottie said, interrupting her internal struggle. She watched him shrug into his shirt, noting his slight wince, as if whatever had sent him to Emergency was still hurting.

"I'm not dressed," she protested.

"You have five minutes." He pulled on boots, then stood to tuck his shirt into his jeans. "I'll bring coffee along with someone who can sort this out."

Marni stared at the closed door for thirty precious seconds, then vaulted from the bed to grab her suitcase.

She didn't waste time with underwear, not trusting that he wouldn't be back any second. Instead she shimmied into a rich charcoal pencil skirt and a pale pink angora sweater. Not bothering with a brush, she scooped her hair up and anchored it with a large clip, then stuffed her feet into her highest pair of black leather pumps. When a girl topped five-four on tiptoes, high heels were a must for facing down bullyboys.

Needing all the advantages she could get, and knowing that she'd think naked orgasms every time she looked at it otherwise, she quickly tugged and pulled at the blankets to make the bed.

She'd just plumped the pillows when the door reopened.

Hottie walked through, followed by—oh, bless him— her favorite porter friend. And quickly moving him up the list of her favorite people, the porter was carrying a silver tray with an elegant coffee set and two porcelain cups.

He set it on the small table, then gave Marni a distant smile.

Her heart sank.

"There appears to be an issue with the berth?" he said,

addressing both her and Hunter. "Miss Clare, it seems you and Mr. Hunter have both booked the same space."

The worry in Marni's gut was so strong, not even the delicious aroma of rich coffee could distract her.

"We both booked it?" Hottie, aka Mr. Hunter, frowned and crossed his arms over his chest.

"I'm sorry, sir. It looks like someone made a mistake. Both bookings came in at the last minute, well after our usual deadline. Sometimes mix-ups happen with last-minute reservations."

"Fine. Just move one of us to a different berth."

"Again, I can't apologize enough. But there are no other berths. Every overflow sleeper has been claimed."

Nooo. Barely managing to keep her protest silent, Marni's stomach sank.

"This is the only berth available?" Hunter confirmed in a chilly tone.

"This one is booked, as well, sir. By both you and the lady."

Heart racing, Marni waited for him to ask who'd booked first. Or to dig out his government credentials and pull rank.

"Fine. We'll figure it out." With a quick tip for the coffee and a nod, Hunter dismissed the man.

Marni wasn't sure who looked more relieved, her or the porter. She knew he hid it faster, though, because she was still smiling when he gave a quick nod. With a murmured goodbye, he hurried from the room, leaving Marni to finish spinning this out.

"Look, I know how special this train trip is. I mean, film noir on a restored vintage train is a once in a lifetime thing, right?" Ignoring his baffled look, she made a show of tapping one finger against her lips in consideration. "Oh, I know…"

"I'll bet you do," he said, his smile just as sarcastic as his tone. He settled into the club chair, crossed one ankle over a knee and gestured for her to go ahead.

"We can share."

"What?" Sarcasm fled, shock taking its place. Marni's lips twitched. Obviously that wasn't the answer he'd been so sure she had.

"I'll share the cabin with you. You'll have to take the top bunk, of course," she said, gesturing to the discreet notice on the wall that indicated another bed could be pulled down. "And we'd need a few privacy rules, just to keep things from getting messy."

She paused, wetting her lip and trying to get a gauge on his reaction. Clearly the guy had gone to the stoic school of FBI training, though. Other than losing the sarcasm, his facial expression hadn't changed.

Should she be worried that she was pretty sure she could stare at that face for hours, losing herself in those deep blue eyes, and never tire of seeing that same considering expression?

"You want to share? This cabin." His hand circled to indicate the space. It was a very small circle, fitting since it was a very small space. "With me. A total stranger, and a man whom you met for the first time, almost naked, less than an hour ago?"

Doubts, tiny ones, started creeping under Marni's cheerful demeanor. It wasn't as if she'd share with just anyone. He was FBI, for crying out loud. But she wasn't supposed to know that. Still, she didn't like looking like a naive idiot.

"Well, I do want your name, and you'll have to give that nice porter a character reference so he can check on you for me," she said with a saccharine smile. "I'll take your picture with my cell phone and share it with my entire family, too, so they know exactly who to look for if anything happens to me. Oh, and from now on, I'll be sleeping with pepper spray under my pillow."

"That a girl." Instead of looking offended, he gave her an approving smile. Then he sucked in a breath and shook his head. "Still, smart as you're being, I don't think sharing a berth for a week is my idea of fun."

Sharing a berth?

Or sharing one with her?

Feminine ire prickling, Marni gave him a hard look. "Did you have any other ideas?"

For just a second, his eyes flicked from her face, to the no longer rumpled bed, then back again. When he met her gaze again, there was a heat in his dark blue depths. Sexual, intense, powerful. Her mouth went dry and her stomach dove into her toes as Marni wet her lips.

This wasn't about sex.

No matter how many ideas he had in that direction.

"Nope," he finally said. She blinked a couple of times. Had he read her mind, and was denying her the comfort of that no-sex lie? She replayed the conversation to try to figure out what he was noping.

He wasn't going to argue about sharing the space?

This was awesome, right?

Immediate and ongoing access to the key source for her story. A chance to sneak in hard-hitting newsworthy questions, maybe cull together some major points to write another article. This one on the mystique of the FBI agent.

She gave a delighted little shiver at the idea of delving deeper into his...mystique.

This was it. Her chance of a lifetime. She could get the hottest story of her career, indulge in her love for writing in-depth character studies and put the polishing touches on her very own launching pad to career success. All at the same time.

"So," she said with a bright, cheery smile. "Looks like we're roommates."

4

HUNTER WATCHED THE PRETTY little blonde pretend that she was perfectly comfortable with his staring.

He figured a few hours of this friendly roommate farce and she'd not only welcome but be falling all over herself grateful for his offer to refund her full ticket cost and put her off the train in Chicago.

In the meantime, he'd just kick it here in this cozy club chair and enjoy the view.

A view that was currently sitting at the small desk, typing away. Waves of gold flowed around a round, dimpled face. A milkmaid complexion combined with thick lashes and big sky-blue eyes completed the picture of all-American beauty. She was too lush to qualify as the girl next door, though. More along the lines of Marilyn Monroe than Jennifer Aniston.

Not that he was paying any attention to that overt sex appeal, even though it was wrapped in a deliciously tight-fitting, fuzzy pink sweater that cupped full breasts and a perfectly fitted, hip-skimming gunmetal-gray skirt. The packaging was pure feminine heat. The kind that made him think of long nights sliding over her body while she moaned in appreciation.

Not that he was affected by lush curves or pretty blue eyes.

At least, not while on the job.

Right now those eyes, partially obscured by black-rimmed rectangular glasses, were fixed on the screen of her laptop as she typed away. He was pretty sure if he tried to read over her shoulder, he'd see nothing but gobbledygook.

Because if there was one thing that Hunter was damned good at, it was intimidation.

Five minutes later, his frown was more irritated than menacing. She hadn't even looked up. Her expression was focused, her fingers still flying over the keyboard. Heck, her breathing and skin tone hadn't changed at all.

What the hell?

Hunter shifted in the chair.

He tapped his fingers on the slick fabric.

He crossed one leg over the other.

Then he uncrossed them.

He scared gangbangers and drug lords.

He sent crime bosses cringing behind their hired guns.

And this pretty little blonde barely noticed he was here. Was she immune to men? Had she gone to an all-girls school or something?

Suddenly, she looked up and gave him a bright smile.

"Oh, just remembered I'm here, did you," he muttered.

A tiny frown creasing her brow, she reached under all that thick hair and pulled a small, wireless earbud from her ear.

Hunter almost growled.

Half his intimidation was based on his ability to sit, silently staring. How would she know he was silent if she had noise blasting through her head?

"I'm sorry, did you say something?" she asked, pulling the other mini-earphone out and shaking both in her palm.

"Nothing."

"Oh."

After a couple of seconds of his death stare, her smile drooped, and then she bit her lip and looked away.

There. He still had it.

The ability to intimidate sweet women. He'd bet he could make babies cry and puppies whimper, too.

"You look grumpy."

Hunter scowled.

"Really grumpy," she decided, closing the lid of her laptop, setting it aside and getting to her feet. She glanced at the clock on the wall, then at her watch as if to verify the time. "I'll bet you're hungry. We haven't had anything but coffee in two hours. Want to get breakfast?"

"Look, you're going to have to let me have this berth," he said instead.

"I'm what?"

"I can't do this roommate thing. It was nice enough of you to offer to share, but it's just not going to work."

"So you're leaving?"

"No, you are."

Her cupid's bow mouth dropped open and she stared for so long, he wanted to blow on her face to make her blink.

"It's my berth. I was in it first. Out of the goodness of my heart, I offered to share it with you. So why would I give it up?"

Hunter considered flashing his FBI badge and going the national security route. But he was seriously tired. Tired and sore and empty. He needed a little downtime. He had a week to build a case that would put away the head of one of the biggest criminal organizations on the East Coast. He wasn't going to do that with people bugging him, asking FBI questions and passing him in the hallway muttering, "The truth is out there."

He could ask her to keep it a secret. But in his experience, women couldn't keep secrets. And she'd have no reason to want to once he'd booted her off the train.

"I was in an accident recently," he ventured, shifting his expression from intimidating to doleful. "I'm feeling some pain. I need space, privacy, so I can sleep when I feel like it, pace at night if I'm hurting too much. I need it if I'm going to recover properly."

Her pretty face creased in sympathetic lines and she poked out her lower lip in a sad pout.

"You poor thing."

"So you'll vacate the berth," he confirmed.

She patted his forearm. Hunter frowned at the heat he felt at her gentle touch. There, another reason to be glad she was leaving. A couple more touches like that and he wouldn't be thinking about the case, about catching up on sleep or about the miserable ache of his screaming muscles.

It was as if he was hardwired after their little wake-up games. She touched, he got hard.

"Sorry, but no." She even added a regretful smile to her refusal.

Hunter frowned, trying to pull some of the blood north to his brain so he could remember what she was refusing.

"You're kidding, right?"

"Look, this trip is important to me," she said, looking less like a china doll and more like an avenging angel all of a sudden. Her chin lifted, her eyes heated and she got that same stubborn my-way-or-else look his mother used to get. "I'm not giving it up."

"I need my rest."

"I need to get to California."

"So fly."

"You fly."

"I can't fly. I told you, I was in an accident. Ruptured my inner ear. I fly, I die." An exaggeration, but he was going for effect here.

"I fly, everyone on the plane dies," she shot back. Clearly she was better at exaggerating.

"Oh, please."

"They will all die. I know they will. I've had horrible dreams for years about crashing, of going down in flames. And my psychic agrees. If I get on a plane, it will crash. I owe it to those other people to not put their lives in danger." She gave a big, tearful sniffle before turning her back to him.

Hunter squinted. She'd played it pretty well, but that had to be a total bullshit act.

When she faced him again, her lower lip was trembling just a little and she'd raised her chin as if putting on a brave face. Hunter almost grinned.

She really was cute.

Until she heaved a big sigh and shook her head.

"I guess that settles it. Unless, of course, you're giving up the berth?" When he gave a scowling shake of his head, she shrugged, then walked over to the little table by the door. He wasn't sure whether to be relieved that she might be going, or wish she'd walk a little more so he could enjoy the view of her hips swaying.

She picked up a small leather folder.

"Breakfast?" She waved the menu in the air.

Hunter frowned. He was starting to get the feeling that she wasn't going to be easy to get rid of. Not willingly.

"How about we settle the room situation first." He folded his arms over his chest and leaned back in the chair, making it clear he wasn't moving until he'd gotten his way.

She gave an elaborate eye roll, leaned against the table and matched his crossed-armed stance.

"And what is it that you suggest?" She widened those gorgeous eyes, pure sweetness and light.

"I suggest you get off in Chicago. Take the next train. I'll cover your ticket and reimburse you for this one." There. Pure generosity. He offered his most reasonable smile to go with it. The one he used when he gave criminals the choice between jail and bodily harm.

"I have a better idea." Her smile took on an irritated edge, toning down the sweetness and dousing all that light. "Why don't you get off in Chicago instead? You're the one with the issue, you can take the next train."

"I have to be in San Francisco in seven days."

"I have to be in San Francisco as soon as possible," she countered.

"Then fly."

"I told you, if I fly, people will die." She gave a stubborn jut of her chin before adding, "Do you need to talk to my psychic? She'll tell you."

Hunter growled. His wannabe roommate didn't even blink. Instead, she waved the menu in the air again.

What the hell? Had he lost his mean-guy mojo in that car accident?

"I haven't eaten yet today," the not-at-all-intimidated blonde said with a wide-eyed look and a pat of one slender hand on her tummy. "And I promise you, the hungrier I get, the less reasonable I am."

When had she been reasonable before?

Hunter all but growled.

He wanted her out. He had a case to build. An explosion to recover from. And a general state of mental health to maintain.

He couldn't work on high-security material with a civilian in the room. He couldn't relax with a gorgeous blonde hovering around his libido. And his mental health was already taking a hit, thanks to her lack of respect for his dead-eye stare.

He could pull rank, flash his badge and boot her out of the berth.

Except for two things.

First, she'd been here first. Booking a ticket an hour before the train left didn't give him the right to steal a bed out from under her.

Second, and as much as he hated to admit it, Murray was right. Another few days without things exploding around him and he'd have been clear to fly. But he hadn't been able to resist hotdogging, trying to wrap up one more case, to tally one more arrest on his record before the big, career-breaking trial next week.

His innate fairness said he couldn't pull rank to get the cabin. It said nothing about not using every trick at his disposal to convince her to leave willingly, though.

"Actually, I'm hungry, too." He rose to his full height and offered a slow smile filled with as much sexual heat as he could muster. Which, given that he was still half-hard from waking to find her sexy little body in his arms, was quite a bit. "Marni, right? Why don't we visit the dining car."

Looking a little flushed all of a sudden, she blinked a few times, her lashes sweeping over those big eyes as if she were trying to refocus. She wet those full lips, sparking a sharp, deep regret in his belly that he hadn't tasted them before he'd been pulled out of the fantasy. Were they as delicious as they looked? As soft? Did they yield, or take control?

"You're hungry?" she repeated, her words a breathless rush.

"I'm starving." He let his voice drop just one decibel above a husky growl and let his gaze slide down her body. As though, if they didn't get out of here now, he wasn't going to be able to resist taking a big, juicy bite.

Hunter was gratified by her shaky breath, but his own libido took a hit at the amazing things that breath did for her fluffy pink sweater. She was like something sweet and sugary, swirled atop what promised to be a rich, decadent treat. But he was just as good at ignoring his sweet tooth as he was his sexual urges while on the job. All he had to do was remind himself of that. A few dozen times.

Hunter crossed the room, taking the menu from her suddenly lax fingers and tossing it on the table behind her. Marni's eyes never left him, her focus so intent on his every move. Beneath the suspicion—smart girl—and an intense curiosity—dangerous if she wasn't careful—there was just enough desire for him to use to his advantage.

With that in mind, Hunter initiated his Evict Blondie plan.

"Babe, here's the deal. You're a very beautiful, very sexy woman." He paused just long enough to enjoy the wash of color over her cheeks and the way her eyes softened. "I'm not a man who's big on denying himself pleasures. I like delicious food, a good Scotch and losing myself in the delights of a gorgeous woman."

He let that hang there between them, as heavy and intense as the erection hanging hard between his legs. His body craved the feel of hers, wanting nothing more than for him to press that hard-on against her curves, to feel her warm welcome. But this was Intimidation 101, not Advanced Sexual Harassment. Hell, if he couldn't scare her into getting off the train, he deserved to share her berth, and he'd have to attend all those stupid dress-up functions the train offered, too.

She wet her lips and looked away. Hunter let himself smile. No worries about tracking down a lame forties-style fedora, here.

Then she shifted her gaze, slowly lifting her lashes as her eyes traveled higher and higher up his body. It was as though she was reaching out and dragging her fingers along his thigh, caressing his throbbing dick, scraping her nails over his flat abs, smoothing her fingers through the hair on his chest, then oh-so-lightly skimming his face.

Finally, as if she'd tired of the torture, her gaze met his. Her eyes were heavy with desire, hot with the promise that the passion he'd tasted that morning was only the tip of the iceberg.

"That's fascinating, I'm sure," she told him in a breathy voice. "But I have every confidence that you're also a man of control. A man who understands the word *no*. A gentleman, through and through."

Shit.

Hunter's expression didn't change, but his admiration for her jumped up a couple notches. So did his determination.

He stepped closer.

She stepped backward.

He stepped again. So did she. Until her back was against the door.

Hunter's smile was wicked as he placed his hands on the door, one on either side of her head. He leaned close, just enough to make her aware of his body, but not touching anywhere.

"Is that what you think?" he challenged.

She thought she was totally in over her head and sinking fast.

Marni's body was on fire. Her nipples were craving

the touch of his fingers again. Her body melted, hooked after that teensy taste of orgasmic pleasure he'd showed her that morning.

Control, her mind screamed. *Get a grip.*

"So you're saying if I don't get off the train in Chicago and let you have this berth, you're going to…what?" She let her gaze drop, her mouth watering when she saw the impressive bulge pressing against his zipper. "Seduce me?"

And how would that go? she wanted to ask. Would he start at the top and work his way down her body? Or begin with her toes and lick his way up?

"I've never forced myself on a woman. Never had to, never been tempted to," he promised. "All you have to say is no."

It wasn't as much the smile accompanying his words that pulled Marni from her sexual reverie. It was the amusement in his tone, as if he was laughing over the idea of her refusing him.

Maybe he was right.

Maybe she wouldn't be able to resist the heat, the sexual energy between them for the entire week. Not if they were sharing this space. Sleeping in the same room, listening to each other breathe night after night. Aware of the other's body, so close, in touching distance.

Her pulse raced.

But she ignored it. Just as she ignored the rest of the possibilities she'd just listed.

This was a job. An important job, with a story that could launch her career. She wasn't going to be scared away from it by sex. Or more precisely, by the possibility of incredible, mind-blowing, body-melting, once-in-a-lifetime awesome sex.

She could resist.

For the story, for her career, she could resist.

Maybe.

"So?"

"So, what?" she repeated, her brow furrowing as she met his gaze again.

"So what do you say?"

She knew what her body wanted her to say. But her ambition was stronger. Determination, motivation and a few cold showers would keep her from doing anything stupid.

"I say…" She leaned closer, close enough that she could feel his breath warm on her skin. Then she reached up with one finger and tapped it gently on the soft curve of his mouth. "No."

Marni ducked under his arms, hurrying across the room as if racing against the possibility of him grabbing her back. Feeling as though she'd just run a marathon or through a horror movie to escape a horde of zombies determined to eat her for lunch, she blew out a heavy breath.

She didn't know if she was grateful or miserable when Hunter didn't follow. As soon as she realized he wasn't going to pursue her, her body sagged into a limp mass of unfulfilled desire against the dresser.

"Fine." He snapped out the word with the same intensity a starving panther would use to snap a slab of raw meat in half. "Let's go."

"Go?"

"Breakfast. We'll discuss this over food."

When she continued to lean on the dresser and stare, Hunter arched one mocking brow. That's all it took for Marni to force her body to move.

Get food. Coffee. Richly scented coffee, she thought as he yanked the door closed behind them. Thankfully, shutting away the view of the bed and the thought of temptation.

Or at least the view of the bed.

Ten minutes later, Marni was having second thoughts. Now that they were out of the bedroom, so to speak, she wasn't sure she could handle going back in there with him.

Maybe she should get off in Chicago, she thought as the waiter led them across the crowded dining car to a small table by the window.

She now had the name of the FBI agent in charge of the case, which was more than the FBI public relations liaison had offered before. She had enough information on the explosion to put together a decent story and, since Burns hadn't been implicated yet, if she got the story in by midnight, it might run before the trial next week. But the story would be speculation that he blew up his own building, without any facts to back it up. It'd be a decent story.

Maybe. If she found some way to build it into more than conjecture and supposition.

But it wasn't enough to be her breakout story.

It wouldn't launch her up the reporting ladder of success.

With a smile of thanks for the waiter holding the leather dining chair out for her, Marni settled down across from Hunter.

She bit her lip, pretending to read the menu while her brain swirled in a million directions at once.

She couldn't get off the train. She needed a big story, not a fair-to-middling one. Hunter was her hook. Her big break. Her provider of the sexiest, most delicious sleeping orgasm she'd ever had in her life.

"What can I get you?"

"Another org…" Horrified, Marni pressed her lips together, not daring to look at Hunter. She could feel his gaze on her, though. Like a laser peering into her soul, searching out secrets and sexual fantasies. "An organic fruit tray, if you have it," she corrected with a bright smile and a flutter of her lashes. They worked as distraction enough for the waiter, who blushed and wrote so hard on his pad that he broke the tip of his pencil.

"Sorry. Be right back," he muttered, hurrying away. But not without giving Marni one last effusive look.

"Do you do that often?"

Steeling herself, Marni shifted her smile to curiously innocent before she met Hunter's gaze.

"Do what?"

"The cute thing. Does it work all the time, or is it a fifty-fifty thing?"

More like seventy-thirty. And only with men. She'd never been called on it before, though. Which meant he was likely in that elusive, unreachable thirty percent who wouldn't see her as just a pretty face. He might expect something.

Like the truth. Her truth.

Something no man had ever looked past her face and figure to wonder about.

"Can I bring you anything else?" the waiter asked as he set the plate of fruit in front of Marni.

It took all her will to pull her gaze from Hunter's intense stare. Marni blinked at the waiter a couple of times, trying to focus her thoughts. Then, not bothering to look at the menu again, she handed it to him and ordered, "Coffee, two scrambled eggs, whole wheat toast and a side of potatoes."

"Right away." He offered an excited smile before turning away.

"Excuse me," she called before he could leave.

"Yes?"

Her lips twitched at his eager reply, and then she tilted her head toward Hunter. "My friend is hungry, too."

"You're something else," Hunter said after the blushing waiter had taken his order and hurried away. "Those eyelashes should be registered as lethal weapons."

Marni batted her lethal weapons.

"But they won't work on me."

She stopped batting.

What would work on him? What was it going to take for him to relax enough for her to sneak a story out of the guy?

Because she'd do it, whatever it was.

Except strip naked and beg him to take her.

Well, *maybe* whatever it took except that.

5

MARNI MENTALLY RECITED all of the reasons it was important to keep her clothes on as she considered the sexy FBI agent across from her while their waiter poured coffee.

There had to be a better—aka less dangerous to her mental and emotional well-being—way to get this story.

She'd spent a little time researching while he'd tried to stare her out of their cabin earlier. With a document opened, she used typing away at her aunt's life story as she knew it as her cover. It'd been a few years since she'd worked on a biography type profile, and she'd forgotten how much she loved it. Curiosity drove all of her writing, but there was an extra spark to a profile, the excitement of digging into the who and why of a person's life that she found fascinating.

She'd been so lost in the joy of writing, she'd had to force herself, between paragraphs, when she was sure he wouldn't jump up and grab her laptop to see what she was doing, to access the FBI media files.

Special Agent in Charge Hunter. No first name on public file. Second generation FBI with more commendations than she had shoes, he was based in New York but had worked out of D.C. and San Francisco over the years, too.

She'd emailed a few contacts, hoping they'd shed more light on the enigmatic FBI hottie before the end of the day. Not just because he was totally fascinating. But because she was going to need every bit of light, every shred of information she could get, if she was still going to be sleeping on this train tonight.

"So what kind of accident were you in?" she asked as soon as the waiter had finished arranging—and rearranging—the china cream and sugar containers. At Hunter's frown, she added, "You said you'd damaged your inner ear in an accident and couldn't fly. That sounds scary."

"I was in a car accident last night." His shrug suggested it was no big deal, but she saw the way his lips tightened a little in the corners at the movement. He must still be in a great deal of pain. All of a sudden, she felt horrible about keeping him from that rest and recovery he'd said he needed. She vowed that once she'd secured her place on the train and gotten a grip on her raging hormonal response to him, she'd do her best to help Hunter feel better. Well, almost her best.

"It must have been really bad to damage your ear," she observed, although she figured *re-damaged* was probably more precise. "I'm surprised you're able to travel so soon after something that devastating. I was rear-ended once and was laid up in bed, bruised and sore for three days afterward."

He shrugged again, either dismissing her concern, or her mini–sob story, she wasn't sure which.

"So what do you do?" he asked.

"I work in fashion, but I want to be a writer." A good lie was woven around the truth, her grandpa always said.

"A writer? What kind of a writer?" His deep blue stare sharpened, as if warning bells were ringing in his head.

"Biographical. I'm working on a wonderful profile right now," she said, thinking of the couple of pages she'd written that morning. Her excitement and love of writing bios almost made her words bounce. "It's about a groundbreaking, prizewinning feminist who flouted family expectations to build a career in a man's world."

The suspicion in his sexy eyes faded into what just might be boredom. Marni frowned. What was up with that? The handful of biographies she'd written were anything but boring. She'd even won awards for them. Her fascination with the bits and pieces that made up the lives of people who'd made a difference, who'd stepped outside the box and forged their own path, came through loud and clear.

She'd debated for a while about sticking with profile reporting. The process of digging into someone's history, of sharing their world and their story, was incredible.

Just not as incredible as being an ace investigative reporter. She straightened her shoulders, pulling her head out of the clouds and telling herself to focus. A biographer was all well and good, and maybe someday after she was rich and famous she'd try her hand at it. But for now, she was after bigger career kudos.

And she needed the man across from her to get them.

"So what do you do?" she asked, propping her elbow on the table and resting her chin on her fist. "Businessman? Big-time CEO of a million-dollar company? Engineer? Ladies lingerie salesman?"

His lips twitched.

"None of the above."

She waited.

He just leaned farther back into his seat and smiled.

"You know, to share the berth with you, I do need more information than just your name and a snapshot of you from my phone's camera," she chided, figuring going on the offense was always preferable to playing defense. Especially with a man like Hunter, who was clearly used to putting people on the defense.

"I still haven't agreed to share anything, though."

"Do you always play hard to get?"

Her laughter faded when his gaze heated, the intense look in his eyes making it clear that he was remembering just how hard he'd been earlier this morning, and just exactly what he'd been so close to getting.

Marni's breath caught in her throat. Her thighs melted, heat swirling low in her belly as the memories filled her head, too.

"Look," she said, leaning across the table and giving him her best don't-mess-with-me look. "We both know that neither of us is giving up that berth. We also know that if you had the power to kick me out, you'd have used it already. So you're stuck. I'm stuck. Let's quit being silly and deal with the reality of that, why don't we."

Hunter's eyes flashed with frustration for just one second, then turned mellow and amused again. She had to give him credit, this was a man in command of his emotions. A tendril of heat sparked again in her belly as she remembered how it'd felt when he'd almost lost control in her arms.

The idea of making a man, a strong, controlled man, forget himself and go wild... She gave a tiny shudder of delight. Oh, that was a sweet concept.

But one she was going to ignore, she reminded herself sternly. Career over sex had always been her mantra. Just because she was potentially sharing a cabin with the hottest guy she'd ever met didn't mean that mantra was going to change.

"How do you suggest we deal with being stuck together?" he asked in a tone she knew wasn't nearly as friendly as he made it sound.

"Let's start with getting to know each other." She countered his fake friendliness with saccharine sweetness. It was only fair. "I told you what I do. What do you do?"

He hesitated for a second, then reached over to snag one of the large, juicy red strawberries off her plate.

"I work for the government," he told her before nipping the berry in half with strong white teeth.

Marni watched his mouth as he chewed, her own watering for a taste. She licked her lips, trying to stay focused. This was definitely going to be a challenging week.

"Government? That's either hellishly boring or terribly exciting," she offered with a laugh, the flutter of her lashes inviting him to tell her which one.

He didn't take the invitation.

"So, what do you do for the government? Are you in politics? Or are you one of those regulatory inspectors, going from business to business, checking to see if they are following the rules?" She forked up a spear of fresh pineapple and nipped off a bite, letting the rich juice slide over her tongue as she waited to see how much he'd tell her.

"I'm in accounting."

"Sounds fascinating."

"Not really."

"Your accident, was that accounting related?" she asked, her eyes not leaving his as she popped the rest of the pineapple into her mouth.

"Accidents are unfortunate happenstance events that can often be tied to errors in numeric calculations."

"Clever." She gave him an exaggerated wide-eyed look of admiration.

Hunter grinned in response.

Then he leaned both elbows on the table and gave her a serious look. "Tell you what. I'll talk to the conductor, make sure he has all the vital information to vouch for me. You check with him, see if you feel comfortable. Sound fair?"

"Sure." Oh, that was smart. She could do the same, instructing the conductor to notify her family with all of that information if anything happened. That way she didn't have to tell them that she was pursuing a hot story instead of a hot guy. "Now that we've settled that, let's talk about the fun stuff."

"I'm on this train to work."

"I am, too," she insisted, honesty giving an extra weight to her words. "I'll admit, I'm excited about the film noir events they have planned, which is why no other train would do." Especially since she'd checked the trains leaving Chicago that'd put Hunter in San Francisco in time for the trial and this was the only one. "Still, it's important that I work this week. That I get this story done. My career, my future, depends on it."

"On this biography?" The skeptical look on Hunter's face made it clear that she'd lost a few points in her argument for them to share the berth. "I didn't realize publishing worked quite that fast."

She almost jumped up and kissed the waiter for choosing that moment to bring their breakfast. Her mind raced while he arranged their plates.

She lifted her fork, ready to use a mouthful of eggs as an excuse not to respond until she'd figured something out. But the look on Hunter's face, suspicious expectation, had her laying the fork right back down. What was it with this guy? Was it being with the FBI that made him so suspicious, or was he with the FBI because he was naturally distrustful? And wouldn't that make a fascinating biography?

"My aunt is in San Francisco," she blurted out, her mind one word ahead of her mouth. "It's her story I'm writing. She's not doing well. The family expects to lose her anytime."

Again, all truthful, given that the family had disowned her aunt when she'd run off to join a commune in order to write an insider view of the free-love movement. Marni had heard her grandparents say time and again that Robin was lost to them.

"I'm sorry." Looking as if he really was, Hunter reached across the narrow table to pat her hand. "Are you and your aunt close?"

"She's my hero." Marni's smile was bittersweet as she spoke that truth. What she didn't share was that because of the family rift, she'd never met the woman in person. Then and there, she vowed that once she reached San Francisco, she was going to remedy that. "I don't think she has any idea how much I admire her, want to be like her. She's lived this amazing life, and is such a strong woman. She deserves to have her story told. Have you ever known anyone like that?"

After a second of hesitation, Hunter nodded. "My father, I suppose. He always inspired me in a lot of ways. I always wanted to be like him when I was a kid. I guess he was a hero, you know?"

"Then you know what I mean. My aunt is so special to me. I need to do this. I need her to be proud of me."

Hunter grimaced, then gave a nod toward her plate as if to indicate she get to eating. Since he dug into his slab of fried ham and three eggs over easy, Marni slowly followed suit. But she didn't take her eyes off his face.

She didn't have to wait long.

"Here's the deal…"

"Yes?"

"We'll share, but there are a few rules." He looked about as enthusiastic as if the words were being forced out at gunpoint. She didn't mind. It wasn't as though she needed him to want to have her around. Not like she would if they were going to have another bout between the sheets. Or against the wall. She swallowed, trying to get past the sudden lump in her throat at the image of the two of them up against the door like they'd been just an hour ago. She imagined his body tight against hers, this time while the train's motion added a whole new level of erotic to their sexy dance.

"Rules?" she croaked, trying to banish that image.

So far, she sucked at this focus-on-business goal of hers.

"I need privacy to work. I'm preparing a classified financial report and can't have you in the room. We'll establish the hours, and during those hours each day, you clear out of the room. You can write in the lounge, or watch movies, or paint a picture for your aunt. Whatever you want to do. But during work hours, the room is mine."

Marni managed to contain her butt-wiggling happy chair dance, instead raising a single brow in inquiry.

"Anything else?"

"Yeah. You take the top bunk. I'm sore and don't want to have to climb into a tiny bed that's too short for my legs."

"And that's it, your last rule?" she asked, her heavy sigh making it clear she knew he was going to toss in another one.

She was right.

After a quick frown, he shook his head and leaned forward.

"Nope. One more. The minute you change your no to a yes, you be sure to let me know."

HUNTER LIKED THIS TRAIN. The old-world feel, harkening back to an easier time, it had a lot of charm. A man of the times, he didn't yearn for the days without 4G, Wi-Fi, instant records checks and string bikinis. But the gritty world of a gumshoe, the cut-and-dried appeal of simpler— though no less horrible—crimes, yeah. He could see why people would drop a pile of money to pretend they were a part of that era.

After he left Marni to finish her meal, he moved through the cars, from dining to lounge, past one renovated into a movie theater and back toward the caboose. He wasn't officially on duty, but he always found it handy when traveling to introduce himself to whoever was in charge, as well as to get a lay of the land. Or in this case, to memorize the layout of the train.

It was standard protocol.

Not as if he was avoiding his new roommate or anything.

That he'd chosen not to walk her back to the cabin had nothing to do with avoiding temptation. So the woman was hot. And sweet. And sexy as all hell. So she did fascinating things to her skirt when she walked.

That didn't mean jack.

Except that she was sexy and sweet and smart.

He'd worked with plenty of sexy women. They never distracted him from the job.

He knew a few sweet women. They rarely made enough impression on him to merit more than a kind word.

He was surrounded by smart women. They had a way of seeing things, an innate understanding of human nature that he appreciated.

So the sexy, sweet and smart blonde waiting in his bedroom shouldn't be a distraction. If he couldn't handle prepping a huge criminal case with a pretty little thing like her around, well, hey, he wasn't much of an FBI agent, then, was he.

Feeling as though he'd just gone the mental equivalent to whistling in the dark, Hunter gave a mental groan. Before he could decide which direction to take his mental lecture, though, his phone rang.

Saved by the cell.

Grateful, even after checking the call display, he answered.

"Hey, Murray."

"Any problems?"

"On a train dedicated to gritty detectives and dames in distress?" Hunter quipped, knowing the irony would go right over his boss's head. "I'm handling it just fine."

"You're going to have to dress the part. Participate."

"No, I'm not." Hunter climbed the steps to the open-air gondola car. Since most people were at lunch or down doing some silly movie thing, the platform was empty but for a dozen glossy benches for relaxing to enjoy the view.

"Yeah. You are. I told you that when I booked it. It's mandatory participation."

"I can ignore mandates just fine." Giving in to the aches in his body and the screaming pain of his cracked rib, Hunter dropped to one of the benches to give his body a time-out.

"Don't want to waste taxpayers money, now, do you?" Murray's words were light, but the edge beneath them was a direct attack on the habit of only turning in expense receipts if he figured they supported whatever official means he offered up in his case reports.

He had a habit of breaking cases his way, though, and

taking the financial hit rather than dinging Uncle Sam for payment. Like the case he'd broken the previous year in Black Oak, California.

Tobias Black, a notorious con artist and master criminal, had, in Murray's view, skated free thanks to Hunter's taking matters into his own hands instead of playing by the rules. Rather than use his own guys to infiltrate the crime ring and try to bust Tobias, Hunter had called on a buddy in the DEA who specialized in the many wicked ways of Tobias Black.

That the buddy was also Tobias's eldest son had been pretty damned handy. Caleb Black was Hunter's best friend since they'd been college roommates. Long after they'd graduated, the two men still had each other's back. Still stayed in touch, were still tight. Hunter had gambled on that friendship, pulling Caleb into the sting operation. Murray had called that a serious breach of protocol.

Then a month later, one of Hunter's own agents infiltrated the crime ring without permission, using Caleb's sister, Maya, as cover. The deputy director had been pissed enough to spit nails when, instead of busting the agent down to checking shipping manifests in the Gulf of Mexico, Hunter had promoted him. But hey, Simon had broken the case open and brought in vital information. Enough information for Hunter to make his next call to bring in Danita Cruz, his protégée at the agency, as a fake hooker. Danita had found the final key to not only close the case, but to bring yet another criminal off the streets in the form of Gabriel Black giving up his con artist ways to marry Danita.

Murray had thrown such a fit, his face had turned ten shades of purple. But the powers that be had done back-flips over the busting of a statewide crime ring, the arrest of a dozen major criminals and the takedown of the town's dirty mayor.

Still, his unorthodox methods had guaranteed Hunter's spot on Murray's short list. But since he'd covered his own expenses, right down to the tux he'd worn as Caleb's best man, the deputy director hadn't been able to do more than lecture him on protocol.

"I'm not playing Sam Spade on a train," Hunter told his boss, who was gloating so hard on the other end of the line he was practically breathing heavy. "I'm here to work, remember."

"You can't do two things at once? Losing your edge?"

Hunter snorted. Was that the best he could do?

"I made sure the agent who's meeting you in Chicago in three hours packed a suitcase with just those events in mind. Be sure to get a picture or two. I'm going to want it with your report."

With those words and a cackle worthy of any cartoon villain, Murray ended the call.

This case was becoming a three-ring circus. In the center ring was a vicious criminal whose ass Hunter had vowed to put away. But he couldn't ignore the other two rings to do that. He didn't mind so much the sexy blonde in one of them, but the political posturing and jealous games in the other were annoying.

Irritated despite himself, Hunter contemplated the view for a few seconds. Then, like he did most things that irritated him, he shrugged it off.

MARNI SAT CURLED ON THE comfy club chair, her laptop on the table next to her, her cell phone in her hand as she juggled texts and emails with the skill of a teenager.

When Hunter had tromped off an hour ago to do whatever he'd muttered he was doing, she'd hurried back here for a little research time. He didn't have any luggage and hadn't left anything in the room other than a faint hint of his cologne. But now that she had his name she was able to tap into a few more sources than she'd had before. She was contacting everyone she knew, both official magazine sources, old friends and even family.

"Oho," she exclaimed when Meghan's text came through. Sammi might be tight-lipped about sharing official hospital business, but Meghan had ways of sliding information out of her sister that was nothing short of twin-tastic.

Hunter hadn't been admitted alone that first night.

Meghan's text read:

Watch it. Hottie you're so in lust over has a girlfriend. He was with her that first night in emergency, so says Sammi. She's worrying about you getting all gaga over someone who's already hooked.

Someone else had been in that explosion last week? A woman?

Marni's brain raced. She was so excited, she tossed her phone on the table and got up to do a fist-pumping happy dance.

This was it. This was a real break.

Oh, think of the story.

Hunter and someone else had been in that building.

Was the someone else another FBI agent? Had they survived? Were the rumored new charges connected somehow?

She had to find out. She just had to know.

Before she could do another butt-wiggling dance, there was a knock. She quickly shut down her email and exited her message app, then with a deep breath, pulled open the door.

It wasn't Hunter.

"Hi," she greeted with a warm smile. "Simpson, isn't it?"

The porter stepped into the room, hooking the door on a chain so it didn't close behind him while he fetched a covered tray of food from the cart in the hallway.

"Right, hi," he said with a big grin. He pushed his spiffy porter's cap back on his forehead, then gave a head tilt to indicate the room. "It looks like this worked out okay. You got the cabin, right?"

"Well, that's actually a problem," Marni said, closing her laptop and shrugging. "With no other berths available, and neither of us willing to leave the train, Mr. Hunter and I are actually sharing the cabin."

A knowing glint lit the young man's gaze. Before he could say anything, though, Marni walked over to the bed.

"Can you show me how to pull down the bunk? Since I'm shorter, I get the top bed," she said with a rueful smile.

"You get...?" The porter frowned, setting the lunch tray on the little table, then moving over to press a button next to the headboard of the main bed. A bed slid out of the wall like something out of a fifties sci-fi movie. Marni grinned, wondering if the bed was covered in Jetsons sheets.

The porter walked to the foot of the bed and opened a small panel, and out twisted a set of steps for easy bedtime access.

"We will set up the bed at nine each night and return it to its cubby during the morning cleaning. You have your own sleep light here." He indicated a small lamp on a wire gooseneck. "The blanket has temperature settings built into the lamp controls, as well."

"Oh, isn't that clever," Marni said, trying to pretend a light and blanket controls would be enough to keep her from wanting to slide into the bed below and have her way with Hunter's body. "Thanks so much."

"So, wow. This really isn't what you wanted?" Looking more upset for her than smarmy over the enforced roommate situation now, Simpson hefted the bunk back into place and latched it closed. "I feel bad. I wish there was something I could do."

Marni bit her lip. Rooming with Hunter was ideal on so many levels. Sure, he was a strange man. But he was a safe strange man. Everything she'd found out about him said he was completely trustworthy. As long as she wasn't a criminal, that was. And since lying wasn't actually a criminal act, she figured she was fine. And if he was serious about spending his days working in here, there were so many possibilities for ferreting out information.

But rooming with Hunter also meant no privacy.

It meant that every bit of time spent in the cabin would either be in his presence or with constant reminders of him. Like now, he wasn't here but his scent floated in the air, forest fresh and inviting.

How could she focus on writing the story of her career if she was spending every night lying awake above the sexiest body she'd ever felt? Wondering what he'd do if she climbed down that ladder and slid over his body in the dark, pressing hot, wet kisses to every inch of his skin?

Marni's pulse skipped a few beats and she was tempted to wave her hand in front of her face to cool off.

"Any chance another berth might become available?" she asked with a doleful smile.

His grimace was all the answer she needed. Not wanting him to feel any worse, Marni patted his arm. "Don't worry about it. I'll make do. But remember, if one does open up, I'd love first dibs."

With that, a big smile and a generous tip, she thanked him for bringing lunch. Looking relieved, the porter turned to the door.

"Oh, one last thing." Simpson all but smacked his palm against his forehead, grimacing as he turned back around to pull a sheaf of papers out of his handy leather portfolio. "This is your role for the Train Whodunit. You and Mr. Hunter are playing a gumshoe and his dame. Your character is one of the main suspects for the murder that will take place tomorrow night."

"Really?" Marni laughed, taking the pages with delight. "I've never been cast as a femme fatale before. I think this might be fun."

Then she saw the drawing. A slinky woman, in glittering spaghetti straps and seductively sweeping curls, draped all over a guy in a hat with six-foot-wide shoulders and a skinny tie.

Her pulse sped up. Hunter had shoulders like that. Wide, strong and sexy. The kind that made her fingers tingle with the need to touch. Broad enough to support the weight of the world, sturdy enough for a woman to hang on to while he took her on a wild, naked ride.

Whew, it was getting hot in here. Marni puffed out a breath, then gave the porter a doubtful look.

"I'm not sure how Hunter's going to feel about all of this," she said. She looked at the pencil sketch of the fedora-wearing gumshoe with the lantern jaw again, then flashed Simpson a big smile. "Is there any way to make mine a stand-alone character? Just in case. After all, for all we know, he hates solving mysteries. Or worse, that he's horrible at it."

"Oh, I think I can handle it."

It was anybody's guess who jumped higher, Marni or the porter. Her heart racing, she glared at the man standing in the doorway, gloating over their reactions. Did he specialize in sneakiness in FBI school?

"Sir, I've got your character dossier here," Simpson said, recovering first. "You're a hard-bitten gumshoe with a soft spot for your secretary."

"A soft spot, hmm?" Hunter took the papers, but didn't release Marni's gaze. His smile was slow, wicked and challenging. "I guess we'll see how well I can pull *that* off."

6

HUNTER HAD SPENT PLENTY of time undercover. It wasn't his specialty, but he was still pretty damned good at immersing himself in the part, losing himself in the role while still keeping his objective clear.

But it was always a job.

This, he thought as he snagged a stuffed mushroom cap from the roving waiter, was ridiculous.

Three lounge cars, one after another, had doors thrown open, giving the image of one very long room. Crystal chandeliers reflected the multitude of lit candles, even though it was only five in the evening. All of the blinds were pulled closed against the evening light, so as not to ruin the ambience.

Most of the people milling about were dressed in forties-era evening wear. Narrow suits, quite a few shoulder pads, and glitteringly slinky dresses filled the rooms. It was a costume jeweler's dream, with fat fake diamonds and strand upon strand of plastic pearls.

A bunch of adults, well-to-do if the cost of this event was anything to go by, all playing dress up on a train? Pretending to solve a fake crime that they all knew was coming?

Yeah.

Ridiculous.

Then his gaze fell on Marni as she wove her way across the room with the skill of a politician's wife. A smile here, a chatty word there, always moving but totally unrushed.

He popped the mushroom cap into his mouth and watched her, pretending she wasn't the sexiest woman he'd ever seen. And that he wasn't anticipating, even a little, how fun it'd be once she reached his side.

"What do you think?" she asked when she reached him. Her laugh was breathless as she looked around the room. "Isn't it great? I've never seen so many people outside a movie screen, theater stage or kindergarten classroom so into playing make-believe."

"You look like you're enjoying it."

She was, too. Artfully made up, her eyes glowed and her cheeks had a flush that went perfectly with the pale pink of her satin dress. Unlike the other women, she didn't glitter. She glowed. Long sleeves hugged her arms, but left her shoulders bare while the rest of her dress wrapped and draped over her curves. His hands itched to slide over that slick fabric, to feel those curves. To cup her hips. To curl over her luscious breasts.

She was so damned delicious. His body tightened, as if his brain needed that reminder that she was sweet sexiness wrapped in pink satin.

Because, yeah, his brain wasn't already imagining the various ways he'd like to strip that fabric off her body and rediscover the delicious treasure he'd held only that morning.

Hardening painfully, he shoved his fists in the pockets of his jeans, wishing he was wearing slacks. Or sweats. Anything roomier.

"When's the murder?" he asked, needing distraction.

A tiny frown creased her brow. Instead of answering, she accepted a flute of bubbling champagne and took a sip, staring at him over the rim.

"Didn't you read your assignment?"

"I skimmed it."

"You might want to update your skimming skills, then. It clearly outlined the timetable. Tonight is a meet and greet, costumes optional. Which is why you are here, in jeans, and nobody is suggesting you go shovel coal in the engine room."

"And the murder?" he asked again. Not because he cared. But it was fun to see her try to school him.

"Even though costume is optional, character isn't," she hissed, leaning closer as a group of women commandeered the chairs next to them. "We're not supposed to discuss the setup or details of the events except in our rooms."

"Don't you think you're taking this a little too seriously?"

"The winner gets a thousand dollars and a trophy," she pointed out.

"Ooh," he teased. Not that a grand was anything to toss away, but money wasn't one of his big motivators. And trophies? Those weren't even little motivators.

She giggled, lifting one shoulder as if in agreement.

"I think it'll be fun. I'd like to win, not so much for the prize, but because I think it'd be cool to figure out the mystery. Don't you enjoy putting together clues, pitting your intellect against others and figuring things out first?"

Hunter gave her a curious look. Her words were pretty passionate, her tone awfully excited for a woman whose life revolved around clothes and dead people. Because those were the things that came to his mind when he thought fashion or biographies. Maybe that's why these mystery events were such a big draw. Every accountant and housewife wanted to be a supersleuth.

"Mysteries are okay," he said with a shrug. Not that he wasn't a fan of piecing together the puzzle. But he got a bigger charge out of outsmarting dirtbags who thought they were above the rules. Who figured they were smarter than the law. Since he *was* the law, letting them know just how wrong they were was his ultimate pleasure.

"I'll bet you're more of a suspense kind of guy," she guessed, tilting her champagne glass his way and leaning close to whisper. "*Die Hard* instead of *Sherlock Holmes?* Blazing guns instead of a magnifying glass?"

"Sexy blonde instead of bespeckled old maid?"

He liked the way her eyes rounded, but she didn't look away even as her cheeks warmed with a soft flush.

"Don't you think Sherlock had something hot going on with Irene Adler?"

"Was she the brunette who drugged and stripped Robert Downey Jr.?"

He liked how she laughed. Full, deep, honest. This wasn't a woman afraid of enjoying life to the fullest. He remembered how she'd felt in his arms that morning, regretting just a little that she'd awoken before he'd found out if she would have enjoyed that to the fullest.

His thoughts must have shown on his face, because her laughter died, her smile faded. Heat, intense and curious, flared in her eyes. She bit her lip. His eyes narrowed. He wanted to step closer, to pull her up on her tiptoes and offer to nibble that lip for her.

She looked as though she'd be pretty cool with that, too.

"Hello, there."

Marni blinked, then shook her head as if her gaze was still fogged with sexual heat. She turned to face the person who'd joined them. Hunter took another second to watch her, not in any hurry to look away.

"Hi," Marni offered with a shaky breath.

Finally, Hunter looked to see who she was greeting.

The woman appeared to have stepped right off a movie set. Low budget and black-and-white.

"Hello," he offered disinterestedly. He wasn't on the job, and she wasn't the type he had any interest in on his own time. Maybe if he hurried her along, he could get back to seeing how hot things could get between him and Marni before one or both of them remembered why it was a really bad idea to stoke that sexual heat.

"Well, well, aren't you delicious." With a sultry smile, the brunette looked him up. Then she looked him down. He was surprised she didn't take a visual three-sixty around his body.

Hunter grinned at Marni's hiss.

"Nice to meet you," he added, more because it was fun to watch Marni's reaction than because it was the truth.

"My pleasure," the vamp greeted, leaning forward to offer her fingertips.

Hunter wasn't sure if she expected him to kiss them or shake them. Since her nails were as sharp as talons and her rings as big as his eyeball, he opted to shake.

"I'm Sugar Dish," she introduced, fluttering her lashes in a pale imitation of Marni's flirty move. "I'm traveling with my aged aunt, a wealthy art collector."

"Right. Sounds good." Hunter knew she was playing the role and expected him to play along. But while he'd vaguely heard of these mystery events, he had no idea what the rules were and hadn't bothered to read the ones the porter had given him.

"And why are you traveling across the country?" she

asked, shifting sideways as if blocking Marni from her view could cut her from the conversation.

"Business."

She blinked those spiky lashes again, then gave him an impatient look.

"What kind of business?"

"Personal business."

He watched Marni's eyes dance with amusement, even as she gave him a chiding look and shook her head.

"Care to have a drink later and share what kind of personal…business you do?" she offered, her proposition more genuine than her bustline.

"No."

"Well." In a huff worthy of any forties seductress, she tossed her chin, turned on one heel and stormed off. She did, however, give his ass a pat on her way across the room.

Marni's grin turned into a glare at the woman's departing back.

"You're not playing the game correctly," she said when they were left in the wake of the brunette's perfume.

"I don't play games." Especially not ones that involved getting his ass patted by strange women.

"Then you really should reconsider getting off the train." She got a stubborn, for-your-own-good sort of look on her face. "This is a themed event trip. Unless you're going to take the rest of your meals and spend all of your time in the room, you're a part of the event."

Hunter gritted his teeth. Damn Murray.

"You're supposed to share the basics of your character tonight," Marni explained. "We're laying the groundwork for tomorrow's big occurrence. The more information you get tonight, the further ahead you'll be when they kill someone."

Could he volunteer to be the corpse? Then he could stay in the cabin and play corpse for the rest of the week. Hunter sighed. If only Murray could hear this conversation. The guy would bust a gut laughing.

"Do you not understand how this works?" she asked quietly, laying her hand on his forearm in what she probably figured was a sympathetic gesture.

Hunter's body went on high alert, though, wanting more than sympathy from her touch. Desire heated his gaze before he could hide it. Those slender fingers tightened for just a second. But she didn't pull away.

"I understand just fine."

He understood that she was more temptation than he'd ever faced.

He understood that she was a complication that he didn't have time for.

And he understood that his resistance to that complicated temptation was hanging from a very thin, very frayed thread, ready to snap at any second.

"Why don't I go through it with you later," she suggested. "They allow people in the same cabin to share their character information. Kind of like working as partners."

He didn't work with partners.

Ever.

Hunter's goal was to reach the top of the FBI, eventually to be director of National Intelligence. An honor awarded to few, appointed by the president himself. He still had a lot of climbing to do to get there, and he moved faster alone.

"I know what I'm doing."

"Do you, now?" The skeptical arch of one eyebrow echoed the doubt in her tone.

"I'm confusing the masses. The less information I offer, the less they can pin on me when the crime happens."

"So you're just going to offer, what? Nothing?"

He considered, then pulled a face and nodded. "Yep."

"I'm not sure that's a winning strategy," she mused.

"I am." Especially since the only thing he planned to win was his privacy.

"I think my way is better."

Better? Than eight years' experience as a decorated FBI agent with an arrest record a mile long? Then Hunter forced himself to remember what this was about and shrugged instead. His methods had netted him plenty of bad guys. He didn't have anything to prove. Nor did he need to brag just to impress the pretty girl.

Especially since he wasn't interested in the pretty girl.

Marni shifted, turning to look around the room. The light glistened off her bare shoulders, making his fingers itch to touch, to see if her skin was as smooth as the satin of her dress.

Okay. So he didn't *want* to be interested in the pretty girl.

"Look, if you're serious about kicking me out of the cabin every day while you work, that means I'm out here." She waved her hand to indicate *out here* was the rest of the train, and all these people. "Since we're partners, so to speak, you'd better play along so you don't ruin my chances to figure out the mystery, okay? Otherwise I'm going to sit in that cabin and stare at you. All. Day. Long."

All. Day. Long.

He wasn't sure he could take her and him in that cabin with her complete and total attention focused on him for that long. The way he was feeling right now, he'd make it maybe a half hour, possibly forty-five minutes before he stripped himself naked and asked her what else she wanted to focus on.

"Well, hello."

Hunter barely resisted snarling as they were interrupted again. What was with these people trying to socialize?

"I'm Peter. Peter Principle. I've been watching you from across the room and simply had to come over and introduce myself."

Smirking at the overblown drama of the guy's words, Hunter tore his gaze off of Marni to see what kind of dress-up dork this one was.

Except he didn't look nearly as stupid as he sounded. His tux was custom, his haircut top dollar and his capped-tooth smile full of wealthy smarm. This guy might be pretending to be someone else, but he really lived the moneyed life represented in this little shindig.

"I'm a wealthy investor, traveling to California for the opening of my newest hotel," the guy lied. Or playacted, Hunter supposed Marni would claim. Hunter liked *lied* better.

"Indeed?"

Hunter frowned when Marni's smile shifted from curious to seductive. His gut clenched and his shoulders stiffened. He glared at the smarmy asshole, wondering how much effort it would take to toss the guy off the train.

"I'm Moira Mystery," Marni offered, introducing her character and letting him shake her hand for way too long.

"Would you like to take a walk? I'd be happy to show you the upper deck of the train and the lovely view in the moonlight."

"It's six-thirty. The moonlight is pretty wimpy with the sun still up," Hunter pointed out.

Irritation quickly chased confusion on the guy's surgically sculpted face.

"You'll have to forgive him," Marni said in a throaty voice, sliding closer to Hunter's side and patting his arm as if he was a crazed old man. "He's ever so jealous when men pay attention to me."

"Ahh, you're a couple?" Smarmy asked, still looking irked.

"He's my boss," Marni said, giving an exaggerated eye roll. "He hates anything that might keep me from focusing on the job, though."

Hunter looked down at her, all cozy and sweet.

Then, unable to resist, he chose stupid over smart, and wrapped his arm around her shoulder to pull her tight against the hard length of his body. She felt so damned good there. Too damned good. Still, he didn't let go.

"Her boss," he agreed. "And her lover."

MARNI'S BODY WAS ON FIRE.

From the side of her forehead, where it was pressed against Hunter's chest, to the bare skin of her shoulder, where his fingers wrapped tight. The parts that weren't on fire were tingling with sexual sparks.

"So, what was your name again? Pete? Yeah, Pete, sorry. But she's not available for any fake midnight walks," Hunter said, giving a little shoo motion with his chin to indicate the guy be on his way.

"Well, that was interesting," she murmured two seconds later when the charming Peter had practically left a cloud of smoke in his hurried wake. "Lovers? Really?"

"Let's go." Hunter started toward the exit, not letting go of her shoulder.

Marni would have dug in her heels, but, big shock, stilettos weren't very sturdy. Instead, she shifted to the right, out from under Hunter's arm.

She didn't like being led, any more than she liked being played. And while she wasn't sure what his game was right now, she had not a single doubt that she was a pawn in it.

Marni wasn't against playing games, but she never played unless she had a firm handle on the rules. Or if the stakes were so high, she couldn't resist the odds.

"We're supposed to go in for dinner soon." Marni wasn't interested in food. But she figured it'd be better to stay in the crowd. Smarter would be to let Hunter leave alone. To put a little space between them until she got a grip on the crazy desires that were rushing through her body like hormones run amok.

"I'm not hungry." His words were flat. Matter-of-fact. But the look in his eyes, hot sensuality, said he had a voracious appetite for something other than food. Something like her, if his heated stare was anything to go by.

"We arrive in Chicago just after they serve dessert."

"Then we should have an hour to settle things, shouldn't we."

"What things?"

He just stared. A patient, calm look that said he knew she was smart enough to figure it out and had no problem waiting until she was brave enough to own up to it, too.

Marni gulped.

She was used to being dismissed.

To being considered fluff. Light and sweet. Her own family ignored half of what she said, all sure they knew her better than she knew herself.

And here was this man, looking at her as if he knew the real her. The her inside. The one that was strong and brave, with enough ambition to reach the stars. The one who knew her own mind, and had the gritty determination necessary to make all of her dreams into a solid reality.

He didn't say another word.

Just turned and walked toward the exit.

As if attached by a string, Marni was helpless to do anything but follow. She silently walked at his side as they made their way through the crowd, both ignoring the attempts here and there to engage their attention.

Shoulder to shoulder, they made their way down the narrow corridor to their berth.

"I'm pretty sure our roles are boss and secretary," she pointed out randomly as he shoved open the cabin door.

"Check the stats. I'll bet a lot of bosses and secretaries sideline as lovers."

"We don't."

"Sure we do," he said, dropping into the chair and giving her a smug look. "Especially if it keeps creeps like that off of you. Go ahead, you can thank me."

She gaped.

"Thank you?"

"Yes, thank me. If I hadn't gotten rid of him, you'd be shoving his lechy hand off your shoulder right now, side-stepping yet another of his tacky attempts to look down your dress and wishing like hell you were here with me, debating how long paint would take to dry if a train left New York traveling forty miles per hour, and the paint-brush left California traveling eighty miles per hour. Because, you know it'd be a lot more interesting than what Creepy had to say."

Marni hated that he had a sense of humor.

Gorgeous and sexy were bad enough.

But gorgeous, sexy and fun?

She was doomed.

"How do you know I wasn't interested in that creep—I mean, that gentleman," she corrected quickly, biting the inside of her lip to keep from laughing.

"Because you have better taste than that. You're not the kind of woman to be taken in by smarm."

It was as if he was wearing magic glasses.

As if she'd lived in a blind world all her life, and he was the first sighted person she'd ever met. It was so cool. And just a little scary. Because her tricks, her usual ways of getting around people and situations, they weren't going to work if he could see right inside her.

And getting around him, hiding her real intentions and keeping him off center were vital if she was going to accomplish the only reason she was on this train. To get that article.

Not, she scolded her body, to get laid.

Before her body could offer a rebuttal, Hunter looked at his watch, then got to his feet.

Her heart raced. Was he going to show her what he did think she'd be taken in by? He crossed the room, but not toward her. Instead, he headed for the door.

"I've got to meet someone at the station," he said, his hand on the doorknob. He gave her a long look over his shoulder before pulling it open. "You have a couple hours. You might want to use them to figure out how you're going to handle tonight."

"Tonight?"

"Yeah. Tonight. You need to decide if you're going to be camped out above me on that uncomfortable bunk. Or if you're going to rethink that no you gave this morning."

With that, and a look hot enough to remind her of every delight she'd felt in his arms that morning and to hint at how many more they had to offer, he left.

Marni stared at the closed door for a long time.

They'd been on the train less than a day. They had six more to go.

Maybe she should reconsider this case.

She'd always figured she'd risk anything for a big career break.

Her body, and the delights Hunter promised, wasn't a bad price to pay.

But her heart?

That was more than she was willing to invest.

7

MARNI BLINKED, TRYING to bring the room back into focus. Her eyes were blurry, her head ached and her body...oh, her poor body.

Lack of sleep bad enough.

But lack of sleep for three days added to an ongoing state of unfulfilled sexual arousal? That was straight-up abuse.

"Another espresso, Miss Mystery?" the waiter asked with a friendly smile.

Marni hesitated.

It wasn't that she had an issue with six espressos before noon. It was the worry that the lack of caffeine boost, combined with almost painful jitters, would be worse than falling asleep at the table.

"Maybe a cup of hot tea instead," she decided. "Earl Grey with a side of lemon wedges, please."

If nothing else, she could suck the lemons.

Maybe the citrus would add a little extra zing to her article.

Marni checked her email, excited to see a note from her editor. He was looking forward to seeing the article and, thankfully, had agreed to cover the expenses of her trip. Marni gave her laptop an affectionate look, all but patting its casing in pride.

Over the past three days, while banished from her cabin, she'd written a damned good article. She'd done in-depth research, not only on Charles Burns, but on the FBI, as well. She'd pulled together an incredible amount of facts, figures and information on Burns, his history, his organization, his marriages, right on down to his addiction to cherry licorice. What she didn't have, though, were the insights that would take this from an exposé to a hard-hitting piece of journalism. It might be a good follow-up for after the trial, buried somewhere in the middle of the magazine. But it still wouldn't net her the cover.

Frustratingly, neither would the pitifully small bit of information she'd been able to cull together on the man who'd arrested Burns in the first place. Because Hunter was still an active-duty FBI agent, there was almost no information to be found—including his darned first name, which had driven her crazy for an entire day. Then she'd shifted focus, spending almost as much time studying Hunter Sr. as she'd spent pulling together information on Charles Burns.

The man was amazing. The more she found out, the more she wanted—no, needed—to know.

She pulled up that document, noting that the word count was quickly heading toward a novel instead of an article. The man was fascinating, both in his adventures with the FBI and in the connections he had outside it. What must it be like to have a father who stood godfather to the child of a notorious con artist? Who'd headed up the FBI, had dinner with presidents and vacationed with foreign leaders? Rick Hunter's story enthralled her.

It'd been through studying his father that she'd garnered the most information on Hunter. She'd talked to people who were happy to share stories about the senior Mr. Hunter, and she had charmed out of them bits and pieces about Hunter's own talent for looking past the obvious and his habit of solving cases through unconventional methods.

"Your tea."

She mumbled a thanks to the waiter as she made more notes on her laptop. This profile of Rick Hunter was probably the best work she'd ever done.

"Well, you're bright-eyed and bushy-tailed this morning. And with a fake murderer on the loose." Sugar Dish, as the brunette had introduced herself three nights past, sidled into the chair opposite Marni with a big smile. Ever since the mystery murder had occurred, everyone had been sleuthing their hearts out. "I don't know how you do it. Must be rough, those all-nighters with your boss."

Marni sighed, and realizing she wasn't going to get any more writing done, shut her laptop cover and gave Sugar, or Carla as she was known outside the train, an impatient look.

"Again with the all-nighters jokes?" She sipped her tea while Sugar ordered a cup of coffee. "You know we're not really a thing."

"And you know I think that's a horrible shame." The brunette grinned and fanned herself. "Because your handsome roommate is worth losing sleep over."

Wasn't that the truth?

Most guys, after a couple of days of constant exposure, lost that initial oh-my-God-gorgeous appeal.

Hunter, though, just kept getting hotter. He was hot in the morning, with his blurry-eyed mumbles and stubbled chin. He was cute in the afternoon, during the one hour he'd designated that she was allowed in the room—as long as she brought a snack. He was freaking sexy as hell in the evening, when he wound down and relaxed, losing a little of that intense edge that always seemed to drive him the rest of the time. He was fascinating and so damned cute, the way he'd share stories about him and his father, the hero worship he'd mentioned once coming through loud and clear.

Was it any wonder she wasn't getting sleep?

Or that each passing night made her think there were much better ways to spend those endless waking minutes instead of staring into the dark, resisting her body's urges.

The other woman thanked the server, waiting for him to pour her coffee and leave the creamer. While doctoring her caffeine with that and enough sugar to give a diabetic a coma, she studied Marni's face.

"Of course, it looks like you're doing just fine on that lack of sleep already. Wouldn't it be better if you were having great sex to go with it?"

Marni snickered into her teacup. She'd been prepared to straight up dislike the other woman. Especially after she'd hit so hard on Hunter that first night. Jealousy wasn't a pretty thing, but it was powerful.

"We're not a couple," she said, trotting out her usual excuse. "We're strangers who happen to be sharing a berth. Just like this train would have seen in its heyday."

"Yeah, yeah." Sugar waved that away. "But you're a smart woman. You've got brains and looks, and enough savvy to know that the only reason the two of you are both lying awake all night in separate beds is because *you* are choosing to."

Something Hunter reminded her of each night.

Not in words.

But in the look in his eyes, the husky tone of his voice as he said good-night. He didn't tease, or play games like some guys would, like insisting he always slept naked and stripping down in front of her. Instead, he respected her no, kept his boxers on and tortured her with the wonder of what was underneath.

She was going crazy.

Just thinking about it got her hot, made her want to wiggle in her seat.

"I'm not a fling kind of gal," Marni demurred truthfully. She could be. She would be, if it wasn't for this article. She wanted to be, given how intensely her body reacted when Hunter was in the room. How her nipples beaded at the sound of his voice. How the few times they'd casually touched, her thighs melted.

She took a deep breath, reminding herself that, as always, career came first. It had to.

And she couldn't, in good conscience, use a guy for a story while riding his body to new heights of orgasmic pleasure.

"I'm hearing a lot of *are nots* out of you," Sugar said with a tilt of her head. "What about the *ares?* What *are* you?"

Horny.

Obsessed.

Quickly sliding toward infatuated.

What she was must have shown on her face, because Sugar reached over and gave Marni's hand a sympathetic pat.

"Sweetie, if you want something, you know perfectly well how to make it happen." With that, and a wink that was as natural as it was in character, coffee cup in hand, the brunette rose, tossed her hair over her shoulder and scanned the room. "Now, I'm off to find out who is allergic to red roses, but loves hot bubble baths before bed. Three days down, three left to find the killer."

She arched a look at Marni, who, figuring one good

turn deserved another, angled her head to the three crimson roses in the bud vase in front of her.

"Oh, good point." Scanning the room to see who had ditched their centerpiece, Sugar gave a little finger wave and was on her sleuthing way.

Marni gave the departing woman a grumpy glare.

She had no problem figuring out how to get what she wanted.

The problem she had was figuring out how to not take what she shouldn't want.

It was exhaustion. That had to be the problem. If she'd had sleep, she wouldn't be having these crazy ideas. Or, at least without the cloud of fatigue, she'd be mentally strong enough to shove them back in a dark corner of her mind where she could more easily ignore them.

That was it. She'd spent yesterday afternoon in the library car, dozing next to a corner bookcase. She'd awoken to the hissing whispers of six people, three of whom were sure Hunter was the murderer, and the other three just as sure he'd been murdered himself in a surprise twist they hadn't heard yet.

When they'd seen Marni was awake, they'd all plastered on their most innocent smiles and pumped her for information on her boss, Lex Lanternjaw.

"He can eat lunch out here," she decided in a grumpy mutter. Scooping her laptop into her messenger bag with a scowl, she left the dining car and stormed toward her cabin. Hunter was making her job harder, her fake job and her real one, by hiding out in their berth. He could get his tush out in public so people quit trying to pump her for information.

And while he did, she could take a nap.

A glorious, deep-sleep, cozied-under-the-covers nap.

It was all she could do not to melt into a puddle right there in the corridor.

With a big smile, her arguments all neatly lined up, she flung open the cabin door.

There, in the desk chair exactly where she'd expected to find him, was Hunter.

Sleeping.

She almost slammed the door shut, just to watch him jump.

Then she noticed the exhaustion on his face.

Looked as though the two of them had his-and-hers matching circles under their eyes.

She sighed, her entire body sagging under the weight of her shoulders. She was so tired, she felt as if her head was floating a foot over her body. She needed sleep.

Marni shut the door with a quiet snick, then laid her laptop on the small table next to it. Sliding off her shoes, she eyed the button that would release the bunk from hell.

If she pushed the button, it'd wake Hunter.

Then they'd have to have the argument over him leaving and her napping. And she was just too tired to argue.

Besides, three nights she'd lain on that bunk. For a piece of mattress-covered plywood, it wasn't too uncomfortable. If she hadn't been constantly struggling against the desperate need to climb down and jump the man beneath her, she might have actually slept okay.

But it wasn't as comfy as the bed. The bed was glorious. The bed was wide. The bed was sleepy-time heaven.

She was napping in the bed.

She stopped at Hunter's side, glancing at the work spread out around him. The laptop showed a lock screen. The papers sitting next to the multilock briefcase looked like they were in code. Even his notes were some form of weird shorthand she couldn't decipher. All she could make out were the initials B.B. here and there.

Snoop?

Or sleep?

No contest.

Silent as a mouse, Marni carefully, oh-so-slowly, pulled the duvet back. Her watchful gaze never left Hunter's face as she slipped under the plush cotton and slowly, as if the sound of the feathers compressing might wake him, lay her head on the pillow.

Oh, mercy.

It felt so good, she almost cried.

Breathing deep, she inhaled the rich scent of Hunter's cologne that permeated the bedding. It was like being wrapped in his arms. Hugged close.

Slowly, so slow she wasn't even sure when it happened, her eyes drifted closed. Her brain drifted into that glorious cloud that was a deep, dreamless sleep. Her last thought was how wonderful it felt, as if she was actually in bed with Hunter.

MARNI WAS FLOATING. Somewhere, high above the level that consciousness could currently reach—higher than she had any interest in checking out—something nagged. Like a thorn in her shoe, it poked at her, trying to get her attention.

She snuggled deeper into the pillow, easily ignoring everything except how wonderful she felt.

Wow. Sleep was awesome.

Warm, delicious and awesome.

And a total turn-on.

Not an unusual state for her these days. It was as if being around Hunter had flipped her desire meter from average to super-high, keeping her in a constant state of excitement.

This wasn't the usual sex dream, though.

Maybe it was four days in close proximity to the hottest guy she'd ever met. Hormones run amok. Constant awareness keeping her passions simmering. Heck, maybe it was just horny overload.

Whatever it was, Marni's body was on fire.

Curiosity pierced her sleepy cocoon.

She pulled herself out of sleep just enough to take stock of what was going on.

She could feel the rumbling motion. So she was on the train.

Warm sunshine glowed behind her closed lids. So it was early afternoon.

The duvet was light and comforting over her body, the mattress soft and giving beneath her. So she was still in bed.

And there was a hard body wrapped around her back, one arm thrown over her waist. Her body was awash in a lusty sort of awareness, her nipples aching and the damp heat between her thighs needy.

She wasn't dreaming.

Her eyes flew open and, without moving her head, she glanced down at the hand pressed against her belly. Just there, within inches of relieving that damp, hot need.

Holy shit.

She was in bed with Hunter.

Again.

How did this keep happening?

She should get up.

She should rip herself out of his arms, jump from the bed and throw a fit. Accuse him of taking advantage of her. Of sneaky napping practices. She should be outraged.

She snuggled deeper instead, breathing deep the scent
of his skin, letting the warmth seep into her muscles, relaxing her even more.

Outrage?

She wasn't sure she could force herself out of his arms
even if the train were on fire.

God, he felt good.

Hard and solid.

Warm and safe.

Comforting and, oh, yeah, she wiggled her butt just a
little against his groin, he felt sexy.

"Do that one more time and you're going to have to deal
with the results," he murmured sleepily against her hair.

Her breath caught in her throat. She was tempted. Oh,
so very tempted.

And in this second, with Hunter's arms tight around
her and his erection pressing its delicious length along
her tush, she couldn't think of a single reason not to give
in to that temptation.

At least, not a single reason she cared about.

HUNTER WAITED, EVERY FACET of his being hoping she'd
wiggle her ass again. Just like he'd hoped, every night on
this train, that she'd hang her head over the edge of that
damned bunk and tell him she'd changed her mind.

That she wanted to strip them both naked and play a
few rounds of count the climaxes.

He knew better.

Over the past few days, she'd been sweet. She'd been
friendly. She'd been fun and entertaining and sexy as hell.

She'd also been sticking to her no.

Still, a guy woke from a dead sleep to find his fantasy
woman in his bed, he was bound to hope.

Hunter was used to catnaps. His was a job of long hours

and odd sleeping arrangements, so he'd taught himself early on to snatch enough energy from fifteen, twenty minutes of shut-eye to let him power through.

He'd opened his eyes, and there she was, like a fairy-tale princess, waiting under the covers.

He hadn't been able to resist climbing in with her. Both to freak her out, because he loved that chiding look she gave him, and because he was weak. Yes, he admitted it to himself. He was weak enough to take whatever chance he could get to wrap his arms around the delicate blonde. To hold her, breathe in her scent, to tempt his body with the feel of her curves.

And yeah, to hope she'd be tempted right back.

Enough to change her no to a hell yes.

He'd been doing a damned good job of avoiding Marni so far.

Focusing on the case. Scouring the files his agents had taken from Charles Burns's secret safes. Delving into the computer drive they'd recovered from a house nobody realized he owned. The information Beverly Burns had turned over was a gold mine. So much so that Hunter was taking an extra careful pass to make sure it was all real. It wasn't that he didn't trust the woman's fury against her husband trying to blow her up along with his building. But Hunter had an innate wariness of gift horses who were angling for a deep cover in WitSec, and a fat payoff to continue the luxurious life they felt they deserved.

He'd be a lot further if he'd been getting sleep.

The first night, he'd blamed it on his body's aches. A taped rib wasn't comfortable to sleep on, and the constant motion of the train was doing weird things to his ruptured eardrum.

The second night, he decided it was that, plus the fact that the only time he slept with another person in the room—unless they'd just had sex—was when he was undercover. So his senses were on automatic alert, keeping him from anything but the most cursory of rest.

Last night, he'd dropped the bullshit excuses.

He'd lain here on this very bed, staring up at the bunk above him, aching to touch Marni. To taste her. To feel her in his arms again.

He wanted her like crazy.

And then she moved.

Just a little.

So little, his brain argued that she might have only been breathing.

His dick argued right back that she'd just tossed aside the no and opened the door to yes.

Hunter hesitated.

And she moved again.

This time, with the sweet pressure of her butt against his erection, there was no mistaking her intention.

"Oh, yeah," he murmured, sliding the silky swathe of her hair aside so he could plant his lips on her delicate throat. He breathed in the soft floral scent of her hair and groaned. "Oh, yeah, baby."

His mouth moved over her skin, sliding, kissing, caressing. One hand was anchored between their bodies, but the other was free to roam. And roam it did. Up the rounded curve of her hip, down the gentle slope of her waist and along the glorious weight of her breast. He cupped the weight, loving how her breath shuddered and her breath quickened.

Needing to make sure this was a genuine yes, not something she could dismiss later with a half-assed I-was-asleep excuse, he swiftly shifted positions. So Marni was flat on her back, staring up at him, those big blue eyes rounded with shock and blurred with passion.

She was gorgeous.

Pale pink washed her skin, making it glow. Those cupid's bow lips were open, whether in shock or invitation, he didn't care. He took them anyway.

His gaze not releasing hers, he kept the kiss soft. Easy. Uncomplicated.

The way he usually liked his relationships.

The complete opposite of this.

Because as soft as she was, there was nothing easy or uncomplicated about Marni.

Her eyes didn't shift, didn't try to slide away. Instead, they challenged. They tempted. They dared him to take it further, to show her what he could do.

Hunter had never refused a dare in his life. But he'd never been as excited about meeting one as he was in this second.

His hands anchored on either side of her head, he took the kiss deeper. His tongue slid along her bottom lip, then traced the edge of her teeth. Passion flared in her eyes, but she didn't blink.

Instead, her tongue, delicate and cool, met his. Just the tip, as if she was testing the taste of him. Her breath was a soft, fluttering inhalation. Then she moaned.

Oh, yeah, baby.

She liked what she was tasting.

His tongue dove deep, pulling hers into an intense dance. Swirling, tangling, thrusting against each other. Hunter shifted, so his body weight was angled between his hip and one shoulder, so his hand was free to roam. And roam it did. His fingers skimmed, light and teasing, over her shoulder and down her chest. His palm hovered over her breast, then slid across the soft cotton fabric covering her stomach and down to her low belly where her shirt was tucked into another one of those sexy, hip-skimming, knee-hugging skirts. He didn't dip lower. Just skimmed. Teased. Reveled in the soft give of her body beneath his hand.

She had the most incredible body.

Welcoming, warm, gloriously feminine.

He wanted more. Needed more. Had been driving himself crazy wondering what more would be like.

Now he was going to find out.

Excitement surged, adding an urgency to Hunter's hunger.

His mouth delved deeper. He reveled in Marni's sweet, rich flavor, his fingers working their way back up her body button by button, freeing each from the fabric and revealing silky soft skin. When he reached her chest and that last button, he couldn't resist. He pulled his mouth from hers to look at the bounty he'd just uncovered.

Like Aphrodite rising from the foam, her breast was encased in frothy lace the color of the inside of a seashell. Lush and rounded, he could see the raspberry tip through the shimmery fabric. His finger traced, light as air, around that tip.

Marni gasped.

He ran his thumb across the pebbling flesh. Once, twice, then pinched.

Marni moaned.

His finger slid between the pale pink lace and her even paler skin, her nipple hardening to a gratifying peak beneath his knuckle.

Marni's fingers dug into him, one hand on the waistband of his jeans, the other gripping his shoulder as if deciding whether to pull him over her or shove him down so she could straddle his body.

Either position was fine with him.

Figuring he should help her decide, he gently tugged the

lace down, revealing one gorgeous breast. He closed his eyes for a second, so blown away at her perfection, then opened them again because, well, he just couldn't resist.

He took that raspberry-red, pouting tip between his lips, twirling his tongue around the sensitive flesh. Her cry of pleasure was almost lost in a pounding sound from somewhere behind them.

Hunter's body tensed, but he didn't stop.

The only threat he could sense was to the end of their pleasure. And he wasn't ready for that to happen.

Marni gasped, though, making as if to pull away.

"Ignore it," he advised against her nipple. To emphasize his point, he nipped at the bud with a gentle scrape of his teeth. Her body arched, shuddering as she pressed her breast closer to his mouth. Hunter sucked, hard, reveling in the taste, the texture, the deliciousness of her.

The knock came again.

Marni's body tensed. He could actually feel her desire seeping away, like a faucet shutting down.

If Hunter's mouth hadn't been full, he'd have clenched his teeth. *Ignore, ignore, ignore,* he mentally chanted. But he didn't say a word. This, like their sleeping arrangements, was her decision.

"You should get that," she finally breathed.

Hunter pulled away to stare at her, biting back the barrage of cusswords. Her eyes were blurry with passion, but her jaw was set. Hunter wanted to argue. He damned near wanted to beg. Instead, like the gentleman he hated himself for being at that moment, he ripped his body off hers and stormed across the room.

"What?" he snarled as he yanked the door open.

"Your, um, outfits for tonight," the porter stammered, his eyes flashing fear. "My instructions were to provide costuming for the big event, that you'd take part in the mystery skit tonight."

"Whose damned instructions are those?"

The kid, his hand trembling, shoved the hangers at Hunter, then started flipping through papers so fast, he tore a couple.

"Mr. Murray indicated when he booked the room that you'd take one of the roles this evening. We assumed—" The kid stopped to gulp so hard, his Adam's apple almost bounced. "We figured that meant both people in the room. You can skip it, though. I mean, I'll make—get someone else to take the parts. You don't have to do it."

Hunter had scared plenty of grown men in his day. But he'd never felt like this kind of jerk.

"No, I'm sorry. I didn't realize what was going on," he apologized. When the kid tried to take the hangers back, he shifted them, then dug into his still painfully tight jeans to find some cash. "Here, thanks."

"The, um, the instructions are pinned to the costumes."

"Okay." Hunter started to shut the door.

"The dinner dance starts in an hour."

"Right." Hunter glared.

The porter swallowed again, then turned heel and scurried away.

Dinner dance. In costumes.

Murray was definitely getting his revenge for Hunter pissing him off.

Shutting the door, Hunter took his time turning around to face the bed and its delightful occupant. He wasn't sure what he'd see on her face, but he was betting it wasn't going to be an invitation to finish what they'd started.

He tossed the costumes, hangers and all, over the back of a chair, then met Marni's eyes.

She looked like she'd been well loved.

Her hair tumbled in a tangled mass of curls over her shoulders. Her eyes were heavy with passion, makeup smudged and lips swollen. She'd tugged her clothes into place and now sat, prim as a schoolgirl, on the edge of the bed. Her feet were still bare, though. Hunter wanted to kneel between her thighs and lift one foot, cover her toes with hot kisses, then work his way up her leg.

"So?" He waited.

She swallowed hard, then lifted her chin. "So that was fun."

"Fun?"

Hunter couldn't help it. He laughed.

"Let me get this straight. You broke the rule by coming into the cabin during off-limit hours." While he had unsecured top secret material out in the open, no less.

"You climbed into my bed. Rubbed your sweet ass against me until I had a hard-on to rival a railroad spike. You drove me to the brink of what had promised to be the most incredible orgasm of my life. And then you forced me to answer the door."

He gave her an are-you-freaking-kidding-me stare.

Unfazed by his rant, Marni batted her eyelashes right back.

"What? And that isn't fun for you?"

8

IT TOOK EVERY OUNCE of her will to keep the glib smile in place as Marni waited to see what Hunter would do. Heck, she still wasn't sure what *she* was doing.

Fun?

She had no idea why that'd popped out of her mouth. Her only defense was that her brain didn't function well on sexual overload.

Heck, one second, she'd been floating on a sea of incredible pleasure. The next, she'd been pounded back to earth. And not in the fun, sexual way she'd have enjoyed.

Her body felt as though it was going to splinter into tiny little pieces. Nerves wrapped around desire, tangling with excitement and overlaid by fear.

And Hunter just stood there, staring.

Unable to hold his gaze, she shifted her attention to the fancy clothes he'd tossed over the back of the chair.

Vividly aware that she was barefoot, as if the sight of her naked toes was the ultimate tease, she rubbed one arch against the other. Hunter's eyes shifted to her feet. Narrowed. Heated.

Marni gulped.

She jumped up from the bed, crossing to the outfit and

lifting the dress as if it were suddenly the most fascinating thing on earth.

All of her attention was focused on the man behind her.

She waited for Hunter to do something. To say anything.

But he didn't.

He just leaned against the wall, his arms crossed over his chest, and stared. She could feel his eyes on her back, like hot lasers equipped with tiny sexual fingers that teased and tempted everywhere they touched.

Her breath only a little labored, Marni pretended she didn't notice. Laying the dress back on the chair, she crossed to the tiny bathroom to get her brush, running it through her pillow-tangled hair. Then, realizing that this would just remind both of them why her hair had been getting tangled on the pillow, she tossed it on the table.

She looked around the room, her eyes flitting from this to that, landing everywhere but on him.

His briefcase and laptop were once again locked away.

The green landscape flew past the window like a blurred watercolor.

The bed—where just a few minutes ago he'd been inviting her to enjoy what was promising to be a pretty sweet orgasm—was mussed, with the duvet kicked to the bottom of the mattress.

Her pulse jumped ahead a few beats.

She wanted that orgasm.

She wanted it so badly, she was afraid she'd do something stupid. Something crazy. Something she'd regret, maybe not in the morning, but within a couple of days. Because she figured that was probably about how long it'd take to return from climactic pleasure la-la land.

"Are you attending the party tonight?" she asked, tossing random words out to try to defuse the tension. "It's the big event, where everyone gets to toss out their suspicions and make accusations. I think it was Peter. He had means, opportunity and motive. What do you think?"

"I'm not interested in games."

Well. Marni pressed her lips together. She was a smart girl. She didn't need an interpreter or a big flashing neon sign to pick up on the double entendre.

Her fingers dug into her palms as she stared at the dress. She wasn't trying to play a game. But she didn't know what she wanted, either. Well, that was a lie. She wanted him. But should she give in to that desire? What was going to happen if she did?

Was she strong enough to separate her physical needs and her emotional hopes? Was she smart enough to keep from hoping for something that she knew was impossible? Something guaranteed to demand more than she could give if she was going to achieve her career ambitions?

Finally, shoring up all her nerve, she looked at Hunter.

He didn't look pissed.

Or impatient, or irritated, or any other negative thing that she'd imagine most guys would feel after finding a willing woman in his bed—twice—only to be denied. And maybe he did feel all of those things, but he was too much a gentleman to show it.

That scored a lot of points in her book.

That, and the memory of his lips on her breast.

She sucked in a deep breath, pulling her gaze away again to finger the beaded fabric of the evening gown.

"So?"

"So?" she tossed back, still staring at the dress.

"So are you going to play dress-up?"

Marni tilted her head, taking in the entire gown. It was one of the prettiest she'd ever seen. The kind that made a girl want to play dress up, to put on her highest heels and fanciest jewelry. To pretend she was a princess.

A fair maiden.

The most desirable woman in the room.

Of course, Hunter made her feel that way, too.

Marni closed her eyes, and for the first time she could remember, decided not to weigh the consequences. Not to put her career, her ambition first.

For the first time, she was a woman first.

She blew out a deep breath, imagining she were letting go of all her fears, every worry and caution.

Then, because she'd gotten what she needed—the space and time to make sure she wouldn't regret her actions— she turned to Hunter with a smile.

It was her most seductive smile.

"Actually, I had a different sort of entertainment in mind," she told him quietly. "One that requires we stay here. Together."

Hunter straightened from the wall. His gaze, so intense she was sure he was peering into her soul, didn't leave her face.

"We keep ending up in bed together by accident," she pointed out, pretending nerves weren't clutching at her vocal cords and making it hard to speak. "Maybe we should see what it'd be like if we started out there together, on purpose."

His eyes flamed bright with the promise of a passion deeper than anything she'd experienced yet.

"You're sure?" His words were low, husky.

Marni's fingers trembled as she slid her hair behind one ear. She wanted to look away. It was so hard to think when he was staring at her. Hard to discern the right choice when she was looking directly into the face of temptation.

"Is it just sex?" she blurted out. She winced, but managed to resist slapping her hands over her mouth in embarrassment. She was equal parts horrified at the neediness of the question, and proud of herself. Hey, if a little honest talk before getting naked scared him away, then so be it. She'd be better off without him then.

She backed up that silent lie with a defiant lift of her chin.

"You're something else." He laughed. "Every time I think I've got you figured out, you change things up."

"Is that a problem?"

Walking toward her, he slowly shook his head. "Nope. I'm all for honesty. I'd rather we lay it all out now, before we get naked. Because as soon as the clothes come off, we're not going to be talking for a long, long time."

Marni's heart raced. Both at the image of them naked and unable to talk for long, sweaty hours. And at his mention of honesty. One excited her like crazy, the other scared the hell out of her.

She bit her lip, twining the fingers of one hand through the other as she struggled with the scary part. Did her being a reporter, here to do a story on his case, qualify as something she needed to confess to merit that honesty he mentioned?

Since the probable reward for that kind of honesty was her tush being tossed off the train, she figured she'd stick with sexual honesty. It wasn't as if she was sleeping with him for the story. She didn't expect him to moan the details of the Burns case while she kissed her way down his body.

Would he be pissed later?

Yes.

Could he claim she'd slept with him to get the story?

She didn't see how. And that wasn't just her horny side

talking. Even though the horny side was doing a few mental cartwheels now that it was sure it was getting its way.

"Finally got it all settled in there?"

"What?" She frowned, wondering when Hunter had moved. He was one step, maybe two, away. How had she not noticed? Heat spun around her like a whirlpool of energy. It was as though all of her nerve endings were standing on edge, waiting.

"Your mind is just as fascinating as your smile. Did you know that? It's like I can see you working through all of the options, debating with yourself and lining up your reasons. Pro and con."

Marni wrinkled her nose. It really was weird to have someone see her, know her, that well. People who'd spent their lives with her didn't see her nearly as clearly. She wasn't sure she liked it. But she wasn't sure she didn't, either.

"If you think you're so smart," she taunted in a flirtatious tone, "can you also see what I decided?"

He stepped closer. Close enough that she could feel the heat, the energy, off his body. Close enough that if she wanted, she'd just have to lift her fingers to touch him. And oh, how she wanted. His smile turned wicked, as if he'd just flipped the locks on a sensual prison and tossed the key out the window. Marni's pulse raced, nerves and desire tangling together in her belly. Excitement was a drug pounding through her system. She was helpless to resist it. She wanted more. She wanted everything.

"You decided to cover your butt," he said slowly, his words so low they were barely discernible over the sound of the train's wheels racing across the tracks. "You want this. Want to see what it's like between us. You probably figure it's a safe bet. We hit California in two days. If the sex sucks, you only have to avoid me for a few dozen hours. If it's incredible, you figure the few dozen hours are enough to immerse yourself in it, but not enough to get addicted."

She'd been addicted since that first morning, waking up to his mouth on her body. Feeling the edgy, needy fingers of desire gripping her as never before. But he didn't need to know that.

"Scary," she muttered, her smile a little shaky. "Do you read minds in that government accounting job of yours?"

For just a second, the heat in his gaze cooled. Shuttered. Like that part of him, the special agent man, had stepped aside. Like he was waiting. Judging. But not involved.

"I've spent a few days watching you. Learning you," he finally said. It didn't escape her that he was completely ignoring her question about where he'd learned his mind-reading tactics. Instead, he reached out, his fingers sliding through her hair. Marni shuddered, her mouth going dry at his touch. "I've spent even more time thinking about you."

Her ego wanted to know what he'd seen watching, what he'd learned. But the woman who was teetering on obsessing over him? All she cared about was that last part.

"And just what have you been thinking about me?" she asked, the words catching in her throat as his fingers skimmed her jaw, then slid under her hair to the back of her neck.

"My thinking has kind of gone like this." His mouth descended.

Mmm.

She really liked the way he thought.

And she really, really liked the way he kissed.

Her mouth opened to his, reveling in his taste. His tongue thrust, strong and hard. Marni welcomed him with a moan, anticipation so intense it was almost painful as she met each thrust with a welcoming glide of her own tongue along his.

His fingers were so warm, his body so hot. She skimmed her palms over his shoulders—oh, baby, she loved his shoulders—and reveled in their broad strength. His body was a work of art. One she wanted to study. To worship. To spend untold hours exploring in great, delicious detail.

"Mmm, now this is even more fun," she murmured as his mouth shifted so his lips whispered over her cheek and along her jaw.

"Fun, hmm?"

"Oh, yeah. Don't you think sex is fun?" she teased, her fingers tunneling into the silky thickness of his hair.

"I guess we're going to find out."

Even though she'd known where this was going from the second he kissed her, a powerful surge of excitement exploded deep in Marni's belly. Her thighs quivered, her nipples puckered. She was so ready to see just what they'd be finding out.

"Marni," Hunter rasped, his lips hovering just over hers.

"Yeah?" She forced her eyelids open, meeting his slumberous gaze.

"It's gonna be incredible."

HUNTER WASN'T A MAN afraid to make promises. He knew how to make things happen. But this was the first time he'd ever promised a woman incredible.

It was the first time he'd ever promised a woman anything.

He didn't know whether to be horrified or excited.

He settled for completely turned-on.

Wanting, needing to taste more, he sucked her lower lip between his teeth. Marni moaned.

"You like that?" he asked, his words a husky whisper as he shifted backward just a little, so he could see her face.

"I do," she breathed, her head falling back. Her hair fell like a soft curtain over his hands. Her eyes were closed, a rosy flush making her skin glow.

He gripped her hair in one hand, tugging gently to shift her head to one side, then took advantage of the move by skimming his lips down her now exposed throat. He nibbled the delicate flesh, reveling in her breathy moan. He reached the juncture of her collarbone, burying his face there for one second and breathing deep her enticing scent.

When he reached her blouse, his patience snapped. Through with the gentlemanly pretense—hell, all of the pretenses—he gave in to his own wants and ripped the fabric aside.

Her gasp, and the pinging of buttons, bounced off the walls. She pressed her hips tighter against his throbbing erection, which was all the proof he needed that she didn't have an issue with the damage.

He made quick work of the rest of her blouse, sending her bra flying along with the ruined clothing. Then he leaned back to take in the gorgeous bounty he'd been dreaming of.

Incredible.

Her skin was so pale, her nipples a rich raspberry. Tight and puckered. He couldn't resist tracing his forefinger over one generous areola. Her breasts were lush, perfectly round and so inviting. His mouth watered to taste her.

Marni's eyes were slumberously sensual as she watched his surveillance. She arched one brow, as if asking what was taking him so long.

Good question.

Hunter cupped both breasts in his hands, weighing their

bounty, lifting the delicious tips for his mouth. His tongue swirled around one, then the other. He sipped, delicate and sweet. Her fingers dug into the small of his back, her breath coming faster and faster.

His dick throbbed, tension spinning tighter and tighter through his body. Giving in to the desperation, he sucked hard on one nipple while his fingers plucked at the other. She cried out, then almost made him explode by wrapping one leg around his thigh and pressing herself tight against his dick.

Hunter dropped to his knees, yanking the zipper of her skirt down as he went. He shoved the fabric down over her hips, then took another second to appreciate the glorious view.

Clad only in a tiny pair of zebra-striped panties at odds with the vintage look she'd been sporting all week, she looked like a modern goddess, offering a glimpse of heaven to the mortal at her feet.

A heaven he was all too ready to enjoy.

His eyes hot, his body desperate, he snapped that black-and-white fabric with a quick twist, leaving her totally nude.

Marni flinched, as if she were going to modestly cover herself. Then, at the look in his eyes, she gave a shuddering sigh and stepped a little wider, as if inviting him to go ahead and look.

He did more than look.

He leaned in close, hitching one of her thighs over his shoulder. He waited just long enough for her to settle her shoulders against the wall for balance, then he dove in.

He ran his tongue over her clitoris.

She cried out, then grabbed on to his head as though she was afraid of losing her balance.

He sipped. He nipped. His fingers reveled in the delicate dance in and out of her hot, wet canal.

Her breath came faster and faster. When he sucked the throbbing pink flesh between his teeth, she cried out. Her body spasmed, contracting around his fingers as she came.

"Bed?" she gasped.

"I don't think so," he responded, quickly getting to his feet. "Every time we land in that bed, this ends."

Her laughter filled the room even as she made quick work of his shirt, seemingly caught in the maelstrom of his desperate hunger.

Hunter wasn't kidding, though.

Hell, he was barely thinking.

He shrugged off his shirt while her fingers reached for the zipper of his jeans. His brain was barely engaged, all of the blood in his body throbbing along with his erection. He had just enough foresight to kick off his shoes so he could rid himself of the denim, then grabbed his wallet out of his pocket to snag a condom.

He knew she was on the Pill. He'd shared a tiny cabin with her long enough that little things like that became obvious. But he owed it to her to make sure she was safe until they could talk. And talking was out of the question right now.

So he quickly sheathed himself, her hot stare making it a little harder to get the latex over his still growing erection. Hell, all it was going to take was a touch of one of her fingers at this point, and he'd blow.

"Now."

He pressed his body against hers, his hands skimming up and down her curves. She gripped his shoulders, her nails digging in tight as she wrapped one leg around his thigh.

He lifted her by the ass, holding her body flush against his. She used his support to anchor her other foot around him, both ankles locking at the small of his back.

When her wet core pressed tight against his straining cock, Hunter lost it. He shifted their bodies so she was caught between the narrow dresser and his hips, using the rounded edge of the wood to anchor her hips as he thrust.

Hard.

Intense.

Deep.

Holy freaking hell, so incredibly deep.

Hunter growled as more pleasure than he'd ever felt pounded through him, even as he pounded into Marni.

Her cries started low and deep, growing higher and keener with each thrust. Her breath came in quick pants.

"Oh! Oh, oh, oh," she chanted, each word more breathless than the last, each one a higher decibel as her voice and her body climbed pleasure's peak.

Hunter thrust again.

Her fingers clutched at his shoulders, nails digging into his flesh. He growled.

She tensed.

Her eyes flew open to meet his demanding stare.

Pupils so huge they drowned out her sky-blue irises, Marni stared right back. There was a demand in her gaze, insisting that he give her more than satisfaction. Insisting on more than just sexual fulfillment.

He didn't know what she needed, what she wanted.

He just knew that whatever it was, he wanted her to have it.

He wanted to give her everything.

Hunter thrust again, holding her gaze.

Then he smiled.

A wicked promise that said without words that he'd meet her demands, and push her for a few of his own.

With that in mind, he shifted her higher.

One hand still on the sweet curve of her ass, he skimmed the other up her silky skin to cup her breast.

He bent his head, sucking the full, pouting tip into his mouth. His tongue swirled, sipping at her sweetness. He nipped, wanting to eat her up, to take everything she had.

His eyes never left hers.

She flew over the edge.

Her body exploded beneath his. Her breath shuddered, her entire being shaking with the intensity of her orgasm.

Beneath the exquisite pleasure on her face, he saw shock. Like she'd never felt anything so powerful. So good.

Yeah.

He grinned, his ego battling his body over which was being stroked harder right at that moment. Then she shifted, moving closer so her mouth closed over his.

Hunter lost it.

His breath.

His control.

His mind.

He was pure instinct.

His body bucked hard, shaking with the power of his orgasm. It exploded, taking him to levels of pleasure he'd never experienced. Never imagined.

He poured and poured and poured into her.

The climax was like a rolling earthquake, it just kept coming.

Finally, so breathless he was seeing spots in front of his eyes, the orgasm retreated to tiny shudders.

His legs were water. His arms shook. He could barely breathe.

Damn.

Never in his entire life had he felt as incredible as he did in that moment.

9

HUNTER CONSIDERED HIS life damned good. He had a great career. He had excellent luck with the ladies. He was financially secure, had good friends and a great father.

He'd never claim to be a humble man, nor was he interested in false modesty. So he'd always been pretty comfortable with the fact that he was good at sex. Damned good.

But he'd never been—the *sex* had never been—this good.

He wasn't surprised, though.

Marni inspired him to new levels of greatness.

What was tripping him out, though, was how fabulous the nonsex was with her.

They sat across from each other at the small table in their cabin, Marni's hair a tumble of curls over her silky robe. The deep blue fabric clung to her full breasts, emphasizing nipples still peaked from his earlier ministrations.

"So who's your biggest life influence?" she asked, dipping her strawberry into a pot of warm chocolate, then nibbling. Hunter's mouth watered, his gaze locked on her mouth.

"Influence?" he repeated absently, shifting in his chair. His jeans, all he had on, tightened enough to make him glad he hadn't bothered to snap them.

"Yes. Influence. Mine is my aunt." Marni continued to eat her strawberries, alternating between the chocolate and fluffy whipped cream. As she nibbled, she talked about her huge family and how her aunt stood out from what sounded like a very intrusive crowd.

"How do you deal with that?" he asked, interrupting her description of a recent family outing that'd turned into a speed dating–style blind date, with four cousins bringing along their version of her perfect man. "The interference, the constant nagging. Isn't family a pain in the ass?"

Marni laughed and shrugged. The movement did delicious things to her robe, the fabric rippling over her breasts, baring a little more of that pale, silky flesh. Hunter shifted in the chair again.

"They're interfering, yes, but they love me. There's something incredibly comforting in knowing they are always there. The ties of family are like a safety net, you know? It's a lot easier to fly knowing they are there."

Hunter nodded before he realized he was agreeing.

"My dad's like that, I guess. He's always had this absolute belief in me. Even when I was a kid." Hunter gave a little laugh, remembering. "I was maybe four when I declared I wanted to be—" FBI. Hell, he was getting a little too relaxed here. To cover his wince, he reached over and stole one of Marni's strawberries. "I'd told him I wanted to be like him. He never laughed. He just sat my four-year-old self down and said if I wanted something, I had to work at it. Then he spent the next fifteen-to-twenty years showing me how."

Twirling the strawberry between his fingers, Hunter watched the juicy red fruit swirl as he remembered all the times, all the ways, his dad had been there. Had influenced him. Paving the way in his career, showing him overtly and silently his unstinting support.

"You really look up to him, don't you?" Marni asked quietly. "I mean, I love my family, but the only one I think I might want to be like is my aunt. But you and your father, that must be a pretty special relationship."

Hunter shrugged, a little abashed to realize just how much he did love his father. And how easy Marni made it for him to feel those emotions without feeling like a jerk. The only other person he'd ever talked about his family with was his best friend, Caleb.

Shifting his gaze from the strawberry to Marni, he noted the sweet warmth in her eyes, the softness in her expression as she looked at him. It was as if she was reaching into his heart and tugging at the strings there. As if she was testing to make sure he had enough depth, enough emotion, to match hers.

Damned if he didn't wonder that himself.

And suddenly, for the first time in his life, he hoped he did.

Like a slap upside the head, Hunter reeled at that insight.

Then, because he knew thinking about it would ruin what they had going here, that the minute he accepted that there was something emotional here, he'd slam the door shut. If he ignored the emotions, he could happily enjoy everything else between him and Marni.

The laughter.

The discussions.

The teasing.

And the sex.

Those emotions, though, kept pounding, pushing, trying to get his attention.

Determined to ignore them, Hunter went the only route he knew would work one hundred percent.

He stood and, ignoring Marni's surprised look, pulled her to her feet. Then he grabbed up the tray of chocolate and whipped cream.

"What are you doing?" she asked, following him to the bed.

"You ate all the strawberries," he pointed out, flicking the belt of her robe open with a quick twist of his fingers. The heavy satin slid down her body, leaving her gleaming, naked, in the dim lamplight. "So I'll have to eat my snack off your body."

MARNI LAY IN HUNTER'S ARMS, her body limp with satisfaction. Forty-eight or so hours of exploring each other's bodies, of playing out ever sexual fantasy that could be played on a moving train, and you'd think she'd be satiated.

She glanced at the floor next to the door, where the daily briefings of the train's murder mystery event had piled up since their first morning together when Hunter had insisted that Simpson slide them under the door instead of disturbing them.

The last one declared the murderer to be Peter Principle, and invited everyone to the final party that evening to celebrate the sleuthing successes.

Which was yet another reminder that the train was due in San Francisco in the morning.

A feeling of panic tried to take hold in Marni's stomach. This was almost over. She needed to get her fill of Hunter. To convince her body that it'd had enough to last the rest of her life.

"That was good," he murmured against the back of her neck. One hand released its gentle hold of her breast to slide down to her waist, but the other stayed, all cozy and tempting, in the warm, damp heat between her thighs. His fingers didn't move. Just set up camp, like an ongoing reminder that he could send her spiraling into a lovely orgasm anytime he wanted. "I think that was good enough to qualify for our top-ten list."

"Which position are you bumping to put it there?" she asked with a husky laugh.

"Hmm, I don't know," he teased, his warm laughter making her hair flutter across her ear. "I'm pretty sure they're all tied for first place."

"Nice answer," she said with a sleepy giggle.

And not one she'd argue with.

Every time they'd made love was a vivid memory. Every kiss, every touch stood out in her mind in bright, intense detail. It was a little scary how incredible they were together.

They'd had each other every way she could imagine, every way he'd suggested. At this point, they'd need to hit Google for position inspiration.

"You know, I think we need a tiebreaker." She reached behind her, her fingers trailing between their bodies to cup his growing erection. The man had the most amazing recovery powers. "What do you think it'll take to top all the other times? You on top? Me on top? Chocolate, whipped cream, scarves? What do you think?"

Hunter's laugh was just this side of wicked.

Seductive.

Marni melted at the sound. She should laugh, too. Make as if it was all in fun.

But he made her feel things inside, the most incredible things. She could handle the physical ones. The emotional ones, though? They were starting to scare the hell out of her.

"Why don't we give this a try," he suggested, his lips

skimming her shoulder before he shifted downward. Marni shivered, reluctantly releasing her hold on his hardening cock. She loved stroking his length, enjoying the power of his reaction to her tactile teasing. Still, she reveled in the feel of its rigid velvet slide as it pressed lower, over her butt cheeks and to her thigh as he kissed his way down her spine.

Marni moaned softly when he reached that delicate spot at the small of her back and nibbled soft, wet kisses over her sensitive flesh. She wrapped her arms around her pillow, curving her body into the mattress and rolling flat on her belly to give Hunter better access to play.

He seemed to have some special sense of when her thoughts were going too deep, of when she was freaking herself out.

Marni knew that part should freak her out, too.

But whenever she got her hand on the handle of that freak-out door, he pulled her back, distracted her with incredible sex.

Her eyes fluttered, the lights of the passing night flashing through the train window as his hands squeezed her breasts, his tongue skimming the curve of her back where it met her butt before continuing downward.

His hands scooped under her body, lifting her hips into the air as he wedged himself between her thighs so they parted wide. Heat, a combination of embarrassed delight and passion, washed over her cheeks—all four of them. He pressed one finger, then two, into her burning, wet passage. Marni whimpered. His tongue slid along her folds, sipping and flicking. She moaned.

He played her as if she was an instrument and he a master musician. Fingers and mouth worked in concert, building the tension in her body to a crescendo pitch. Marni's back arched. Passion tightened, curling like a taut spring between her legs.

All it took was one extra pluck of his finger, his teeth scraping over her aching bud. The climax swept through her body. Marni buried her face, her cries muffled by the soft pillow. Her body shook with the power of her orgasm, tiny tremors going on and on.

She felt Hunter move and tried to catch her breath, to prepare for the next round. Hands grasping her hips so she couldn't move, though. Then he plunged.

Hard.

Powerful.

Marni tried to meet his thrust, to intensify the driving friction.

But he held her captive, his fingers stabbing into the soft flesh of her hips like a vise.

She whimpered.

He slid in, then out.

Slow, wet, deep and hard. He was so big, so incredible. And totally in control.

Marni's fingers flexed, as if to reach back. But she didn't. She kept her hands on the pillow, her body at his mercy. This was a part of the game. To see how long she could last before trying to wrest back some portion of control.

She didn't make it more than a minute, maybe two, before the next orgasm exploded. Lights flashed behind her closed eyes, like fireworks matching the heat deep in her belly.

Before the scream had cleared her throat, he flipped her over. His hands gripped her thighs again, this time anchoring them high, so her ankles draped over his shoulders.

Through passion-blurred eyes, Marni stared at his face. Tight, controlled. And right there on the edge. She knew the signs now. The taut pull of the flesh around his eyes. The fire in his gaze as he demanded without words that she put it all out there, that she give over everything. Because he'd do the same.

The thought of that, the knowledge that he was willing to put everything he had into this connection between them, that it was so much more, bigger, deeper than just his very talented dick in her very well-pleasured body, flipped her trigger.

Marni arched, gasping.

She couldn't close her eyes. Couldn't tear her gaze from his. But she flew over the edge, soaring higher because he smiled, his look pure triumph.

Then, because she knew it drove him crazy, she called on the last vestiges of her own control and gave him a sultry smile and a flutter of her lashes.

His explosive climax sent her flying over one more time, her gasps mingling with his guttural cry.

Oh, yeah. The man was amazing.

THE TRAIN WAS STILL. They must have arrived in San Francisco, Marni realized when she awoke the next morning.

And she was still wrapped in Hunter's arms.

With a deep, satisfied sigh, she gave herself a moment to revel in how good it felt. Better than anything she'd ever experienced. Not just the sex, which was mind-blowing. But this, she realized, snuggling closer. Feeling so connected, so safe. So loved.

Her eyes flew open.

Her heart stopped for a quick, panicked second.

What had happened? Or a better question would be, What the hell had she been thinking? Or not thinking, clearly. If her brain had been engaged instead of her body reveling in indulgent pleasure for two days, she'd have seen this coming. She'd have been able to sidestep it.

Maybe.

But it was too late now.

Terror took hold in her belly.

She'd gone and done it. Brilliant, career-focused, got-her-shit-together and nobody-was-going-to-stop-her Marni Clare had absolutely gone and done it.

She watched as the room did a slow, murky spin, even as her mind grappled with the truth.

She'd fallen in love with Hunter.

Holy cow. How could she fall in love with him? She didn't even know his first name.

She shifted. Slowly, so as not to wake the man who she was suddenly terrified of. As if he were an explosive device that any quick move might set off, she put every bit of her concentration on getting away as fast as she could without waking him up.

And tried to pretend she wasn't turned on by the feel of his hair-roughed thigh sliding over hers, of the heavy weight of his arm as she carefully lifted it off her waist.

As she slid from the bed, he muttered something in his sleep, then rolled facedown into the pillow.

The urge to climb back between those sheets and cuddle against his warm body was stronger than anything Marni could remember feeling. Stronger than her desire to protect her heart. Stronger than her ambition and career goals.

It was like getting hit upside the head with a giant cartoon frying pan. Marni swore she could see little birdies flying in circles around her head, all singing to the demise of her dreams. Tweeting their goodbye to her career.

Terror buzzed in her ears, gripped her stomach in a tight fist.

She had to get out of here.

Not to protect her heart.

Hell, that was already guaranteed to be shattered. She'd have to deal with it no matter what.

But if she didn't leave now, didn't get away from the Novocain-like effect Hunter had on her ambition, she'd give it all up.

And end up hating herself.

She dressed in silence. Constantly reminding herself to pull on each item of clothing quietly, as if a single sound would waken not only Hunter, but waken a Hunter who would immediately start spouting off verbal demands that she wasn't prepared to meet. Questions.

She was the one supposed to be answering questions. To be searching for information, building a story.

Some ace reporter she was. The only prize she'd had her eye on for the past two days was the one between Hunter's thighs.

She wet her lips, her gaze sliding over his body with regret for the blanket covering that prize. One more peek, one more taste, was that too much to ask for?

God, she was ready to come again just thinking about his dick. She realized in the past couple of days, this gorgeous man had unknowingly provided her with years of sexual pleasure, whether he was present in the flesh or not.

As she held on to the table to steady herself while slipping into her boots, she averted her eyes, glancing at a sheaf of papers Hunter had forgotten to put away when she'd surprised him the previous night. As before, the writing was a bizarre mess, somewhere between Middle-earth runes and sloppy shorthand. Was that an FBI thing or just how he wrote? Smiling a little, she imagined Hunter as a schoolboy, explaining to his teacher that his report was illegible because he was gonna be a government agent when he grew up.

Even though she knew she couldn't read anything there, she flipped through the pages as if they were a fan. Then, frowning, she flipped back to one that'd caught her eye.

B.B.

Beverly Burns?

Beverly Burns had disappeared. Nobody knew what had happened to her. Rumors abounded, everything from a runaway wife to Burns locking her in a cellar somewhere.

Marni had talked to the doorman of their building right after the explosion. He'd told her that the couple had a major argument the night before, a screaming match right there in the middle of the lobby. It'd ended ugly, with the missus slapping her husband across the face, then storming out. When Marni had followed up with the same doorman four days later, he still hadn't seen the pretty young Beverly. Nor, he'd whispered, had someone come to get any of her treasured possessions. At least, not according to the maid who cleaned their apartment.

Marni actually knew Beverly Burns from her work in fashion circles. Using her husband's money, she'd launched her own designer line and was obsessed with being the next big name in fashion. The woman was a vain namedropper who lived for her clothes and valued each button more than any single person in her life. She wouldn't have taken off without her fancy wardrobe.

Had Charles done something with her?

Or was she the woman Hunter had escaped the exploding building with? Had Burns left her for dead before blowing up his own building? Was she still alive? Meghan had said there was a woman, but not whether she survived or not.

Holy cow. That'd blow her original story idea out of

the water. Tying Burns to attempted murder? She could start working on her Pulitzer acceptance speech as soon as she turned that article in.

Trying to curb her excitement, Marni frowned at the notes again, but couldn't make heads or tails of more than the initials. Then she spotted the letters *SF* and the word *Paris*. She turned the paper over, noting it was a hotel receipt dated three days ago, again with the initials B.B. She glanced at the bed quickly to make sure Hunter was still sleeping, then shifted a couple of the papers covered in his unreadable handwriting to see if there was anything she could understand.

Did this have anything to do with the case? How? Burns was strictly U.S. From what Marni had been able to pull together, the guy had a major phobia of the ocean. He refused to fly over water, so hadn't ever left the continent.

So what was all the information on fashion and Paris for? Was Hunter looking into being transferred to Europe? Did they even have FBI operatives overseas? In the fashion industry? Her brain raced with possible answers, a million more questions and a ton of directions of inquiry. She wanted her laptop. She wanted her phone. Like a nagging, impossible-to-ignore need, she had to get to the bottom of this.

All of her excitement came to a painful, screeching halt in her mind. She sighed, feeling as if someone had just poured a vatful of misery over her head. Getting to the bottom of this meant using this information she'd just found. And that meant betraying Hunter.

Frowning, she looked over at sleeping beauty, his soft snores muted by the pillow cushioning his face. Marni's gaze softened as her eyes traced the strong lines of his back. Her fingers itched to touch, her mouth watered for another taste.

She'd never get enough of him.

Her stomach clenched, terror hitting her like a brick wall.

This was supposed to be a fun interlude. Great sex. A once-in-a-lifetime experience. Hot times with a sexy federal agent. That was the kind of thing that looked great in a fascinating biography looking back over the adventurous life of a prizewinning news reporter when she was, oh, say seventy or so. The sexy chapter, guaranteeing reader delight.

What this wasn't supposed to be was a way for Marni to ruin her life by falling in love.

She'd always said she was too smart to put her career behind some guy. Despite the fact that her entire family had always ignored her vow, she'd always said she wasn't marrying, because she wanted her career to come first.

And the best way to avoid the trap of marriage was to evade the complication of falling in love.

She knew that.

She'd vowed it.

Her knees went wonky.

And she'd gone and done it anyway.

If she wasn't afraid the sound would wake Hunter, she'd smack herself in the forehead.

Instead, she did the only thing she could think of.

The only thing that made any sense when faced with the huge, mind-blowing realization that she had just gone and fallen for a man so strong, so intense and so powerful he'd make her second-guess her every career decision. Hell, at this rate, if Hunter offered her six orgasms a week and a quickie on Mondays, she'd probably agree to don an apron and play housewife.

She shuddered at the terrifying image.

As quiet as a mouse under the nose of a starving cat, she packed her bags and gathered her things.

Then, after one last, desperate look at the man sleeping in a fog of sexual satisfaction, she ran away.

HUNTER WOKE SLOWLY, irritated before he'd even opened his eyes but not sure why.

He'd fallen into a sexual stupor, exhausted and satisfied, hours ago. Now? He forced his eyes open to a squint and gauged the light coming through the window. It was morning. Time to get up.

Alone, he realized as he rolled to the edge of the bed, looking for Marni's warm, soft body.

Suddenly alert, he shifted, looked around. Where the hell was she? The sliding bathroom door was open, and the rest of the room took less than a second to peruse.

One thing he'd learned from pre-awesome sex with Marni was that she wasn't a morning person. She didn't slide quietly and happily from bed. Nope, she arose in a grumpy state of clumsiness, banging into walls on her way to her shower.

So where was she, and why wasn't she here, sharing that endearing grumpiness?

He showered and threw clothes on in record time, determined to find Marni and haul her back into bed. He didn't care how much she needed her caffeine. He wanted morning wake-up sex, dammit. And he wanted her, there, where he could see her, touch her. Be with her.

As irritated with himself for that deep, intense need as he was with her because her absence forced him to admit it, he yanked open the door.

And stopped short.

"What the hell are you doing here?"

All of a sudden, Hunter realized the train was still.

He'd been so obsessed with finding Marni, with getting her back in bed, it'd totally escaped him that they'd already arrived in San Francisco.

"I'm here to make sure you didn't screw up the case," Murray said, his smile bland as he stepped around Hunter and into the cabin.

Hunter would have shot back a pithy remark about never screwing up anything. But there was something in his boss's stance and expression. A taunting sort of triumph that said the guy thought he had something embarrassing to gloat about.

Frowning, Hunter cast a fast look around the cabin, making sure Marni had all her stuff tucked away as usual. He relaxed. Other than her scent, there wasn't much sign of her.

"Screw up? Based on what? You weren't happy with the amount of info I got for you this week? Something wrong with me building enough evidence against Burns to add five more criminal counts to the charges? Including suspicion of murder."

That last one had been a major triumph, as far as Hunter was concerned. He'd dug deep enough into the email files Beverly had provided to find three instances he suspected were execution orders. He'd forwarded the information and his suspicions to the New York office for his guys to track down. He'd heard just last night that they'd found enough to tie Burns to one, possibly two of those murders. Hauling the guy up on murder one without bringing the wife he'd tried to blow to smithereens into it? Success in Hunter's book.

He waited to hear what it was in Murray's, though.

"You spent the entire trip here in this cushy berth?" the deputy director asked, twirling his finger to indicate the cabin.

Hunter leaned one shoulder against the wall and shrugged the other.

"I thought participation in the events was mandatory," Murray continued, his smirk a reminder of why he'd booked Hunter on this particular train in the first place.

"I think we've established that I'm okay ignoring rules that get in my way," Hunter shot back.

Murray's smile was replaced by an irritated grimace. Then, saying the words as if they were painful, he told Hunter, "Looks like your refusal to follow directions paid off in this case."

"Because you didn't get any photos of me looking like an idiot?"

"Because I got a tip that there was a reporter on the train. She's been asking questions about the Burns case, digging around. I don't want this story broken on the cover of some magazine."

Hunter grimaced. Damn. Unlike Murray, he didn't begrudge them doing their job. Hell, there were a lot of times their job made his a lot easier. Still, this case was as sensitive as a teenage girl with self-esteem issues. The extra charges could fall apart over the slightest detail. The last thing the FBI needed was some half-assed article on the case to put a screw to the works.

"Who's the reporter?" Everyone he'd met had been using their mystery event pseudonym, so he probably wouldn't recognize the name. Still, it was good info to have.

"Marni Clare," Murray said, consulting his pocket computer. "Writes for *Optimum* magazine."

What the fuck?

Hunter's expression didn't change.

His body didn't shift from its casual stance leaning against the wall.

But his mind?

Well, it took a good ten seconds to get past the vicious swearing for his mind to engage.

Marni was a reporter?

A freaking reporter?

He mentally put his fist through the wall, cussed up a storm and heaved a chair out the window. In his mind, he threw a fit so ugly, hardened criminals would hide.

But, thanks to years of practice, on the surface he kept it casual.

He cast another glance around the cabin. This time he noticed that Marni hadn't tucked her bags away, keeping things neat. She'd tidied herself right out of there. Her suitcase wasn't under the bed. Her lotions weren't on the tiny bathroom shelf.

"Nope. Didn't meet anyone claiming to be a reporter, or anybody asking questions about the case," he said honestly. His brain raced, reviewing the week. She'd never mentioned the case, or even hinted that she knew anything about the Burns case. Either Marni was a hell of a lot better reporter—or actor—than any he'd ever met, or she had no clue that he was FBI.

"Figured you kept it under control, but I had to check. Wanna get coffee before the official debarking time?" Murray suggested, glancing at his watch.

A vat of it might kick-start his brain, pushing him past this mental stuttering shock that the woman he'd been falling for had used the hell out of him.

Hunter still kept his expression neutral, but his gut churned with fury.

He'd love nothing more than to get coffee and find his erstwhile roommate for a few words, except he was sure she was long gone. Which meant she wouldn't be outing him as an idiot to his boss.

Still, discretion and valor and all that crap deemed it smarter to just get the hell out of here.

"Let's just go. Meals in this place are a circus, complete with sideshows. We'll check into the hotel and load up on room service." To emphasize his choice, Hunter grabbed what little he'd unpacked and started tossing things into his suitcase.

His eyes fell on the bed, still rumpled from his and Marni's last mattress tussle. The image of her face, glowing and tight with passion, filled his mind.

Watching her fly over the edge, listening to her laughter, seeing her curled up asleep next to him... He'd finally understood how a guy could put his career in second place for a woman.

Damn, he was an idiot.

Murray poked around the cabin. Cozy when it'd just been Hunter and Marni, with two large men—one of whom was bristling with barely controlled fury—the space was more fitting to a dollhouse.

"Yeah, let's go. I'll bet you're tired of this cramped space, right? Done with the whole train experience?"

Packed bag, briefcase and laptop in hand, Hunter offered a bland smile.

"You have no idea how done I am with this entire affair."

10

SHE SHOULD BE EXCITED and filled with anticipation. She was about to make one of her dreams come true. Meet her hero, the woman who'd inspired her every career decision since the second grade.

Marni stared at the looming town house, as elegant as the rest on the steep San Francisco residential street. But the flowers flanking the steps were a blurry yellow, difficult to focus on through eyes that kept tearing up.

She'd done the right thing—for both of them—by leaving Hunter.

She'd done the right thing—for her career—by tracking down the information from that hotel receipt, pulling every string she had to find out who had been in that hotel suite in the week after the explosion. While she hadn't been able to get a photo or name confirmation, she had gotten a physical description from a room service waiter describing the temperamental redhead who'd thrown her chocolate cake at the back of the head of the guy who, as the waiter put it, looked like an extra from *Men in Black*. Marni was sure that redhead was Beverly Burns, and that the cake-splattered suit-wearer was FBI or someone from WitSec.

She'd spent two days writing an edgy, hard-hitting article that would break open not only the case against Charles Burns but also point to the games the FBI played.

She should be thrilled.

Instead, she felt ill.

She should be exploring the excellent San Francisco shopping venues to choose a perfect edgy reporter wardrobe.

Instead, she was wearing her oldest jeans and a T-shirt as black as her mood.

Telling herself to focus on now, instead of crying over then, Marni wiped a nervous hand on her hip. Taking a deep breath, she climbed the steps, raised her hand and knocked on the bright red door.

"Yes?" the woman answering greeted. Her hair was as blond as sunshine, the creases around her eyes deep and cheerful. Slender and stylish, she looked at least ten years younger than the forty-eight Marni knew her to be.

"Robin Clare?"

"That's me. You selling something? I hope it's cookies. I'm partial to those chocolate mint ones."

Marni answered with a smile and a shake of her head.

"Actually, I don't have anything to sell. I'm here to meet you."

"You a reporter?"

How cool was it to be recognized as a reporter by one of the best in the business? A tiny thrill tickled its way up Marni's spine, but was chased back down by a trickle of doubt. Because she wasn't sure she had what it took to deserve that recognition. Not yet. And for the first time since she was eight years old and had started the *Gradeschool Gazette,* she wasn't positive she had what it'd take to be a great reporter.

"I'm Marni Clare," she answered slowly, her words as

hesitant as her confidence in a warm reception. "Melinda and Jason's daughter."

Robin's eyes, the same blue as her own, rounded for a second before narrowing to inspect Marni.

"Are you, now? Did something happen? Last I checked, everyone was healthy, hearty and whole."

"You check on the family?" Marni asked in surprise. Didn't *estranged* mean you locked that part of your life in a dark closet somewhere, pretending it didn't exist except in middle-of-the-night-insomnia-induced memories?

"Course I do. Better to know all the facts, even when you don't plan to use them." After letting Marni mull that for a second, Robin waved her inside. "But I can see from your face they're all fine. So you must have some other reason for crossing the country to show up on my doorstep. C'mon in. We'll talk."

Marni followed her aunt into the chic condo. Red walls, white trim, stark black leather furnishings all made a vivid backdrop for... Marni squinted to be sure. Was that art? Tall and slender, short and squat, black metal sculptures dotted the room like scary shadows waiting to jump out and yell boo.

"Be comfortable," Robin suggested, pointing at a thin leather bench and taking the one opposite. Marni perched on the surprisingly comfortable seat, still looking around.

"This is an incredible space," she finally said. Incredibly scary, but that little clarification was probably too rude to mention during their first meeting.

Robin looked around with an assessing and indulgent eye before nodding. "It is incredible, isn't it. I'm about finished with it, though. I've got my eye on a Persian theme next. A lot of carpets, silk pillows, gilt and tassels."

"I beg your pardon?" Marni shook her head, confused.

"I get bored. Oh, the constant travel helps, but it's not

enough. I used to move every two years. But staying in one condo is financially smart given the real estate fluctuations. Instead, I redecorate. Well, not personally. I couldn't tell a Chippendale from a chifforobe. I hire a decorator. They send me a catalog each year, I choose a theme and by the time I get back from my next story, the entire place is redone. Right down to the sheets." She wrapped her hands around her upraised knee and gave a satisfied nod.

Marni could only stare.

It wasn't as though she came from an unsophisticated nowhereville. She lived in Manhattan, for crying out loud. But she'd never heard of anything like that. It was so, well, indulgent. So impersonal. She frowned, looking around again, wondering if it felt as empty as it seemed.

Marni's nails dug into the tender flesh of her palms as she tried to pull her emotions back where they belonged. This was crazy. She shouldn't be second-guessing her choices because her aunt had a bizarre decorating style. She should be excited, craving the same privileged life. That was her goal. Freedom, fame, the ability to create a life that was perfectly suited to her own particular tastes.

Still, all of a sudden, she missed her mother's china cabinet. The one that had been in the family since before Marni was born. The one her mother wished, time after time, that she could get rid of because it was so huge and ugly, but wouldn't for sentimental reasons.

"So. You'd be my niece. Marni, right? That makes you the fifth girl from the oldest."

Marni started to correct her since she was actually the eighth oldest of her thirteen cousins. Then she did a quick count of just the girls. Devon, Meghan, Sammi, Carrie, her. Then Kyra, Lannie, Sheila and Marla.

Wow.

"You really do keep up with the family, don't you?"

Was that because she missed it? Her heart a little heavy at the idea of her aunt being so shut out, Marni almost reached over to give the woman's arm a pat.

But Robin's shrug didn't seem sad. More...disinterested.

"You're not here to borrow money, are you?" Robin asked, her affable smile fading a little. "I've got a strong policy against lending."

Borrow money? Horrified, Marni opened her mouth to protest, then snapped it shut. Was that better or worse than asking for career advice?

Before she could decide, Robin wrinkled her nose and added, "But family is family, so I might be willing to re-consider once I hear your story."

Holding out one hand in dismayed denial, Marni shook her head so fast, she whipped herself in the face with her own hair. "Oh, no. Thank you, but no, I'm really not here for money."

Robin arched one perfectly groomed brow, leaned back on her own bench and waited.

"I'm here to ask about your life," Marni blurted inel-egantly. She winced, pushed her hand through her hair. "I mean, I want to know more about you. About your ca-reer. What it's like, leaving the demands and expectations and, well, the burden of everything you grew up with and chasing your dream?"

"Exhilarating. Have you ever jumped from an air-plane?"

"No. About the closest I've ever gotten was maybe jumping on a trampoline," Marni offered with a weak smile.

Robin dismissed that with a wave.

"The drop from the plane, knowing you're completely at the mercy of fate, it's fabulous. That you can depend on just yourself, your equipment and the elements… That's the life, Marni."

Marni didn't get it. What did willingly stepping out of a perfectly sound airplane to plummet to the earth, dependent only on a flimsy piece of fabric and the wind, have to do with being a reporter?

Her confusion must have shown.

Robin leaned forward, her hands hanging loose between her knees, the look on her face intense.

"That's what it's like walking away from family. Leaving behind the safety net and demands. It's like diving into the unknown. It's fabulous."

"Couldn't you be the same reporter, have the same drive and success if you hadn't walked away, though?"

"Not a chance. There's no way I'd have pushed as hard, or felt as free if I hadn't closed that door."

Marni bit her lip. Well, then. Maybe she could settle on a similar career, with half the success, and keep her family ties. Just sort of distance them a little. Like, from the opposite coast. California, from what she'd seen since getting off the train that morning, was pretty.

The train.

She sighed.

And Hunter.

She was standing in a tidal wave of misery. As if she'd just wrenched open that door and let all the pain she'd tucked away pour out. She'd left him there, sleeping. She hadn't said goodbye, hadn't left a note. Nothing.

He'd figure it out, she knew.

The man was FBI. All he had to do, if he cared enough, was run her name and he'd know she was a reporter. Would figure out that she was a liar.

That she was a heartbroken, miserable liar was still her own secret, though.

"Can I ask a personal question?" she blurted.

"All questions should be personal. Otherwise they're a waste of air," Robin declared.

Right. Marni grimaced.

"You want a drink?" Robin offered after a few seconds of pained silence as her niece tried to figure out how to word her nosy question so it didn't come out like a waste of air.

Tequila would be nice.

Marni settled for ice water.

And used the couple of minutes while her aunt was gone to pull herself together. She wasn't a sucky reporter, dammit. She was just an emotional mess after leaving the man she loved. She was pathetic, not talentless. There was a difference. This was an interview, not a desperate plea for some answer that would paint a clear path for her own life.

Treat it like a biography, she decided. She was writing Robin Clare's life story. What information did she need to tell it right?

With that perky little pep talk ringing in her head, Marni lifted her chin and offered a bright smile of thanks when her aunt returned.

"So, my question is about relationships. You've achieved so much with your career. The stories you've broken, the places you've traveled, they're remarkable for anyone, let alone a woman who began reporting when it was a completely male dominated field."

"World's still dominated by men, girly. Don't let anyone tell you different," Robin broke in.

Marni made a mental note that her aunt still faced gender bias, wondering if it was as strong now as in the past, or if her views were a by-product of years of fighting prejudice.

"Did you feel you had to choose between your career and your emotional life?" Grimacing, she wet her throat with her ice water, then reframed that. "What I mean is, did you ever have a man who wanted more from you? Who resented your career?"

That wasn't quite the same as asking if she'd ever screwed over the man she loved for a hot story. But Marni figured that was the kind of question you eased into.

From the knowing look on her aunt's face, she'd picked up the subtext without much trouble, though.

"I made a decision early on that my career was my priority," Robin said slowly. As if each word were a bomb she was carefully setting on the painted concrete floor between them. "Because of that, all of my relationships have been based on a framework of distance. On the knowledge that I'd need to pick up and go at a moment's notice. That when I'm focused on a story, it gets all of my attention. I've had plenty of wonderful men in my life. But none took precedence over the story."

Marni looked at her hero. In her forties, Robin had seen and done everything Marni dreamed of. Except maybe that jumping out of the airplane thing. And now she was facing the rest of her life without the emotional accomplishments the rest of the Clare clan deemed mandatory. Family, marriage, children.

She didn't seem to mind.

"Do you regret it?"

"Regret it?" Robin's eyes rounded in shock, as if Marni had just asked if she'd offered blow jobs in exchange for inside scoops. "Girly, I love my life. I have success, travel, money. I'm living in one of the most exciting cities in the world, I mingle with the famous. I have lovers when I want, and privacy when I'm through with them."

"I take it that's a no."

"Not just a no. That'd be a hell no."

Misery settled in Marni's stomach.

She wanted to hear that it sucked.

That the life of an ambitious reporter, totally focused on chasing stories, on climbing the career ladder, was empty. Was lonely. Heck, she'd been hoping for a little sorrow.

"Seriously? It's that great?" she asked.

"Seriously." Robin gave her a rueful smile. "I can tell that's exactly what you were hoping to hear."

Marni's own smile was a little weak around the edges.

"I guess I'd hoped you'd tell me that giving it all up was a mistake. That family, a relationship, love, that they all trump ambition."

"Can't tell you what I don't believe." Robin paused, watching Marni over the edge of her own glass as she sipped her drink. "But I can give you a little advice if you want it."

That's why she was there, wasn't it? Even as her shoulders sank despondently, Marni made a bring-it-on gesture with one hand.

"Your climb up the ladder is yours. Not mine. You get to choose your baggage. And you might be better at carrying certain things. A relationship, kids, all that stuff isn't at odds with a great career. I've interviewed plenty of people who have both. I've worked with a few, too."

Hope was like a tiny seed trying to sprout against all odds. Marni had never before thought it possible, but suddenly she wanted to believe she could do it all. That she was strong enough, clever enough, dedicated enough to balance the successful career of her dreams with other things. Things like kids, family. Love.

Hunter's love. She swallowed hard against the painful lump in her throat.

"Would you put a story aside if you knew it'd cause a problem for someone you cared about? Ever?"

Could she set aside this story, sit on the news that Beverly Burns was still alive, no thanks to her husband? Could she ignore the information she'd discovered that proved Charles Burns had tried to blow up his wife, along with that building? But that a sexy, dedicated FBI agent had dragged her out of there before she'd been decimated? Could she pretend the FBI wasn't hiding the rumored late Mrs. Burns away, in exchange for as much dirt as they could get on her husband?

Marni wanted to think she could.

For love.

But she wasn't sure.

"Set aside a story for a man?" Robin mused, her face screwed up as if she'd just tasted something nasty. "I've never met a man who made me ask myself that, girly. If I did, though, I have to think he'd make the question moot. Because if he was the man for me, he'd know I couldn't take that path. The story, the truth…it's everything."

Not for the first time in the past couple of days, Marni was beset by doubts. Her stomach churned, misery making her ill. What did it say about her ambition, her dedication, if she wasn't willing to break a story because it might upset someone?

Shoulders as heavy as concrete, she wondered if she'd been fooling herself all these years. Because now, when faced with a shot at the biggest story of her life, she didn't want to take it. Not because she was afraid of success. But because she didn't want to betray Hunter.

"You've got some big choices to make," Robin observed quietly.

Marni met her gaze with her own troubled one, comforted by the sympathy in her aunt's blue eyes.

"You make them while worrying about how others will live with your decision, and you'll never be happy." The older woman set her glass aside, then after a visible hesitation, got up and crossed the room to sit by Marni. "You make them by asking yourself if you can live with them. Then, whatever others think, you'll know you've done what's right for you."

"Even if it hurts someone?"

"Girly, we all get hurt. That's life."

HUNTER CLIMBED THE STEPS of the federal court building, his briefcase in one hand, coffee in the other.

His gut burned as he downed the dregs, and he found no satisfaction from crushing the cardboard cup and spiking it into the trash.

He was getting used to that dissatisfaction. Caffeine and fury had fueled his past forty-eight hours, and as far as he could tell, the rage roiling in his gut wasn't going to dissipate anytime soon.

It was a toss-up what had infuriated him more.

Waking to find the train had arrived in San Francisco and Marni had disappeared. Not a word, not a note, nothing.

Or finding out she was a reporter.

So far, she'd turned in jack, though. At least, his sources hadn't been able to dig up a whisper of any story, except for that initial call to her editor that Murray had filled him in on.

Didn't mean she wasn't writing one.

The question was, what did she have to fill the pages? Supposition? Public knowledge?

He hadn't said anything about the case.

She hadn't asked diddly.

But his instincts, those vital intuitive flashes that not

only saved him from disaster, but often gave him the brilliant insights that put his case close rate at the top…those instincts said she had plenty.

Hunter shoved the heavy glass door open with enough force to send the oak bouncing against the marble wall and earned himself a few glares. He ignored them as he stormed his way through security and to the courtroom.

He tried to argue down his instincts. There was not one exchange between them that involved what he called business. Not directly, not overtly, not discreetly. The only interest she'd shown was in his body. Not his job.

Stopping in front of an eight-foot oil painting of the East Bay, he gritted his teeth. Well, hell. Had he just crossed over into his-ego-doth-protest-too-much land? It wasn't as if he'd never been pursued for a case. Or as if he'd ever thought a woman was more interested in him than she really was.

He stared blindly at the blur of land beyond the Golden Gate, forcing himself to face reality. None of those times mattered. Not on the job, not off.

Because, dammit, this was the first time it'd hurt.

And if she broke that story, it'd hurt a hell of a lot more than his embarrassingly fragile emotions. It'd send his career into a tailspin, ruining everything he stood for. Everything he'd dreamed of, worked for, his entire life.

"Special Agent Hunter, good to see you."

Glad for the interruption, more than happy to sideline his obsessive mental circles, Hunter blinked the concern off his face and turned to greet the prosecuting attorney.

"Denton," he said to the dapper blond man with a nod. They'd worked together on a few cases, and Hunter knew that beneath the cordial smile and frat-boy looks was a shark with an ambition addiction. There was nobody he'd rather have arguing this case.

"The opposing counsel is meeting with the judge now. We'll know of their decision within the next fifteen minutes."

When presented with the extensive additional charges two days before, Burns's team had been faced with the option to take their chance trying the case with the new charges. Or call for a mistrial and let their guy stay in jail while they regrouped and gave the FBI enough time to keep digging through suspicious information until they found solid facts. Aka, searching for bodies that'd turn those suspicion of manslaughter charges to murder one. Either way posed a risk. To Burns, that was.

Hunter wanted this case moving. Now.

He was one hundred percent sure that the feds would get the proof they needed to take Burns down if it was put on hold.

What he wasn't one hundred percent on was what his sexy little roommate knew, or what damage she could inflict on the outcome of the case, or quite possibly the life of Beverly Burns.

Focus, he mentally snapped. Worry did no good. Second-guessing and prognosticating was a waste of time. *Set it aside and focus on the damned job.*

"What's the temp?" he asked the attorney, wanting to gauge the chances that the lawyers would choose to move forward with the trial.

"Burns isn't liking his current accommodations. He's cocky enough to know that suspicion of murder isn't proof." Denton shrugged, as did Hunter, his gaze locked on the courtroom door. "My money says we're eating crappy courtroom cafeteria lunch today."

It didn't take more than five minutes before they were called into the courtroom. Denton spoke with the leader of the pack of lawyers flanking Burns, then nodded. His face was passive, but Hunter could see the look in his eyes. Countdown to shark attack. Looked as though they'd be sticking around for cafeteria jello surprise.

Then, and only then, did Hunter let his eyes shift to the crime boss. Broad and badass, the guy sported an iron buzz cut, a sharp jaw and a suit that'd cost Hunter a month's pay. Cocky and confident, Charles Burns didn't show an ounce of concern.

Perfect.

More than ready to take on Burns, his fat-cat attorneys and, hell, the entire criminal justice system if necessary, Hunter dropped to his seat and gave the crime boss an ugly smirk.

Yeah. This was war.

Six hours later, after a hearty lunch of that jello surprise and a questionable burger, Hunter took the stand.

"State your name for the records."

"Special Agent Michael Hunter, FBI." With that, Hunter raised his hand, recited his oath and settled into the game.

The questions were softball at this stage. Establishing his authority, outlining his role in the investigation. The defense wasn't stupid enough to try and take a hatchet to his reputation. They were going to try to limit his effectiveness, make his testimony irrelevant.

At ease, his expression and body language making it clear he was as comfortable as if he were lounging in his own living room, Hunter rarely took his gaze off of Burns.

Finally, while Denton and Burns's head shark yammered over a point of procedure, Hunter let his gaze wander.

It landed on a pretty blonde in the back of the room, seated behind a huge mountain of a guy, seemingly trying to hide.

He should have kept looking at the crime boss.

It was as though the floodgates burst. All the fury, the anger and frustration that'd been dogging him for the past two days pounded through his system again.

His responses became clipped. His attention split.

The chilly distance that was his usual testimony style took a hit as that anger started sparking at the edges.

Burns shifted in his seat.

His attorneys started scribbling a lot faster.

Murray frowned.

Denton tried to hide his grin.

Hunter didn't give a damn about any of that. He met Marni's wide-eyed gaze across the courtroom.

He watched her gulp. But brave little reporter that she was, she stood her ground. Or given that she was seated on one of the hard wooden benches, sat her ground. Lifting her chin, she met his glare with a calm look of her own, then probably because she couldn't resist, she fluttered her lashes.

He was torn between fury and laughter.

Over the top of that, though, was the dueling need to storm across the courtroom, grab her curvy butt and toss her over his shoulder. Whether he'd verbally rip into her or physically dive into her when he got them to privacy was the only question.

11

MARNI GLANCED AT HER watch: 10:00 p.m. You'd think the terror-inspired headache she'd earned seeing Hunter in the courtroom that afternoon would have faded by now. She'd only managed to stick around for ten minutes, leaving before he was freed from the safe haven of the witness stand.

Her head throbbing worse now from the combination of self-disgust, a very loud restaurant and one glass past her limit of wine, she opened her hotel room door, tucking her key card into her purse. She stepped out of her heels right there in the doorway, not bothering with the lights.

She shouldn't have gone to dinner with her aunt. She hadn't been good company. She'd felt lousy after sneaking in to watch part of the trial. She'd expected to see Hunter, of course. But she'd figured she'd be staring at the back of his head. That he'd be facing the judge, not taking the stand. The shock of his eyes meeting hers still ricocheted through her body. It'd been all she could do to sit down and take notes instead of run from the courthouse in tears.

She'd learned more watching him on the stand than she'd learned in all her research. Not more than she'd learned by stripping him naked and nibbling her way down his body, but she didn't figure any of that knowledge was relevant to her job.

In the end, she'd hurried out of that courthouse confused, upset and overwhelmed.

But as miserable as she'd felt, she hadn't wanted to risk the tenuous new family bond with her aunt by canceling their dinner plans. So she'd popped a couple painkillers, slicked on her brightest lipstick and pretended that her life was peachy keen for three hours.

Now all she wanted was some relaxing music, a hot bubble bath and her pillow.

"You're out late."

Her scream ricocheted off the walls. So did her purse when she heaved it across the room. The responding grunt told her she'd aimed true. She spun toward the door, grabbing the handle and preparing to scream bloody murder.

"Aww, is that any way to greet me after all we've been through? All we've done with each other. To each other."

Marni's body went into a Pavlovian sexual meltdown at the sound of that voice coming through the dark. Even if she hadn't recognized the shadow across the room, her body recognized the husky laugh.

But even as her body was screaming at her to turn around and launch it onto that gorgeous body, her mind was whispering caution warnings, while her instincts danced around waving flashing danger signs.

All things considered, she figured her mind and instincts were the smarter choice right now. Her body, already warming, was obviously biased.

"Don't you want to stick around? There's so much we have to talk about. What you were doing at the courthouse today. What we do for a living. Why you ditched me on the train."

Wrapped around the door handle, her fingers spasmed.

For a second, she wanted to continue her flight out of the room. To run from this confrontation and her own heart's needs. She closed her eyes, trying to pull together her nerve to face Hunter for the second time that day. As long as he didn't know she was a reporter, she could pretend she'd snuck into the courthouse to see him one last time.

But if he knew…

She shifted closer to the door, halfway turning the handle. Her ears rang and black dots did a wispy dance in her vision. She was really, really sure that running away would be the smart move right now.

"I'll just come after you. I'm a stickler for taking care of unfinished business. You might have figured that out, though."

Marni sucked in a deep breath. Pretending her heart wasn't pounding so loud in her head that she could barely hear him, she plastered a serene look on her face and turned around.

"Why on earth would you think I'd figure that out?" she asked, making her tone both light and incredulous while sticking close to the exit. "I think I'd be more interested in figuring out how you ended up in my hotel room."

A dark, private hotel room. With walls thick enough that she could moan and whimper and scream her pleasure without worry of facing a trainful of smirking faces the next day.

Lust drowned out fear crazy fast.

Marni's thighs turned to water, her nipples beading beneath her simple white T-shirt. She felt as if she'd had a gallon of those eight-hour energy drinks, all at once. Her nerves stood on end, her body zinging as if it were going to fly apart any second. At the same time, a languid heat seeped through her veins, desire heavy and aching in her body.

This was just one more reason why Hunter was bad for her. He confused her body, her mind and her heart, dammit.

"Like I said." He moved away from the wall he'd been leaning on, his face shadowed but his gorgeous body vividly clear in the pale light filtering through the window. Marni's heart sped up again, this time spurred by passion rather than fear. "We have some unfinished business to take care of."

What business?

Her anxiety intensified.

She glanced at her laptop, neat and tidy on the desk across the room. Even if he'd poked through it, he wouldn't have found her Burns story or any notes. Once in college she'd had a breaking story about the various methods students used to cheat on their exams stolen from her computer. Losing that byline had taught her to keep everything close, that passwords were easy to crack and that when it came to breaking a story people would steal without compunction. She eyed her purse, where it lay in a sad heap on the floor, innocuously hiding a jump drive holding her story notes and the provocative draft she'd already written in a fake lipstick case.

She was sure he'd figured out she was a reporter. Was that why he was here? She bit her lip, wondering how fast she could run barefoot. Probably faster than if she were in heels, at least until she reached the pavement.

Or, her heart whispered, maybe he was here because he'd missed her. Maybe he'd disregarded her privacy, tracking her down because he couldn't let things end between them. Perhaps he was as crazy about her as she was about him.

Yep. And the tooth fairy could be real and Santa might be chilling at the pole. A girl could always hope.

Marni wet her lips, not sure what to do if she wasn't going to defend herself when he started flinging accusations.

So she did nothing, except wait.

"So?" he prompted, his smile on the wicked side of intimidating. As if he figured he just had to stand there and look sexy and she'd spill all of her secrets across his feet.

Marni lifted her chin, stubborn determination glossing over the ugly nerves.

"So, I'd think a man as sophisticated as you would have figured it out. Wake up, woman gone, affair over. One, two, three." She ticked the countdown off with fingers that only shook a tiny bit. "I'd say the business is all finished, wouldn't you?"

"Nah. I wouldn't say that. I might say sneaking out is cowardly. Or I could outline a few etiquette basics, such as waiting until a guy gets his pants back on before you call it quits." His words grew harder with each syllable, the smile gone as he leaned closer. Even with three feet separating them, Marni felt he was pushing right into her personal space.

She resisted the urge to back up. Instead, she dug her toes into the carpet, pretending they were holding her in place.

"I'm not playing this game," she decided with a dismissive sniff.

"Babe, you already anted up. You can't walk away now."

"I already walked away. Consider it me folding, if you'd like," she suggested with a stiff smile. She didn't care if she sounded like a chicken. Why shouldn't she? She was nervous enough to sprout feathers.

Then, in a move she'd never imagined from a man who held control with such a deft hand, Hunter lost it.

Before she could blink, he stormed across the room, kicking the chair out of the way. She didn't even have a chance to uncurl her toes and turn to run before he grabbed her by the arms and lifted her off her feet.

Marni squeaked. Now her toes were grabbing at air.

"We aren't finished yet," he growled, his minty breath washing over her face.

"Finished? With what? Were you shorted an orgasm or two? One more obscure sexual position suddenly occurred to you and you felt cheated by not getting to try it out?" The words tumbled past Marni's lips so fast, she sounded like she was stuttering. As if the faster she talked, the sooner she'd find solid ground. "We'd reached San Francisco, Hunter. The end of the line. What could you possibly think we still had to finish?"

Besides honesty, forthright truths about their jobs and the case he was currently testifying on, of course. But she swallowed those options along with a tiny whimper of pleasure as he pressed her back against the wall.

Frustration tightened his face, his eyes narrow and his jaw clenched. Fury flashed like a lightning storm, fast, intense and fascinating.

Her heart raced, and her body melted. Because even that sudden fear carried a sexual edge, deep and needy.

"What do we have to finish?" he repeated, his words so low she felt them rather than heard them. "This."

HUNTER TOOK MARNI'S mouth with vicious greed. He had to have her. And he'd be damned if he'd take no for an answer.

All of the frustrations, all of the fury and hurt and betrayal he felt was channeled into that meeting of their lips. It was too raw, too greedy to be called a kiss. It was too carnal to walk away from.

After a second of shocked hesitation, she moaned against his lips, then tunneled her fingers through his hair, holding tight. She tried to shift, wriggling her body between the hard—and getting harder by the second—body and the wall. Other than enjoying the hell out of the results on his own body, Hunter ignored her squirms. Then she slid one leg, still a half foot off the ground, along his. Her bare foot arched along his thigh, then wrapped around so her heel dug into his butt cheek.

He exploded, like gasoline being poured over a fire. He reached down to cup the warm, soft flesh of her thigh, then slid his hand up under her short denim skirt to grab her butt. She wiggled closer, anchoring the hot core of her passion against his throbbing erection.

He left her mouth to race his lips over her throat in huge, biting kisses. The scent of her, rich and floral, filled his head. Surrounded him in the memory of every bit of pleasure they'd brought to each other.

He was a proud man. A strong man.

But he was pretty sure that if he didn't have her, right now, he'd break down and beg.

The fragile softness of her T-shirt was no defense against his need. He simply tore it out of his way with one quick rip.

Her gasp echoed, bouncing off the walls as her fingernails now dug into his shoulders. Pain and pleasure twined, tight and powerful.

Her skirt was just as easy, short enough that he easily shoved the denim up her hips. He wrapped one finger around the fragile lace of her panties and yanked.

Bare to him, her body was hot and pulsing.

His fingers drove into her welcoming wetness.

Her gasp quickly turned to a moan, deep and throaty. Hunter took that as an *oh, yeah, c'mon.*

With a quick flick of his wrist, he had his jeans unzipped and the hell out of his way.

He gripped her butt, shifting back so her weight was
balanced between the wall and his hands, and plunged.

Hard.

Intense.

It was like coming home.

Over and over again.

Marni's heels dug into his hips, anchoring her body to
his as she met each thrust with a little undulation that sent
his body soaring even higher.

"Michael," she breathed, her words a whisper that
began in his ear and quickly sifted its way into his soul.

Michael.

That's all it took. One word that reached in and tore
him to shreds.

With an eager growl, Hunter dove deeper. The edge
was still razor-sharp. The need was still desperate. But
his heart, closed and protected before, was wide-open and
vulnerable for the first time in his life.

Marni's body convulsed, clenching around his cock.
Her fingers bore holes in his back as she arched, wringing every drop of pleasure from her orgasm.

He watched her fly over the edge, the flush painting a
pink glow to her skin, her eyes hazed with satisfied passion. Her delight flipped a switch, removing all restraints
on his own.

Hunter exploded. His entire being poured into her in
a pulsing stream. His growl turned to a groan, low and
throaty. His body convulsed. Pumping, feeling more incredible than he'd ever felt before.

Instead of reveling in the power of his orgasm, though,
a feeling he'd never felt before grabbed hold.

He stared at Marni's pretty face, flushed and damp

with proof of her own pleasure. He'd been shot at, blown up, chased by a bear and marked for death by a vengeful crime boss.

But this was the first time he'd ever been terrified.

IT WAS LIKE FLOATING in a cloud. A pleasure-filled, mind-numbed, delight-induced cloud. All Marni could do was feel. Feel her breath, ragged and hot as it labored from a throat raw from screams of pleasure. Feel her pulse, pounding like a freight train, fast and out of control. Feel her heart, melting with more love than she'd ever felt for another person in her life.

She sighed. Her shoulders drooped against the wall, all of her fears, all of her worries sinking away. Whatever their differences, she and Hunter could work it out.

As if he heard her thoughts, and strenuously objected, Hunter released her butt so abruptly her feet slammed to the floor. He shifted, moving away from her body so fast she was chilled by the quick gust of air.

Her mouth dropped open. Shocked, she stared, but before she could ask what was going on, he'd stormed into the bathroom. The door shut with all the finality of an exclamation point.

She knew something had just gone horribly wrong, but she didn't know what. Her brain just wouldn't engage. On autopilot, she moved to her suitcase and found a shirt, pulling it on and tugging her skirt down to cover her still pulsating privates.

"How'd you know my given name?" Hunter asked when he stepped out of the bathroom.

Marni stared, her mind still numbed from the quick slide through a sexual fog.

"What?"

"You said my name. Just then." He gestured to the

wall where he'd just screwed her brains out. Without said brains, she wondered, how was she supposed to respond? Marni pushed her hands through her sweat-damp hair and shook her head.

"We spent a week on a train together, had more sex in that time than I had in my entire four years of college. You don't think I know your name?"

Tucking his shirt into his jeans, Hunter gave her a bland stare. And waited.

God, she hated the waiting.

It was even worse with this heavy expectation in the air. Hunter's unspoken demand. As if she were some recalcitrant child who'd easily fall in line with a wag of his finger and a disapproving look.

She'd be damned if she was going to cave to his tough-guy intimidation.

Marni lifted her chin and pressed her lips together.

He arched one brow, as if to say it was a little late for her to close her mouth, he'd already been there.

"So what'd you do? Use your contacts to dig into my FBI files? Poke into my college records? How deep did you go?" he snapped, his fury unabated by what had been—at least for her—a mind-blowing orgasm. "That's what a good reporter does when working a story, right? Opens every door, peeks into all the closets."

Marni caught her breath, trying to control the jolt that slammed through her body. As though she was standing on the edge of a high dive, knowing she was going to plunge at any second and trying to be prepared. Then having someone come up from behind to shove her right over the side.

Still, she reminded herself, she was a damned good swimmer.

So she waited a beat, using the time to steady her quivering nerves. She made a show of crossing one leg over the other and brushed a nonexistent piece of lint from her skirt. Then, her smile as chilly as his words, she shook her head. "I was in the courthouse when you gave testimony, remember. You were sworn in using your full name."

His face going blank, he stared. Calculating.

"And that's your excuse?"

"My excuse for what? Getting a little too emotional while you did me against the wall?"

"You know, I think I liked it better when you were doing that unobtrusive sweet act," he decided, crossing both arms over his chest and giving her a frustrated look.

She didn't bother to deny that it had been an act.

"Was that when you were pretending to be an unassuming government pencil pusher?" she asked instead, offering an arch smile. "How'd that budget go? Was your boss happy with the way you crunched the numbers?"

"Clever. I guess that comes in handy, your ability to play with words and craft shrewd questions."

"So you know I'm a reporter," she said with a shrug, making as if she didn't care. "And you are a big, bad FBI special agent. I guess we're even."

"Even?" He straightened, looking scary again. "You think so?"

Afraid he'd grab her for another round of wild sex, Marni jumped up from the bed. No point making it easy for him. She scurried—yes, she was ashamed to admit it to herself, but this quickstep was definitely a scurry—across the room.

"Yes, we're even. You lied, I lied. You hid truths, I hid truths. You aren't what you said…" She paused, then tapped her finger against her lips and shook her head. "Oh, wait, I'm exactly what I said. A writer. So I guess you're right. We're not even."

Suddenly she was tired of being scared.

Scared of Hunter's reaction.

Scared of her own emotions.

Scared of making a choice.

Enough was enough.

Marni didn't know what she was going to do about any of it. But she did know she wouldn't figure it out with Hunter looking over her in glaring fury, working his government-learned intimidation tactics.

"We have a few things to settle," he said, sidestepping her comparison of their job claims.

"Do we?" she asked, now crossing her own arms defensively over her chest. Hindsight said it'd been insane to sleep with the man central to the biggest article she'd ever written. Her judgment was compromised, her every decision biased by their relationship. Even now, when she knew damned well she'd written the biggest, strongest article of her career, she worried about turning it in. Worried that she'd hurt Hunter's career, jeopardize his case, make him look bad.

But even as she mentally screamed at herself for making such a huge mistake, she still couldn't regret it. Because her time, her relationship, her feelings for Hunter, they were once in a lifetime.

Even if they were, thanks to reality, now over.

He stepped closer, giving her a long, searching look.

"You've been asking questions about Beverly Burns," he accused quietly.

Marni blinked. Then, because she knew he was watching for it, she tried to keep her expression absolutely neutral. She couldn't stop her fingers from clasping around each other, though.

"So? We knew each other from the fashion circuit.

Maybe I was putting together a piece on her latest clothing line."

"And maybe you're digging into things that are none of your business."

"Hmm, isn't facts and stories that interest the public exactly the business of a reporter?" she mused, making a show of tapping her finger against her chin.

Hunter scowled.

"You've got nothing," he decided.

Marni didn't know why his assurance made her so angry. Maybe it was years of her family doubting her. Maybe it was her own questioning of her decision with this article. But it was as if he'd just blasted her in the face with a water balloon. She was drenched with irritation.

"I got the facts," she snapped back. "Facts like the FBI is covering up Beverly Burns's supposed death."

Reaching out as if to grab the words back, Marni winced. She'd never make it as a spy. Or secret keeper, for that matter. She was a reporter because she was nosy, not because she was good at keeping things quiet.

"Shit," he muttered, frustration, anger and regret all flashing across his face. Then, with a deep breath through his nose, Hunter straightened. As if he grew three extra inches, and not in a way that interested her, he was back to a menacing threat looming over her.

"Whatever you think you know, forget it," he suggested in a tone all the more formidable for its quiet. "You're risking lives if you keep digging. I'm not going to let you put an innocent woman in danger."

Let her? Marni couldn't tell which was stronger. Her anger at the idea that he'd *let her* do any damned thing. Or the sudden spurt of jealousy spinning through her system, green and toxic. From everything she'd found out, Hunter had made Beverly Burns his own personal pet project. Because he was just that kind of guy? Or because she was a sexy, gorgeous redhead?

"Oh, yeah. Such a poor, sweet, innocent woman." She gave a derisive scowl. "You're talking about the wife of a known mobster. Beverly Burns's own father was indicted on racketeering charges. She's got a reputation that's nearly as vicious as her husband's."

Something he should keep in mind while he was *protecting* her.

The look on Hunter's face wasn't possessive or affectionate, though. It was resolute. He stared long enough to make Marni want to squirm. Then, suddenly, he seemed to pull the plug on the scary aura. In the blink of an eye, he wasn't daunting FBI Agent Man anymore, he was the sexy guy she'd fallen in love with. But the sexy guy who looked crazy serious, determinedly grim.

"She's a dead woman if you let it be known that she didn't go down with that building," he said quietly, crossing his arms over his chest and frowning as if the weight of that was pressing down on his own shoulders.

Marni rolled her eyes, wanting to dismiss it as an exaggeration. But she knew Hunter didn't exaggerate.

"You're going to put Burns away. Between that and her family contacts, I'm sure she'd be safe enough," Marni hazarded.

"Her family is small potatoes compared to Burns. And you're not naive enough to think he won't have almost as much power behind bars as he would as a free man." The look Hunter gave her said if she was thinking in that direction, she should stick with reporting hemlines.

She had to suck in her lower lip to stop herself from pouting. It wasn't that she was naive. She just hadn't thought about it like that. So maybe she'd earned a few more articles on shoes, but definitely not hemlines.

"Just let it go," he ordered, as if he instinctively knew he'd made his point. Or, since she was such master spy material, he'd read it on her face.

"I'm not dropping anything," she shot back, shaking her head and reminding herself of everything she had on the line here.

"Marni…"

"What? What are you going to do?" she challenged. "Arrest me so I won't write the story?"

He gave her a long look, emotions swirling in the blue depths of his eyes. A shiver ran up Marni's spine as she realized that, yes, that had probably been his intention. If that story ran, she'd be jeopardizing his case. He was a man who worked outside the rules whenever it suited him, as comfortable using unconventional methods to close a case as he was calling the shots.

"You need to ask yourself this," he said, leaning in so close she could almost feel his heartbeat. "Are you willing to sentence a woman to death just to feed your own ambition?"

With that, and a look that clearly stated that if she was, she wasn't the woman he thought her to be, Hunter turned on his heel and strode out of the room.

His words echoed through the room.

He didn't look back.

Marni didn't know how long she stared at the closed door, not seeing a thing.

All she knew was that she couldn't face the mirror.

Because she couldn't handle what she'd see there yet.

12

HUNTER SAT IN THE CORNER of the dimly lit bar, glaring at his Scotch.

"You stare at it long enough, it might even be palatable."

He slid his gaze sideways, blinked in surprise to see his best friend standing there, then he shook his head.

"Not much makes rotgut palatable," he said, shrugging and pushing the glass aside. The rickety table wobbled. As appealing as it was, getting drunk wasn't a very good answer to his woes. But a better one might have just hitched himself onto the adjacent bar stool.

"This is a surprise," Hunter decided, keeping to his habit of understatement.

Caleb Black's eyes gleamed gold as he gave a wicked grin. "Consider it an early birthday present."

Hunter made a show of looking past his college roommate's shoulder, as if searching for a gift, then gave him a slow once-over. "You got a bow on you somewhere I don't see?"

"You asking about my package?" Caleb quipped. He looked as if he'd just dropped in for a drink and friendly hello, but Hunter knew him well enough to see the intensity in his oldest friend's eyes.

Hunter'd had enough rotgut to smirk, but not enough that he felt obligated to answer the questions in his old friend's eyes.

"You're a long ways from home. And my birthday is in November. So what's the deal?"

"San Francisco isn't that far from the Santa Cruz Mountains." In the years since they'd left college, Caleb had left an illustrious career with the DEA to settle in as sheriff of a small California town, but the two men were still tight. Probably tighter now, since Caleb wasn't spending half of each year undercover, and more likely to send Hunter dirty emails and regular texts. Or, like now, show up out of the blue. Caleb dragged the bowl of peanuts closer from the middle of the table.

"I heard you'd be here testifying, thought I'd come up and spend a day or so," he said. "I thought it'd be fun to watch you do the feebie dance, put a bad guy behind bars."

"He's not locked up yet."

And the case wasn't nearly as open and shut as Hunter had hoped. It wasn't that the feds' prosecutors weren't good. It was that Burns's money was paying for a top-notch team of sleazy sharks with the predatory skills of starving jackals.

The prosecution was winning. But it was taking a hell of a lot longer than any of them would like. Hunter knew from the increased frustration on Burns's face each day that he hadn't thought this would take more than a day or two, either.

Every day Hunter sat in that courthouse, ignoring the stink eye Murray kept throwing his way, trying to convince himself that keeping Beverly Burns in a safe house and out of the case wasn't a bad plan.

All the while he had this ticking time bomb in the form of a gorgeous, sexy blonde. He had no idea if she'd go off. No clue when. But the minute that story broke, the defense was going to call a mistrial, and very likely Burns would slide out from under the charges like the snake he was.

"So what's the deal? You're not usually the sleazy-bar drinking-alone type. Did the ferns die in all the preppie bars and this was your only option?"

"This case is getting to me," Hunter confessed, his words so low the tinny jukebox tunes almost drowned them out. "I called the strategy on it, and it's looking like it might blow up in my face."

Caleb pursed his lips, contemplating the far wall as if he could see the future in it. Maybe he could. His pretty little wife specialized in woo woo. Finally he slid his gaze back to Hunter.

"Worst-case scenario, you crap out at the FBI. I've got an opening for a deputy. You can come work for me."

After staring for one stunned second, Hunter threw back his head and laughed until his stomach hurt.

"Right. That's what I'm going to do if my career plunges into free fall. Plant myself in a tiny town, surrounded by known criminals."

"Suspected criminals," Caleb corrected with a grin, breaking open a peanut. "And given that two of them are married to FBI agents themselves, I'd say it's unlikely you'd have to worry about arresting anyone when you sat down to Sunday dinner with my family."

Now that was quite an image. Still grinning, Hunter let himself imagine a big, fancy Black meal with the guests lined up on either side of the table like cops and robbers. Paired off, boy, girl, boy, girl. And then there'd be him.

Alone.

No career, and no girl.

His grin slid away.

"What the hell is it with women?" Hunter finally asked. He peered at Caleb through eyes dimmed by enough rotgut to guarantee he'd feel like crap in the morning. "Why do they have to be so complicated? Or worse, so freaking obstinate."

"That's part of their appeal," Caleb mused, cracking open another peanut and popping the meat into his mouth. "Don't forget irritating, exasperating, confusing and, oh, yeah, sexy as hell."

Yep. That was Marni in a nutshell.

"You ever regret everything you gave up?"

"Gave up? For Pandora?"

Hunter nodded.

"I suppose you mean other than all the gorgeous women who'd constantly throw themselves at my feet?"

This time Hunter's nod was accompanied by a smirk.

Caleb lifted the basket of peanuts to poke through them, shook a couple into his hand and considered the question.

"It wasn't a matter of giving anything up. I'd already resigned the DEA, so the job wasn't in question. I might not have moved back to Black Oak if she wasn't there, but I've actually gained a lot from being there." Caleb chose a few more peanuts. "There are drawbacks. My father. Pandora's mother. They're more work than the criminals."

Hunter didn't doubt it. His own father had spent years trying to build a lock-tight case against Tobias Black, Caleb's dad. The man was a con extraordinaire. But a con with a heart of gold.

"What's her name?"

Caleb still had plenty of contacts in the DEA, and his own resources as a California sheriff. A name was all he needed to put together the entire story. Since Hunter was playing fast and loose with his stomach lining trying to decide if he'd done the right thing, he figured it was probably better not to offer up that information just yet.

He didn't insult either of them by playing stupid, though. He just shrugged.

"She tied to the Burns case?"

Hunter slanted a glare at his old roommate, wondering just how much digging Caleb had done before tracking him down.

"What's your interest in the case?" he asked instead.

"Not a whole lot other than wanting the trial to finish up quick enough that you still had time while you're on this coast to visit Black Oak."

"It should be this week. We've got him on the ropes, but his team is dancing fast. Still, unless something huge breaks, we'll be hearing closing arguments by Friday," Hunter hazarded, more open to discussing the realities of the case with Caleb than he'd be with any fellow FBI agents. Or even himself.

Especially since the biggest reality was that one juicy story hitting a national magazine could derail the entire thing.

He tossed back the Scotch with a pained grimace.

"You gonna come down this weekend, then? It'd be good timing. Maya and Gabriel are in town to celebrate the old man's birthday."

Once again numbed by the Scotch, Hunter smirked.

"You want me to attend your father's birthday party?"

Caleb matched his smirk with one of his own.

"Why not? Your dad will be there."

Shit.

Tension pounded.

"I'm not sure I'm up for seeing either one of them," he admitted.

Caleb didn't say a word. Just tossed back a few more

peanuts, then signaled the waitress for a beer. He gave Hunter's empty Scotch glass an assessing look, then lifted two fingers.

It seemed Caleb thought it was time to switch up his drinking preferences. Since he was swimming on a comfortable sea of booze already, Hunter didn't mind.

The scantily clad waitress, her hair a brassy shade that made Hunter miss Marni's soft flaxen curls all the more, dropped two steins on the table, held out her hand for Caleb's cash, then sauntered away.

Caleb took a drink, then pulled a face. Hunter probably should have warned him that what they had on tap in this place was a step up from horse piss. Then again, Caleb had been in enough dives to know that. He was just getting soft.

"It's never easy living up to certain reps, is it?" Caleb mused, referencing the comment about their fathers. "Or down to them."

Meaning their respective fathers.

Hunter shrugged like it didn't matter.

Then, Scotch-induced honesty forced him to admit, "I never figured living up to my old man was a problem. I mean, I had it figured out, you know? All the advantages he didn't have, a clear plan and a lot less holding me back."

"Like a wife and kid?"

"I'm not saying it was a bad idea for him," he shot back, grinning. "I think the results worked out pretty well. But for me? That kind of commitment would put a stranglehold on my trajectory."

"Or give you a nice cushion against your slightly obsessive drive to win."

Hunter frowned.

"Did you just call me obsessive?"

"Did you just claim you won't open your life to a wife

and the possibility of kids because they might slow down your climb up the FBI ladder?"

Hunter's head spun a few times clockwise, then once counterclockwise. Once it landed, he sighed.

"Okay, maybe I've been known to be obsessive. But that's what it takes, right? I want this career, and if I want it to shine, then I've gotta make sacrifices." Choices. Like letting the potential destroyer of his career move ahead with her story, just because he couldn't bring himself to play badass with her.

He'd listened to so many of her stories, watched how she lit up when she talked about writing, he knew how important her career was. But unlike him, she didn't have a strong family support system. Didn't have anyone who believed in her ability to make it happen.

No matter what it cost him, he couldn't be the one to crush those dreams. To intimidate the hell out of her so she was afraid to take a chance at them. Instead, he'd just cross his fingers and hope she didn't screw up his career on the way to making hers?

It was all Hunter could do not to drop his head into his hands and groan. He'd hit heretofore-unimagined levels of pathetic-ness.

"You're a mess," Caleb observed with his usual tact and diplomacy. "You never worried about trials before and usually take tough cases in stride. You want to talk it out?"

Hunter didn't know how to explain, even to himself, why he'd walked out and left Marni with the option to take her information public. He wasn't a do-gooder. Nor was he the kind of guy who left huge decisions up to other people, banking on his faith in humanity. Hell, he figured most of humanity was on the take, out to screw over the next guy.

Since he was clueless to explain the mess in his head, he shrugged instead.

"So you're saying I gotta go to your old man's birthday bash this weekend if I'm gonna get my own birthday gift? Isn't that called dirty pool?"

"You'll actually get the gift in November," Caleb clarified. The only thing missing from his canary-eating grin were a few feathers. "I'm just giving you the official heads-up this weekend."

Hunter narrowed his Scotch-blurred gaze.

"You might want to spill it before you burst."

"You might want to wrap up this case before the end of the year." Caleb tossed another peanut into his mouth, crunched, then grinned. "Because we're gonna want you in Black Oak then. You know, since Pandora wants you to stand as godfather."

The Scotch blur faded from Hunter's brain in a flash.

"Pandora's having a baby?" He grinned, feeling good for the first time in a week. He clasped Caleb's hand in a hard shake. "Seriously? Congrats, man. That's great."

Caleb shrugged like it was no big deal, but his beaming smile screamed his joy.

Hunter reveled in his friend's happiness for a few seconds. Then the alcohol haze lured him back to his own black thoughts.

"How do you do it? Juggle the demands of your career, marriage and now a kid?"

"I'm not undercover anymore. I don't think I could do it if I was. You lose yourself. Lose your life."

Hunter nodded, having done enough undercover to know what Caleb meant.

"Otherwise, juggling is just like anything else. If it's something that matters, you make it work." Still straddling the chair, Caleb leaned forward, so it perched on two legs. It creaked in protest. "So, what're you thinking about?"

"I'm not thinking anything," Hunter dismissed.

"Right." Caleb ate a few more nuts, then let his chair drop flat to the floor. "Look, you've done me a few favors. Now, officially we're square since I did you one last year. But in the name of friendship, I'm going to spot you another."

"That favor, as you call it, was what snagged you the pretty little wife you're so crazy in love with. So I think we're even."

Caleb waited.

Finally, Hunter shrugged. "Yeah, okay fine. I'll owe you one."

It spoke to what a solid friend he was that Caleb didn't smirk. He just nodded, dropped his arms to the table and leaned forward.

"You got it bad for this woman. Bad enough that you're questioning things you've always seen as black-and-white."

Hunter didn't need to ask how Caleb knew.

"The thing is, relationships, women, they always dance in the gray. They aren't going to simply fall in line behind your career. At least, the right one won't." Caleb stared into his beer for a second, his big dorky grin back. Then he met Hunter's gaze and shrugged. "You just gotta ask yourself what matters. What's life like with this woman in it? And what's it like without her."

Hunter shook his head, wanting to dismiss the idea of anyone lining up ahead of his career with an easy smile.

But the image of Marni's face kept flashing in his brain.

"Then what?"

"Then you accept the inevitable. You're in love enough to ask the questions, you're in love enough to find a way to live with the answers."

MARNI PACED.

From the tall black statue shaped like a menacing umbrella, then back to the squat one resembling a demented rabbit. Back, forth, again and again.

She pushed her hand through her hair, her fingers tangling in the unbrushed curls. She was a mess. Three days of alternating between pacing, writing and crying hadn't left much room for grooming and tidiness.

"Well?" she finally asked, unable to stand the wait any longer. Or the view. These statues were getting uglier by the hour.

Robin didn't seem to care about her torment, though.

The older woman held up one finger and continued to read. Marni went back to pacing. She only made it to squat and ugly, though, before her aunt set the pages aside.

"Well?" Marni asked again. She sat on the black leather bench opposite Robin. Then, too worried to take the news sitting down, she jumped up and started pacing again.

"Well…" Robin gave the printed pages another look, then hummed.

Marni had only met her aunt five days ago, but she'd already figured out that while the woman was quick to ask questions, she was slow to answer them. She weighed each word like it was gold, and she was a miser. It was harder to use a quote against someone if the words went unsaid, she'd informed her niece over dinner the previous night.

Still, frustration surged through Marni's system. It was all she could do not to dig her fingers into her hair and tug.

Finally, Robin pushed the papers away and smiled.

"I think you've a great deal of talent. You have a spark in your writing, an edge and humor that are balanced by a depth of emotion that tugs the reader in before they realize it."

Oh. Eyes huge, Marni started to smile. That was nice.

"You need editing, of course. You're a little wordy in

places, meandering in others. But the core is here, and the impact is huge."

Marni's mouth opened, but no words came out.

Wordy and meandering were editable. Huge, with a core and impact? *Holy cow.* She wanted to dance with the tree. To throw her arms wide and embrace the entire weird room. To curl up on the leather bench and cry.

She'd spent three days working on that piece.

Three days of second-guessing every word, of lecturing herself five ways from Sunday over making a major mistake. She'd searched her soul and spent endless hours trying to decide if she was making a mistake.

"So you think I'm doing the right thing?"

Robin sighed, then, looking so much like her brother that Marni hunched her shoulders like she did when her father lectured, the older woman folded her hands in her lap.

"I think the right thing is a subjective question. You have to live with the results, girly. You're the one taking a huge step and quite possibly shifting your entire career." She unfolded her fingers to tap the pages again. "If this has the impact I think it will, you're going to see some huge career opportunities open. It's smart to be sure you want to accept those opportunities, and their repercussions, before you submit this."

As if her aunt had just pierced a balloon, the words sucked all the energy out of Marni in a shockingly fast swoosh. She dropped to the bench and wrapped the fingers of her left hand around the fingers of the right, trying to figure out what to do. She switched hands, staring at her manicure but not seeing the chipped pink polish.

"If I write this profile instead of the Burns article, I'm taking my career in a completely different direction. I love writing biographies, but they will never get the same kind of attention hard-hitting stories would." Marni pushed one hand through her hair, her fingers snagging on the snarls. "Am I doing it because I think it's the right thing? Or because of Hunter?"

"Only you can decide that. Life is made up of choices. And choosing is tough. Anyone who tells you different is lying, girly." Robin sighed and gave a jerk of one shoulder. "As for right or wrong, I don't know. I really don't. I've never met anyone who I cared about as much as my career. I've never had a lover I could imagine lasting as long as my career. I've never met a man who made me feel as special as being a reporter does."

Well, there ya go. As much as Marni had enjoyed weaving a fantasy around the idea of happy-ever-after with Hunter, she knew, really, that it was just that...a fantasy.

And just because she was feeling an overwhelming deep emotional onslaught that she wanted to call love, that didn't mean it really was. Nor that it would last. Nor, her gut clenched, did it mean that Hunter had any reciprocal interest.

Given how they'd left things—or rather, how he'd left things when he'd stormed out—she'd be tiptoeing along the edge of insanity to think there was something solid between them. Something strong enough to build the hopes of a future on.

Marni chewed on her thumbnail, the tiny flakes of polish leaving a nasty taste in her mouth. Giving up her career ambitions, making a serious one-eighty in her goals for the remote, so-slim-it-was-barely-existent possibility of a future between her and Hunter?

She'd have to be insane to do that.

Her fingers tightened around each other so hard, her wrists were numb.

Wouldn't she?

"I guess depending on a career is a lot smarter than banking on a relationship," she finally said, her words hoarse and painful. She cleared her throat, then met her aunt's gaze with her brightest, fakest smile. "Which is what I've always said. Always believed. That just confirms it."

As if she'd seen something painful in that smile, Robin grimaced. Then she sighed and lifted both palms to the heavens, as if asking for guidance.

"Look," she said, her words halting, as though she had to search for and weigh each one, "I'm not saying that's the right choice. It's the choice I made. But I made it based on the options in front of me. If I had a man who made my toes curl, who made me think and made me laugh? That'd be harder to resist. If he was a guy who understood me. Deep down, totally got me... I've never had that, Marni. But if I had, well, that'd be a hard choice to make."

With each word, Robin leaned closer, looked older.

Marni shoved her hand through her hair, trying to process all of that.

It was like laboring for years, pushing and climbing to get to the top of a mountain. Then breathlessly, painfully reaching the top, only to have the grand guru of all that was bright and shiny offer a shrug and a dismissive *Nah, it's not all it's cracked up to be.* She was torn between sympathy, pity and horrified tears.

"I told you once, I've told you a bunch of times, girly. You have to make your decisions based on your baggage. And sometimes that baggage looks pretty damned awesome in the beginning, but loses its appeal after living with it a few years. Or a few months." Her aunt waved a hand at the statues standing in stark relief against her bloodred walls, as if they were the perfect example.

Marni grimaced. She wasn't so sure of equating Hunter

with baggage or butt-ugly artwork, but she was sure he qualified as pretty damned awesome.

The risk was huge.

This wasn't a choice she could backtrack on. Whatever she did, regardless of the results, she was stuck with it.

"I want him," she murmured, finally looking up to meet her aunt's patient gaze. "Even if this doesn't work out, even if I'm making the wrong choice for my career, I still want Hunter."

Robin bit her lip, as if she was bursting to say something. But she settled on a nod.

"What?" Marni prodded. "Please? I came to you for advice, I'd really like to hear your honest thoughts."

"You don't know me that well, girly. And despite the fact we share blood and looks, I don't know you." Robin got to her feet. Now it was she who was pacing from ugly statue to ugly statue. Marni dropped her eyes back to her nails, preferring to see her mangled manicure to those monstrosities.

"Look, I hate giving advice. I'm a selfish woman. I live my life for me, for my goals. I've dedicated myself to my career on purpose. Not because I don't think a woman can't have it all. To hell with that kind of thinking. Women can have anything and everything they want, if they work their asses off."

Marni agreed, but didn't want to set Robin off on another rant about gender equality. So she settled for a silent nod.

"I chose to go it alone because that's who I am," Robin finally said. She dropped back onto the bench, making it safe for Marni to look at her again. "I am ambitious, selfish and lazy. I'm also terrified of failure."

Marni shook her head.

"Ambitious and selfish to make those ambitions a reality, maybe. But I don't buy the rest."

"Like I said, we don't really know each other yet."

Marni's lips twitched, and she gave a gracious nod, acknowledging the point.

"You've got a lot of me in you, girly. You're ambitious, too. Clever with words and you have an eye for seeing the story within the story. An eye that'll take an average piece to excellence."

"Do you think I'd be making the wrong decision?"

"Doesn't matter what I think. The question is can you live with making that particular decision?"

"As long as Hunter can, I can," she decided.

"And if he doesn't?"

Marni lifted her chin, pressing her lips tight together to keep them from trembling.

"I'll just have to convince him, then, won't I?"

"You think it's gonna be easy to convince a guy like that to accept you doing this to him?" Robin asked, waving the pages of Marni's story in the air.

"Nothing about him is easy. But I'll make it work," she vowed.

Because she wasn't taking no for an answer. She'd do whatever it took, use whatever tools were necessary to convince Hunter to forgive her. To give them a chance.

If he wouldn't listen to reason, she'd fall back on the one thing she knew he couldn't resist.

She'd strip naked and offer to show him her pole dancing skills.

13

IT'D BEEN A LOT OF YEARS since he'd been stupid enough to inflict a hangover on himself. The hotel room curtains still shut against the painful morning sunlight, Hunter squinted at the mirror as he knotted his tie.

He wasn't due in court until afternoon, but sitting here in the hotel room would just drive him crazy. He had other cases he could be working, could drop in the San Francisco offices and see a few old faces. He didn't want to socialize, though. He just wanted mental distractions to keep him from obsessing over Marni and the long list of what-ifs.

As if hearing his thoughts, someone pounded on the door.

Hunter clenched his teeth, the sound echoing hollowly in his head.

Murray? He was supposed to be heading back to Washington, having deemed the Burns case a failure since the lawyers hadn't hit it out of the park yet.

Caleb? He was probably already cuddled up with his sweet wife, having decided to drive home the previous night instead of waiting until morning.

Didn't matter who it was, Hunter didn't feel like talking to anyone.

He yanked open the door, ready to tell whoever it was to get lost.

Marni stared back at him, her big blue eyes assessing.

He had to work to keep his glare in place.

"I'm here to talk to you." She ducked under his arm and stepped into the room. When she'd reached the desk by the window, she set a leather messenger bag on the chair and faced him.

Damn, she looked good.

Her hair fell in a sweep of blond over one side of her face, a sexy reminder of the forties era the train trip had embraced. But her outfit was totally up-to-date. A blessedly short black skirt and matching tights, boots that ended at her ankles, and a flirty lace blouse in bubblegum-pink.

Her face was serene, her smile a friendly curve of those lush lips. He didn't see a hint of worry in her big blue eyes.

But her fingers were tangled together, twining and untwining, as if she was strangling them.

"What'd you want to talk about? I'm not giving you information on the Burns case," he said, putting the snarky words between them. More because he didn't think he could handle it if that was the only reason she was there, rather than because he wanted to be mean.

Marni's easy smile slipped for a second, hurt flashing in her eyes. Hunter cringed. Could he be a bigger jerk? Before he could apologize, though, she reached for the bag she'd set on the chair, unbuckled the flap and pulled out a file.

Holding it out toward him, she said, "I'd hoped to talk about something else first, but if you want to get the issues about the story and Burns out of the way first, here."

He wanted to toss the papers aside. He wanted to grab

her close, press her body against his and take her mouth in a God-it's-been-too-long kiss. He wanted to demand she tell him what that something else was she'd prefer to talk about, because it sounded like something he was going to much rather hear than anything to do with their respective jobs.

Instead, calling himself a wimp for the first time in his adult life, Hunter took the folder from her.

He didn't open it, though. He just kept staring at her.

She was gorgeous.

Sexy, sweet and so damned appealing.

He thought of Caleb's words the night before.

You're in love enough to ask the questions, you're in love enough to find a way to live with the answers.

Was he in love enough?

He'd lain awake most of the night, his head swimming in Scotch, asking that question over and over again. He hadn't come up with an answer, though. He'd never been in love. What did he know about those deeper emotions? And how could he know it was real, that it'd last?

Now, looking at Marni, the questions all fell away.

The worries, too.

He loved her. It was that simple.

And, he glanced at the file in his hands, that complicated.

"Go ahead," she insisted. "Look at it."

"What's this?" He riffled through the papers, his frown sinking deeper with each paragraph. By the time he'd reached the last one, his frown was fierce and furious. "Where'd you get this?"

Marni wet her lips, looking nervous for just a second before squaring her shoulders. She stepped forward and reached for the pages. Hunter almost didn't let them go, but figured he was between her and the door, so he'd have plenty of chance to tackle her to retrieve them if necessary. She didn't take them away, though. Instead, she shuffled through until she reached a particular one, then handed the stack back.

"In putting together the story about Beverly Burns, I talked to a lot of people. This guy here, he was her current lover until her disappearance. He doesn't know what's going on, of course. Figures she dumped him, so his ego is whining. He spilled all kinds of stuff, including that bank safety-deposit box he said she put files in under his name."

Hunter could only stare. Not at the name of their breakthrough on this case. But at Marni. She'd pulled off what he and a slew of trained FBI agents couldn't. She'd got what was very likely the final nail to pound into the coffin of a major crime boss.

"You checked the safe-deposit box yourself?"

Marni hesitated, then shrugged.

"I should have. That'd be the right thing to do, of course. But I didn't want to leave California." Didn't want to leave him, her expression said. Marni wrinkled her nose in a self-deprecating way, as if she knew she'd said more than she should, but wasn't going to take it back.

"So you sent some stranger to poke through vital information?" He'd heard a lot in his years with the FBI. You'd think he'd be immune. But sometimes he still wanted to drop his face into his hands and groan.

"Not a stranger, no. I sent my cousin."

Hunter gave in to frustration, rubbing at his forehead as if he could ease the aching throb between his eyes. She'd had her cousin do it.

"Marni, you know this is a federal investigation, right? The stakes are sky-high and you let a stranger, someone without any clearance at all, poke through the information? I know that might be okay for a story, but it's putting this case at major risk."

She nodded, looking totally unabashed at his words. Instead, she just looked calm. What the hell? He knew she cared about doing the right thing. She wouldn't be bringing him this otherwise. Did she not get the importance of confidentiality and timing in a case like this?

"Did I mention that my cousin goes by the name Sister Maria-Louisa with the Sisters of Charity?"

"Your cousin is a nun?"

Hunter cringed just a little, suddenly very aware of all the things he and Marni had done with, to and on top of each other. Was there some rule against that?

She didn't seem very intimidated, since she laughed with delight, clearly reading his discomfort.

"She is. And according to my mother, she still follows the family marriage dictate, as she's a bride of God." Marni pulled a face, then shook her head as if she were trying to shake off her irritation at that fact. "Maria-Louisa is also great at persuading gigolo wannabes to show her the contents of their safe-deposit boxes. She didn't read anything there herself, she just took pictures with her cell phone and sent them to me."

Hunter stared. Maybe it was the hangover. Or the fact that Marni was right here in front of him, close enough to pull close so he could bury his face in her hair. But his brain just couldn't wrap itself around what she was saying.

"Your cousin, the nun, has a cell phone? And she convinced a hood rat like Giuseppe Laredo to let her take photos of the goods he was hiding for his girlfriend, the wife of a known mobster?" He shook his head. "Seriously?"

"Well, yeah. Who better?" Marni shrugged, pulling another folder out of her magic messenger bag and handing it to him. He flipped the cover and saw a stack of eight-by-ten photos. "She's the queen of that spiritual guilt thing, but so sweet about it that you end up feeling guilty for being guilty, you know? She promised Giuseppe she wouldn't let the information become public, though. That's why I made you promise you wouldn't use it as evidence."

For the first time, she looked anxious.

"You won't, right? I mean, you'll keep my word?" Marni grimaced, then shoved her hand through her hair. "I know that's not fair, but, well, she's a nun. I can't lie to her, even after the fact."

Hunter stared at the photos.

Triumph surged. His grin was both excited and just a little vicious. They'd nail that son of a bitch to the wall with this. Listed right there on that photographed-by-a-nun page were the hit orders, the details of the deaths the prosecution wanted to bust Burns on. He didn't need to use these photos as evidence. With these names, he'd have the hit men, their girlfriends, hell, their mothers, all rounded up within an hour. It wouldn't take long before someone flipped on Burns. That's all he needed, one flip, and he had the guy solid on murder charges.

His hand was halfway to his pocket to grab his own cell phone when his gaze landed on the photo's date stamp.

"You had this when you came to the trial. When I—" *screwed you against the hotel room wall* sounded so tacky "—surprised you in your hotel room."

From the wash of pink coloring her cheeks, Marni got the subtext without a problem. She shrugged, then shook her head.

"Maria-Louisa went to the bank that same day and took the photos, yes. But I didn't receive them until the next morning."

After he'd guilted her over the danger to Beverly Burns.

"You said you're still writing the story?"

"I sent my story in yesterday," she confirmed, her smile a little shaky. Not out of nerves over his reaction, but with excitement.

He set the file aside, needing to have nothing between them for this next question.

"But you said you promised her the information wouldn't be made public. How can you do that and write the big-hitting story that's going to make your career soar?"

She took a deep breath, puffed it back out, then offered a cute shrug.

"I pivoted on my story," she confessed.

Pivoted.

For him? Because he'd guilted her into it? Because she didn't want to put a questionably innocent woman in danger? Why?

A million thoughts raced through his head. A million hopes took hold of his heart. But Hunter didn't show a single one. The same as he'd always done when he was in a position that put his life on the line, he kept his expression bland, his nerves on the catatonic side of mellow.

Even as he hoped beyond words that her answer would be the shot he wanted, he didn't bank on it.

Instead, he simply asked, "Why?"

MARNI'S MOUTH WATERED a little as she stared at the man who, the last time she'd seen him, had given her the strongest, most body-shaking orgasm of her life. The look in his eyes was so strong, so demanding, it was as if he was looking straight into her soul. Again. Maybe that's what made her so crazy for him, that he saw her. Beyond the hair and the clothes and the curves, he saw the real her. And demanded she be the real her.

"Marni?"

"Hmm?"

"Why?" he asked again.

Well, there's the million-dollar question. Marni's throat was so tight, she had to swallow three times to get the air past it and into her suddenly aching lungs.

"Why?" she repeated, buying time.

"Yeah." His voice as calm as his face, he leaned his hip against the dresser and gave her a look with about as much expectation as if he'd just asked her for the time. "Why'd you make a promise like that? What'd you pivot your story to? And what good is this information to you if you can't use it?"

Maybe he should be trying the Burns case instead of those fancy lawyers. Between those kinds of questions and his ability to see directly into her mind, he'd have already gotten the conviction. She bit her lip.

"I could have used it. I mean, I did make my initial promise to Maria-Louisa with the caveat that she couldn't hold me to it if the case involved murder. She agreed, since, you know, she's big on the commandments." Marni offered a shaky smile, waiting to see if he'd join in on the joke. He just stared. Okay, then. Her heart pounded. She almost pushed a nervous hand through her hair again, then reminded herself of how long she'd spent getting prettied up for this meeting. So she wrapped her fingers together instead and shrugged.

"If I break this story, it ruins your case. I know one lost case won't ruin your career or anything. Your reputation is too good, your record too impressive for that. Still, it felt, well, wrong."

"Why?"

"You keep asking that," she said in exasperation.

"Go ahead and keep answering."

Marni opened her mouth to tell him.

She tried to push the confession past her lips.

But she couldn't.

Not without having any idea if he'd reciprocate her feelings. Not without a clue if he cared about her, too.

"Why didn't you stop me? You knew I was working on the Burns angle and his wife being alive." Her nerves exhausted from the constant spin of emotions, Marni lifted her palms in question. "So why didn't you stop the story? Have me detained. Intimidate me into running back to hemlines and fashion shows."

There. She'd put the *why* right back in his corner.

From the look in Hunter's eyes, he didn't like it there very much. Frustration and something else, something deep and intense that made her stomach clench and her heart race, lurked in those blue depths.

Why? What didn't he want to tell her?

Marni held her breath, waiting to find out.

"I can't have you arrested for breaking a story. You know that."

"You could have made my life very difficult. You could have played the intimidation card," she countered.

"You don't think sneaking into your hotel room, slamming you against the wall and having wild-man sex with you wasn't intimidating?" he asked, the bitterness in his words clearly self-directed.

Marni frowned. Unable to help herself, she moved closer, reaching out to take both of his hands. His hard, strong fingers closed, warm and solid, over hers.

"I hate to break it to you, wild man, but I wasn't intimidated by that. Turned on, blown away, satisfied, yes. But scared and intimidated, no."

He arched one brow and waited.

Marni rolled her eyes.

"Okay, fine. Maybe I was overwhelmed, nervous and

a little freaked out. But not intimidated. Not enough to sideline my ambitions and sit on the biggest story of my as-yet-growing career." She bit her lip, and then, because she hated the idea of him turning what had been incredibly exciting and totally consensual sex into something he was ashamed of, she tightened her hands on his and shook her head. "But I never felt at risk, you know? I knew, no matter how angry you were and how important this case is to you, that you wouldn't cross any lines. I'm safe with you."

All of a sudden, the only real fear Marni had when it came to Hunter fell away. The fear that he'd break her heart. Tension poured from her body, leaving her feeling a little limp and teary-eyed. It didn't matter whether Hunter returned her feelings or not. Whether he was interested in a future together or separate.

Whatever happened today, she'd walk away knowing she'd be okay. That she had the priorities between her self, her heart and her career in an order she could live with.

Marni gave a silent sigh.

There. Now that she'd got all that touchy-feely stuff straight in her head, she squared her shoulders and prepared to make damned sure this went her way. Because she wasn't leaving this room until she'd got her man.

"You feel safe with me?" he repeated, clearly having spent a few seconds mulling that and, if his frown was any indication, not being thrilled by his conclusion.

"I didn't call you a harmless, fluffy bunny rabbit," Marni said with a soft laugh. "I just said I don't believe you're a bully. Not a physical bully, since I was right there enjoying that wall-banging with you. And not a mental bully, since you didn't play head games to try to intimidate me into falling in line on the story."

"The story." Hunter glanced at the desk, where he'd tossed the papers, then back at her. "So what's the deal on that, then? You claim I didn't influence your decision in writing the story. You also say you promised a nun, which is a big promise even if you did grow up together, that you'd keep this information from going public."

Marni took a deep breath and, because she needed to move to keep her thoughts from stuttering, slipped her hands out of his and stepped away.

She poked at the papers, then walked to the window to tweak the curtain open and let some light into the room.

"You okay?" she asked when Hunter winced. He nodded, then gave her an impatient look. *Hurry up with the details,* his eyes screamed. Okay. Time to get this over with.

"I actually did write a piece and submitted it yesterday. My editor contacted me this morning. He's blown away, really excited. He said they'd not only be running it, but he's moving me out of Style."

Hunter's eyes chilled.

He crossed his arms over his chest, steadied his feet as if he was bracing himself, and tilted his head for her to go ahead.

"It's not this article, though," she said, pointing at the deskful of papers. Starting to feel nervous again, she paced between the bed and the window. "Look, before I tell you about the piece I wrote, there's something I need to say."

Hunter waited.

Marni bit her lip, wishing he'd switch off the FBI face but knowing why he couldn't until he knew where the article situation stood.

"I did get on that train because of the Burns story," she confessed. "I knew through, well, a little sleuthing, that you would be working on the case prep. That you'd be a captive source, if you will."

She waited for his anger, but he kept staring, those blue

eyes calm and patient. Marni's stomach churned and she paced faster.

"I didn't poke into your files, though. I didn't search your luggage or try to hack into your laptop or listen to your phone calls, or anything like that."

Still, he stared.

Her pace increased.

"I didn't sleep with you to try to get information. I wouldn't use you like that, or cheapen this thing between us." She waved a hand back and forth between them, like the *thing* was right there, in all its three-dimensional glory. "I have high standards for myself, Hunter. I don't share myself with a man unless I have really strong feelings for him."

She hesitated, then, forcing her feet to stop running between the furnishings, she wrapped her fingers together and gave Hunter a shaky smile.

"I tried to resist this thing—" she gestured again "—between us. I knew it'd ruin my focus. Make me question my judgment in writing the story I was there to write. And worse, that it'd make it seem like I was sleeping my way to success."

He just kept staring.

She was tempted to kick him in the shin just to get a damned reaction.

Finally, he tilted his head as if acknowledging her point.

"I don't think the sex between us had anything to do with your story or my case," he said quietly. "I know you better than that."

Okay. Marni bounced a little in her boots. So far, so good. She could leave it at that, actually. Just clear the air, make sure things were copacetic and be on her way.

She swallowed hard, pretending her feet were nailed to the floor, and called on every bit of nerve she had.

"You know me better than anyone," she confessed. "I come from a huge family, a close family. But you're the first person who listens to me, who gets me. Who really sees me for who I am." She wet her lips, then shrugged. "But maybe that's just a by-product of your job?"

She held her breath, trying to keep her expectant look more interested than desperate.

"Are you asking about my feelings toward you?" he asked, narrowing his eyes. She hated that she couldn't tell what was going on behind them. He had that special agent face on.

Yes, she wanted to cry. Please, take over this conversation, grab the lead and pull the responsibility off her shoulders. She'd be happy to respond to his confession instead of making her own. That'd be so much easier.

She opened her mouth to say that. Then snapped her lips shut. Not because she changed her mind. But because she had no idea how the hell to put it into words without sounding ridiculous.

"I guess I'm trying to explain my own feelings toward you," she finally said, her words low and hesitant. "I wouldn't have slept with you on the train if they weren't strong. I could have resisted the physical attraction between us, but not the emotional one."

He closed his eyes, then reached up to rub two fingers against his temple. What? Was she giving him a headache? But when he opened his eyes again, they were glowing with a delighted kind of joy.

Enough to have her spilling out the rest of her confession.

"I admire you, Hunter. I admire your dedication to your job, and even more how you do the job your way. How you stand for people that others wouldn't. I'm in awe of your mind, at how you think." All of the energy that had made her need to pace, to bounce or move, seeped away. She stepped closer, once again taking his hands in hers as she met his penetrating gaze.

"You make me laugh. You make me think. You're pretty amazing in bed, or against the wall." She grinned when his lips twitched, and then she sighed deeply and confessed, "I love how you see the real me. And in seeing me, how you not only accept me, but encourage and celebrate who I am. You make me feel strong."

Hunter was shaking his head before she'd finished the final word.

"You don't give yourself nearly enough credit for your strength, Marni. I saw it before I knew what your job really was." She winced, but he kept going. "But after I looked into your record, saw the things you've done—and the odds you faced—I was even more impressed with your drive and focus on building the career you want."

Marni's heart melted, going as gooey soft as chocolate in the bright sunshine. She sighed, tilted her head to one side and gave him a tremulous smile.

"I love you," she murmured. "I really, really love you. I love your dedication, your strength, your smile and how you make me feel. Inside and out."

For a second, one miserably long second, Hunter's face went blank. His eyes dimmed. His smile faded. He seemed to freeze in place.

Marni's gooey heart froze, too. For that interminable second, she held her breath, trying to prepare herself for the easy letdown. Trying to convince herself that it wouldn't hurt nearly as much as she kept imagining.

Then, before she could call herself out for being a liar, Hunter pounced. He released her hands, grabbed her by the waist and spun her in a circle before pulling her tightly into his arms.

"I take it you think this is good news?" she asked, her words muffled against his chest.

"Good news?" He pulled back enough to give her the happiest grin she'd ever seen on his gorgeous face. "This is fabulous news. I love you, too. I never thought I'd feel this way. Never thought I'd care so much about anyone, let alone care so much more than I do about my career. I love you. Like I love nothing, no one, else in my life."

Delight and relief surged so strong, Marni almost cried. She managed to laugh instead, giving him the biggest, brightest smile and running her palm over his cheek in a gentle caress.

Her laughter died away at the look of intense passion in his eyes. His kiss was a promise. A bond. A pact that swore their love would not only get a chance, but that it'd flourish and grow. That it was now the most important thing in this powerful, committed man's life.

She didn't realize she'd actually started crying until he pulled away and wiped one tear from her cheek with his thumb.

"Happy tears," she mumbled.

His laugh was sweetly understanding. Then he glanced at the files again.

"I understand if you need to write that story, Marni. I respect people's right to know the truth. Even if I don't always like the timing and how it affects things. Don't put it aside just because of us."

"Oh." She wrinkled her nose, then figuring he wasn't going to take his love back once he heard what she'd done, she shifted out of his arms and offered a lash-fluttering smile. "Well, thanks. But I told you, I wrote a different sort of story."

Hunter sighed, leaned back against the desk and made a gimmee gesture with one hand. His smile stayed mellow, but his eyes were intense, not letting her look away. Marni puffed out a breath, then pulled the story file out of her bag and handed it to him.

"Just so you know, this isn't open for editorializing," she said, wiping her suddenly damp palm on her skirt. "I've already turned it in to my editor, he's already accepted it. It'll run in the next edition of *Optimum*."

He gave her a long, assessing look. As if he was debating whether or not he was okay with that. Then, with a contemplative look on his face, he flipped the folder open.

His eyes rounded with shock. Marni gnawed on her lower lip. His gaze narrowed as he read. Marni pressed a hand to her churning stomach. Not because she was worried he'd be mad. But because she wanted him to be proud.

After a minute or two, she wanted to rip the papers from his hands and read it aloud to him. Hurry, hurry, hurry.

Finally, just about the time she was sure her head was going to explode from nervous excitement, he flipped back to the first page, then closed the file.

"Still love me?" she asked with a shaky smile.

He gave a wordless shake of his head, lifting the file as if to say *wow*.

Good *wow* or bad *wow?*

"You are something else," he told her. "You wrote a profile on my father? You make him sound like, well, like the hero I always think of him as."

Hunter looked away and cleared his throat. Then he tossed the file on the desk, took her hands again and lifted them to his lips in the most romantic gesture of her life.

"I don't even have the words to thank you for writing such an incredible story. I've always been proud of my father, of his work. But I'm honored to see it laid out in such a remarkable way."

Relief surged so strong, Marni's knees almost gave out.

"I have to ask, though. Why did you change your focus? I know you talked a lot about biographies and stuff, but I thought that was just a cover."

"It was and it wasn't. The thing is, the more I talked about it, the more I worked on the profile of my aunt, just in case you happened to peek over my shoulder, the more I remembered how much I loved writing them. The more I researched for the Burns story, though, the more I dug into your history, and your father's. I was fascinated." She thought of those days with her aunt, their talks and the decisions Robin had helped her make. "I realized that while I might be good at hard-hitting news, it was the people in the news that captivated me. That's what I wanted to focus on."

She wet her lips, then touched the tips of her fingers to the folder before giving him a smile.

"I sent the piece on my aunt to my editor, too. He's excited to run it, as well. Instead of becoming one of the minor players in the news department, I'm being given my own segment each month. Profiles, by Marni Clare. And I couldn't, wouldn't have ever done it without you."

Just saying it made her shiver.

But not as much as the look of pride and delight on Hunter's face as he drew her closer. His fingers tangled in her hair while he gently took her lips in a tribute. Marni fell into the kiss, delighting in the passion flaming between them, the commitment whispered in that soft meeting of their mouths.

Slowly, so deliciously slow, Hunter pulled his mouth away from hers. She forced her eyes open, needing to see his face when she asked her last question.

"So, you're really happy about the story?"

"I'm really happy about the story," he assured her.

"Good. Because your biographical profile will run next month." When his mouth dropped, a horrified look skating through his gaze, she grinned and fluttered her lashes. "What can I say? I love you so much, I had to share how wonderful you are with the world."

Epilogue

MARNI HAD THOUGHT TELLING Hunter she loved him was scary. And she'd been crazy nervous over his reaction to her new career focus, and his special place at the center of it. But those nerves, that fear, had nothing on the acrobatics going on in her stomach at that very moment. It was like butterflies, bats and dragons were square-dancing.

"I really shouldn't be here," she murmured from her safe, cozy spot in the passenger side of the car, her seat belt still firmly in place despite the fact that Hunter had shut off the car and had one hand on the door latch.

"Of course you should. Besides the birthday bash, we need to celebrate you helping me put Burns away for life." Hunter gave her a knowing look, then reached over to unwrap her fingers from themselves, so her hand was twined with his instead. "This is my family. I want them to meet you. To know the woman I'm in love with. And I want you to meet them."

"I get that your father is family," she said, half turning in her seat to give him a curious look. "But I didn't realize you were related to the Black clan. I found a ton of information on them when I was researching the articles." A ton was an understatement. "I know you were college roommates with the oldest sibling, Caleb, right? Is that why you consider them family? Because of that?"

"The connections crisscross and bisect. My father spent half of his career trying to nail Tobias Black. Somewhere along the way, they became tight friends. But you know that. You wrote the profile." After giving her an appreciative smile, Hunter glanced at the house, a two-story Victorian complete with fancy gingerbread and a colorful garden. "And like you said, Caleb and I were roommates. His sister, Maya, is married to Simon. He's FBI and was one of my agents at one time."

"I thought the family, except for Caleb who was DEA, were all con artists," she interrupted, drawing her knee up and turning more fully. Her fingers itched for a pencil. This family was the stuff fiction was made of. Or seriously enthralling profiles.

"Yep. Well, officially, Tobias and Maya retired years ago. Gabriel was still on the take when I brought him in last year."

"You arrested your best friend's brother?"

"My protégée did. Danita Cruz. Or Danita Black now, I guess."

She hadn't found that out in her research. Marni knew her eyes were round to the point of falling out, but she couldn't help it.

"Gabriel Black, con extraordinaire, is married to an FBI agent? One who arrested him?"

Hunter laughed. "Be sure to use that phrase with him. He'll love it."

"One of the most notorious families of con artists, and each one is tied in some way to a federal agent?"

"Sure." Hunter shrugged. "You're going to love them. And the food. Pandora serves up some great eats. There are bound to be aphrodisiacs, so this will be fun."

Paying no attention to her jaw hanging on her chest, Hunter gave her fingers a squeeze, then let go and exited the car. Marni had no choice but to follow.

Aphrodisiacs?

Curiosity fought with nerves. They all sounded fascinating. And, she tried to swallow past the lump in her throat, totally intimidating.

Do-si-do, and here we go. She pressed one hand against her churning belly, then took a deep breath and plastered on her brightest smile, hoping the strength of it would shield her a little.

As she joined Hunter at the sidewalk, Marni started to head up the walk. But he caught her hand before she took a step and pulled her back into his arms.

Marni sank into the kiss, her nerves dissipating quickly as passion left no room for anything else in her body. But just as her lips were warming and her body heating, Hunter pulled away.

She murmured her protest, slowly opening her eyes and giving him a questioning smile.

"What was that for? Afraid to introduce a nervous mess to your family?"

"Maybe I just wanted to remind you that you love me before you face the craziness and question your choice," he teased. Then, his smile still in place, his eyes cooled. He glanced quickly toward the door, then, for the first time since she'd known him, looked a little worried.

Marni's earlier stomach churning do-si-do turned into a spastic jig as her nerves returned with a vengeance. Was he worried about his friends and family reacting to her? Nervous for her to meet them? Concerned over bringing a reporter into their midst?

Sucking in a deep breath, she pressed her palm against her stomach to try to calm the frantic dance.

"There's something I want to do before we go inside," Hunter said, his words so quiet they were almost carried away in the wind. "Something I want to say."

"Okay." Needing a little distance to brace herself, Marni stepped back just a bit.

And was instantly horrified when Hunter stepped back even farther. Could she just dive into the car and wait until this little birthday celebration was over? Then, after another quick glance toward the house, he puffed out a deep breath and grabbed her hands before she could make her dash for the safety of the car.

"I love you," he said.

That's all it took for Marni's nerves, fears and urge to flee to disappear. She gave him a bright smile, ready for whatever follow-up he was going to offer.

"I want to marry you."

Her brain stopped.

Hunter reached into his pocket and pulled out a small velvet box, flipping the lid and holding it out.

Her mouth dropped.

Her eyes shot from the ring, sparkling in the setting sunlight, to Hunter's implacable face, then back again.

She couldn't find the words.

She couldn't even find her breath.

Frowning, he shot a glance at the house again, then shook his head at her.

"You really should say yes. Avoid all of those what's-your-relationship-status, why-haven't-you-introduced-a-woman-to-the-family-before questions when we go inside," he suggested, sounding a little nervous.

Marni blinked.

"You want me to agree to marry you because you think it'll make your family behave better?"

That broke his stoic expression, making him bark with laughter.

"Hardly. I want you to marry me because I love you. Because I want us to spend our lives together, to build a future together. To celebrate this love every single day."

Her heart, already his, melted with love. All Marni could do was whisper yes, reaching one hand up to cup his cheek as she stood on tiptoe to brush a kiss over his mouth.

Hunter wasn't having any of that gentle, sweet stuff, though.

He grabbed her close, taking the kiss from gentle to intense with one swift thrust of his tongue. Marni's body joined her heart in the meltdown.

"Yes?" he clarified, shifting back just a little.

"Yes," she repeated, laughing.

As if afraid she'd change her answer, Hunter quickly slid the ring onto her finger.

Before she could even get a good look at it, though, he pulled her right back into the kiss.

When she finally eased back to beam up at him, Marni noticed there were at least a half-dozen faces pressed to the house's front window. Her laughter rang out, even as Hunter groaned.

Still laughing, Marni snuggled tight into his arms, then sighed with delight.

"Just so you know," she warned quietly, tilting her hand this way and that to watch the last of the day's sunbeams dance off the diamond, "our engagement is going to make my family crazy. And they aren't nice enough to wait behind a window. They'll grill you, nag you and drive you absolutely batty."

"They can't be that bad, can they?"

Marni brushed a kiss over his mouth, then, with her

hand snuggled in his, headed up the walkway to meet the people he loved.

"Oh, they can. You've been warned. But you can't get out of it," she said, curling her fist tight over the ring.

Hunter stopped to kiss her again, then shook his head.

"Sweetheart, I promise. We're in this together, forever."

* * * * *

The Royal
HOUSE OF KAREDES

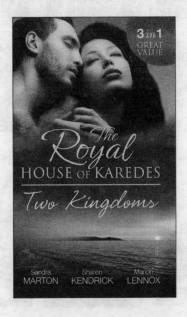

**TWO CROWNS, TWO ISLANDS,
ONE LEGACY**

One royal family, torn apart by pride and its lust for
power, reunited by purity and passion

**Meet the Karedes now, at:
www.millsandboon.co.uk**

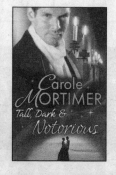
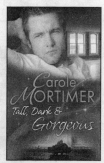
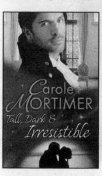
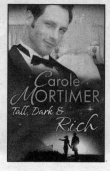
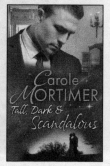

The World of Mills & Boon®

There's a Mills & Boon® series that's perfect for you. We publish ten series and, with new titles every month, you never have to wait long for your favourite to come along.

Blaze.

Scorching hot, sexy reads
4 new stories every month

By Request

Relive the romance with the best of the best
9 new stories every month

Cherish

Romance to melt the heart every time
12 new stories every month

Desire

Passionate and dramatic love stories
8 new stories every month